PRAISE FOR

THE STAR SPANGLED CONTRACT

"CHILLING...SUSPENSEFUL...A FIRST-RATE THRILLER CHARGED WITH MENACE....It will keep you glued to the printed page and, better still, make you think."
—*John Barkham Reviews*

★

"MOVES AT THE SPEED OF A HIGH-POWERED BULLET....For readers who enjoyed James Grady's *Six Days of the Condor.*"
—*Library Journal*

★

"POWERFUL AND SHOCKING...A MAJOR WORK."
—*Charlotte Observer*

★

ALSO BY JIM GARRISON

ON THE TRAIL
OF THE ASSASSINS

PUBLISHED BY
WARNER BOOKS

THE STAR SPANGLED CONTRACT

JIM GARRISON

WARNER BOOKS

A Time Warner Company

WARNER BOOKS EDITION

This Warner Books Edition is published by arrangement with the author, and was previously published by Warner Books in June, 1977.

Cover illustration by Michael Racz
Cover design by Diane Luger

Warner Books, Inc.
666 Fifth Avenue
New York, N.Y. 10103

W A Time Warner Company

Printed in the United States of America

Second Printing: March, 1992

10 9 8 7 6 5 4 3 2 1

For my mother
Jane Garrison Gardiner

THE STAR SPANGLED CONTRACT

1

The limousine moved through the first turn, slowed for twenty yards, then accelerated to parade speed. At the last turn, a sharp left, the car slowed to seven miles an hour for thirty yards—and then increased speed again.

Then came the crack of rifles—the first two shots so narrowly spaced that the ear heard one, the third and fourth shots smacked the echoing air in tight succession three seconds later.

The figure slammed sideways in the rear of the limousine—then it lay slumped in the corner of the seat.

Reiner, sun flashing off his field glasses, nodded approval. "All right," he said. "But the forward shooters are hitting more accurate than the shooters behind."

"The boys behind got the hard shot," Bittman said. "Just about twice as hard when you figure the droppage—the droppage factor."

Reiner touched his forehead with his handkerchief, his owl's face pasty, a man plainly uncomfortable in sun and dust. The sun, the heat, seemed enormous to him; it was the immense sun and heat of desert, not of the Illinois woods.

"We know all about droppage *factors*," said Reiner. "We planned for *factors*. We did not plan well enough."

Using the trees as cover, pausing motionless now and then, Colin McFerrin made his approach to the mock-up site in a crouching trot, now moving again, starting his final run to the edge of the clearing a hundred yards distant. He stopped behind a wide oak, caught his breath, rested briefly. Then he stepped out —and as he did he heard, behind him, a twig snap. McFerrin jumped to the side, whirled. The rifle butt just missed, just grazed his face, and before the man in fatigues could recover his stance, call or fire in warning, McFerrin kneed him in the groin. The man in fatigues went down, went over backward, mouth wide, eyes wide, but not screaming, not seeing. McFerrin took a measured step—then, feet together, he vaulted. Feet together, he came down in the center of the man's chest. The sound was like the crushing of a sack of wet sticks.

In the clearing, Bittman glanced at the positioning of his riflemen, then turned to Reiner. "It's whether the car is on a line going *away* from you or coming *to* you—that's what makes the difference, Mr. Reiner. There are factors to be considered, sir. The shooters from behind are just as good as the front shooters. But it's not just the target's moving away from them that doubles the trick for the boys behind." Bittman, a tanned, big-chested man, pointed first to one tower, then the other. "Those boys are up there sixty feet and seventy feet. That doubles the hit for those boys."

Reiner slowly turned, studied the two wooden towers—one to the right and rear of where the driver had stopped the limousine, the other tower more directly rearward. Ladders led up to the shooting platform atop each, each set at the precise angle and distance to target as would be the actual firing stations in the General Motors Building and the Petroleum Product Tower on Dulles Street in Foley Square.

Reiner sniffed. The acrid smell of gunpowder stirred a feeling in him. It was good to be on the line again, out with the firing of weapons and not merely lecturing about firepower and the rest of it. He sniffed the air again and said, "You're quite the fella on factors, aren't you?" And then he raised his field glasses to the forward shooting station, a hill built just to the right of the dirt road and measuring the exact elevation of the grassy knoll at Foley Square. Skip the frosting, and the entire mockup was a precise practical duplication—distances, turns, angles. Even the dirt road, as it approached the practice hill, had been dug lower to duplicate the exact dip in Dulles Street as it passed the grassy knoll, a dip that sent Dulles Street below the railroad overpass a block or so down Dulles from Foley Square. At the practice site, it was dimensions that counted, and the dimensions were near perfect, whereas incidental details were merely suggested— the hastily constructed wooden fence fronting the mock hill giving the rough effect of the actual picket fence. As for the target zone on the dirt road, it was brightly marked at its corners by four yellow

11

flags on surveyor's sticks, two on each side of the road.

"That driver's some cute cookie," said Reiner. "You lay a bad shot in there, it takes his head right off."

"You bet," said Bittman. "But he's okay. He knows those boys are precision shooters, because he's a shooter too. We got it worked out so he alternates if someone turns up sick—so he shoots from each station regular, to keep him sharp on the hit." Bittman studied Reiner's face, saw the bad flesh in it. "These boys don't get squirrelly," Bittman said. "They know the kill, how it goes. They don't know who yet, but they won't care. They're not the worrying kind."

"Everyone's the worrying kind," Reiner said.

"These boys?" Bittman said. "Shit, they've done terminations—important ones. They're killers, Mr. Reiner. These are five solid boys."

"It's going to take solid boys." Reiner moved his shoulders impressively. "I want closer to the action on the next run. I want to see the shots hitting."

"But I can't allow it, sir," Bittman said. "I don't want these boys to see your face."

Bittman, the assault-team commander, knew that Reiner wasn't Reiner's real name, just as Bittman wasn't his. Reiner was Bittman's sole link to higher up, the cutoff to General Underwood. Though it was Bittman who would supervise the assault team at the time of the termination, he would never hear the name Underwood mentioned in connection with the operation; nor would he ever see the man from whom all planning and control radiated. A former C.I.A. field-supervisor, Bittman would surely recognize the name of the former deputy director of the Agency—but Bittman would never know he was again working for the same man.

"I want in closer," Reiner said.

"Let me think about it," Bittman said.

McFerrin checked the clearing. Nothing seen, nothing heard, everything normal: the limousine was circling back to start point for another run. He scanned the woods around him. Nothing. Had the guard been alone? McFerrin tried to breathe evenly, heart pounding still. Then he took up the guard's rifle and moved out in a crouching trot again, the silhouette of his large, lanky frame low in the strong light. He did not look back at the dead man. There was nothing McFerrin needed to see. And if by some crazy miracle the man were still alive, no sound he made would be audible more than a foot away—and it would not be a sound that meant anything. McFerrin closed with the clearing. When it was fifty yards off, he dropped to the ground and began his belly-crawl forward, the rifle laid across his arms.

"How insulated are these boys?" Reiner asked.

"All the way," Bittman answered.

But Reiner already knew the answer to his question, the answer to all his questions. The shooters would be men with tunnel vision, a trait high on the list of selection criteria. What the shooters knew was that their employer was an outfit called Mid-Century Corporation, that it operated out of Chicago and Vegas, that they would be paid handsomely for long periods of idleness and more than handsomely when they at last did their number. That's all the shooters knew—except, of course, that they were five dead men if they talked. What else did they need to know? Nothing. Besides, they weren't interested.

"I'm Coppersmith so far as they're concerned," said Bittman. "Everything I carry says Coppersmith. They know I work out of Vegas, and they know it's through me Mid-Century does the deal. I do my job, mister."

"I'm the worrying kind," Reiner said. "I'm the number one worrier."

Reiner knew that Bittman had done his job. But Reiner's job was making sure. And even if it weren't Reiner's job, he'd do it anyway. Bittman would be the only operative at Foley Square who knew Reiner, whether by that name or any other cover identity. As for Reiner, he knew Underwood, and that was as far as his knowledge went. Nor did Reiner know that an alternate team of shooters would be available from the Los Angeles pool, whereas the rifle team sweating ass out here came from the Miami pool. Neither team would know whether they would be called into action until the very last moment.

Making sure was Reiner's job. But Reiner knew there was plenty he did not know. The less a man knew, the longer a man lived. Those in control made sure all concerned were informed on *this* score. It was in your interest, and in the interest of the total enterprise, that what you knew was no more than what you *had* to know to perform your task. On this point, there was no misunderstanding—and the clarity of the rule kept Bittman and Reiner each at a respectful distance from the other man's ground. Neither man knew the parts of the operation beyond his function. Underwood's cutoff and decoy system worked vertically and horizontally. And it paralleled an intricate tracery of fear—up the chain of command from shooters and across the chain from supervisors of one sort or another—yielding an incredible Byzantine arrangement of capsulations and cutoffs.

For example, those operators—"baby-sitters" Arthur Underwood called them—whose job it was to work the patsy (Zero) and who were now supervising his activities to provide for a profile that would seal his "guilt," would know neither Reiner nor Bittman nor anyone else in the termination force, and similarly no one connected to the termination force would know any operators handling the baby-sitting—and on it all went, in every direction, a triumph of ingenious insulation, until it reached the top: General Arthur Underwood, Reiner presumed.

"I believe you've amply demonstrated accuracy with standard frangible shells," he said. "Now let's see what you can do with the new bullet."

"You want it, you got it," Bittman said. He jogged off to where the driver was standing in the shady area across the road from the fabricated knoll. Bittman huddled with the driver, and then the driver turned away from Bittman and spoke to one of the two riflemen behind the knoll. Then the driver backed the limousine to the towers and shouted up instructions to the shooters positioned on the platforms.

McFerrin crawled toward the clearing. There were fewer trees now, less cover. He hugged the ground, bellied forward, the rifle cradled in his arms. At the border of the clearing now, he slid in behind a low scrub oak. The field of tall grass lay before him and

15

then, just beyond, the practice site. Sweat burned down into his eyes. His shirt was soaked, his exhaustion overwhelming. He forced his breathing to slow, his large body stretched flat to the earth. He rested this way for a long time, and then he raised up on his elbows and studied the rifle. The M-16. McFerrin knew the weapon better than he knew his mother. And why not? She'd given him life, but the M-16 had made sure he still had one to take out of Nam. McFerrin removed the shell from the chamber. Damn light, even for a frangible. Something oddball about it.

He checked the number of shells in the clip—five altogether. He shoved the first bullet back into the chamber. Then he emptied the clip of all the shells except one and replaced the clip, leaving one bullet in the chamber and one at the top of the clip. He put the other shells in his pocket. Two bullets would handle it. Three he'd carry home.

Again McFerrin scanned the woods. Other guards? None. So far, so good. He turned his attention back to the practice site. There was nothing to do now but wait. He wanted a smoke, could feel the desire for it rising in him, but knew he dare not light up. He waited.

The driver waited for the signal to make his next run while Reiner continued to press Bittman.

"Your shooters, these solid boys you have, they make the transition from standard frangibles to the new bullet okay?"

"Well now," Bittman said, his face trying for a studious look, "I guess you know we had some trouble that last time you were here. But we put water in the way you said we should. Of course, mercury fulminate makes the best filler for frangibles. But the specifications for the job were that it had to be set up for a one-man explanation————"

"You see," Reiner said, taking on his own air of importance, "your lone assassin seldom comes up with mercury fulminate."

The two men chuckled knowingly.

"The water give you more wind-buffeting stability?" Reiner continued.

"Made all the difference," Bittman said. "But I don't fill the shell all the way. Too much water, too much tensile strength. Then you'd have no breakup, and a hollow bullet that doesn't break up is almost as much a giveaway as mercury fulminate. I fill about two thirds, leave a third air."

"You getting good accuracy with that?"

"Damn right I am. Especially with the M-16's."

Reiner raised his eyebrows. "M-16's are coming out ahead of the Mausers? That's news," he said.

"Yes, sir. News to me too. The Mausers looked better with the heavier bullets, but the M-16's turned out more accurate with the water bullet. You just watch this run. It'll be the freak ammo this time—that and the M-16's," Bittman said, unable to hide his excitement.

"All right," Reiner said. "I love a parade." He grinned, pleased with himself.

Bittman signaled. The limousine moved.

McFerrin, prone behind the scrub oak, watched the car move out. He jerked the rifle into line and centered the dummy in the sight. Over a hundred yards, he estimated, and goddamn far without a scope. But not too far. He threw up a few blades of grass to test the wind and then scaled the sight up to the 100-yard reading. He had the dummy keyed in, and he was tracking it well as the limousine made the last turn. He curled his finger lightly around the trigger, kept the target centered, and when the dummy was blown across the seat, an instant before the sequenced cracks of the rifles sounded in McFerrin's ears, he had the head square. But this was just play. He didn't want that head.

Now he hefted the gun for the feel of it, checked the selection fire lever to make sure it was set for single shot and not for automatic. He figured the M-16 firing time for two accurate distance-shots at three to four seconds maximum, most of that for targeting time. All right, he could put two good ones in there easy, enough of their firing on either side of his firing to cover his double with room to spare. They would hear nothing.

McFerrin studied the scene before him. His back itched from the heat, itched from the grass, itched from what he knew and wished he didn't. And it itched too from what he did not know, only wondered at.

He wondered, to begin with, how many other domestic intelligence forces had by now duplicated the C.I.A.'s termination techniques. He figured the Defense Intelligence Agency for one, and probably the National Security Agency, now that it had quietly branched out from its original communications function into operations. The shooters, the driver, you could inject them with sodium pentothal, hypnotize them, give them lie detector tests—and you would find out nothing because they would in fact *know nothing.* Nothing you could make a case out of. Sure, they'd know who they had hit—but that would be it.

What the hell was going *on* out there? Why weren't they moving? McFerrin hugged the ground and held his attention on the firing-team supervisor, the man Bittman, a field operative, a specialist in action intelligence. As for the man Reiner, Underwood's arms expert probably and a man with access to the top. At least to Underwood. For it was from the stakeout at Underwood's place in Georgetown that McFerrin had followed the trail to these woods—by following the man Reiner. *Reiner.* His pallor betrayed office work or laboratory work: a technician of some kind. But why a technician where a regular field agent would make more sense? The curiously light bullet? Perhaps.

McFerrin flicked off the safety.

"That was splendid," Reiner said. "The hits look truly splendid. But for all I can tell, it may be one of the shooters from the front that's making the head hit, while the other shooters are hitting the upper back and shoulders. If that's the case, I want to know it. I want all the head hits we can get."

Bittman made an understanding face.

"Moreover," Reiner said, "next run have one of the tower shooters put the new bullet in the trunk of the car. And I want to see the effect close up, make sure those frangibles are disintegrating against metal." Reiner gave Bittman a hard look. "Don't you worry about those jokers getting a good squint at me. You let *me* be the big worrier, my friend,"

Reiner said, his tone clearly announcing he meant business.

Bittman shuffled a bit, then yielded his ground. "Any way you want it. We can go right up by the flags if you want."

"Check," Reiner said. "That's what I want."

Bittman instructed the man on the rearward tower to lay the light shot in the trunk.

"I think you're going to like the way this bullet pulverizes," he said to Reiner as the two men walked toward the target zone. "It's bound to leave a dent, of course. But the main thing is, it won't leave a hole—at least nothing that looks like a bullet hole."

They reached the side of the road by the marked-out area. Bittman gave the signal. The big limousine began its run.

McFerrin raised the M-16. The limousine made the first turn, slowed, then accelerated to parade speed. Now it slowed again, to make the sharp left. Holding the rifle lightly, almost tenderly, McFerrin steadied himself and began counting. Reiner's doughy face was centered in the sights.

Reiner grinned as the limousine rolled smoothly toward the target zone. As the huge black car heaved nearer, Reiner said, more to himself, really, than to Bittman: "Jesus, God, I'd like to see the sonofabitch now. You know, the real blow-away?"

This was the last thing Reiner said, and the last thing Bittman heard. At the instant the limousine's bumper lined up with the first flag, McFerrin squeezed off. The explosion was terrific, the gun jumping hard. The first cracks of the other rifles were sounding in his ears as he geared down on the other man. He centered on the head and squeezed off. The second explosion was followed by the crack of the last of the practice shots.

The perfect bullet sandwich, goddamnit! Motionless in the grass, the rifle hugged under him, McFerrin surveyed his work. Reiner and Bittman had been dropped where they stood. McFerrin saw the first to move was the driver, who stood away from the car and started screaming at the riflemen on the knoll. The two shooters from the knoll came running, and now the shooters from the towers were climbing frantically down the ladders.

Still flat, McFerrin began to inch backward. Working his large body backward faster now, dragging the rifle in one hand and clutching the one ejected cartridge in the other, McFerrin kept his eyes on the men now gathered around the two sprawled bodies. None of the shooters had bothered to check out the area. Instead they were shouting, cursing, clearly frightened and bewildered. And probably ready to shoot each other in suspicion. McFerrin kept crawling backward until he reached the first cove of oak trees. Now he got up into a crouch, and keeping to the trees as cover, he backpedaled even faster. He never looked away from the men, but the men never looked up. McFerrin's last view, as he backed away into the woods, was of the five of them, down on their knees, poking at the dead men's heads. He had got them where he wanted, then. Head shots. Death shots. Then the trees and brush grew too dense, and he could no longer see the clearing from his crouch.

He heard it before his brain had a chance to classify the sound. He threw himself down. It was a helicopter. Prone, he flipped onto his back. He got a glimpse of its belly and guessed it was a two-seater traveling southward at an altitude of about fifteen hundred feet. The aircraft was directly above him now—over the woods rather than over the clearing, and sufficiently high up and far enough off to the side of the clearing that the pilot might have missed the scene at the practice site. McFerrin held his breath. Finally the helicopter banked sharply north and headed out. Was the helicopter connected in some way to the termination team? Who the hell knew? He wiped at his eyes. The sweat was pouring off him; his clothes were stuck to his skin. Now he turned his attention to locating the dead lookout, and found the body about thirty yards deeper into the woods. The man was flat out, eyes closed—and alive! From his chest came a soft groaning, and from his mouth a trickle of blood!

McFerrin pulled out the man's shirttail, used it to wipe fingerprints from the empty cartridge, and then dropped the cartridge in the grass. The other empty cartridge in the rifle's chamber McFerrin wiped off carefully and replaced in the chamber. Now he rubbed grime from the chamber of the rifle and pressed it into the man's right cheek. He then lay the rifle across the man's belly, taking the limp left hand and forcing it under the wooden grip in the front—thumb to the left, fingers to the right, standard grip. He held the hand there and pressed. Now he took the right hand, arranged it around the forward part of the stock and the trigger guard, and then very carefully placed the index finger on the trigger, holding it there for a moment. Satisfied, he gave the rifle a push off onto the grass with the back of his hands and tucked the shirttail back in place. He leaned close to the man's ear. He whispered: "You're a tough old critter, and I want you to know that I admire you for it. But, you know, good buddy, in less than five minutes you better quit all this struggling, because the way I see it you'll be dead."

McFerrin stood up, looked carefully around, and then he ran.

He found the tan Chevy Nova he had rented at O'Hare exactly where he had parked it in the grove of trees. He dragged himself behind the wheel and turned the ignition. He would make it out on the first plane. It was risky doing the obvious — heading straight for the airport, backtracking — but it was riskier to try for a less immediate escape route. He turned the air conditioner up high and drove with his left hand while he combed his fingers through his hair. And then he used his handkerchief and spit to get most of the dirt off his face. He took a look at himself in the mirror. Not bad. He could finish in the men's room at the airport, an hour's drive away.

He got rid of the car at O'Hare, paid Avis in cash, and went first to the novelties counter and bought the child's version of the Delta bag. In one of the stalls in the men's room, he dumped the three shells in with the flight bag candies. Then he went to the bank of baggage-check lockers in the lobby, stuck a coin in one, locked the toy bag inside, and placed the key in his pocket. He bought a pack of chewing gum. Then he went to the United counter and purchased, in cash, a round-trip ticket for the next New York flight. He booked his Chicago return for departure from New York two hours subsequent to his scheduled arrival at La Guardia. He made this transaction under the name L. Jensen, a different phony from the name he'd used with Avis.

It was not until the plane was airborne that McFerrin permitted himself to consider his fatigue. Now he lay back, exhausted, too weary even to light up a Schimmelpenninck, one of the small boltlike cigars he favored. It wasn't worth the effort, he decided.

He was utterly spent. He closed his eyes, and for the first time in days he allowed himself to drift. He had almost fallen asleep when he heard the stewardess ask if he would like something to drink.

"Bourbon," he said, but when she returned with the drink minutes later, Colin McFerrin was deep in sleep.

2

McFerrin started awake as if to a crash alert when the plane touched down at La Guardia. He shouldered into the aisle and out of the aircraft. He headed for the signs to the Washington shuttle, took his place in line, and within the half-hour he was in the air again on his way to the nation's capital.

His large frame was regathering its poise as he sat heavily back in his seat and let the plane carry him to cruising altitude. In his early thirties, nearly as strong as he had ever been, and he had been very strong, McFerrin was still close to his old football and wrestling weight. He'd wrestled unlimited class at Iowa and been one of the best running backs in the school's history. He knew his reflexes were still fast, his judgment still sharp.

As for Illinois, he knew he had done what he had had to do. He had acted on intuition, on instinct, made decisions on the spot and under pressure. It seemed right. It would take spontaneous action, explosive action, to keep off balance the large, complex thing he was up against. He had handed some agency—which agency?—a setback. It pleased Mc-

25

Ferrin to consider the chaos and alarm that would erupt from the discovery of his skirmish in the woods. Yes, that was the word he liked in this— *skirmish*, a little skirmish.

Yet it worried him now to feel the extent of his fatigue. Fatigue always followed killing—he knew that. Killing, as he had learned years ago, would leave you tired—tired for days. But he had never felt quite this tired. He felt—for the first time since he had quit intelligence service—a clenched feeling, and he felt a slamming weariness, a strangely persistent disquiet and sluggishness, as if he were half asleep and half adream in some unshakable waking nightmare.

It was then that the realization hit him, and it was like a splash of icy water. *He'd made a mistake.* The details wouldn't surface yet. But that was it: a mistake! The excessive fatigue was psychological. He knew and yet he refused to know—that was what made him so tired. But *what* mistake? What was the error that eluded his effort to grasp it? He probed. He tried every device of memory. *A mistake in Illinois.* What had he done wrong? Had he left a lead, something, behind? What had he *done* or *not* done that would unravel to his discovery? He knew there could be no mistakes. Not one. There was no margin for error. It was zero defects if you wanted to stay alive.

He kept repeating to himself, as a sort of magical chant that would reveal what he sought: *somewhere back in Illinois.* But what? Something *done* or something *not* done? What? True, he had taken a risk in carrying with him the key to the O'Hare locker where he had left the weird ammo. He checked again. The key was still firmly in place: stuck to the front of the heel of his right shoe, encased there in a wad of gum. He sat back, his mind working feverishly. What mistake? Where? When?

He was still probing relentlessly when the stewardess announced the approach to National Airport. The information went through McFerrin with the force of a blow. He sat straight up. *National!* He was landing at National—when his tailing of Underwood from Poucher's Virginia home and then Reiner from Underwood's Washington home had led him to Baltimore-Washington International Airport, not National. His car was parked *there*—not at National!

All right. Stupid, of course, but just an inconvenience. He would have to send someone with the parking ticket and the key. Dan. Dan could do it. McFerrin would send Greenfield—first thing.

No, the blunder was something else, and the hint of error behind him continued to plague McFerrin as the shuttle jet banked and then curled into its approach pattern. The Potomac flashed by below. As the aircraft descended to the rush of the runway and its sudden testimony of speed, McFerrin felt events racing, and his pulse quickened to keep pace. All right. He was one mistake over his quota. What it was and where it was logged he didn't know. What he *did* know was that, whatever it was, it would catch up with him. That he could count on. But in the meanwhile, all right! He was one over his quota; he would go no higher.

3

He poured Jack Daniels, added one cube, and drank
off half of it. Then he lay down on his living room
couch, his long legs propped on the armrest, eyes
closed, hoping to go blank for a while but knowing
too much was pressing around him to ease off,
knowing that this was the way it was going to be for
the rest of his life. And the knowledge that his life
might be very nearly ended overwhelmed him. He
had been so *sure* he was through forever, through
with the crazy circus of government working against
government, agency against agency—my God, agencies working secretly against themselves! And he
was sick of it—the whole mean, grinding wheel of the
new and invisible fifth estate, a dimension of government yet undiscovered in its magnitude by the media,
its hidden power still undreamed of by the people.
In even the most fanciful schemes of intrigue
favored by the most insanely radical paranoids, there
was nothing described that scarcely approached the
width and depth and mad architecture of the new
reality that had installed itself along the power
planes of America. Colin McFerrin *knew*—and there

28

were some times when he thought the knowledge would spill him into suicide or madness—but there were no times when he did not realize that the knowledge could get him killed—and that the action he was now taking *because* of what he knew had so heightened the odds against him that he was taking no bets. It was what he thought most about: their killing him. Oh, he knew how the wheels turned, how it went with intelligence murders. It was the hallmark of the new hidden national government, the orchestral deceptions that concealed the murders, deceptions devised by the best minds—hell, the best minds with an assist from the best computers. Yet the press could not even guess at what was really going on, at the power coordinates that had emerged with the advent of the Cold War. The long-nurtured, well-attended machinery had now so spread itself and so deepened itself and so concentrated itself that the installation of a new force from hub to radiating spokes was in fact invisible, *incredible*—strange and unreal—*weird*, really.

But it was specific death that got to Colin McFerrin—his own, first of all. He thought about it all the time. And he thought about Fred Macomber's—which, unlike McFerrin's, was no longer problematic. A jump from the window of his room at Bethesda Naval Hospital, widely featured in the news as a suicide. Macomber, a robust man, a big future in the cards, fair-haired boy of the C.I.A., an assistant director in his early forties, but let the record show he had become "depressed and paranoid." And now you would find nothing to dispute the record. Which agency handled the termination? McFerrin didn't know—and what did it matter? A potentially powerful man was targeted for elimination from the political arena. That was the size of it, and the size of it was taken care of—with such sleek and impervious methodology that McFerrin, himself a professional in the clandestine arts of government by finesse and force, couldn't help but admire. They kill your buddy and you admire their style. Christ! And no matter how hard McFerrin tried to get his mind off it, he always came back to the worldly incidentals, the nuts and bolts. What kind of sedation had Fred's doctor prescribed? How many operatives had been used to throw Fred out that window? Probably four, McFerrin liked to think. They would have taken no chances on such a high-level termination, a pre-executive termination. And *which agency?* Always: *which agency?* You never could tell.

And when McFerrin thought about Fred Macomber, it was always a short step to Henry Watts, a Pentagon-employed accountant who, on his own, had discovered and turned over to the General Accounting Office—and thus, in effect, to the press—the billion-dollar overrun the Air Force was encouraging its fighter-plane manufacturers to accrue each year. Well, of course the upper brass at the Air Force had become a trifle miffed at Watts. And so this one was called, in the trade, a "termination with prejudice." Funny, McFerrin thought, but I'm not laughing.

A low-category target, Watts was, as targets went. But attached to the assignment had been the verbal guidance of "strong interest at higher levels." That meant that Hank got it but good: fast and thorough.

So the police called to the scene of his death (on a bed in a rooming house that happened not to have

30

been where Watts lived) took one sniff. Ether, they declared—and the strongest whiff you get is precisely at the nose. Then they see the open ether can by the bedside. Ah, well—another "ether freak." End of case? Could have been, but wasn't. An assistant coroner making a routine autopsy finds arsenic in Henry's esophagus. In fact, he finds quite a lot of arsenic in Henry's esophagus. Far too much for any man, no matter how dedicated to self-destruction, to have gotten down into his esophagus—much less into his mouth. So this enterprising assistant coroner shows the autopsy report to good old Colin McFerrin because good old Colin McFerrin happens to be hanging around the morgue on C.I.A. business.

"Murder," good old Colin McFerrin volunteers, and enterprising young assistant coroner nods. Two dummies.

Murder it was not declared. Henry Watts had inspired the displeasure of Air Force high brass, and, even with him dead, there weren't going to be too many breaks coming Henry's way. When assistant coroner contacts Washington police, informs them he finds a murder on his hands, police don't seem very interested in the contents of assistant coroner's hands. Case already closed. Classified "suicide." Assistant coroner protests. He is very enterprising, very young. In fact, he protests so much he catches attention of Air Force high brass and the agency it used for Watts' termination. Assistant coroner is charged with incompetence. Assistant coroner is fired. Watts is buried. Truth is buried. Assistant coroner realizes it may not be very healthy to wonder too much about what the fuck is going on. Assistant coroner goes off to do his assisting somewhere else.

He wises up to a new understanding of the rules of enterprise—cardinal among which is *stay alive*. Case really closed now.

Ordinarily, of course, even where government could not accomplish outright ownership of the coroner or a key pathologist on his staff, most coroners avoided being so assiduous in their work as to step on the government's toe, much less on a corn. Government knew this and counted on it. There had been exceptions, of course: Deutsch in Pittsburgh, Akassi in Los Angeles, Callahan in New York. But for the most part it had been McFerrin's observation that government regularly managed to obtain sufficient autopsy control. The Watts case had been an exception. And McFerrin's helping it to be one helped him on his way out of C.I.A.

McFerrin moved his feet on the armrest and stretched his long body and sighed heavily. He was feeling more himself, he thought. He let his mind run, thought of Sciambra, his instructor in Clandestine Operations training at the Farm in the Virginia hills. "Give us the coroner," Sciambra had said, "and we can control the city."

McFerrin forced a look at his watch. He sat up, ran a hand through his hair. And though he'd never seen it, he had a flashing image of the thing that tracked him, a house-sized computer. *Walnut*. A spike of fear entered him and brought him off the couch into an aimless movement around his apartment. He was massively tired again. He went to the bathroom, washed his face. He brushed his teeth. He changed his clothes. He tried watching a talk show. He tried fooling around in the kitchen. He made his crazy brew, Turkish coffee with sage.

32

But it was all no use. He was afraid. All right, so he was afraid. He'd get used to it. In the morning he'd call Dan—get the car, get the memos and the other stuff going. And he'd call Val. In the morning it would be Saturday and he'd call Valerie. Valerie, he said to himself. Over and over. And that made it possible to sleep.

4

In the morning, when the congressional press room finally answered the phone, McFerrin got Dan Greenfield on the wire and told him to hurry over. Greenfield showed promptly, his dark, bony face lined with concern. He poured himself a hooker of Scotch and listened while McFerrin explained about the car. Then he shrugged. "All right, man, I'll get your car. But what's the action, for crying out loud?"

McFerrin made his voice severe. "You go ahead and do this for me, pal, you hear? Then I'll have some other stuff for you. Okay?"

"Okay, okay," Greenfield said, and downed his drink. "Anything you say, chief." He started for the door and turned. He smiled. "I was your main man in Nam, baby. I couldn't figure you then, and I can't figure you now—but I was always there, right?"

"Check," McFerrin said, and for some crazy reason tears welled up in his eyes.

"Okay, okay," Greenfield said, embarrassed. "I'm going. Later, cousin, okay?"

"Yeah," McFerrin said, and turned away.

After Greenfield left with the keys and the claim

ticket, McFerrin locked the door and lit up a Schim. He had to restrain himself from calling Valerie until he'd taken care of what he'd been too exhausted to do last night.

He went to the kitchen, took a knife, and with soap and water he freed the key to the O'Hare locker and dropped it into a carton of milk and put the carton back in the refrigerator. He kept the knife and rummaged through the kitchen drawers looking for a candle, and when he found one he stepped into the bathroom, shaved, and then lit the candle and let wax drip onto the blade. He spread wax over the right side of his face, from his chin up past his cheek and well around his cheekbone and then around the right side of his eye and up across his temple and all over his ear. He kept melting wax. He coated the inside of his right hand, forefinger, thumb, the crease between. When the wax had fixed, McFerrin peeled it off, washed his face, and rubbed at it vigorously with a towel. Then he repeated the entire procedure just to be sure, right side of face, right hand, cool, peel, wash, rub. What was left of the candle he cut up into small pieces, and he flushed these down the toilet with the used wax.

Then he washed the knife with cleanser, dried it, replaced it in the utensil drawer in the kitchen. He made himself a cup of Turkish coffee and went looking for where he had left the sage.

He sat on the kitchen stool, sipping, thinking, reviewing again. At least now, if he were given a paraffin test to determine whether he had fired a rifle, it wouldn't come up nitrate positive—as it would otherwise do even days later. About the goddamn neutron test McFerrin felt less confident.

All right, there was Quiller to be seen. McFerrin would have to set up the meeting as soon as the inflammation faded from his face and Greenfield had returned with his car. He made a second cup, sprinkled in the sage. Then he tried Valerie. No answer. He kept on trying Valerie's number all morning. Nothing. When Greenfield got back with the car, McFerrin tried again. Still no answer. All right, he'd call her after Quiller. She could wait. Quiller couldn't.

McFerrin told Dan he'd check with him later—and then they both rode the elevator down, and McFerrin put out his hand for the keys and took off.

5

McFerrin entered Arlington by the North Gate and parked. Before him spread the rising vista of the great green hill. He glanced at his watch and saw that he was early. He walked uphill toward the summit.

It was mid-July. With summer in Washington already in full flush, the cemetery seemed humid with death. Again McFerrin felt tears rising in him. What the hell was the matter with him, this emotion that was lately rising up in him, waves of uncontrolled feeling? White markers on the rolling green spread as far as the eye could see. It was a vast garden of fathers, of sons—dead men marked by petals of white stone.

How many could recall the reasons for the wars? But the dead in Arlington were dead, anyway. And Vietnam seemed as long ago as World War II. The Age of Nixon was well in the past now, although the patterns it established were of course more powerfully etched along the institutional interface. The National Security Agency—invisible enough to most Americans—had spun off the even more invisible Security Control Agency, whereas the Federal Bureau of Investigation was now augmented by the National Interior Reconnaissance Agency. Had things evolved all that much since Vietnam, since Nixon? Shit, McFerrin answered himself, how about *beyond recognition* just for starters!

He strolled past the graves, hands in pockets. The fatigue swept in upon him relentlessly. If he could only have back those years, all those years of doing the Agency's lunatic work, all the years chasing after a mission and being chased by death. It was true that he had hungered after accomplishment, that he had thought it all amounted to something, but that illusion had long since fallen from him, and almost all that Colin McFerrin had in actual fact to show for the lost years was a specialist's skill in killing.

The July morning had been very warm, but now a cool breeze brushed him, and he heard the rustle of leaves in a nearby tree. He looked up, saw that clouds were drifting into the summer sky.

Just up ahead he recognized the sycamore tree. And over the small hill beyond it, he found the headstone he was looking for. "William McFerrin," it read, "1945–1969." He hunkered down, flicked away an old clutter of leaves. A wave of emotion washed up in him again. But what's so extraordinary about wanting to cry at your brother's grave? Not a damn thing, McFerrin assured himself. There was too much memory, that was all, and McFerrin turned away from the grave. He stood up again, not easily, and walked briskly westward toward the sector where he knew he would find the Blackburne headstone.

McFerrin entered upon a battalion of small markers whose shut-down dates were all 1861, the numerals fading now—he was approaching the grave of Brigadier General Clarence Blackburne. The wind was rising, and this time it brought a gust of rain with it. McFerrin wiped at his face. He picked his way through a grove of trees.

The President's man was waiting.

"You look lousy," Quiller said.

"Same to you," McFerrin said.

Thunder rolled across the sky. Quiller glanced up. "You never were much on wit," he said. "Let's get moving. My car's over by the gate."

They started ahead quickly toward the North Gate. When the rain came in earnest, they broke into a trot. McFerrin could feel his legs complaining.

McFerrin had met Quiller at Yale, where McFerrin had gone for postgraduate study in history after quitting the Agency. Quiller was famous even then, and a chance to pick up on his popular course in constitutional law had put McFerrin in Quiller's class. Their friendship had begun slowly because of McFerrin's midwestern distrust of Ivy League types: he had seen a bit too much of the old school ties back in his C.I.A. days.

But Franklin Quiller had turned out to be something more than a rumpled J. Press sport coat with leather patches at the elbows. Quiller had turned out to be a commanding figure. And this was reflected in his face—the face of a scholar and of a man of character and humane purpose. McFerrin had found Quiller's intellect immensely appealing, and there had been something irresistible in his dreamer's conviction that there was no disease in American life that would not yield to the radiant medicine of the

39

Constitution. For a time, in fact, Quiller had worked hard at trying to talk McFerrin into going into international law and diplomacy. But McFerrin had had enough of government in any form. A law professor then, Quiller was still a law professor—although he had meanwhile become a distinguished special advisor to the President of the United States. He was a top man at the White House and busy as anyone else there; yet he managed to give a weekly lecture on constitutional law at Georgetown, the attendance at these talks limited to heavy-gun scholars and to movers and shakers of a political type. If ordinary lawyers had been let in, Radio City couldn't handle the gate.

McFerrin folded himself into the small English roadster. Quiller settled himself comfortably and took out his pipe. "Okay, let's get right into it, Colin."

McFerrin hesitated. He wasn't at all sure how this man, with his deep belief that every problem gave way to a legal and equitable solution, would accept the killing that had been necessary.

McFerrin longed to convert Quiller into a man who understood necessity as well as he understood constitutional law and political philosophy. McFerrin shrugged—and plunged ahead. He left nothing out. When McFerrin had finished, Quiller was silent, his majestic eyebrows furrowed in concentration. Quiller simply chewed his pipe, kept frowning, kept driving. At last McFerrin said, "Goddamnit, where are we going?" His knees were jammed up against the dashboard. He reached down under the seat and found the lever and tried to shove the seat back. It wouldn't budge. Quiller, as big a man as McFerrin, perhaps a little taller even, seemed enormously comfortable. He drove, silent. McFerrin lit a Schim. Finally, Quiller let out a long, low whistle.

"Yeah, sure," McFerrin muttered, "now where the hell are we headed?"

"Nowhere in particular. We'll just drive and talk while I think this out. I'm an old cow, Colin. This is tall grass you're feeding me, and if you don't mind I'll just run it through all my stomachs before I come up with the milk you want."

There was another long silence. And then McFerrin said, "I gather you're unhappy I got involved in a little action."

"A little action? Is that what you call it?" Quiller turned off toward the National Observatory Park. "You can't expect me to be happy about this. You know how I feel about solving problems by force. Force is what we're against—doing things the way Poucher and his mob do." At length he added, "Yet I will concede, Colin, that I'm not sure you really had all that much choice. For if you hadn't shot up the place then and there, you would never have had another chance—and maybe this will scare Poucher and Underwood off."

"You're a prince," murmured McFerrin. "Anyhow, that's my thought too."

"But we seem to have stumbled into this thing ass backwards," Quiller continued.

"Nothing's perfect," McFerrin said. "Everything about this thing is ass backwards. You said go to hell on out there after Reiner and do what I could. All right, I did what I could."

"Well, let's look at it this way. Aren't we now in

the position of having yanked out a few of the shark's teeth but having lost the shark itself?"

"Not exactly," McFerrin said. "We know there *is* a shark, an actual operation underway, just as you suspected. And now we know for certain that General Underwood was managing, and possibly General Poucher sponsoring."

"All very well, all very well, old son. But you tell me: *Who* is managing Poucher?"

"Look, Frank, we didn't know *that* when we started watching the bastards. We just played a long hunch and it paid off. So what the hell have we *lost?*"

Quiller took his own time answering. He pulled on his pipe and then he said, "Colin, I want you to consider this thing more broadly, that's all. I want you to see that what I'm worrying about is the possibility that your little action, as you call it, may have triggered the wrong reaction. Think with me in this, my friend. That's all—*think.* Maybe what you did will work out all right. But maybe it won't. I just want you to examine the possibilities—be prepared to reflect on them, that's all."

Quiller seemed satisfied with the lesson. He puffed on his pipe. McFerrin took the stub of the cigar from between his teeth and said, "Let me say it this way, Frank: Go to hell, please. Don't you think I know all this?"

Quiller waited a dramatic moment and then said, "If you *know* it, old son, why all the annoyance with my saying it?"

Quiller turned off into the park. Clusters of bright yellow lilies began to move slowly past the window. McFerrin crushed out his cigar in the ashtray. The little roadster was thick with smoke, and Quiller kept his windows closed against the driving rain. McFerrin pointedly rolled down his window. "I did what seemed to me to need doing."

Did Quiller hear him? McFerrin couldn't tell. McFerrin often couldn't tell with Quiller. The man was—the word was *enigmatic*, that's it. "I said ——" McFerrin began, but Quiller made his speech as if not a stroke had been skipped.

"Oh, there's no doubt that Underwood's the grand master at assassination—in a country that can boast more than its share. Of masters, I mean. That means he's pretty far up—in *some* structure. But in *which* structure? C.I.A.? Underwood retired from the Agency years ago. But is Poucher using Underwood to bring in other C.I.A. people, or is Underwood enlisting from D.I.A.? Or even someplace else? And Poucher—is Poucher working this for the Pentagon and the Joint Chiefs, or for some independent outfit or D.I.A.? And from the picture you've given me of the interplay between our various agencies, our esteemed General Underwood and our no less esteemed General Poucher might not even be genuinely integral parts of the structure backing the assassination. They might merely appear to be center stage —and believe the roles themselves—while the crucial scenes are being played backstage. That's straight out of McFerrin's Intelligence community playbook, isn't it?"

"A classic," McFerrin said, all business now. "Underwood could be working for an insulated group, thoroughly capsulated from some parent organization. But that would require a remote-control action, and it would be damned expensive for any agency to do that when instead it could use its own men, already on the government payroll, familiar with that agency's particular mode of operations. And Underwood would have to feel pretty damn uncomfortable handling a farm-out from an insulated sponsor. That would mean the long-range strategic decisions would have been made even before the mission was turned over to him. Poucher? Made by Poucher?"

Quiller shrugged and kept the car moving smoothly along. "Of course decision making is always available once there exists the will for the venture. Capital too. To know an assassination is going to occur is to be able to predict otherwise unpredictable changes in foreign policy. And that means you're talking about billions of dollars, not millions. Megamoney, so much money that a sizable fee for Underwood or an interest for Poucher wouldn't even register on the long side of the decimal point."

McFerrin impatiently lit a new cigar. Quiller was drifting off into grand theoretical speculations. "Shit, Frank, every goddamn agency invests in the stock market on a regular basis —and if they're orchestrating an international incident or something of the sort, they go for a real ride. They've got more conduits available than they need—dummy foundations, cover corporations, you name it."

Quiller was all smiles. "That's what I mean, old son. So you see, an Underwood and a Poucher would be cheap money in the long run. Which leaves us with our original problem, trying to identify the ultimate sponsor."

McFerrin was finding the whole exchange somewhat quaint, just a beat too cute. He liked Frank

Quiller, he really admired the man; but he did not like Quiller's patronizing him, and McFerrin did not like his own willingness to play into it.

Quiller drove past the National Observatory and took the next turn, deeper into the park. The rain was thicker, the air in the car heavy, even with McFerrin's window open.

"How about we start with the elementary question," McFerrin said. "I don't want to insult that big brain of yours, Frank—but we might just begin by asking: Who gains? Who gains if the President dies?"

Quiller regarded McFerrin balefully, tolerantly, master teacher hearing the obscenely innocent question that comes at the start of every semester. "Of course," he said, too patiently, "but that's not really the problem, Colin. When you're considering the prospect of a President being assassinated, the problem is not his enemies but his friends. And the President has many, many friends."

McFerrin knew better than to respond. Instead he waited for the inevitable rhetorical question and the pompously stated answer that would follow.

"And why should this be?" Quiller began. "Because assassinations are distinctly unlike all other varieties of murder. The usual motives—greed, hate, revenge, whatever—you can dismiss, at least as primary motives. Assassinations of chiefs of state are invariably motivated by principle. And when men see themselves as motivated by some high principle —such as national security, or what they conceive to be national security—it is infinitely more satisfying to them to knock out a man they're fond of rather than one they hate. Because," Quiller continued, "when you bump off a man you're fond of, you prove

45

all your principles are of the highest order and earnestly held. After all," Quiller said, deftly making himself a new pipe with one hand while guiding the wheel with the other, "what greater satisfaction can there be for men who already wield great power than to demonstrate to themselves their own power *over themselves?* Perhaps it is not the President's enemies but his *friends* whom we must consider."

"Friends who disagree with him on principle," McFerrin added in perfunctory fashion, knowing he was expected to provide a line not unlike the one he'd uttered.

"A relatively reliable conclusion, Colin. Now, just who would such friends be?"

McFerrin studied his friend's face. He noticed that the white tufts of eyebrows were raised, as always, in anticipation, Quiller feeding a pet student an easy question to give himself the pleasure of hearing it correctly answered.

McFerrin blew out a needle of smoke. "Jesus *Christ,* Frank, will you cut out the goddamn patronizing!"

Quiller seemed amused at this outburst. "I'm sorry. Damn old teacherly habit is all."

McFerrin was annoyed with himself for letting his annoyance show. "That's okay, Quill," he said. "Forget it, for Christ's sake. I'm kind of off my stride. Tired."

"I shouldn't doubt it," Quiller said. "That game you played out in the woods must have been a bit of a strain, to say the least."

"Yeah," McFerrin said, irritated again, resenting the formal nod of sympathy.

"Look," Quiller said, "you really don't seem at

46

all yourself, Colin. I mean, you really do look lousy —so what do you say we close down for the time being—pick it up tomorrow, say."

"Up yours, Frank. I feel *fine*, in the pink. And if I could see you through the smoke screen you're hanging out, I guess you wouldn't look so hot, either."

"Sorry," Quiller said quickly, and casually rolled down his window.

"Thanks," McFerrin said.

"No sweat," Quiller said, and occupied himself with his driving.

McFerrin couldn't resist it: "You're his friend," he said. "Let's not forget that, Frank. You're Edward Burlingame's best friend, now that I think about it."

Quiller smiled. "True, true," he said. "Perhaps I should be suspected."

"All right, Quill," McFerrin said, "I'll keep you under suspicion."

"Good," Quiller said.

"Then there's Danforth," McFerrin said, looking out his window.

"Exactly," Quiller said. "The Secretary of State —another close friend of the President."

Quiller seemed distracted now, or so McFerrin thought. McFerrin shook his head. "Danforth's the only one I *don't* suspect. The man has *always* fought the good fight, and now that he's Secretary of State, he's still doing it. That guy is okay, Quill. And don't hand me this shit that you suspect *him*. You're horsing around with me, and I don't like it. I don't have, *we* don't have, time for horsing around anymore, Frank—and you know it well as me—just as you

47

know as well as me Danforth is clean. The man is beyond question."

Quiller gestured with his pipe. The theatrics of it filled McFerrin with an unexpected loathing for the man. He knew it was crazy, but McFerrin suddenly hated Quiller, was convinced that he had always hated Quiller. Perhaps his skirmish in the Illinois woods had affected him more than he realized.

Quiller was nodding, and poking the air with his pipe.

"Colin, you *must* be off your stride," he said. "For there is no one, Colin, *no* one who is beyond question. Not Danforth, not me, not the President himself."

"Oh, fuck off, teach," McFerrin snapped.

Quiller blinked. "All right, old son," he said, and smiled. "Now to the point. The issue is Greece. The President is determined to support the popular government there, while Poucher and the Pentagon are pressing the President to help put the Greek military back in power. Naturally, with the Greek military back in, the U.S. would have more control. The pressure on the President is strong. Control of the Middle East oil is involved, the Mediterranean as a base for the Sixth Fleet, et cetera. The usual," Quiller said.

"So, who's pushing hardest?" McFerrin said, hoping Quiller was going to give him a chance to apologize, for McFerrin was already sorry about his outburst, already ashamed of his anger.

"Poucher, the Joint Chiefs," Quiller said.

"That puts us right back where we started," McFerrin said. "Poucher and crew can't get what they want because the President stands in the way—so they hire Underwood to make the President lie down in his grave. You're so smart, you took us in a circle, teach. So you're *not* so goddamn smart!" McFerrin said.

Quiller exercised his abundant eyebrows, laughed —and then McFerrin laughed, and when the two of them had recovered from laughter that had nothing to do with the remark that released it, they grinned at each other, and McFerrin said, "Sorry for blowing my stack, Quill—I really am."

"That's okay, Colin," Quiller said. "You're bushed. I know."

"I am," McFerrin said, feeling leaden and selfconscious. He stubbed out his cigar in the ashtray.

Quiller glanced at him sympathetically. "You want to go back?" he said.

"Right," McFerrin said, and kept his eyes fastened on the foliage as the car made its way out of the park.

As they neared Arlington, McFerrin abruptly laughed. He found himself laughing hard and a little hysterically.

"Easy now," Quiller said, but McFerrin kept on laughing, swept along on the wave.

"It's funny," McFerrin finally said. "The net effect of the whole goddamn Illinois number is going to be fucking-A *zero*. I mean, so whoever the hell it is just goes back and plans again and blows me up, too. What I'm beginning to see in this is that maybe the only way to save the President is if they snuff me first and it opens them up, you know? That's funny, isn't it, Quill, old top? I mean, one guy trying to save another guy has to get himself snuffed to maybe do it?"

"Easy now," Quiller said, and that was all he said until he said, "It happens all the time, Colin."

"What?" McFerrin said, no longer thinking of what he had said, thinking now only of getting back and getting Valerie.

"One man giving his life to save another's."

McFerrin did not answer. He was thinking about the memos. He wasn't going to tell Quiller about it. Quiller might quarrel with the notion. But McFerrin knew he was right. Quiller was okay so far as Quiller went. But instinct, intuition, invention, were guiding McFerrin—and now that he'd gone this far with it, he was going all the way. *His* way.

"What?" McFerrin said again. "I missed that."

"I said," Quiller said as McFerrin climbed out of the car, "there's ample precedent for one man giving his life to save another man's life."

"Yeah, Frank, I've read some history, too," McFerrin said, and shut the door.

6

McFerrin drove back to his apartment, annoyed with himself for his display. It troubled him to have been so visibly impatient with Quiller, so obviously irritated by the man's inability to grasp the reality of what had happened in the Illinois woods. And all that endless high-toned speculation had drawn him to the edge of hysteria. From McFerrin's point of view, the entire affair—from his coming across the spoor of Underwood, and perhaps Poucher, on a tip from Quiller, to his dancing all over a fatigue chest and burning Reiner and Bittman was wild enough to make anyone crazy. Still, he had not behaved well with Quiller.

He changed his clothes after a shower—the soap stinging his face where the wax had been used—and then splashed some bourbon into a glass, thought better of it, and made coffee instead, the Turkish concoction he'd gotten a habit for on some goddamn Agency trek, he couldn't remember which. He drank the thick pungency down in two swallows, skidded some specks of sage from his teeth to his tongue, and spit them into the sink.

It was to happen in August, the first of August, when the President spoke in Kansas City. That was all Quiller had heard, all he had told McFerrin—that and that Poucher and Underwood might be in some way involved. Quiller had warned the President, but the President seemed unconvinced. "Too much paranoia these days," Edward Burlingame had protested. So Quiller had called on McFerrin to track Underwood and Poucher, to find out more, to see what might be done. And why not? McFerrin had been one of the best when he was an Agency man, and Quiller knew that—knew the skills and loyalties of his old student. And McFerrin had done what he could. Now he would do more. He called Greenfield and set up the memos. Then he dialed Valerie's number again. No answer. He held the receiver while he counted rings to twenty—she could be in the shower or on the patio, in the sack with the man who was arranging the murder of the President, who the hell knew?—and then McFerrin hung up. A moment later he raised the receiver again and dialed. Still no answer. He drank the bourbon he had poured, and then he drank a second hooker. He sat down on the couch. Then he lay down on the couch. Then he rolled onto the floor, pulled a cushion from the couch, and then pushed the cushion away and did forty push-ups and then eighty sit-ups. Then he showered again and changed his clothes again. And at last he dialed Valerie's again—but her phone still refused to answer.

He knew he needed Valerie. He knew he needed to hold her, to talk to her right away—before he wound up talking to himself. McFerrin wanted to talk about his fear, his fatigue—and he wanted to talk about *Walnut*, Poucher, Underwood. Underwood, the bastard. The Master they called him—still The Master, though he was retired. Bullshit! Effective senior Agency officers never really retired. They only appeared to. They might receive fewer assignments, and they might show up at Langley Field very rarely, but these hugely skilled men, experts on the scale of Underwood, worked and were worked until they were dead. One agency's "retired" expert would become a highly paid specialist for another agency —even while he drew retirement benefits from his original outfit. Underwood really retired? Like hell he was! You couldn't sell that bullshit if it were lifeboats in a flood.

But McFerrin was tired of thinking, tired of contradictions, tired of ironies, and tired of longing for Valerie, her throaty voice, her ferocious body. He ate a little supper and then lay down on the couch with a copy of Sandburg's *Lincoln*.

7

It was almost midnight when he awoke. He was on the floor, next to the couch. Had he fallen asleep here? Fallen asleep on the couch and rolled onto the floor? McFerrin couldn't remember. He felt leaden. He sat up and then eased back down. He was awfully groggy, would have to come gradually awake, move gradually. He stretched out on the rug, and then he felt it, a *presence*, and in one motion he bucked to his feet and stood poised, ready to spring.

The two men were sitting on the couch, quite comfortably, altogether blasé. The one to the left leaned well back, with one leg on the coffee table. The other sat primly, despite his large size, with his legs crossed. McFerrin instantly surmised that neither man could make an action toward him without first adjusting to a stance from which to spring forward. The man to McFerrin's right, the big one, wore an extravagant grin, whereas the man to McFerrin's left sat back in the couch, his face inexpressive, his posture languid. The black .45-caliber automatic he held pointed its snout at McFerrin's belt.

"Forgive me for not being awake to hear the doorbell," McFerrin said.

"No problem," the smaller man said. "We just came on in."

"Didn't want to disturb you," the big one said, and grinned more broadly.

"He needs his beauty rest," the small one said.

"That's it," the big one said. "We could see you needed your beauty rest," and he laughed.

"Enough shit," the small one said, and waved the automatic. "You park your pretty ass over *there*," he said, indicating a chair.

McFerrin shrugged loosely, moved to the chair, and sat down. "I don't know you boys," he said. "Tell me, are you friend or foe?"

The man with the gun gave a nod to the big man. "Clyde," he said, "it's dial-for-dollars time."

The big man got up and walked to the phone. He was a powerful man, his heavy shoulders drawing the jacket of his brown suit tight across his back. He dialed with thick fingers. McFerrin listened for the digit count while he studied a point midway between the two men.

The big man spoke into the phone. "Clyde. He's here. Okay." He hung up. "He's on his way," the big man said.

"That's nice," the small man said. "Can't play bridge without a fourth."

The big man laughed. "You're too full of shit, Ben," the big man said, and then he turned to McFerrin. "Colin!" he said. He grinned, showing enormous yellow teeth. "Where'd you get a fruity name like Colin?"

McFerrin said, "Well, you see, when the big fella

in heaven who hands out names had used up 'Clyde'
on all the imbeciles, he——"

"You're a regular scream, McFerrin," snapped
the small man.

"Yeah," the big man said, "fruitface is a laugh and
a half."

"Up your gigantic asshole!" McFerrin said, not
really looking at either man, his attention still equi-
distant between them.

"Colin McFerrin," the small man said. "Age
thirty-two, born Cedar Rapids, Iowa, to Alice Mar-
shall and John McFerrin. Graduated McKinley High
School; B.A., University of Iowa, in three years.
Year of postgraduate work in history at Yale. Two
years with the Green Berets." His toneless rote
issued out of him mechanically, as if he had a tape
player and amplifier built into his larynx.

"How come fruitface didn't go to *Har-vard?*" the
big man said.

"You went there in a bottle, Pluto?" McFerrin
said.

"Served in Nam two years," the small one said,
"then attached to Central Intelligence. Specific
assignments to be made available. Whenever he can,
he gets his pecker into one Valerie Craig, *Mrs.* letter
T., Fort Meade connection National Security Agency,
clear-channel rating; white female, home address
5340 Gwinett Street, Washington, D.C. Started
getting nooky off her while still associated with
C.I.A."

"Fuck you," McFerrin said.

"Tut, tut," the big man said. "Fruitface got a
naughty mouth."

"Left C.I.A. after five years," the small man went

on. "Appointed assistant professor of history at Commonwealth State College, Philadelphia."

"Impressive performance," McFerrin said, "but what's the matter with lard ass? Brain still out for a lube job?"

"Oh, he's dumb, all right," the small man said. "You know how it is with these big guys, heads made out of stoneware."

"Right," the big man said. "I ain't smart like Professor fruity-name McFerrin." And now, almost automatically, he began his own recitation. "Defendant in three arrests: one at New Haven, Connecticut, while postgraduate student at Yale University. Charge: intoxication. Charge dismissed in city court, insufficient evidence. First traffic arrest, Des Moines, Iowa. Speeding. Fined twenty-five dollars. Second traffic arrest, Philadelphia. Violation of stop sign. Fined twenty dollars."

McFerrin laughed. "You fellas must be nuts. Those last two weren't arrests, for God's sake. Those were traffic tickets. Is that why you busted into my apartment? You aim to scold me for outrageous conduct behind the wheel?"

"Oh, yes," the small man said. "We are going to scold you all right."

"Member, Philadelphia Athletic Club," the big man recited. "Occasionally plays tennis at city park courts. Present status: still attached to faculty at Commonwealth State. Promoted to associate professorship. Permanent residence: 2736 Monroe Street, Philadelphia."

McFerrin slowly began to stand up. "How many entrances to my Philadelphia apartment?"

"Three," replied the big man. "One front, one

side, one back. And get your fucking keester back in that chair."

"Thank you," said McFerrin, sitting down again. "I remember that question on the census form last year. So it's in the computer, in *Walnut* already. Used to be a two-, three-year lag. Things are looking up."

Ignoring him, the big man continued: "Tends to be a loner. Reads extensively. No homosexual tendencies established. Ha, ha. Fruitface ain't a queer—*yet*. Society and association memberships: not known other than Philadelphia Athletic Club, as indicated."

"Hey, Homo!" McFerrin called to the big man. "You and the girl friend here belong to any clubs together—you know, the Knitting Auxiliary, Sewing Circle, Needlepoint Nances, stuff like that?"

"You may continue now, Clyde. We are amused, Professor McFerrin. Please understand that Clyde and I wish you to know that we are tremendously amused by the lofty character of your wit."

The big man grinned and began again. "Travels often. When in New York, usually stays at the Plaza; when in Los Angeles, usually stays at Century Plaza; when in Chicago, usually stays at the Palmer; when in Iowa, usually stays with relatives or friends."

"Great going," McFerrin said. "That must be really handy to have that great stuff at your fingertips."

"Subscription to radical magazines," the big man said. "None indicated. Memberships in subversive organizations: none indicated. Reason for current presence in Washington: not yet determined."

McFerrin said, "Hey, Ben, excuse me, but I took a crap this morning. You want to get that down there just in case there's maybe a code in my turds, you know?"

"One more cuteness from you, Professor, and I am going to have to scold you a little," the big man said, staring at McFerrin with impassive eyes.

"You scare shit out of me, Pluto," McFerrin said.

"Clyde," the small man said pointedly, "I don't believe the professor has yet learned the virtue of patience. Perhaps we'd best proceed to business." He turned to McFerrin. "All right, my friend, let's get to the subject at hand. You do not belong in this city. Your sweet ass is not wanted in this city. Now you tell good Clyde and me precisely what it is you are doing in this fair city."

"What in hell are you talking about?" McFerrin said.

The small man shook his head with exaggerated weariness. "It seems I cannot communicate with him, Clyde. Do you imagine you can?"

The big man moved heavily to where McFerrin sat. He stood massively over him. "We want to know your business here. You tell me your business here, little darling, or I tear your rectum out and give it back to you for a wallet. I am not funning, little darling."

"Tell you *what?*" McFerrin said. "I got these carrots in my ears and I can't hear you."

McFerrin rolled just ahead of the blow, but the force was nevertheless immense. The right side of his head seemed to explode in light. When he came to his senses, he could hear the small man laughing softly.

"On your feet, babycakes," the big man said. "Uncle Clyde wants to lay some real good wood to

you now. Upsy-daisy, babycakes. Upsy-daisy now."
McFerrin felt himself being lifted by the belt, and
when he thought he was upright, that he might be
on his feet, a pillar of cement rammed him full in
the stomach, and he heard a sound like a rubber
ball slamming against a brick wall. Then, what
seemed hours later, he heard someone speaking to
him, in a gentle, coaxing way.

"Get up, get up, sleepyhead—get up and tell me
your pretty dream." It was the big man, McFerrin at
last realized, and McFerrin decided to do as he was
told. He got up very slowly. The big man stood there,
grinning proudly. But the big man now stood between
McFerrin and the .45. How nice, thought McFerrin,
how thoughtful. And just as he was coming up from
his crouch, McFerrin locked his hands together and
brought them up under the big man's chin. He let
his chest go into it, blasting upward, his locked fists
a block of spectacular force. The big man's head
snapped back strangely, and McFerrin heard the
familiar click. The big man sagged, a split sack of
salt with the grains racing out.

McFerrin took him under the arms and let him
down onto the floor. He turned and very quietly sat
back down in his chair and very deliberately pulled
out his flat tin of cigars and removed one of the
Schims. He was gambling, he knew that. But what
else could he do? Whoever was coming was coming
to see him alive and would not be pleased to find
him too much less than that.

McFerrin was shaking, his heart heaving from the
exertion and his head roaring with pain. He wondered if an organ might be damaged; he was afraid
to think what might be loose and bleeding in his gut.

"You fool," the small man said, frozen in place, clearly stunned by the exceptional theater he had just witnessed.

McFerrin faced him. "I beg your pardon?" he said.

"You are unintelligent," the small man said.

"Sorry," McFerrin said.

"What did you do to him?" the small man said, somewhat hoarsely.

"Oh." McFerrin glanced down at the big man, piled into a mountain on the carpet. McFerrin blew out a narrow stream of smoke.

"I believe I broke poor Clyde's neck. May even have severed his spinal column."

"You broke his what?" the small man screamed, standing up, suddenly very excited.

"His neck," McFerrin said calmly. "You know. Da haidbone connected t' da shoulderbone—you've heard that one. Bet you sang it when you were a cute little fella in knickers, even tinier than you are now. Well, right between the headbone and the shoulderbone comes the neckbone, and it is my belief that what your friend Clyde has experienced is an abrupt fracturing of his neckbone."

"And what am I supposed to do now?" the small man virtually whined.

McFerrin drew on his slim cigar. "I don't know what your instructions are. But if you want my advice, little man, I'd worry. I could worry with you if you wish. We could worry together while we passed the time until whoever you called comes, and when he gets here we could all three of us worry together."

The small man seemed very confused. He nodded toward the big man on the floor. "He dead or not?"

McFerrin leaned over and felt for a pulse. Then he felt the back of the big man's neck, probing with his fingers. "I really don't want to venture a guess. Let me say," McFerrin said, "that he teeters on the brink."

"We'll wait for instructions," the small man said aloud.

"Of course," McFerrin said, sitting back comfortably in his chair. "It's perfectly all right with me if you wish to stay on the premises—but I really must see some credentials, you know."

The small man jiggled the automatic. "This is my bar mitzvah certificate," he said, collecting himself now, putting his foot up on the coffee table again.

"Oh, but it's not adequate," McFerrin said, "not acceptable at all. You see, if I take that gun and shove it up your asshole—which I imagine I will have to do if I don't see some sort of official identification and fast—then that rig of yours is going to hurt like the dickens going in sideways. I want to see your authority for being here," McFerrin said. "I want to see some government credentials of some kind."

The small man shrugged. He reached into his breast pocket with his left hand. "If it will civilize you," he said. "At least this will give you some idea of the size of the wringer you've caught your tit in." He flipped a black credential folder to McFerrin and held the gun trained carefully on McFerrin's beltline as he moved his hands up to catch.

McFerrin studied the credentials closely, saw the big blue Federal Bureau of Investigation circular seal, saw that the thing appeared to be legitimate, saw that the photo was clearly that of the small man.

McFerrin looked up. "So you're F.B.I.—so what the fuck is the beef?"

"I'm F.B.I. and you are unintelligent," the small man said.

"Sure, you're F.B.I.," McFerrin said. "You're F.B.I. and I'm Shirley Temple." He leaned forward slightly and tossed the black folder into the wastebasket.

The small man sat transfixed in astonishment, his face coloring, tense with fury. His gun hand started shaking.

"Easy, sister," McFerrin said to him firmly. "Get hold of yourself. You burn me and you're in big trouble. Use that thing before your buddy gets here, you'll be cleaning toilets in Leavenworth."

The small man sat glaring at McFerrin, the rage in his face giving way to uncertainty.

"You see, Ben," McFerrin said, "you're at an awkward stage. You're caught in an era of tremendous transition in the uses of authority—and that's created a problem for you. And of course for our friend Clyde down there as well." McFerrin interrupted himself for a moment, reached down, and felt Clyde's pulse. "Still teetering," he said, and smiled sympathetically. "Anyway, as I was saying, your problem is that you're caught between two eras, which puts you in a damnably clumsy position. And it's for the same reason that the regulations you're operating under and the instructions you've been given are just a little too vague to cover the unconventional situation in which you now find yourself. Am I right, Ben boy?"

At length the small man said, "That describes it very neatly, yes."

"Of course," McFerrin said, with an expansive wave of his hand.

The small man shook his head slowly. "Jesus," he said, "this is crazy."

"Of course," McFerrin said. "You've got it now. It's crazy."

There was a long silence, the two men staring as if considering something. Then the door buzzer sounded. The small man got up and walked quickly across the floor. "Hi," McFerrin heard the small man say.

But McFerrin did not turn to see who stood at the door. Instead, he sat comfortably in his chair and faced the far wall. He knew that for the first time in days, he was utterly relaxed, deeply calm. It was *happening*—it was opening up.

8

McFerrin had a sudden sense of being a misbehaving child waiting fearfully while elders conferred in the matter of his insult to society. He heard Ben and the new man muttering as they approached. And when they were standing before him, McFerrin had an impulse to put out his cigar, as if his smoking were the offense for which he was now waiting reproach or punishment.

The new man was big enough, very smartly dressed, a gray silk tie waved handsomely over a very white, very starched, shirt. In the dim light, his face at first seemed soft, undercooked, set off only by the zigzag of a deep, short scar on his chin—an oddly flat face, the nose plainly broken at least once. But when the man moved into better light, McFerrin could see that this was a face like none he had ever seen before—the parts vaguely out of place, the cast of the skin and its taut texture like gelatin over bone. The man's face was hideous—a shelled hard-boiled egg gray from long refrigeration, with slits for eyes and mouth, and a little hill of flesh for a nose.

The new man stared at McFerrin and then looked

casually down at the big man's body where it lay on the floor.

"What is this?" he said, his voice gutted of all emotion.

McFerrin's mind skipped through the possibilities, like index cards flashed by fingers. Was he dealing with the C.I.A.'s Special Division—which investigated the Agency's own security problems—or with the D.I.A.? Who the hell *was* he dealing with? With something like twenty Federal agencies policing for the Government, the permutations of the probabilities were endless.

"I hurt your man," McFerrin said. "Your man insisted that I hurt him."

"Call Agajadian," the new man said to Ben. "Tell him I want a cleaning unit over here."

Then the new man sat down opposite McFerrin. While the man Ben used the phone, the new man sat silently contemplating McFerrin through bemused eyes. McFerrin wanted to look away from that face, but he did not. He returned the new man's stare. After a time, McFerrin said, "Your friend might live, but he'll need a permanent good buddy to catch his crap in a cup."

The new man made no reply. When Ben finished at the phone, the new man said, "Just what is your problem, Mr. McFerrin? Are you trying to prove you're a tough fellow, Mr. McFerrin? I advise you not to try to prove that with me. I will crush your nuts, Mr. McFerrin. Understand me? Now then, are you having a bit of awkwardness answering questions? Is that your little problem, Mr. McFerrin?"

"My problem is someone busts into my apartment

and tries to fuck me over. And someone pretends to be F.B.I. and isn't."

"Just who," asked the man, "has pretended to be F.B.I. and isn't?"

McFerrin nodded to Ben. "Your man right there."

"What makes you think my man right there is *not* F.B.I.?" the new man said, his eyes relentless, the awful color and composition of his face making McFerrin want to look away.

"Bureau agents don't use .45 automatics. Starting with their Quantico training—and from then on—they use .38's. That's for openers. I could give you nine other reasons, but why bother?"

"Mr. McFerrin, I won't waste words with you. I suppose you know you're in serious trouble for assaulting a Federal agent. Frankly, I think you exercised extremely impeachable judgment for a former Government agent and for a man with such a good combat record." The man examined his fingernails, well manicured in contrast to the scrambled quality of his face.

"Frankly," McFerrin said, "I don't give a rat's fart what you think."

Now the man gave McFerrin a deadly gaze. "You can't say I didn't warn you. You will learn, Mr. McFerrin, that no matter how smart you think you are, the Government is a damned sight smarter. No matter how tough you think you are, the Government is tougher. You are going to learn this, Mr. McFerrin. I want you to understand me. *Do* you understand me?"

McFerrin didn't answer, asking himself how much the man knew.

The door buzzer cut through the silence.

"Ben," the new man said, "I want you to go along with Clyde."

The small man went to the door and held it open while three men in street clothes carefully lifted the big man and moved him to a rolling stretcher and smoothly scooted it out. Before he closed the door behind him, the man named Ben called to McFerrin, "Bye-bye, patty cake!" Then he reversed his direction and came back into the room, walked to where McFerrin was sitting, took out his .45 by the muzzle, and tapped McFerrin smartly on the forehead with the gun butt. He replaced the gun in his shoulder holster, stepped quickly to the wastebasket, picked out the black folder, and returned to the doorway. "Bye-bye, patty cake," he called again, and left.

When the room was quiet, the new man spoke. "My name is Montague. You wanted to see credentials." He pulled a black folder from his pocket.

"Defense Intelligence Agency?" McFerrin asked as he reached for the folder.

Montague nodded curtly.

McFerrin examined the credentials. They were genuine. They indicated that Montague held the rank of assistant inspector. That was a high rank in a major investigative agency. It was happening, all right.

He handed back the folder. He said, "You mind if I see to this?" indicating his forehead, where the blood was seeping down, finding the creases in his face, and dripping now, in two widening stains, onto his lap.

Montague shoved his chair closer to McFerrin. "Question number one," he said. "You visited the

White House a few weeks ago. Who arranged for your visit there?"

"I am bleeding rather badly," McFerrin snapped.

"Clyde is the father of three fine boys," Montague said, his voice colorless. "Now, who arranged your appointment at the White House?"

McFerrin hoped he didn't show his relief at the question. It concerned merely the visit to the White House, hardly anything grave; yet Montague was clearly a seasoned interrogator. This could be a chess game.

"Obviously," McFarrin said, "I was invited to the White House. I can't tell you who invited me."

Montague brushed the answer aside. "Question number two. What was the purpose of that visit?"

"There you go again," McFerrin said. "I said I can't go into that." He waited to see if this was to be the entire subject area or if it was just a little warming-up exercise.

Again Montague seemed to ignore the answer. "Question number three. You live in Philadelphia. Why have you rented a Washington apartment?"

McFerrin was incredulous. But he tried not to show it. Was this really to be the direction of the questioning? Was it possible that he actually had not yet been connected with anything more precise than the visit to the White House? He decided to take the offensive again. "My head's bleeding, buster. How about you let me clean it up and fix us both a cup of tea?"

Montague remained impassive. "Question four," he continued. "Are you presently affiliated with any Government agency?"

McFerrin laughed. "Are you kidding?"

Montague stood up. "Where's your whiskey?"

"In the cabinet over there," McFerrin said, still dubious and, now for the first time, a little confused. He watched Montague as he opened the cabinet, took out a bottle of vodka and a bottle of Jack Daniels, and then stuck his head back in the cabinet. Montague turned around. "Beefeater?"

"No gin," McFerrin said.

"Shit," Montague said.

Montague took the Jack Daniels out to the kitchen and came back with the bottle and two glasses filled with ice. McFerrin studied the man's face. There was no deciphering an expression in that mess.

"Say when," Montague said, pouring.

"That's good, right there," McFerrin said.

Montague handed him his drink, then poured his own.

McFerrin fingered out the ice, dropped it to the rug, and drank off his whiskey. He started to stand, saying, "Look, I don't guess you mind if I see to this busted head your little friend gave me?"

Montague took his place again, motioned with his eyes for McFerrin to sit down. "Back in that chair, Mr. McFerrin," he said, "or I will kill you, one shot. I'm a one-shot man, Mr. McFerrin," Montague said, patting his pinstripe suit high on the breast. "I warrant you that I am fast. There is no one clocked faster in my division. You might say, Mr. McFerrin, that I'm the fastest gun in the East. You really might say that. Would you like another drink?"

"No," McFerrin said.

"Now getting back to the questions I asked you, surely you understand that you must answer them."

McFerrin shrugged. "Okay," he said. He tipped his

head back to slow the bleeding. "Answer to number one: I was invited to the White House because I'm a close friend of Franklin Quiller's. I had a class with him at Yale. Answer to question number two: My purpose in going to the White House was simply to visit Quiller. Quiller had some influence on me in school, and I like the guy. Answer to question number three: I'm in Washington on summer leave from Commonwealth. I'm using the library here for research to do a paper on good old Abe Lincoln. Answer to four: no government connection."

"Splendid," Montague said. "Now that wasn't so bad, was it?"

While Montague made some brief notes in a small notebook, McFerrin tried to figure out just what was happening. Montague closed his notebook and returned the gold ball-point to his pocket. "Your answers really weren't bad answers," he mused aloud. "And I'm perfectly willing to assume they're true. But they're not *good* answers, either. They don't go far enough. If they are entered into your dossier like this—sooner or later someone will come across them and recognize that they don't go far enough. And the Government will be back at your door again. Your answers leave too much imprecise, too much potential for too many questions for too many investigative agencies. And, of course, Clyde's misfortune complicates matters terribly."

"I'll drink to that," McFerrin said, holding out his glass.

Montague stood and fixed his stance shrewdly as he poured more bourbon into McFerrin's glass. McFerrin drank some off, then lit a fresh cigar.

"How come, just to play safe, you don't get your

71

weapon out?" he said, eyeing Montague's spoiled face.

"Oh, I *am* playing it safe, Mr. McFerrin, never you worry," Montague said. "Now, do you happen to have any evidence that you're really working on a paper?"

McFerrin motioned to the desk with his cigar. Montague stood up and moved to the desk. He opened the drawer and took out the folder of notes. He hefted the folder in his hand. "Not enough for nearly two weeks in Washington," he said. "That's obvious to anyone. Let me suggest you take a few days out next week, get some real notes in here. Make it thicker. Now, where are you doing this research?"

Am I going crazy? McFerrin thought. "Most of it in the Library of Congress and in the Archives," he said. "Some in the public library." I am crazy or he is crazy, McFerrin explained to himself.

"All right," Montague said. "Drop around to those places more often—even if some of the visits must be short. Make yourself familiar with the people at those places so they'll remember you. Incidentally, what is your research about?"

"I told you. In general terms, Lincoln. More specifically——"

"That's enough." Montague waved away the rest of McFerrin's reply. "The President's more or less a Lincoln buff, isn't he?"

"Yes, I think so," McFerrin said. "I've heard something like that, yes."

"Good," Montague said. "Now, let me give you the better answers to the first three questions, answers more likely to end interest in further inquiry. And let's understand that what I'm telling you is between us. Right?"

"Right," McFerrin said, puzzled by the change in the man's tone.

"All right," Montague said. "Quiller is regarded as dangerous. He's regarded as dangerous because of his insight, because he can't be gotten to, and because, unlike the President, he has had the time to try to develop some protective structure, some form of help for the President that's more meaningful than any he's had up to now. On the other hand, while the President's intellectual capacity is not underestimated, it is recognized that he's not a particularly practical man. His thinking is more of a theoretical nature. Moreover, his natural inclination is to trust when he should question. Most particularly, he is disposed to leaning toward solving problems 'over the long haul'—an approach that will benefit those people who—well, let's say those people who do not have the President's greater interests at heart. Above all, the President is so overloaded with administrative work and policy decisions that he actually doesn't have time to do better than to react. But Quiller *does* have the time, and he's a deeper, more organized, thinker than the President is. The whole thing comes down to who has been evaluated—by the most skilled human judgment *and* by computer —as dangerous to the bureaucracy, the *most* dangerous, and the answer is Franklin Quiller. Are you following me, Mr. McFerrin?"

"You bet," McFerrin said, completely confused now. "I'm right with you." He felt his forehead; it was still bleeding. Montague could clearly see it was still bleeding, seriously bleeding.

"Consequently," Montague was saying, "those answers you gave about going to the White House at the invitation of your longtime friend Quiller, while essentially harmless, would have the effect of putting you dead center. Certain distrustful persons somewhere in Intelligence would have you classified— however *incorrectly*, you understand—as a defense operative Quiller has lined up to help the President. In short, your *truthful* answers would have the effect of targeting you. Am I communicating? You understand me, Mr. McFerrin?"

"Completely. But I would understand a lot better if you let me fix my forehead," McFerrin said.

Montague took a sip of his drink, then said, "Therefore, Mr. McFerrin, your answer to question number one will be: 'Because I knew Quiller casually since college, he invited me to meet the President—because the President is a Lincoln enthusiast and I am engaged in research on Lincoln.' Which explanation puts you apart from Franklin Quiller. I trust that sounds more acceptable—and wise, Mr. McFerrin. It does, does it not?"

"I suppose so," McFerrin said. "At least the way you put it." He studied the man, now wildly curious about his game.

"A pity I must waste valuable time rehearsing your replies to a handful of simple questions." Montague rose from his chair and set his unfinished drink on a table. "You know," he said, pacing the floor thoughtfully, "I once knew a fellow as dense as you. In Nam. He worked for me, as a matter of fact. Off and on. Demolitions expert—who now and then did a little job for Intelligence. A hotheaded kid. Very bright, very attractive. Wouldn't listen, though. Not your team player, if you know what I mean. Took a hit north of Am Loc, as I remember it. Totaled him."

McFerrin stirred, opened his mouth to speak. But Montague ignored him and went on.

"Damnedest kid. Thought he knew it all. Wouldn't listen, mind you. You just couldn't get that kid to listen."

Now McFerrin broke in. Very quietly, very coolly, he said, "I just hope the last thing he saw wasn't your dickhead face."

"Well, your brother Bill sees *nothing* now," Montague said, and selected a business card from his wallet. He sat down and wrote on the back. "First number's my inside office number. Second's my home number. Call me if you need me for anything." He looked and winked. "That means anything, you understand?"

McFerrin simply gazed back in return.

Montague stood up again. "Sorry to keep you up so late, Mr. McFerrin." He put out his hand and then thought better of it. "You've been wonderfully co-operative, Mr. McFerrin, and I want to say that I and my people are very grateful. Stay where you are, Mr. McFerrin—I'll see myself to the door." Montague slipped his elegant leather notebook in his breast pocket, and in the same motion—the effect seemed magical to McFerrin, a rabbit out of a hat— he slipped out his hand, and it held a small, squat pistol of an exceptionally large caliber. McFerrin had never seen anything like it, the gun's design and the weirdly dreamlike way Montague had produced it. Now Montage shifted the queer-looking pistol to his left hand and extended his right to McFerrin. His face expressionless, Montague said, "A distinct pleasure to meet you."

"Sure," McFerrin replied.

"We'll meet again," Montague said.

"Sure," McFerrin said.

"Now, stay where you are," Montague added. He stepped briskly to the door and reached for the doorknob.

"My best to Clyde," McFerrin called.

"Naturally," said Montague.

"And one more thing. That piece—is it home-made?"

Montague glanced down at the gun in his left hand as if he had just discovered its presence there. "Why, yes," he said, "you might say that, I suppose. It's a little invention of a man named Reiner. Quite the crackerjack in weaponry design, he was."

"He's dead, this Reiner?"

"Did I say that?"

"You said *was*," McFerrin said mildly.

"I can't imagine what gave you that impression," said Montague. He pulled open the door and left.

McFerrin waited a moment, then went quickly to check his forehead in the bathroom mirror. It was an ugly wound, the flesh gaping, hanging in ragged bits. He pressed a towel into the bleeding. As he drove to the hospital, he kept repeating to himself, until he no longer was aware of his words: "It's happening, it's happening."

In the emergency room McFerrin sat impatiently while the attending physician took four stitches and kept asking McFerrin to please put out the cigar, hospital regulations.

"Oh, yeah—regulations," McFerrin said, and continued smoking.

9

The celebrated native product of the country just south of Chicago is extremity of weather, and in no section is this more true than in Cartwright County— icy wind in winter, scorching wind in summer. But there was nothing at all changeable about Cartwright County's sheriff, a World War II former supply sergeant named Melvin "Slim" Anderson. Because it assured his re-election time after time, and because holding office thus allowed him to pursue his foremost interest—sloth—Anderson was as constant as the earth's rotation in the matter of communism: He was against it. He was *very* against it, vigilant against the least hint of Marxist-Leninist thought, in books, in movies—by God, even in the records they played on the radio. Anderson was four-square against the dirty little boogers and their Godless crusade. It was a good thing to be against, as Anderson proved to himself every two years: it regularly got you re-elected sheriff with the least expenditure of thought or effort. On the other hand, Anderson did spend some time at his desk because it was as good a place as any to browse through the paper and swap stories and to keep an eye out for any Commies that might be trying to overthrow the government of Cartwright County. In any case, he had been flawlessly successful in keeping the county free of Communists, for no one in Cartwright County had ever, by force or will, admitted to being a Communist, not in all the years of Anderson's public service. A few fault-finding characters—you know the kind, never satisfied—did occasionally bitch and whine that Sheriff Anderson seemed to have significantly less success ridding the locality of bootleggers. But despite this clutch of malcontents, Anderson had persevered and had triumphed again and again into office, his guardianship of the people sanctioned for yet another term of preserving the American Way.

Like the radical and discouraging weather, the radical-hating and undiscouraging Melvin "Slim" Anderson was a product of Cartwright County. As a boy, he had fished the length of the Kankakee and the Iroquois rivers, and whatever kind of fish he had not caught had never swum in those rivers. Anderson knew the whole of this county better than the city dweller knows his block, and Anderson knew the citizens of his county even better than that. And the citizenry knew Slim Anderson as a well-balanced enforcer of the law, a man not likely to cause any particular law to fall into disrepute through its overzealous prosecution.

A big, red-faced man with a belly and a big nose lacy with purple veins, Slim Anderson was not his usual jovial self this hot July Saturday afternoon. He was alone in his office with his chief deputy, Sy Heckman. Trousers tucked into boots, Anderson's feet were flung up on his desk top; his hat—white semicowboy, sides rolled—was in the far corner of the room where he had thrown it. But his mood was where he didn't want it to be.

"Let's see," Anderson said pensively, "Back in February, the kids took over the high school. Kept the principal locked in his office. For three days. Then came April, early April, Major and Mrs. Jarvis go deer hunting, and she takes the major for a deer. Then—last month it was—three hippie jerk-offs breeze into town, knock over the bank for fifty big ones, and breeze back out again. And what's coming up November? Merely election time, that's all." Anderson belched, point made. Heckman farted, point understood.

"And now," said Anderson, "we got this—" and again he belched. He opened his desk drawer and pulled out a bottle of Maalox tablets. "We got," he continued, "this sack of moose shit out by the Long Hill Conservation Area—or what we thought up to a couple of days ago was the Long Hill Conservation Area. Naturally it has to happen in that section of the Conservation Area that sticks over into my county—not in the other nine tenths that's down in Eddie Schwenker's county. Nothing ever happens in Eddie Schwenker's county. Birds fly *singing* over Eddie Schwenker's fucking county and wait until they cross over into *mine* to take themselves a dump. So anyway, we got three dead old boys in the middle of nowhere—on *my* side of the county line. We got Armbruster, hole in the head, Baltimore address turns out to be a phony. And we got Coppersmith, hole in the head, Memphis address turns out a phony. And we got some sucker with no name at all,

80

phony or otherwise, with a chest like a matchbox an elephant did a somersault on. Am I right, Sy?"

"Yes, sir," the chief deputy said. "Down the line, Slim."

"Thank you, Sy. Now, the Cook County crime lab gives us a real helping hand. The Cook County crime lab informs us that while two of those boys got a *bullet hole* in the head, neither one's got a *bullet* in his head. Just little itty-bitty pieces of metal. Right?"

"You're hitting it fine," Heckman said.

Anderson swallowed a handful of the Maalox tablets.

"So then," Anderson said, "I had me what was the greatest idea of my career. My idea is it's a Federal problem—the Long Hill Conservation Area is *Federal* property. So I check the county records office just to make sure—and it turns out the United States Federal goddamn government sold the part of the Conservation Area that's in my county eight months ago—so it is my problem, God bless it! The name of the outfit they sold that piece of woods to, Sy? I want the name."

The deputy clucked his tongue, squinched his eyes. "The Foundation for the Preservation of Wildlife."

"Oh, yes." Anderson said. "Oh, yes. Ain't that a lovely thing? The Foundation for the—oh, piss on it! That outfit's doing a lot better with wildlife than it's doing with people. That outfit is doing so good it doesn't even *exist!* Nobody around here ever heard of it; nobody in the next county ever heard of it. It ain't on the tax rolls, because it's a frigging foundation. It ain't anywhere or anything but a pain in the

81

ass. But, hell, do I worry?" Anderson said. "Because come Monday we can call Springfield and get the dope from the F.B.I. on that Foundation. And we can maybe get the dope from the F.B.I. on Armbruster and Coppersmith's prints—seeing as how those boys just maybe did a service bit or something bad. Why, hell, Sy, why should Slim Anderson ever worry his ass about thing one?"

Anderson slapped down some more Maalox tablets and munched a while in deep thought. "Shit," he said when he'd thought enough. "We ain't going to get the dope on *nothing!* You can put me down on record as saying come *Monday* it might as well be Saturday, which is today, Sy boy!"

Anderson rumbled up and retrieved his hat from where he had thrown it. Then he sat in a slump on the edge of his desk. "Oh, yeah, Sy boy, come Monday, come *nothing*, and don't you forget you heard it first from me—because I'm the one telling you, I'm telling you *now*, all Monday's about to show is us walking blind in a shitstorm. Your sheriff is telling you he can smell that cow flop yeasting up nine years from Christmas, and he's telling you it's going to blow good and proper. Now, you know what Springfield's *also* going to tell me come Monday? You watch if old Slim ain't right. Because Old Slim's going to bet his chief deputy it come Monday Springfield's gonna say those two boys was shot by that other boy with the caved-in chest—only the boy with the caved-in chest just happened to be dead or dying before he shot them. You watch. Now, Sy, you tell your sheriff, has he summed up this here situation right on up to the hair on its tit?"

"You done all right, Slim," the chief deputy said.

And then, because he chose to seem shrewd, he said, "It looks like you maybe done all right."

"That's what I thought," Anderson said, and considered his hat. At last he arranged it on his head and led the way out, allowing Heckman to catch up in time to perform the service of opening and holding the door while the sheriff passed importantly through to the world outside, a world he had always suspected of colossal mischief, of filthy conspiracy at every turn—and which, Sheriff Melvin "Slim" Anderson was now willing to guess, was about to prove him right.

10

General Underwood tasted his Scotch and water and found it passable. Since he kept no written notes of even the obscurest sort, nor permitted anyone key to do so, it was his practice to deploy his memory to a recitation of every feature of the plan at least once a day. Underwood was a perfectionist—in his work, such a trait was minimal expectation, bottom line— and no one worked for Underwood who did not perform at minimal standard: perfection. The mental calisthenics Underwood daily performed in lieu of notekeeping, all key persons in his cadre also performed—daily. At least that was the routine responsibility, and Underwood was more than reasonably confident it was, to a man, lived up to. Underwood liked the little ambiguity in that—*lived up to*. He had waited until the DC-10 had leveled off at crusing altitude, had waited patiently until his Scotch was poured and savored, and then he began his cerebral calisthenics. It was an exercise of staggering effort and duration, he was pleased to observe, and *he could do it;* he could enumerate the least element of the total design, the grand and confounding sche-

matic, the *mosaic*, all of it, in its rococo amplitude,
as easily and accurately as counting to ten by two's.
Incredible, he congratulated himself—and by the
time the plane was halfway along its agreeable
course from Kansas City to Miami, the General had
completed his regimen for the day.

Underwood smiled and, with the last of his
Scotch, drank a toast to himself and to the hasten-
ing of all he was working toward. *Planning* was
everything, he mused. That was why the Joint Chiefs
of Staff had retained him. Because there was no one
else who could plan as precisely and thoroughly as
Arthur Underwood could. Poucher knew that, And
so did the rest of the Joint Chiefs. Everyone knew
that Underwood was the best, The Master!

But as to the day's receipts, Underwood was a
shade disappointed that Reiner had not made the
scheduled telephone contact before Underwood's
departure from Kansas City. Hardly a matter for
great concern—since Reiner was sheerest perfection,
and if there was something that had dissatisfied
Reiner at the practice ground, then surely it would
be typical of the man to work out that last kink *even*
if doing so meant missing a contact point, one that
was, admittedly, of negligible importance.

The General ordered a third Scotch. Miami lay
ahead. Splendid. Sunshine and work. Kansas City
lay behind. Splendid. Wonderful friends, wonderful work. All this was the painting of the scenery,
the positioning of the actors, the *blocking*, which
term the General understood to be the appropriate
theatrical expression. Good work, *excellent* work.
Well, after all, they used to call him The Master, did
they not? Did they still call him that? he wondered.

Of course they did. Perhaps an even more enviable honorific was now abroad among his former colleagues. Perhaps they now saw him as the great artificer he was. Did they perhaps have the wit to call him The Black Prince? The General would have liked that, yes, but this was absurd to expect of them at so early a juncture. It would take a century of close scholarship for the account to yield the true artistry of his achievement. Exactly. But then it well might be The Black Prince! With that, General Underwood gave himself over to the appreciation of his mediocre but, yes, increasingly companionable whiskey. And after a moment or two of teasing himself with anticipation, he also gave way to his first Havana of the day.

With great ceremony, the General cut and lit the cigar, first toasting its length with the marvelous German lighter his Agency secretary had given him on the occasion of his retirement, flaming the cigar's finely wrapped leaves to the degree that was his custom.

Had he drawn from its unparalleled humors more than three puffs when the bitch presented herself, mumbling stupidly, at his elbow?

"Young woman," the General finally said, "I did not understand one word you said. Mind speaking more distinctly, sugar?"

"Sir," the stewardess said, "you will have to extinguish your cigar."

"I cannot smoke a cigar on this airplane? Is that what you are telling me, little girl?"

"Yes, sir. I'm sorry. It's regulations. You can smoke cigarettes," she said hopefully, clearly too hopefully to back the General down.

He drew grandly on his cigar. Then he eyed her closely. "What is the name of your captain?" he said. "I want your captain's name, missy."

"It's Captain Johnson, sir," the stewardess said, glad, it seemed, to be giving ground.

"Captain Johnson is it? Good," the General said. "Now, I want you to tell your Captain Johnson that General Arthur M. Underwood is aboard and that General Underwood is smoking a cigar on this aircraft and that when General Underwood finishes smoking this fine cigar, he is going to smoke another one. Now you go tell that to your Captain Johnson, honey—you hear?"

"Yes, sir," she said, and stood unmoving, not confused or startled so much, it seemed, as frightened.

"That's good, sugar. Now you go do it; you go tell Captain Johnson, and if this makes him unhappy or disturbs the routine of your aircraft in any way, you tell Captain Johnson that General Arthur M. Underwood suggests he get on his nice radio there to General Roy Emerson, who is head of our government's Federal Aviation Agency, sugar, or else to Mr. Donald R. Mims, who is president of this airline, little lady, and you have him say, you have your Captain Johnson say, that what he has is General Arthur M. Underwood aboard and that the General is asking politely to smoke the best cigar a white man ever smoked, but your Captain Johnson is choosing to interfere. You got that, sugar?"

The stewardess grinned inanely and moved off to the front of the cabin.

"That's fine!" he called after her. "Now, you go have a talk with that nice boy up there, you hear, honey?"

87

Underwood adjusted himself for greatest comfort in his seat. He was feeling very good now. The Scotch, the cigar, the relaxing glide of the plane, the reassuring exchange with the stewardess, all contrived to establish the exuberance of his mood—but most of all, it was his recognition that the termination enterprise was thriving which sent his spirits soaring. Oh, he was not so mindlessly euphoric as to let himself entirely forget Reiner's silence when a contact had been prearranged. But the exception had been accounted for, after all, *had* it not? Had the General not analyzed the infraction and perceived it as owing merely to Reiner's diligence, to his thoroughness? Was this not a simple case of one obligation pre-empting another? Reiner could be counted on, of course. To be sure, the General reminded himself, *what couldn't?* When you had fixed it, *what*, after all, could not be counted on? Why, he was even going to count on that stewardess for his first night in Miami. Hadn't he, in a way, fixed it as soon as he'd decided her rump was passable—mediocre but passable?

11

QUESTION: All right. Now I want to hear about Underwood in Kansas City. Was your work successful?

ANSWER: Yes. Not a hitch. It went very well, yes.

Q. With whom did he have contact in Kansas City?

A. Including friends? Or just—associates?

Q. Be as thorough as you like.

A. Well, there were women. Two of them.

Q. Which nights?

A. No, they were, you know, *together*—the two of them together—one night.

Q. Oh. All right. These were prostitutes? He purchased the services of prostitutes?

A. No, I don't think they were prostitutes, really. Students—at the university—two friends. One was married.

Q. A married woman and her friend—both students. Is that correct?

A. Yes. He was, you know, *with* them.

Q. Where? Where was he *with* them?

A. They came to his hotel. He made a telephone call, and they came.

89

Q. And stayed the night?

A. Yes. Until five A.M., anyway.

Q. And were there other social contacts of this kind?

A. No—but there were—

Q. Other social contacts?

A. Yes.

Q. Please.

A. A couple of local oilmen. And a man in ranching *and* oil. And one other man, a lawyer—he was— is, I mean—in a lot of things, has some interests in TV in Tulsa and K.C., some real estate, dabbles in antiques, and, I don't know, this and that, and, yes, he's also something with the university —a consultant or a professor or something.

Q. All right, then—these summarize all of Underwood's nonbusiness contacts during his stay in Kansas City?

A. I think so, yes. So far as I know.

Q. Now, with respect to *business*—what can you tell me of Underwood's activities during his stay in Kansas City?

A. All right—may I refer to my notes?

Q. By all means.

A. All right. He called Fort Worth and Miami. Eight calls to Fort Worth. Six calls to Miami.

Q. You can supply dates and times?

A. Of course. If you'd like to see them now . . . ?

Q. No—go ahead. No more calls?

A. One other—to Albion, Illinois. And yes, another to Las Vegas.

Q. No local calls?

A. Just the one I told you about—when the girls, the women, came.

Q. All right, what else?

A. He spent a lot of time with a man named Darby—Roger Darby.

Q. This is the man's real name—you have confirmed that?

A. No—it could be an alias. I only know the name Roger Darby. I can't tell you if it's authentic.

Q. This Darby's function?

A. Kansas City control, the way I figure him.

Q. A conduit, then, to other Kansas City operatives?

A. I guess. Darby's it, so far as I could see. Under Darby comes Reiner—at least when he's in the Kansas City area—and it's Reiner who's going to be supervising the Kansas City storage of the shooting team or teams, I couldn't tell how many. I mean, the first team looks like it's coming out of one of those places—Miami or Chicago or Los Angeles but there's no telling which is the first team and where their present storage is.

Q. But do you know that the action's set for Kansas City and that Darby is the one handling whatever's happening there now?

A. Right—it all works through the Foundation for International Trade, which is Darby's outfit—you know—his cover. Reiner's been there to set up the domiciles and local covers for the shooters and whatnot, and Reiner's expected back.

Q. Good. Now, how much time are you going to tell me this Darby and Underwood spent together?

A. I have the total precisely. Forty-seven minutes. Three contacts coming to a total of forty-seven minutes.

Q. And you know what was discussed?

A. Of course not—are you crazy? I don't take that kind of chance.

Q. There are those that do.

A. I wasn't engaged on those terms.

Q. Quite right. I merely thought——

A. I realize. But you're getting what was assigned. I perform to expectation—I can't go beyond that. The percentages aren't in it for me.

Q. Understood. Now, what else are you reporting?

A. Dooley.

Q. Dooley?

A. The pigeon. The one they call Zero. The setup.

Q. Yes, of course. Billy Joe Dooley.

A. Yes, but not the real one. The real one is either in Miami or Fort Worth, I don't know. But Dooley doubles are at the gun clubs and the shooting ranges all over K.C., just hanging around and shooting a bunch of bull's-eyes.

Q. You determined this through surveilling Underwood?

A. Most of it, yeah—but some I got after Underwood left for Miami—some I got when I picked up Darby again.

Q. But the actual Dooley, you can't say where he currently is.

A. I cannot. Miami or Fort Worth—no way of telling without looking closer. But my guess is not in Kansas City yet.

Q. Then you will look closer.

A. I will *not*. I contracted for Underwood in K.C.—with an agreement to sniff out what could be smelled from far enough off—which is why you got Dooley and Darby. I'm out now. Kansas City was it.

Q. No problem. Then you're out. My assistant, Miss

Agajadian, will hand you an envelope. Are you staying in Washington?

A. I leave in two hours.

Q. For where? Where are you going?

A. Are you kidding? Here's the report and my notes.

Q. Thank you. A pleasure.

A. It's been an honor, sport.

Q. He has his envelope, darling?

A. Yes. Counted every single bill.

Q. And you heard—two hours?

A. Yes—I was listening—and I made the call.

Q. Good. A little bonus payment on his fee.

A. Nothing additional, then.

Q. No. He added nothing. Darby and Dooley. Nothing we didn't know.

A. Nothing lost, however. We have him and we have the envelope.

Q. Of course. It's wise to run backups, though.

A. Of course. Miami called, by the way. Dooley's still there.

Q. I imagined as much. Still the same?

A. Yes—handing out his circulars and so on—making a noisy display, play square with China and the rest of it. And they've got him the job now.

Q. At the G.M. Building?

A. Yes, he had the letter this morning.

Q. Fine.

A. All fine, then?

Q. I suppose.

A. You worry, darling—stop worrying.

Q. Of course. I shall stop worrying.

A. Then do it, please. If you must worry about something, worry about Underwood—at his age, two at a time.

Q. That, my lovely, inspires not worry but envy. But that was your point, wasn't it?

A. Silly, let's get out of here, and I'll do something for your envy.

Q. Darling, I've got a meeting in an hour. You might repair my feelings faster were you to press the lock on that door and come over here.

A. On the chair?

Q. Darling, would you please? I've got a ferocious schedule, really.

A. Let mama sit on your lap.

Q. Yes, darling, please.

12

Valerie touched the bandage on his forehead, very tenderly, and then took his large brown hand and kissed it and kissed each fingertip. "Wake up," she said softly.

McFerrin opened his eyes. "How long did I sleep?" he asked.

"An hour. Maybe a little more."

"Jesus, honey," he said, "why did you let me sleep so long?"

"What's long about an hour? For God's sake, Colin, you're exhausted."

He rose on one elbow. "Yeah," he said. "Believe me, I know it. Baby, I've never been so worn through in my life."

She moved closer to him and nuzzled his ear, and he could feel the warmth of her breath, almost feel the fragrance of her body. Then she leaned across his chest and put her mouth on his. She ran the point of her tongue over his lips. "I am your woman," she said. "I like saying that, darling—saying I am your woman. Do you like to hear me say it?"

He did not answer her but took her chin and guided her lips to his again. Her eyes were wide as she came to him. He kissed her hard, and then he rolled to his side and lifted away the sheet that lay over them and drew her by her hips against him and felt the high heat of her body bring his senses awake. "What it is, lady, is we wasted an hour," McFerrin said, his mouth against her neck.

He took her breast into his hand and let his fingertips slowly trail down her chest, her belly—touching her lightly as he went—until he had a hold of the crisp triangle of ginger hair and could feel the warm wet of her there and feel, too, her pressing herself against his hand.

"Love me again," she said, her voice husky now. "Please, Colin—love me hard."

"Yes," he said, and as he entered her, she closed her eyes. "Open your eyes," he whispered. Her eyelids came open and her eyes stared into his. In the half-light of the room, her eyes seemed stunned, surprised, and then they closed again and stayed closed.

"I'm coming," she said, and he said it too, and held her close to him now, feeling the shivers run through her body and gradually subsiding. They dozed off a time, and then he forced himself awake. When she felt him stir, she kissed his chest with particular tenderness—and then she said, "I really *am* your woman, Colin, and I am only a woman with you."

It was nearly noontime when they parted downstairs, going off in separate cars—McFerrin to meet with Greenfield at the Marriott Inn; Valerie, she said, to go home, straighten her place, catch up on household chores, and be trimmed away before her husband returned from Boston on the noon train out.

McFerrin drove at a leisurely pace. He felt a degree or two calmer now—but he had no conviction it would last. Twice he drove against the signs on one-way streets to confirm that there was no surveillance. No cars followed—but McFerrin was not willing to be convinced that this confirmed anything.

The Marriott, off the beaten path of Washington officialdom, made for a reasonably acceptable place to meet. McFerrin took the elevator to the fourth floor, walked the length of the hallway, fingering the key as he went. He knocked twice, paused, knocked twice again. When there was no call from behind the door, McFerrin let himself into 415, looked in the bathroom, and then returned to the one armchair, stood next to it, read his watch, and then sat. He got up to check that the door had automatically locked and then went again to his place in the chair.

McFerrin reached over and flipped on the television, then turned it off. Where was Greenfield? Did he get in and out of the Illinois bush okay? McFerrin stuck a Schimmelpenninck between his teeth. Who else could he have asked to take that kind of risk? Dan was his best friend from their Green Beret days —Dan and John Douglas—in Nam and again in Greece. What had happened to Douglas anyway? Probably still in the Company—a big man now. Shit, maybe he should have gone back to Illinois himself. McFerrin lit the Schim and was rising to turn on the television again when he heard two knocks, then pause, then two knocks again. He called *"In!"*

and waited, his right hand poised behind him, at the beltline, his feet somewhat in stance.

Greenfield strolled in the door, tossing the key in the air as casually as if he'd just been down to the corner drugstore. "How's the head?" he said, slumping into a chair.

"Okay," McFerrin said, his hand going to the bandage, a little wetted tobacco left there when he took his hand away.

"Still hurt?"

"Aches like hell now—and it itches," McFerrin said, moving to a seat on the bed, stretching his long legs out in front of him. "Forget all that. Tell me what happened."

"All right," Greenfield said finally when he'd sprung loose his tie and had a cigarette going. "It all went fine. *All* of it. Number one: I got the shells at O'Hare. Number two: I dropped the D.I.A. credentials right where you wanted. Number three: They hadn't had any rain, so I didn't have to wet the folder. Number four: I stuck one of the funny bullets in the folder. Number five: I rubbed it in the dirt and so on. Number six: Yes, the place was watched, but only by a couple of local jelly-beans. So no hassle getting in and getting out. Is there a number seven? I don't believe so. I believe six items accounts for it."

"Whose typewriters did you use?" McFerrin asked.

"For the original and copy of the Israeli memo to Underwood and Morgan Drexel, the Associated Press typewriter. Nice big electric one. For the letter to Poucher, a small electric portable from one of the foreign correspondents just back in town."

"Anyone in the press room when you did this?"

"Just a chick from C.B.S. A dippy little broad who does color, woman's angle, et cetera. No sweat, believe me."

"You were careful handling the paper?"

"I was careful," Greenfield said, and from a large manila envelope, he produced three smaller envelopes, holding them delicately by the edges. "Here," he said. "In envelope for Underwood, your memo from Israeli Intelligence. In envelope for the C.I.A. Director, for Drexel, duplicate of memo to Underwood. In envelope for the Chairman of the Joint Chiefs, letter you wrote. I added a few touches here and there."

Greenfield lit another cigarette. "I burned the carbon paper in the press room head, washed ashes down sink."

McFerrin took the envelope, gingerly, by the edges, and sat at the head of the bed by the table and lamp. He selected the Underwood envelope. He held it flat while he used a small penknife to slide out the sheet inside. He read it. "What you added—what does it say?"

"It says, '*Sh'mor tsa-ad-cha may-o-hev shesar may-dar k'cha.*' "

"Yeah, sure," McFerrin said. "So what does it say?"

"You wanted something in what you called 'Israeli'—something in the general tenor of the message. So that's Dan Greenfield's personal solution. I came up with the right sort of phrase, converted it to Sephardic Hebrew—what your average goy professor calls 'Israeli.' But I had to type it phonetically, right? No sweat. An Israeli Intelligence operative wouldn't be lugging around a Hebrew typewriter, right?"

McFerrin looked woefully at the ceiling. He said, "Look, good buddy, I want to know what the goddamn thing *says*."

"It says," Greenfield said, " 'beware of old friends who steer by a different star than you do.' "

"Hey, man, that's okay," McFerrin said.

"Thanks," Greenfield said.

"I mean, it's really good," McFerrin said.

"Yeah, thanks," Greenfield said. "We try to serve, you know—you're pleased?"

"I'm pleased," McFerrin said. "It'll drive the sonsabitches nuts." He laughed. He thought it his first satisfying laugh in weeks. "That's the only friendly Intelligence agency in the world our boys can't get on the horn to and huddle with their chief. The C.I.A. has its red button to K.G.B. and every other damn place; the Pentagon has one to Red Army Headquarters. And N.S.A. can get to anyone anywhere. Everybody's sweethearts. But no way can they get to the Israeli honcho, because there's nobody—not even Israeli military knows who he is until the day he resigns."

McFerrin stood and circled the little room, his pleasure obvious, his excitement high. "Jesus, man—this is really good," he said. He sat again, stoked up another little cigar, and then slid the next letter from its envelope, poking it free with the point of his penknife. He read, smiled. "Where'd you get all the details on Poucher?"

"Public library," Greenfield said proudly. "There's a complete history on the Seventh Army in France and Germany. Try reading a little history sometime, old buddy; it won't give you warts."

"Yeah, you're right," McFerrin said, and thought of Montague's counsel. Or was it a warning? Either way, McFerrin could not figure it, and he did not want to think about it now.

"Hello, hello! Anybody home?" Greenfield said.

"Sorry. Right. I'm with you." He stood and went into his pacing again, his long legs covering the length of the little room in so many strides.

Greenfield watched for a while. When he'd seen enough, he rose and stood to block McFerrin's path.

"You sure you're really with me, man? I mean, I'm wondering if you aren't losing a few marbles over this—and, baby, I'm sorry but I've got to wonder. It's my ass, too, in case you forgot. I don't all that much mind hanging my hide out so long as I know you're quarterbacking with your head on the game. Am I coming through, man?"

"I hear you, Dan. So what's the beef? You think I'm whacking out? Is that what you think?"

"To be flat-out honest with you, old buddy, the notion *has* crossed my mind," Greenfield said. "I've got a right to ask, Colin. I'm hanging it out there for you, and I just want a little assurance."

McFerrin puffed on his cigar, and then he set it between his teeth and said, "You want a crazy man's reassurance that he's sane?"

"Yes, I do," Greenfield said. "I guess you're still the best judge of that."

"Fair enough," McFerrin said, and stepped to the window and gazed out to the street. After a time he turned, his face grave. "I'm okay," he said.

To make conversation, to get back to business,

Greenfield said, "You never stop to think what *Walnut*'s got on you?"

"I've got a pretty good idea," McFerrin said. "I think about it some—like morning, noon, and night, for openers."

"I'm only asking," Greenfield said, "because it's just a matter of time before some sharpo figures to feed *Walnut* the question."

"Ex-Agency men who can shoot like that?"

"*Shoot* like that and *kick ass* like that, yeah."

"About eight to a dozen," McFerrin said.

"That's just what I was thinking," Greenfield said.

"But I wasn't primarily a field man," McFerrin said. "So that improves the odds. I mean, they'll probably put me pretty low on the list, anyway. As a matter of fact, lower than you—because you were pure field operations, good buddy."

"I was," Greenfield said, sober now, "but I never checked out on long-range firearms. And I never totaled a guy with any dancing routine."

"Everybody was taught that," McFerrin said.

"Sure," Greenfield said, "but you name me one other agent we both know about who's ever actually done it. And *you*, you old pal, did it *twice* before—in Indochina, the crazy colored dude, that huge freaking French guy—and then again in Turkey, right?"

"It was stupid," McFerrin said. "Reflex. Stupid, I agree."

"*Walnut*'s going to kick your card right on top, son."

"I never figured you for a mother, Dan."

"I'm not mothering you, buster," Greenfield said. "I'm mothering my own sweet hide, don't forget. They nail you, the hammer's going to be a big enough one to splat whatever's near enough by. And I'm pretty goddamn near enough."

"Then quit!" McFerrin said. "Quit it and shut the fuck up with nagging me!"

"I'm quitting nothing," Greenfield said. "Just want you to know what a big hero I am before it's too late to make any difference. So—all right—orders. What you got?"

McFerrin went to the bathroom, splashed cold water on his face, dried it gently. His face still pained him where the candle wax had sucked skin from his cheek. And he'd gotten his bandage wet. He studied himself in the mirror. He was piling up attention: the slightly reddened skin, the prominent bandage, the fatigue-crazed eyes.

"I want you to telephone Albion, Illinois," McFerrin called out to Greenfield. "Not from here though. From a box on the street or something. Albion, Illinois. Ask for the county sheriff. His name's Anderson. You use a phony, something Italian, Scarlotto. . . ."

13

Greenfield left. He took with him the large manila envelope. Inside were the three smaller envelopes—and inside two of these were two of the three water bullets he had ferried back from the O'Hare locker. McFerrin stayed behind, trying to collect himself, trying to hold his rage within until Greenfield had closed the door and marched briskly down the corridor.

McFerrin kept to the room for a half-hour or so, letting his rage thin out, glad he had hidden its dimension from Greenfield. Because Greenfield was right, had guessed what McFerrin had entirely overlooked.

Walnut!

Walnut would *know!*

McFerrin drove his fist into the mattress, spun, and then smacked the air with short, brutal, gutting blows.

That was the Illinois mistake, the disquieting hint of something amiss in the woods!

That! And it was not something dismissable, the odd correctable detail—but instead a large and blue-ribboned fuckup.

And *Walnut*, never sleeping, converting thousands of volts of raw juice into the collection, collation, and correlation of the stuff that thoughts are made of —*Walnut* would *know*, would never overlook what it was not *possible* for it to overlook, what even *Greenfield* had not overlooked—but what, Jesus God, McFerrin *had!* For had he not put that sonofabitch out with a chest jump? And would *Walnut* not have him already down for *two* of those little high-flying numbers?

Walnut would flip out his card right on the ever-loving top of the deck—and deal it first and foremost to the desk of some section chief who also would *not, could not, conceivably* overlook McFerrin's handsome delivery of his ass as the A-number-one probability.

"Shit!" McFerrin said aloud. He shook with fury. Of all the infinite styles of killing, it had happened that the one little beauty that could nail him was the little beauty he'd picked to nail that kid in the woods.

"Jesus," he groaned, the tide of rage against himself receding now, backing slowly away into a sea of suffused and unspecific anxiety—"Jesus Christ, *Walnut!*"

He reached behind him, yanked free the gleaming Voroshilov revolver, checked the chambers—now *nothing* would go unchecked and double-checked!—and returned it to the belt pack.

All right! It was happening in earnest now! So be it! It might take him by surprise. But he was going to take a sweet hunk of it with him!

He walked eight blocks before he found a pay phone that he judged isolated enough, protected enough. He used a dime to area code 312 information, got the number, and hung up. Then he called Garfinkle's Department Store and in an offhand, stern voice barked, "Outside line!" When he had the tone, he raised a black box the size of a cigarette pack to the speaker and punched out the electronics on the tiny keyboard. After a pause, he could hear the numbers registering and then he heard the ring.

"Cartwright County Sheriff's Office, Officer Browns speaking."

Before he spoke, McFerrin activated a blue button in an array of colored buttons that ran along one side of the box. He touched the black box to the speaker. He held it there, and then he spoke.

"Give me the sheriff," McFerrin said.

"State your business, please," the voice said.

"You got three dead men in the boonies, mister. I know who did it."

"Hold on, please—I'm putting you through to Chief Deputy Heckman."

"Get me the sheriff," McFerrin said. "I won't talk to anybody but the sheriff."

"I'll have to patch you into the radio phone," the voice said. "It'll take a while, okay?"

"Okay," McFerrin said, "you've got thirty seconds. Start patching."

He leaned back against the booth, checking his watch.

"Twenty seconds," he said into the mouthpiece, and the voice said, "One moment, please, the sheriff will be on any second now."

"You taping this?" McFerrin said.

"Yes, sir; I am, sir—you will hear the intermittent tone coming in fifteen seconds, sir."

"All right, Good boy, Browns," McFerrin said, knowing that the black box's electronics would distort his voice, that no oscillation print would ever identify him.

"This is Melvin 'Slim' Anderson. Can you hear me?"

"You're sheriff of the county containing the town of Albion?" McFerrin said. And then he abruptly hung up.

He waited thirty seconds. This time he called the number of Sears, asked for an outside line, and was on his way again. This time he was through to Anderson promptly.

"We were cut off," McFerrin shouted. "You can hear me?"

"Who's calling? Who's speaking? This is the sheriff. Yes, Albion is in my jurisdiction. Who's speaking? Please identify yourself. Your name is safe with me. I personally guarantee it," the voice said, fading somewhat.

"Can you hear me, Mr. Anderson?" McFerrin said.

"Yes, I'm Sheriff Anderson. I can hear you," the voice said, still weak.

"I believe your guarantee, Sheriff—but I am not going to tell you my name because it would only make things worse for you if you knew it."

"I hear you," the voice said.

"It could mean trouble for you!" McFerrin called loudly into the phone.

"You have nothing to fear," the voice said.

"I know," McFerrin said. "But you do."

"Why are you calling?" the voice said, still very distant, its color rinsed out.

"Sheriff, I am Government. Do you understand?"

"Government?"

"Sheriff," McFerrin said. "I am what you would call an agent—but I can't tell you which agency."

There was a long pause. McFerrin could hear the fair-warning tone sound twice during the long interval. Finally, the voice said, "I see."

"Yes," McFerrin said. "I hope you understand."

"I understand," the voice said. "Now, what do you want?"

"Credentials," McFerrin said. "One of our people mislaid his credentials in the Long Hill Conservation Area—do you understand? His credentials," McFerrin said. "They were dropped in the area where the killings occurred, somewhere in that area—do you read me?"

"Yes," the voice said. "Yes."

"Good," McFerrin said. "Now get them."

"What were your people doing in the area?" the voice said, very distant now.

"I can't tell you that, Sheriff," McFerrin said, shouting. "You understand me, don't you?"

"I do," the voice said.

"Get those credentials, Sheriff, and mail them registered to Martin Scarlotto, Box 1274, Atlanta, Georgia."

"A man by that name called us about five minutes ago. He just called up and gave his name and hung up."

"That's right," McFerrin said. "Scarlotto, S-c-a-r-l-o-t-t-o. Do you have that? 1274, Atlanta. Please write that," McFerrin said.

"We're taping," the voice said.

"Write that," McFerrin said.

108

"One minute there," the voice said, and then it said, "that's S-c-a-r-l-o-t-t-o. Right?"

"That's right," McFerrin said. "Get it and do it."

"I will," the voice said.

"Officer Browns," McFerrin said, "are you still taping?"

"Yes," the first voice said.

"Good boy," McFerrin said, and hung up. He returned the little black box to his pocket and stepped out of the booth. Walking back to his car, he grinned with the thought of his little exercise in false leads. —But was he thinking straight in doing all this? Even though he had ample voice distortion on the tape, he was willing to believe there would exist some goddamn gadget that could reassemble a clear voice print.

Was this really hysteria? McFerrin was uncertain.

Could they perhaps do it? McFerrin was certain it was not possible.

But he was also certain that what is not possible is simply what has not happened *yet*.

14

ITEM: Subject (?) observed 10:40 A.M.–11:23 A.M., E.S.T., 22 July, sidewalk fronting Burdine's Miami, distributing handbills (specimen attached).
ITEM: Subject (?) observed 11:20 A.M.–12:43 P.M., C.S.T., 23 July, Kans. City Rod and Gun Club, Kans. City, on range with Browning .303 and Smith and Wesson .32 pistol.
ITEM: Subject (?) observed 11:30 A.M.–12:00 P.M., C.S.T., 23 July, Bob's Sports Emporium, Kans. City, purchased three boxes .22 long-rifle ammo.
ITEM: Subject (?) observed 4:23 P.M.–7:00 P.M., E.S.T., 23 July, Vic and Lil's Gaiety Lounge, Miami Beach, in company of two white females and one mulatto male. (See file on Vic and Lil's Gaiety Lounge in re pro-China mimeo press.)

During the previous winter, *Walnut*, a computer maintained by the U.S. Intelligence community, a machine installation of such mammoth proportion and immense complexity that it has no known equal in the world, had been programmed to print out the names and dossiers of a number of men whose physical characteristics of age, race, height, weight, and general physiognomy would be proximate to one another within a range of $+$ or $-$ 2.

Walnut delivered the names of eighteen men.

The median man in this grouping was given a score of 0 (zero).

The median man's name was Billy Joe Dooley.

Walnut then eliminated from the grouping men with scores of greater than $+$ or $-$ 1.25.

The resultant grouping was a population of seven men.

Six of these men (not Dooley) were given the code designation *Primus*.

Dooley was assigned the code designation *Zero*.

Through the following spring and early summer, Primus was maintained "on program." Primus was monitored and "deployed" in such ways as to develop a "significant" behavior. Primus[8] showed "resistance" to control, displayed suspicion of monitoring. Primus[8] was eliminated from "on program" and terminated. Primus[5] was eliminated from "on program" and terminated when his employer and spouse displayed suspicion of monitoring. Spouse of Primus[5] was also terminated in the same event.

Primus[1,2,4,6] continued "on program" to present. Control action has been gradually withdrawn. Primus remains monitored. Control action currently distanced from Primus by a maximum factor of 10.

Zero "on program" since 11 February. Subsequent evaluations: 3 March, 6 May, 8 June, and 1 July. No significant "display." Redesign of Zero's vita evaluation for progress and reliability same dates. Progress and reliability scores match or exceed program projection. *N.B.:* Failure to achieve cooperation of (1) high school vocational counselor; (2) teammate high school boxing club; (3) Marine Corps drill instructor; (4) stepfather (see attachments and transparencies A-Q); corrected dates corresponding as marked on attachments. All event actions satisfactory in re effect and aftereffect and side effect (none).

Zero control, 24 July, Miami.
Fort Worth "receiving package" ready this date. Zero now trans. to Kansas City control. Primus maintains visibility level Kansas City. Termination Primus 2 Aug.

"How dare you show me these!" Underwood screamed.

The man sitting opposite, his face almost concealed in the shadow cast by the large potted palm, quite enough at least to spare the General from having to divert his eyes from the vile color of the skin, simply said, "They're from memory."

"How dare you!" Underwood shrieked again.

"I recorded them this afternoon," the other man said. "I swear. It was all from memory."

"My instructions," Underwood screamed, "are my instructions! They are not subject to change! They are not subject to overruling! They are not subject to your goddamn initiative!"

"Perhaps I was showing off," the other man said, and began to reach for his cigarette case.

"Burn these," the General said, and threw the sheets of paper onto the floor in front of him.

"All right," the other man said. He rose, came forward, and knelt to gather the papers, one sheet eluding his grasp for a time as it skittered across the carpet on the rush of air blown by the cooler-fan. When Montague stood up with the sheets in his hand, he saw the General pointing to the bathroom.

"In there!" Underwood said. "I believe, sir, you are able to perform so elementary an act in the appropriate fashion!"

Montague said nothing. He pushed open the bathroom door. Underwood—in bathrobe and slippers—padded to the television and changed the channel and then he changed it again. The volume was barely audible. The General sat back down, stretched out his legs and crossed them at the ankles, and brought his hands to his chest and moved them there in a massaging motion. When Montague emerged from the bathroom, Underwood looked up at him with an expression of unparalleled disgust. Then he returned to massaging his chest, his attention fastened on the television.

"Just look at them spics play ball," he said. "The little monkeys are beautiful to watch!"

"I used to play a little soccer myself," Montague said.

"Sir," Underwood said, not looking at him, "you used to do a number of things, all of them well. You used to be my outstanding employee, sir. I'd be the first to say so. But, sir, Mr. Montague, sir, you can't do shit now."

"Perhaps I thought it would please you," Montague said, making the necessary accommodation. "Perhaps it was foolish, wrong."

"The sin of pride," the General said. "Oh, my, I declare, the sin of pride will get you every time."

"Invariably," Montague said, lighting a cigarette.

"Look at those little monkeys kick that ball, would you?" Underwood moved his hands to his thighs and made the same massaging motion. "These legs," he said in disgust, "they're as disagreeable as that face of yours," and for the first time since Montague had returned to the room, the General gave him his attention. "You are a terrible sight, my boy," Underwood said. "Folks tell you that all the time, I suppose. I suppose you scare the living bejesus out of all but the blind and those going in the same direction."

"I don't mind," Montague said, ignoring the provocation.

"I do," the General said. "As a purely personal matter, on aesthetic grounds, you might say, I can't suffer the sight of you. On the other hand, Montague, if you weren't despicable to me this evening on account of your going against my specific instructions, I guess I'd still say you are the best employee I ever had."

"Thank you," Montague said. After a few thoughtful puffs on his cigarette, he turned away to take his seat in the shadow of the palm again.

"Don't sit," Underwood said, massaging his calves now.

Montague stood where he was.

"Get your briefcase and get the hell out of here," Underwood said, rubbing his calves methodically and smiling at the events that unfolded on the large color screen.

"I don't go back until the morning," Montague said.

"I am aware, sir, of your schedule and your itinerary," Underwood said.

"You don't want me further tonight?"

"I do not," the General said. "I want you out of here."

"Yes, sir," Montague said. Then he turned abruptly, his manner almost comically military save that no one seeing him would risk the insult of a laugh, and strode quickly toward the door. He picked up the briefcase that lay on the table nearby. Again he turned to Underwood, shifted the briefcase to his left hand, and made an informal salute.

"I won't see you again, then, until after," he said.

"You won't," Underwood said.

"I wish you luck."

"Thank you."

"I contact you three days after, I remind you, sir," Montague said, with an almost officially impersonal deference.

"The Dunes in Vegas."

"I know, sir."

"I know you do."

"Thank you, sir," Montague said, saluted more formally this time, and left.

15

Greenfield drove from the Marriott Inn to the nearest Holiday Inn, parked his car, entered the lobby, went directly to the pay phones, and dialed the number for Metro Rapid Courier. He gave the name R. P. Works, Room 254, Holiday Inn, and requested immediate pickup service for a delivery to McLean, Virginia, and the charges for such service. He made a note of the amount and said he would remit payment in cash to the boy, adding that he would meet the boy in the lobby in order to expedite service.

Pickup was promised within fifteen minutes. Greenfield cut the connection and then dialed Bonded Messenger, Inc., gave the name Mr. Ben Avrum, Israeli embassy, and asked for a messenger to be sent around to Chesapeake Street for a pickup in precisely one hour and ten minutes, billing to be made to the embassy in accord with the usual diplomatic discount. When Bonded Messenger protested that they had no experience with a "diplomatic discount," Greenfield wrangled for a bit, arguing that a discount was routinely observed by the other messenger services, that he could scarcely understand

116

why Bonded, an established and thriving concern, was unaware of the practice, but, nevertheless, however, yes, inasmuch as Metro, the Embassy's usual conveyor, was tied up for the next several hours, all right, come ahead, we'll pay the full rate, but under duress, mind you, and never again.

"In one hour and ten minutes exactly," Greenfield said. And when he had this assurance, he hung up and took a seat in the lobby facing the main entrance.

When the boy from Metro showed up, Greenfield had the large manila envelope in his lap and one of the smaller envelopes resting on it. He spotted the uniform, called to the boy, and as the boy approached, Greenfield stood and held out the large envelope fastidiously, as if presenting a platter of elegant *hors d'oeuvres* to the most exacting palate.

"All out and ready to go," Greenfield said.

"Mr. Works?" the boy said.

"Yes," Greenfield said, indicating the small envelope with his eyes as he offered the platter to the boy's hand. The boy snatched up the small envelope, slipped it into his satchel, and then took an order pad and ball-point from his pocket.

"Going?" he said.

"General Mark Poucher," Greenfield said. "Fourteen Greenwood Lane, McLean, Virgina."

"Twenty dollars," the boy said. He took the two tens Greenfield handed him and began to make out the receipt.

"That's R. P. Works," Greenfield said, "care of Holiday Inn, Washington, D.C."

The boy slapped the receipt into Greenfield's hand, said, "You got it," and off he went. Greenfield waited a moment and then followed the boy outside, got quickly into his car, and headed for Chesapeake.

He parked a block from the embassy, checked his watch, and when five minutes remained, he left his car and headed toward the embassy. He walked slowly, eyeing the street for the boy from Bonded. Greenfield was paces from coming abreast of the embassy when he saw the motorcycle turn onto the block. Greenfield moved to head him off, and as the boy approached on foot, Greenfield was waiting for him with his platter extended.

"Ben Avrum?" the boy said.

"No," Greenfield said, "his secretary. Take these, please."

The boy took the envelopes that were proffered and got out his order pad.

Greenfield said, "As noted on the envelopes, one is to General Arthur Underwood, 2232 Lauren Court, Georgetown. The other goes to Occupant, 16 Baker Hollow, Arlington."

"Occupant?"

"Occupant," Greenfield said. "Occupant will do nicely, thank you," Greenfield said. He turned away and started toward the entrance of the embassy. When he'd taken a few steps, he stopped, bent, and retied a shoelace. He did not straighten up until he'd heard the engine of the motorcycle fade from the block.

"Cute," Greenfield muttered to himself as he set off for his car. "Very cute." It amused him that *Occupant* in fact signified the Director of the Central Intelligence Agency. For Greenfield had worked for the Company quite enough to be in possession of the opinion that the high office of Director was more or less filled by a mindless, impersonal presence rather than by someone worthy of the dimension implied by a real honest-to-God name. It was all, in Greenfield's view, pure function, tasks programmatically executed without the stamp of human involvement, tasks performed by a sort of characterless, mechanistic consciousness, by someone, some*thing*, that might as well be called "Occupant."

But his amusement quickly left him when he thought again of McFerrin. Greenfield had never seen McFerrin in such a state—not in Indochina, not in the course of their years with the Company. Not in all the time and through all the stress they'd shared had Greenfield seen McFerrin come so close to skidding over the edge of control.

He wondered would it help to talk to Valerie—but he'd only met her once, he leaving, she entering, Colin's apartment in Philly. He really didn't know her, could scarcely approach her on a matter of this kind—and, besides, she probably knew nothing, or *should* know nothing, of what Colin was into. No, not Valerie. And hadn't Colin said she was married? Or separated or something? At any rate, she was in no position—that was certain—to get herself further involved. But *who* really was?

Quiller? Greenfield had *never* met Quiller, probably would not be able to get to him if he tried.

And there was no one else, no one who could hear the thing that frightened Greenfield more than did the prospect of death that was beckoning urgently before him. For if McFerrin *were* crazy—either made crazy by what he suspected or crazy *for* suspecting it in the first place—then Greenfield was dealing himself into an utterly bizarre piece of theater. Getting a cannon hole in your chest was one thing: we all had it coming, so what did it matter how it came? But acting out a role in a drama written by a madman, that was in all respects very scary—for one's world was in effect being turned on its ear, the points of the compass wrenched off center, the pitch of reality brought into question, and baby, all bets were off!

But there was no one to talk to, Greenfield realized. But he realized, too, that this was no longer unusual. In the ambiguous world that was being created all around him, a man was pretty lucky, Greenfield concluded, if he could talk a little sense even to himself, could trust, more than a little bit, even *himself*.

16

When Officer Browns tried to explain further and the man listening could hear better just how drunk Officer Browns was, the connection was cut and that was that. So Officer Browns got himself even drunker. But no matter how drunk he was, it was nowhere near the state of alcoholic paralysis achieved by Sheriff Melvin "Slim" Anderson. The sheriff had phoned just about everybody Federal he could phone, saying: What the hell is this I have in my hand that somebody tells me to mail to Atlanta? No one on the other end of the phone, no one in fourteen tries, was going to tell him. So Sheriff Anderson had to make up his mind about something, which was which did he think was crazier: doing what the man on the phone said or doing what he figured *should* be done? Which was nothing. So he decided to rack up a really heroic drunk, always the best means to a sound act of making up one's mind.

While Sheriff Anderson laid back a quart of Early Times in a period of two hours, the word he had launched into the Washington stratosphere had already spread to its four corners and would soon drift into the Federal ionosphere as well, all this three hours and sixteen minutes in advance of Sheriff Anderson's passing out on his office floor.

Chief Deputy Heckman let him lie there. Let sleeping sheriff's lie, Chief Deputy Heckman figured.

Valerie Craig was home, neatening, readying herself and her surroundings for the arrival of her husband, Tommy. She tidied the kitchen, she tidied the bedroom, she returned to the kitchen and started a chicken roasting. Then she went to the bathroom, undressed, dropped her washable into the hamper, and drew a bath. She sprinkled in something violet, crystals that looked like coarse salt, and then she poured in something amber, an oil of some kind. She followed these ingredients into the tepid water and let herself down against the dark blue porcelain.

Let Tommy discover her here, she thought—everything tidy, dinner on, wife long and languid in aromatic waters.

She reached to a brass basket that stood out from the tiles, selected some silvery items, and these she used to arrange her long brown hair into a graceful frosting at the top of her head. Then she stretched to her full length in the water and let herself admire the marvel of the body that was hers. Not that it mattered any to the man who was her husband, not that anybody mattered more to him than things, than his business, what he called his "pantheon" of great antiques.

She closed her eyes and touched herself, and eyes closed, touching herself, she summoned the memory of McFerrin.

She was an accomplished woman and she knew it.

At thirty-two Valerie Craig was a deputy division head at Fort Meade, a cryptoanalyst of such proven gifts for decoding and administration that she now supervised a team of twenty-three operators and was the author of two N.S.A. handbooks in use as learning manuals in random-process symbologies and computer-based schematics. To be sure, she was near the top of her profession, it would seem, in the company of a well-armed W.A.C. captain bodyguard whenever she wished it, in receipt of a Lincoln limousine and driver whenever she wished it, and in prospect of a stout pension and related benefits whenever she wished to call it quits. That she was also imprisoned in a condition of unalterable marriage to a successful, if inattentive, husband seemed to her no great hardship, considering—considering, that is, her handsome accomplishment in full-time work and part-time love. She had no choice. She needed marriage to assure the promotion that was promised her, and Tommy was the best that was quickly available. It was all hasty, and she didn't really regret it. Her work mattered to her more—and besides, now she had Colin McFerrin, a bed partner of stunning talents by anyone's standards, the kind of man a woman passed in the street—and would think, Yes, him, he could turn me inside out.

So life with Tommy was—tolerable, not so bad as all that. She had her career, her freedom, she had Colin—and the smell of him and the taste of him flooded her as she touched herself and stroked harder and faster and thrust her hips from the water and pressed it *hard* and then, oh, *sideways* at the last instant the way, oh, *he did* and trembled and shook with the spasms that split from her loins and raced to her legs, to her arms, and held her transfixed for a long, long instant.

She sagged back into the warm wallow of water and let herself drift. "Colin," she said aloud, very softly, adream now. She was still saying Colin, though now in her sleep, when her husband turned the key in the door, set down his overnight bag in the foyer, and called, "Valerie, I'm home." And when at last he poked his head into the bathroom, slightly irritated, and said, "I said I'm home," she had roused herself enough to reply.

She was very beautiful, the steam rising around her, her head turning to him on the elegant stalk of her neck, her throat so—womanly, her eyes misted, large, liquid, the pearly beadlets of moisture glistening on her skin.

"How was Boston, darling?" she said.

17

.McFerrin waited. He checked his weapon. He checked his watch. He checked the Charger's gas. Full tank. Good Greenfield—a man you could count on. He checked the ashtray. Also full—Dan's cigarette butts. McFerrin dumped it out. He checked his watch again. He made it three-twenty. He subtracted fifteen minutes, then another ten to be on the safe side, then he added the estimated time from the Marriott Inn to McLean, Virginia, and then he moved.

He pulled out of the parking lot and headed into the Sunday traffic toward the Beltway. His destination was Poucher's stately Georgian house in McLean, and his objective was the surveillance of that house—more precisely, to keep an eye on the place to see who came and went once Poucher had taken the weight of the memo, been jolted by the sheer tonnage it would deliver. Who would Poucher call to him? What would the General do? If you wanted the answers to these questions, there was only one way to get them when you didn't have an army of agents to get them for you.

Go take a look. Yourself.

McFerrin made it into the Beltway, and it was then that he thought to check in his rear-view mirror. From here on in he was taking no chances without covering himself from all directions. Sure, he was going with the play, taking large risks. There was no other way. But he was also going to take large precautions.

Nothing in the mirror, nothing that signaled anything out of the ordinary, anyway. McFerrin knew that the show behind him was developing, that presently the other actors would be gaining on him again, joining him on stage. And there was no getting off the stage now, not until all the acts had been played out and one could sit down and figure out what the thing meant, what it was really all about. In the meanwhile, you stood sweating it dead center on the stage, pretty much solo, with your eyes darting to the wings to see who was coming on there with you— and you did your best to learn your lines as you went along, and you did your best to watch out for what was coming up next.

Nothing in the wings now, nothing suspect showing in the mirror. But McFerrin knew it was only a matter of time before something hard and ugly smacked its blunt reality down onto the stage where he was standing.

The Dodge Charger was a sweet car, too sweet a car to have abandoned at Baltimore-Washington International, whatever the risk. It handled, it delivered, and McFerrin was moving it at a pretty good clip, just starting onto the downslope of the McLean off-ramp when he saw the long Lincoln staff car heading up the opposite grade of the on-ramp.

It was Poucher!

McFerrin's timing was off—for Poucher had already taken the jolt and was already moving with it, reacting faster than McFerrin had anticipated.

The black limousine was onto the access road now, and now the siren was sounding as the Lincoln stood paused and nosing at the busy mouth of the highway, poking the traffic out of the merge lane and pressing now into the stream of cars, the little fender flags whipped back as the big black limo *went*.

McFerrin jerked the Charger up onto the embankment, cut the wheel hard, and slammed the whole business into a murderous about-face over the median. He didn't gear down at the merge lane, but *went* too. He couldn't see the black car ahead, but he had the Charger hitting it and was snaking from lane to lane, gaining, *knew* he must be gaining. But he couldn't see the limousine yet, couldn't see the big ass of that big black machine *yet*. But then he could hear the siren's moan getting louder now. And he knew the staff car must be just ahead. He floored the Charger and laid on some real fire and was just edging on through, gripping the wheel at ten and two, and straining to see the black car, when a dark green Ford sedan started to take him out of the play.

The dark green Ford sedan that was chasing cut down on the Charger from behind. Then it came alongside, and then it jammed itself in front of the Charger and laid itself against the Charger's fender, forcing McFerrin to take the Charger down and brake steadily to the right. Like dancing partners in a precision-step routine, the Ford dropping behind the Dodge now, the Ford herding the Dodge like a

127

reluctant calf, the two hurtling automobiles slowed into a tandem sweep to the right, then farther right and up onto the embankment to a stop.

McFerrin's heart was roaring, blowing apart in his chest. He went behind him and got from the belt pack the stubby silvery Voroshilov and laid it in his lap. Then he watched the show develop in the mirror. The two men sat there, not moving. He tried to see if they were conferring, but they seemed to be silent, each gazing ahead, faces indistinct at this distance. They simply sat like that—and McFerrin sat too—the Charger's engine idling between the gasps that came at widening intervals.

Then the horn of the Ford gave two short reports as if in signal—and in proof of this the front doors of the Ford fanned open and the two men stepped to the ground. They came forward at an even pace, closing on the Charger and veering apart to take it from both sides. McFerrin saw the action, saw that he either stayed put and hit it, slammed the Charger forward and away, or got out and stood his ground with the one man, holding the other man to a handicapped offense by virtue of the shield that was the car. But he did neither. He sat. He let the action happen, let the play come unfolding *at* him—and concentrated all his awareness on the exact weightedness of the glittering weapon centered on his lap. And then both doors were pulled open and both men were touching him and McFerrin saw who they were.

"Spread your knees," Montague said, his hand coming down clawlike across McFerrin's belly and raking the pistol onto the floorboards.

"I want you sitting over here," the other man said

from the passenger side, leaning in and smiling, touching McFerrin's shoulder, a mere coaxing. It was the small man, the man Ben.

McFerrin shifted to the far side in his seat and watched Montague's fluid insertion of himself into the place just created behind the wheel.

"This is mine now," Montague said, reaching under the dash and ripping. The engine fluttered and died.

"It's his," Ben said. "Can you see that now? You can see that now, can't you?"

"He's mine, too," Montague said.

"That's right," Ben said. "I think he understands that now," the small man said.

"Of course he does," Montague said. "How could he not?" Montague smiled agreeably, an uncle pleased with a favorite but wayward nephew just persuaded of reason and prudence.

McFerrin smiled perceptibly in return. He felt an extraordinary, uncanny calm.

Montague was speaking—and as he was doing so, he was also lifting from the floorboards the pistol he had swatted there: "It is said that at forty a man's face is the one he's earned. That is what is said— and you see mine, and I am well past forty. I would like to think the point is not lost on you, Colin."

"Colin is not going to let that point escape him," the man Ben said.

"One hopes so, one wants to believe so," Montague said. "But Colin's so damnably preoccupied, so tremendously much on his mind."

"True," the small man said. "That's very true. Colin is not paying attention. Had Colin been paying attention, been alert enough to our passionate concern with his comings and goings we would not have his scabby nuts in a hydraulic vise. He would have seen our nice, clean, sedate automobile behind his souped-up kiddie car all the way from that second-rate motel."

"You weren't behind me—you were behind Poucher," McFerrin said.

"It speaks!" the man Ben said.

"Put yourself like this," Montague said, and reached his arms out so that his hands descended to just below his knees. Then he brought the insides of his wrists together in a kiss between his legs.

"Colin," the man Ben said, "we're demonstrating this for you because we don't want to see you make a mistake on your first try." The small man produced a pair of manacles and a come-along from behind his back. "Now, when you feel yourself ready to do this, Colin, and you think you can really do it right, I want you to go ahead. I'll wait until you think you're ready, and then you just nod your head and start doing it when you're ready."

"That's good," Montague said. "I don't think anyone ever had clearer, more patient instructions than that. Does he understand we only use this sort of brutish device for your true plug-uglies? Your gorillas and your apes and your Blank Panthers and your hippies and your vicious junior professors of history —your savage of the Liberal Arts school? Does our beast understand? Because your low order of field critter must be given every advantage of knowing what's expected." Montague squeezed the Voroshilov into his trouser pocket. "That's right, Colin," he said. "Take all the time you need."

"All right," the small man said, "he's going to do

it now," and as the small man gestured by inclining his head, McFerrin's movements coincided and he arranged himself in accord with the lesson he had been given. He was so arranged and waiting and very ready when the man Ben moved in and snapped each manacle in place and was just moving out to make the chain taut—and *the slack was still there*. It was then that McFerrin came bellowing alive to the performing of that single action, the movement that would whirl the chain into a looped and traveling noose. And—*there!* McFerrin wrenched the goddamn thing around—and *dove*—and had Montague chained by the neck and coming out the car door and had the small man going down under his right shoulder. The small man was screaming in the crush of the two men that were the weight that was crushing him, while the two men above scrambled and struggled on the field his small body made for their combat. The small man was screaming and still gripping the come-along, and his holding on like that kept the tension on the noose that was strangling Montague—and all McFerrin had to do was keep scrambling and struggling in frenzied moves, enlarging the scale of those moves until neither man was any longer struggling, until both lay quiet against him, the one below, the other above, but Montague sliding, collapsing off now, off onto the ground.

McFerrin kicked himself up, then went back down to one knee. With both hands that were locked this way, he tore pocket and thigh from Montague's trousers and took up the stainless steel revolver yanked the chain from the design it made on the sprawled forms below him, and hunkered fast and low along the grass to the dark green Ford sedan. He rolled in and took the wheel in his hands at six-thirty. The motor was going—good!—and it needed only a shift into "Drive." The emergency automatically released, and McFerrin was moving out of there —taking it forward to the high side of the Charger and getting the man Ben wherever he could, first a tire in front and then a tire behind, and then McFerrin barreled down the incline and onto the highway and into the traffic that was streaming there in its pursuit of the capital city ahead.

18

This was the Gold Room—so named for the color of its walls and of the leather cushioning that adorned the five tall armchairs circling the round white table that stood austerely center. Normally, ten places ringed the stately table, for normally each Chief of Staff was joined by his highest-ranking aide.

But this was not a normal session of the Joint Chiefs of Staff. There was nothing normal in any of this—and aside from the passing observance of Pentagon protocol governing the order of entry into the room, all formalities had been suspended.

General Poucher entered first and occupied the seat of the Chairman. When he had situated himself, the others sat—Keller, Air Force; Grissle, Army; Jark, Navy; Thorne, Marines.

Poucher waited; he would begin at the exact hour: the occasion seemed to solicit the historic element. He would wait out the better than two minutes that remained. He removed his watch and set it on the table before him. The table was otherwise bare, and the heavy chronometer seemed decoratively placed against the field of uninterrupted white.

"Ashtrays," Admiral Jark said.

Poucher activated a call signal under the carpet at his feet. In reply a stern buzzer sounded in the room. In answer to this, Poucher pressed the carpet twice. The sole door to the room opened, and a security guard saluted and stood waiting for instructions.

Poucher said, "Ashtrays."

The M.P. strode to the utility cabinet against the wall and then advanced to the table, carrying five large brass ashtrays, each bearing the appropriate insignia of service. He placed these accordingly, snapped a salute, stepped smartly to the door, turned neatly, again saluted, opened the door, and closed it firmly behind him.

Poucher looked at his watch. Forty seconds.

"Your communications units are negative," he said. "There will be no notes. You will forgive my saying this, but as officers and gentlemen I want each man's word that he is not recording. Do I have it? I will have an oral statement, by the man. Thorne?"

"Negative."

"Jark?"

"No."

"General Keller?"

"You have my word."

"Grissle?"

"I am not recording, General."

"Very well," Poucher said. "And you, sirs, have my oath I am not recording."

"Thank you, General," Commandant Thorne said.

Poucher checked his watch, bent to the floor beside his chair, and removed an envelope from his briefcase. He flipped open the envelope, took out the sheet of paper it contained, and placed it before him. He slipped eyeglasses from his pocket, carefully adjusted them, glanced at his watch, and began.

"The document before me was hand-delivered to my home at approximately fifteen hundred thirty hours today. Its signature is, I quote, 'A Former Comrade-in-Arms.' I will read it now."

"Question," Admiral Jark interrupted.

"Yes, Admiral," General Poucher said, making an elaborate show of lowering the paper.

"Has it been run for prints?"

"Yes, Admiral."

"And?"

"Negative."

"All right," General Grissle said. "Please, proceed."

"The item was processed here at P within the last half-hour. It proved negative," General Poucher said.

"By whose people?" Admiral Jark said.

"Our own," General Poucher said.

"D.I.A.?" Admiral Jark said.

"No," General Poucher said. "The new group. By E.S.A. ident lab and our *Walnut* annex.

"All right," General Grissle said. "Please read."

General Poucher surveyed the faces before him, saw that there was no further discussion to be managed, and then cast his eyes down to the sheet of paper he held.

"It begins without a greeting. I am reading now, quote, 'I served under your command. I think I might say I was among your most trusted officers. I was with you at (1) Mannheim, (2) Heidelberg, and (3) Heilbronn, as well as other actions, but mention these three to prove the authority of this letter—to wit, below you will find, for each of the actions cited, a detail of fact known only to those closest to you at that time. I have keyed them to the numerals given in each case.

" 'Let me begin:

" 'I am informed that the execution of the plan has been placed in the hands of the Central Intelligence Agency—more precisely, that the assignment resides with elements of Covert Operations Division, C.I.A.—although Agency top management is ignorant of the operation.

" 'I am informed that management of the assignment is the responsibility of former C.I.A. Deputy Director General Arthur M. Underwood, who has control of essential Agency units despite the unawareness of Agency headquarters.

" 'I am informed that there now exists a fracture in C.O.D. of C.I.A. with respect to the execution of the assignment, and that an element in C.O.D. is now moving to interdict the execution of the assignment.

" 'I am informed that this effort has succeeded in causing significant interference as a function of an effective destroy-action which occurred at the Long Hill Conservation Area.

" 'You will wish to know that the success of this destroy-action owed to information passed by an officer of C.I.A. sympathetic to the splinter faction. You will wish to know that his motive is to discredit D.I.A. by involving D.I.A. through specious evidence at the destroy-action site. You will wish to know that this officer is in the act of conveying gross facts and attendant distortions to the news media, clandestinely and in a professionally designed "story line" package.

" 'You will wish to know that the motive of this officer extends to the discrediting of the Joint Chiefs of Staff and, most specifically, to you, Sir.

" 'It will not go unnoticed that C.I.A. personnel are engaged in war acts against C.I.A. personnel. It will also not go unnoticed that the interagency combat with D.I.A. promises to bring to ruination your objectives and your personal destiny.

" 'I cannot, dare not, reveal to you, Sir, how I come to be in possession of these facts. I may only say that as a man who served alongside you in the Great War for Christian Freedoms, a man who was prepared to lay down his life for the principles you led us to champion against fascism and socialism, I gladly tell you what I know, in the prayerful hope it will serve to protect you and your high aims. I would be proud to add my name but must, in prudence, only sign, Respectfully,' et cetera, et cetera," General Poucher said, and lowered the paper to the table and smoothed it with his hands. Then he clasped his hands over the paper, and said, "Gentlemen?"

Admiral Jark was the first to speak.

"Jesus fucking Christ!"

The great white table was now empty of all but the five brass ashtrays that held smoldering pipes and cigars, and in one case, Admiral Jark's, a dozen or so cigarette butts—and the tall armchairs of golden leather upholstery were wrenched away from their earlier symmetry.

"The hour is nearly up," General Poucher said. "I think we can all agree that discussion has taken us as far as it will. I ask, then, that conclusions be proposed. Since we are all in this together, I think it furthermore proper that each man be permitted the honoring of at least one of his assessments. Commander Thorne?"

The Chief of Staff of the Marine Corps prefaced his remarks with the scarfing out of his pipe, tooling out the residue with a miniature spade. He said, "D.I.A. is not involved. Underwood would not use D.I.A. He might have brought in subcontractors for this or that bit of piecework, but I know Underwood—and I say Underwood would keep the thing lined up along manageable channels. The man is too experienced to risk the tension of interagency competition." Thorne punctuated his statement with harsh little blasts of breath to clear ashes from the bowl of his pipe.

"Thank you," Poucher said. "General Keller, please."

"My thoughts are not very clear yet, I must say. Until they've crystallized, I want only to point out that it was long ago agreed to incubate D.I.A. from this action in order to keep it hygienic for a further, more ambitious, action. Arthur knew our thinking in this regard as well as any man at this table.

138

Arthur concurred in the thinking. I even seem to recall his encouraging this vein of thought. No, gentlemen, I say we're okay with Underwood, and I also say D.I.A. is not in it. My conclusion is Arthur's being set up. My conclusion is D.I.A. is being set up. My conclusion is not to worry."

"Not to worry!" Admiral Jark said. "Excuse me, General Poucher, I wish to speak next in turn."

General Keller continued. "To finish my remarks," he said, "we all agreed C.I.A. has limited utility. We all agreed its utility was to be drastically diminished in the years ahead. I remind you all that we ran a *Walnut* annex program on this and received the same net appraisal by *Walnut* annex. I remind you gentlemen that we then agreed to locate the assignment with C.I.A. as its last major undertaking, preserving D.I.A.'s capability for future action. Arthur spearheaded that decision, let me remind every one of you. I therefore conclude that Arthur remains one hundred per cent and that the nigger hides elsewhere in the woodpile. I trust I make myself clear, and I trust Admiral Jark wasn't overly pained to hold his water."

Admiral Jark crushed an empty box of Du Mauriers and dropped it in the littered ashtray before him. "Mark," he said, "please buzz security. I'm all out."

"For God's sake, David," Poucher said. "Does someone have a cigarette for him?"

General Grissle offered Admiral Jark a cigar. Jark made a face but took the cigar and quickly lit it. He puffed deeply and began:

"The whole affair stinks. It stunk from the start.

I begged you. I made it eminently clear I had no quarrel with the objective. But I begged you to work out the termination with all D.I.A. personnel, our own people. This Underwood was C.I.A.—and C.I.A. cultivates men who think too much. Fancy types. For my money, we're getting just the kind of ass wound we deserve. I think it's going to fester until there's gangrene up our bungs and a chink's fart will smell good alongside the rot we'll all be shitting when they strap us in and throw the switch."

"Admiral," General Poucher said, responding to the annoyance that was signaled from around the table. "We want your assessment—a description of history is not deemed productive. Please, David, where do you say we go from here?"

"I've said my piece, Mark," Admiral Jark said. "I have nothing productive to add." The Admiral stubbed out his cigar and rose.

General Poucher said, "David, please sit down. I cannot allow you to leave this room yet. Please sit, David—and please compose yourself."

"I'm not asking to leave, General," Admiral Jark said. "I just want to stand a bit, if that's all right."

"By all means," the Chairman said, and turned to the Army Chief of Staff. "You, sir."

"Underwood—I say finish him," General Grissle said. "One, Underwood *was* O.S.S. Two, I say Underwood is *still* O.S.S. and maybe has a little side-venture going. Three, I say even if I'm wrong on one and two, the base rate of probability would weigh on the side of minimizing risk. It comes down to probability—minimax and maximax. Minimax thinking—and minimax thinking is the *only* thinking that works

140

here—minimax thinking says finish Underwood. End him."

Admiral Jark appeared panicked. He turned back to the table and gripped the headrest of his chair. "Ask *Walnut* annex! Get a probability and guidance-yield from *Walnut* annex!"

"Finish him!" General Grissle said. "Fuck *Walnut* annex! My guess is C.I.A. has insinuated its wiring into our banks, anyway. They're over the *Walnut* fault-line, I tell you, and are laughing their goddamn heads off. They're into us, man—and I'll tell you something else. The minute they got us to rent that leg of the box from them, that was the minute they took our sweet eggs in their faggotty hands! They're crushing our cubes with that motherfucking box, and that's where the trouble *began*. If you all had listened to me and stayed with D.I.A.'s box, we wouldn't have that creep Underwood with his finger up our ass, and we wouldn't have O.S.S. diehards putting dirt in our eyes, and we wouldn't have all this motherfucking *shit*! Burn Underwood, I'm telling you, and get out of it! Clean it out! Clean it all out!"

"That's your thinking?" General Poucher said.

"You bet your ass it is!" General Grissle said.

General Poucher seemed pained. He leaned well back in his armchair and laced his fingers under his chin.

"I will make my statement," he said. "I assess as follows: We presume the letter's legitimacy. We preserve Pentagon supremacy at all costs. We terminate General Underwood. Arthur was a good soldier. I ask you to join me in regarding him as an heroic soldier. Good soldiers, heroes, prove themselves remarkably mortal. I believe we will be convinced to see this as a death in battle, a comrade —valorous, certainly; misguided, possibly; corruptible, likely enough—a comrade fallen in the field. Regrettable but, in the long term, expectable.

"Lest we blame ourselves overmuch," General Poucher said, "it was early known that we could never achieve a thoroughly hands-on feeling for the termination procedure. We saw the hazards in getting in a professional, but we determined the gain justified the risk. We rolled the dice, and fortune's folly, gentlemen, they went against us. We attempted to ride the horns of the brute, and now he has rudely gored us. But not mortally, gentlemen, not mortally . . .

"At this time, I have nothing more to say, gentlemen—save, of course, thank you, each of you, for his keen and sincere contribution to these deliberations."

Even Admiral Jark nodded his assent to this—and General Poucher was obliged to raise his hand to quiet the side remarks that were beginning.

"One moment more, gentlemen," he said. "We will forgather here tomorrow morning at nine hundred hours sharp for the drafting of instructions to our cadre. The rules of order and security will be those that obtained this evening."

Admiral Jark said, "All right, Mark—I'll go along with that—but when I want a smoke, I'm going to get it." He laughed, a little hysterically.

"Come provided," General Poucher said. "That is my advice to you, David—come provided."

And all the men chuckled at that and by and by

rose and shook hands and it was at this stage of things that General Poucher remembered to announce the meeting adjourned.

19

It was big.

Those who claimed to know about these things said it was the biggest. The word they used was *mammoth,* and they were right—no installation of similar purpose occupied so much blunt space. For sheer volume it was one of a kind. Yet volume was not the whole story, not the thing that made it the colossus it was. For its virtues of speed and complexity were unrivaled. There were conflicting reports of its precise location, some identifying it as a heavy industrial consortium research-and-development center situated within a fifty-mile radius of the Pentagon; others insisting it would be found in the Great Salt Lake Desert servicing the paper of major financial institutions.

What little else of it was known or alleged, fact or rumor, was the following:

—that its construction was begun in the mid-sixties and its completion achieved in the next decade;

—that an elite corps of engineers was borrowed from I.B.M. and Burroughs and Honeywell but that

144

this group was later dismissed in favor of two men from American Machine and Foundry;

—that the sixteen technicians who were said to service its manifold chambers never left the place it was housed, that this was probably a frivolous speculation—but of course could not be disproved;

—that these sixteen persons understood their individual assignments but were given a false idea of total design, yet even so were sworn to secrecy;

—that its residence was at a depth of at least six hundred feet, beneath a lay-over barrier of alternating concrete and lead thirty feet thick;

—that it could outperform any combination of linkups constituted of the capacities of any number of other known machines;

—that its mega-properties had, of themselves, generated the potentiality for "liquidic" behavior, computation without reliance on solid materials;

—that it had been designed to allow for the patterning and repatterning of an infinitely intricate compartmentalization, an ever-shifting mazelike embroidery whose planes of division were called "fault-lines";

—that its capabilities of storage and retrieval, of contemplation and decisioning, of data span and spec-thought were employed on a "share-space" basis by government and supragovernment entities, and that the space of each "renting" entity was secure from that of every other "renting" entity by a "membrane" of continually altering planar configuration: the fault-line;

—that the recasting of fault-lines, the program generating their ever-changing character, was *aleatory*: an automatically rendered randomizing;

145

—that its operation was executed from consoles situated above ground, and that the manning of these consoles was the responsibility of persons marked by severe physical handicap;

—that no fewer than six but no more than ten of these consoles existed, and that one was somewhere in Kentucky and another in an unmarked aircraft that was always airborne;

—that consoles had been miniaturized down to the bulk of a family-sized package of bread;

—that its chief "renter" was C.I.A., who was also its sole "lessor";

—that any "subrenter" from the Agency had to be a member of the U.S. Intelligence community;

—that it was fundamentally a rather "simple" machine commonly known as a "digital computer";

—that it was called *Walnut* and had been assigned this playful identification because of its unique rivering of ridges and fissures: fault-lines;

—that to some whimsical scientist given to making capricious analogies, the impression of the interior action of this giant must have seemed very like the food of the same name.

And *Walnut*, this fundamentally simple machine known commonly as a "digital computer," on-programmed 2:21:34 A.M., Monday, July 25, and off-programmed 2:21:42 A.M., Monday, July 25. The hi-yield of this eight-second enterprise consisted of the name *Colin Robert McFerrin*.

The "renter" requesting the output package was delivered names in three categories, as specified: *lo-yield, med-yield, hi-yield.*

In the first, the names numbered three.

In the second, the names numbered nine.

In the third, *one*.

And at 2:21:43 A.M., Monday, July 25, *Walnut* —which is to say the "premises" belonging to the "renter" who sought and had this single name— went on to handle more difficult, and perhaps more important, business.

20

Underwood sat in his Barcalounger, head back, eyes closed, listening to Franck's Symphony in D Minor, the brooding strains sounding from the four speakers recently installed in his library. He was pleased with the progress of his plan despite its minor interruption. The trip to Kansas City and to Miami had proved rewarding, and, on the whole, things were proceeding very nicely, one might even say superbly, all things considered. The apparently sinister activities of Billy Joe Dooley and his doubles, ranging across every suspiciously radical, left-wing antic, were achieving wider and wider attention. The record was being established, the pattern revealed. It would all be there to point the finger and to tie the noose when the time came.

Yet it must be admitted that Reiner's continued absence troubled Underwood. Was Reiner not a perfectionist? How then his failure to keep to his appointed contacts? Unless of course the man had to choose between two commanding duties and chose to stay so close to his coverage at the practice site that contact with home base had to be delayed, regrettable as the negligence might be. Yes, that was it! One duty overriding another, Reiner being forced to choose between two urgencies and choosing, it seemed, the more immediate one. Patience, Underwood counseled himself, and let the flooding music wash over him.

At last he rose, and from the humidor on his desk he selected a long tan Havana, held it to his nostrils, savored the fragrance of the leaf. He lit the cigar, taking short, even puffs to start it on a proper burn. Yes, yes, patience, he instructed himself, and smiled at his wisdom in having just the right teaching for himself. He returned to his chair and set to massaging his legs, drawing on the excellent cigar between his efforts with his calves and thighs. Damn that Reiner! What had gotten into the man? Ah, well. The music! That was the trouble. Too—too unsettling, these somber tones. He rose again and this time moved to the turntable and lifted off the Franck. After a bit of sorting through, he decided on the richer melody of Strauss—something from *Rosenkavalier*. What a difference the right music made. He felt better already. Reiner's silence was nothing to fret over, a small matter that would doubtless explain itself in due course. Ah, no. Nothing at all, really—nothing to arouse any serious disquiet. And the music. Ah, yes. Very good, very—comforting. Underwood sat back in his Barcalounger and let himself dwell on the excellence of his Havana cigar.

Goddamn that Reiner! This is insufferable, really! Absolutely intolerable! Perhaps some moderate check on the situation was in order. He would give that some thought—nothing hasty, nothing hasty. Patience, you know. Ordinarily he would send a contact man to wherever it was to learn what the holdup was. But in this case, too risky. He had kept the operation on a "need to know" basis, and he would continue to keep it just that way. Reiner *was* the contact man on the Long Hill coverage. One could not have a *second* contact man. That would compromise security, would it not?

Underwood caught himself suddenly wondering how Morgan Drexel would proceed in a situation of this kind. Your contact doesn't contact at the appointed time—what do you do? What would *you* do, Morgan Drexel? Ah, but Drexel was no match for Underwood. Was Underwood not the acknowledged Master? The greatest architect of intrigue the Intelligence community had ever known? Whereas what was this Morgan Drexel but a bureaucrat, an overly cautious, timid, unimaginative creature mired in administrative and budgetary drudgery and probably happy to be so. Put a snaggle in the plans of a Morgan Drexel, and the poor rabbit would no doubt take to his sickbed while aides summoned a physician expert in the afflictions common to the dull and the weak. No color in the man, no flair. All *business* —a veritable bookkeeper-accountant of a man—a perfect mouse! Not, surely, an Arthur Underwood. Not a bold and creative spirit. It took an Underwood—an artist—to orchestrate the termination and disposal of persons who proved themselves a threat to national security—as this innocent, this Burlingame, had become. Especially when that innocent was the President. It took a Poucher to know *that*. To know that an Underwood was your man, not a Drexel. It took a military man, like Poucher, to know that your old O.S.S. fellow had it all over these C.I.A. clerks that billed themselves as agents. Agents, hell! They were mere footmen, consorts, retainers, bookkeepers, and accountants! Yet it was better that way, Underwood mused, better really for all hands. The more of a figurehead the director was, the further insulated was any particular capsule working on a termination. Yes, the Pentagon knew what it was doing. They came to *me*, right? They know! Poucher and those fellows, they know that if you want some serious work done, work that takes grit and genius, you don't go to a butler like Drexel. Well, yes, by God. You came to Arthur Underwood—and the work was done *right*! Ah yes, now he felt ever so much better—the Strauss, the cigar, the fine decor of this room, the plan. The plan? Great Christ, that clod Reiner! What was wrong with the man! A schedule is a schedule, damnation! A brandy! That would help—a little Hennessy—yes. Good.

He was just sampling his first swallow of the biting liquid when he heard the doorbell. The doorbell? News?

Damn maid! Where the hell *was* she? The bell again. Underwood put the brandy snifter down and went to the door. A messenger, yes! Would Reiner dare?

Underwood took the envelope, tipped the boy handsomely, and returned to the library. He took up his cognac from the table next to his chair, took a long sip, put the glass down again, and tore open the envelope.

Not from Reiner, no, goddamnit! Some kind of goddamn memorandum instead!

Underwood started in on it, reading casually at

first—and then no longer casually but agape, stunned, disbelieving! He had to go back to the beginning again—he could not believe what he was reading! *Amann*? Israeli Intelligence operating in the United States! He'd heard of this Amann, silent and lethally effective successor of the Haganah and the Stern Gang. But even if the damn thing *were* operating here—which seemed doubtful—why would it be sending a confidential memo to him? Underwood plucked his cigar from the ashtray beside him, and now, word by word, he read the memorandum from beginning to end.

He finished. My God, he finished! And still could not believe. He read again, even closer this time, even more scrupulously. He finished reading for the second time. Inconceivable! Inconceivable, Underwood virtually thundered aloud, that *any* outsider could have learned these things! But then he felt the hard lump stuck down in the corner inside the envelope. He reached in. The bullet! The goddamn frangible bullet! So delicate, it broke up upon entry—so deadly, its work inside you could not be undone by a dozen master surgeons—and so convincing as evidence that the plot had been uncovered. Underwood went limp with fear. He reached for his glass and swallowed off the rest of the cognac.

Again he looked at the list of those sent copies. "Good God!" he muttered. "Morgan Drexel!" Had a copy really been sent to the Agency Director? Jesus! He came out of his chair as if it had delivered an electric shock. He went quickly to the telephone, and after considerable difficulty he at last reached the Cook County coroner at home.

"I'm terribly sorry to disturb you at home," Underwood said. "But I've received some sort of crank message, and I need your help in clearing it up."

"Go ahead," said the voice on the other end.

"My name," said Underwood, "is Hastings. My company manufactures and tests rifles and small arms. Some days ago two of my people went to one of our testing grounds south of Chicago and I haven't heard from them since. I thought perhaps——"

"Your testing ground?" the voice said. "Are you talking about the woods in Cartwright County?"

Underwood shut his eyes for a long moment. Finally, he answered. "Yes," he said.

"We have three bodies recovered from that location," the voice said. "Now, what did you say your name was? And the name of your company, please?"

"That's all right," Underwood said. "Not important——" Foolishly, knowing it was foolish, he could not bring himself to hang up yet.

"Who is this?" the voice said. "What's this all about?"

"Never mind," Underwood said. "It's not important, really——" And then, feeling not only frozen with fear but ridiculous as well, Underwood broke the connection and replaced the receiver. He went back to the lounger and sat again, motionless. He stayed that way a long time. Finally he spoke in a whisper. "That goddamned Poucher."

He picked up his cigar. It had long since gone out. He stared at it a long time as if not understanding and then threw it across the room. He picked up the snifter, started to sip from it. Was it empty? How?

He set it back down with such force that he cracked off the stem. He went to the bar, dumped ice in a glass, then filled the glass with Scotch. He emptied the glass with large swallows, then poured more Scotch.

The phone rang. He looked at it as it continued ringing. "Morgan Drexel," he said aloud. He went to the phone. "Copy to Morgan Drexel, Director!" he yelled. He just stood there and let the phone ring until it stopped ringing. "Goddamn, goddamn," he said, his voice entering upon the heights of a scream. "Goddamn Poucher!"

Tears suddenly welled up in Underwood's eyes. He tried to calm himself. He tried to let himself flow out into the music and the liquor. He drank Scotch in long swallows, and he tried to force his mind to the burning in his stomach and the flooding sensation that was suddenly moving over him. From the alcohol? From fear? He felt immensely drowsy —the sort of lulled focus of attention they say overtakes a man going into battle—the way you feel before you step out of the plane into the fire fight below, or sitting in the landing craft thrashing through the waves to the beach, the way you feel *then*, rifle clutched desperately in your fists but your mind oddly elevated elsewhere. He fell asleep this way, the whiskey glass in his hand. It fell to the carpet hours later.

The doorbell sounded.

The doorbell? It was almost dawn! The doorbell at this hour?

Great God, the thought raced through him, Federal marshals, Secret Service: Oh God, he thought, and then thought of the pistol he kept upstairs in the bedside table.

But no—don't be absurd, man. You will ride this through as effortlessly as you've managed every other damn snafu in your life: You led a brigade through the Siegfried line, you sure as hell can beat this thing! Easy does it, now. Relax, relax. It's the liquor! Be calm, man—be calm!

Where in the name of God was that goddamn maid? He started for the door, and in the brief time it took to get there he had already established a way out. If it came to that, he had a way out! How easy it was, really! So simple—simply perfect!

The thing had been solely a Pentagon operation. Luckily he had picked up some information about it, had become curious and made certain inquiries through his extensive contacts. The D.I.A. had learned of this and, when something went wrong, had manufactured and disseminated the Amann Intelligence memorandum in order to strike back at him. A simple matter of envy and competition. That position would hold. He would make it hold.

He opened the door. Three men stood before him, all neatly dressed, all smiling pleasantly.

"Good morning, sir," one said. "I hope we didn't disturb you."

"Not at all," Underwood said.

"May we come in?" the man said.

"Your business?" Underwood asked.

"Government business," the one man who was doing the talking said.

"I see," Underwood said, trying to steel himself. *It has all been a plan of the Joint Chiefs. He had—luckily he had—picked up some information, had become cur——*Everything was emptying out of his mind. The liquor? The fear? *Had become curious,* *made certain inquiries*——What? Who would believe such a thing? Oh God! he cried to himself.

"Yes, do come in," he said. And then he thought to say: "Why don't we all have a drink, at the outset?" And then his hysteria surfaced somewhat, and without wanting to, he said, "Perhaps, as a matter of protocol, I should look at your credentials. Purely routine procedure, of course." Now why the hell had he said such a thing? Oh God, *let them leave.*

"Of course," said the man talking. He nodded to one of the other men. "Mayberry, show him our credentials."

The man called Mayberry pulled out an identification folder, came across the threshold, and held the folder out for Underwood to see. As Underwood tried to focus his vision on the official-looking card, virtually trembling at the mere display of an emblem of authority, the other silent man glided across the threshold and took up a position on Underwood's unattended side.

At last Underwood made out something that looked like the credentials of the Intelligence Division of Internal Revenue Service. Underwood stood there, stunned, staring. "I.R.S.?" he finally said. "What on earth——"

They did not let him complete his little exclamation of surprise. The man at Underwood's left stepped behind him and laid a wide strip of adhesive tape over his mouth in the same moment that the man to Underwood's right was clamping his head between powerful hands clapped to Underwood's ears. When Underwood reflexively raised his arms to jerk away the grip that held his head, his wrists were caught by the third man, the talker, who now, with a force that there was no struggling against, lowered Underwood's arms to his side. The man who had handled the tape produced a strap, and the length of heavy leather was swiftly circled around Underwood's middle so that, when the strap was yanked tight, his arms were bound to his sides.

He was a package now—he knew it. The sweat poured off him, and his mind kept crazily repeating one phrase: When I was O.S.S., when I was O.S.S. . . .

They lifted him like the sack of meat he had become and carried him upright deeper into his foyer, and then, turning him level, they laid him out on the fine oriental rug. The talker went back to close the front door. The man who'd managed the tape and the strap now took a syringe from his coat pocket, removed the plastic safety cap, and motioned with his head to the other silent man, who now cupped Underwood's chin in his hand and pulled back his head so that the full field of Underwood's neck was exposed. The needle was inserted about midway and somewhat to the side. It went in with no resistance, and the fluid that was expelled ran quickly from the glass cylinder. It took very little to do the job, but they always used somewhat more—just to be on the safe side.

"Thirty seconds," the talker said, his wrist up to follow out the time on his watch.

Underwood's eyes bulged. But he did not fight it. His mind raced with the words: When I was O.S.S., when I was O.S.S. . . .

The talker wandered to the door of the library and looked in. "Nicely done out," he observed.

Then he strolled back into Underwood's line of sight and studied him. He placed his hand tenderly on Underwood's forehead, a mother testing for fever. He stifled a yawn, then glanced again at his watch. "I give him ten seconds to go," he said.

But Underwood did not hear this. He heard none of the sounds the three men made now. If he heard anything at all, it was the sound of his own inner voice saying, "I was O.S.S., I was O.S.S.," and then he didn't hear even that anymore.

"He's done," the talker said. The other man removed the strap and the tape while the talker bent to check Underwood's pulse.

"Right on time," the talker said.

He raised his hand to Underwood's face and gently felt along the skin where the tape had been. "That's good," he said. "The General's got him a regular he-man beard. That itty-bitty tape won't show none. But you wipe him with alcohol now, Mayberry—all right?"

A little vial was brought from a pocket, a wad of cotton placed against its opened neck, wetted, and then the swab was rubbed across Underwood's lower face.

The man who did this returned the used swab to his pocket, nodded to the other two men, and then the three of them left, closing the door softly behind them.

"The wife?" the talker said when they had reached the sidewalk and were walking slowly south.

"Still in New York shopping," the strap handler said.

"The maid?"

"Probably asleep in back," the strap handler said.

"I wish the nigger had come on out," the third man said, speaking for the first time.

"Forget it," the talker said. "And you," he said, nodding to the strap handler, "you make sure our man at Reed is ready."

The maid discovered the body shortly after eight in the morning, and by nine-fifteen the autopsy had been completed, a piece of work that was accordingly done at Walter Reed Army Hospital inasmuch as Arthur M. Underwood had enjoyed a distinguished career in the military service of his nation.

The procedure was concluded with a complete fluids drain, special attention to the emptying out of all blood and spinal material. No samples of these liquids were kept, and no sign whatever remained of the Anectine, the most potent derivative of the curare plant. The pathologist who conducted the autopsy dictated that death was due to "natural causes," that the fluids had been drained for routine embalming preparation since preservation of the corpse would be a key detail given the status of the deceased and the expectation of a major funeral that might take a week or better to arrange. He instructed the stenographer to type the autopsy protocol and prepare it for his immediate signature, which he executed in the appropriate places after stitching up the deceased and calling for his removal to the morgue.

Since the maid was unable to reach Mrs. Underwood in New York, it was not until her return to her home the afternoon of this day that she was informed of the disposition of her husband, his sudden and grievous demise. She was a proud woman, a proud widow, and indeed did foresee the propriety of a grand funeral procession, full military honors. She set about making plans, and when it was apparent to her that the sort of occasion of pomp she contemplated would require a bit of arranging, she fixed the funeral ceremonies for the latest possible date, the second day of August. She could already see the honor guard in all that beribboned, stately ceremony marching the colors through the spacious concourses of Washington, D.C.

21

QUESTION: Is it your judgment they're into our leg of the box?

ANSWER: With *Walnut* there's never any telling.

Q. Yes—but what is your best judgment?

A. Impossible to do, speak in terms of "judgment" where *Walnut* is concerned. The thing is wholly self-operating. No one knows—or at least no one *we* know—knows all the ramifications of its operation and therefore how an interlope might happen. This isn't a simple power grid like national electricity of the Bell System.

Q. You mean so far as *we* know, nobody can.

A. I just said that.

Q. You misunderstood me. What I was suggesting is that someone might know how to make an interlope happen, how to effect a pentration into our leg.

A. You mean how to cut across a fault-line?

Q. That is what I mean.

A. Well, I can conceive of some incredible kind of scientist knowing—some sort of theoretical-thinker type—overcoming the barrier-array that

161

was built into the box. But even if there were someone like that, how would he get access to the box? Can't be done.

Q. I don't accept that There is nothing that cannot be done.

A. Well, let's say that the probability in this case is out there a nickel phone call from infinity. Access to the box is by remote units, right? That's how we get to it, and that's how everyone else gets to it. And you know how many filters there are between us and our own access—so imagine how the hell you'd get to someone else's—and even if by some fantastic means you could do it, then what? What could you do with the goddamn remote unit once you had it in your hands?

Q. I nevertheless see profit in speculating. Now, follow me in this. If one turns it around, if one has established—or let's say *thinks* he has established, by discovering the corruption of material *outside* the box—in other words, if one has reason to believe that he has exterior *evidence* of penetration, then it follows that from that penetration *may* have occurred *inside* the box, *before* the material was generated. There's every logic in *that*—now, isn't there?

A. I agree. But when you're talking about *Walnut*, you're not talking logic. It doesn't operate according to such rules. Now, do *you* see the *logic* in *that?*

Q. Of course I do. I'm well aware of indeterminacy—but where the human factor still exists—

A. And that's exactly *it?* The human factor does *not* exist in this.

Q. I think that's arguable.

A. Doubtless it is, but I'm not up to it. Besides, we're both over our heads with this. Neither of us is experienced in philosophical mathematics, and that's what this cookie is all about.

Q. Be that as it may, we must still ask the question.

A. Ask the question all you want—but in my opinion you're beating a dead horse. Or pissing up a tree trunk or whatever the hell the expression is.

Q. When the course of history depends upon it, I will beat every dead horse in sight. But the hour is very late. We're naturally both very tired and irritable. Let's call it a night.

A. You don't want to know about the Zero check?

Q. Dooley?

A. A program check was run late this afternoon.

Q. Splendid. And Underwood?

A. Poucher's reacting. The whole pack of them are. The history professor is teaching everyone a lesson.

Q. By now I should certainly hope he is. So long as he's running—so long as he's scared.

A. I'm doing my job. I'm doing it rather well, thank you.

Q. You *are*, darling. And I *do* thank you. I'm very grateful, really.

22

It wasn't long after the boy from Bonded had made his drop-off that Morgan Drexel left for Langley Field. Drexel made three phone calls and then buzzed downstairs and had his maroon Mercedes sedan brought around. Despite the urgency he felt, Morgan Drexel took the time to shave first, using the Rolls razor he always used, yielding to the habit he'd always yielded to. Drexel was a punctilious man, meticulous in all his customs, and shaving before any public appearance, as thoroughly and methodically as it was possible to shave, was high among the Agency Director's many customs.

The two security guards at the Langley gate recognized Drexel at once. Yet they asked for his I.D. and inspected it closely before waving him on. He moved the Mercedes down along the road that led through the majestic greensward that fronted the main building of C.I.A. headquarters. Dark, lush forest growth bordered this clearing, but no one would mistake its presence as proof that the agency whose installation it surrounded had chosen the site for natural beauty.

The surrounding forest growth was here for secrecy's sake. Everything here was here for its function, the landscape not excluded. And nothing and no one was greater testimony to this reverence for pure function than Morgan Drexel himself. In appearance, manner, and motive, Drexel was the living embodiment of this Agency ideal. There was no waste in the man, and the man wasted nothing.

Drexel entered the building, walked briskly to his office—greeting no one en route and being greeted by no one except at those four additional security check-points, displaying his credentials and at one check-point replying to the password interrogative with a three-word sentence—and at last took his place behind his immaculate desk. The room that enclosed this desk seemed more the setting of a thoroughly absorbed scholastic than of a chief executive, more the environment of a fussy, inward scholar than that of a man who wielded enormous power in the public sector.

Drexel removed the envelope from his jacket pocket, slipped out the paper, and then tilted the envelope to spill out the bullet it held. His waxen hands spread before him on the patinated surface of his antique desk, Drexel examined these items with a concentration that seemed nothing less than ferocious. A bloodless man in his late fifties, his skin the lifeless color and fleshless texture of parchment, Drexel was devoted to work with the intensity most men reserved for the lustier passions. His milk-white hair and his bleached blue eyes and his colorless, papery skin all underscored the sense of a man who spent his days in rooms with things that had no life, things remote from the world of people trying to live and die and just get along the best they possibly could.

Drexel did allow himself one slight indulgence, a long-standing interest in things very old, objects that were burnished by the handling of history, of which the nineteenth-century French Boulle desk, inlaid with tortoise shell, was an outstanding emblem. But Morgan Drexel was a scrupulously cautionary man too—and had earlier arranged with the Agency's security systems contractor, United States Safety and Protection Corporation—to have a crew on hand for the arrival of the desk, so that it might immediately be outfitted with extraordinary security devices and, given the piece's fragile character, a special high-density steel stronghold to be concealed behind the desk's one drawer. In the two or so years of Drexel's tenure of the desk, little went into that stronghold. For Drexel reserved its space for material of the utmost secrecy, records and artifacts of such immense importance that even the classification "Eyes Only" and the listing thereafter of two or three of the nation's most eminent names would not in itself have been sufficient notice to gain the sanctum of the stronghold. The four wall-safes in his office held the materials others thought secret. But the stronghold in the ancient desk held what *Drexel* thought secret—and at this moment its contents numbered only one document, a single sheet of paper on both sides of which there were abbreviated notations in Drexel's own hand, the sum total of an eighteen-month personal effort to catalog the inventory of every *Walnut* "renter's" critical programs.

Since these "renters" constituted a group of one

hundred and four line-agency, hypo-agency, supra-agency, intra-agency, extra-agency, and blind-agency organizations—not to mention the larger user, both "renter" and "lessor," the C.I.A. itself; hence, really a group of one hundred and five—Drexel had his work cut out for him in sheer numbers and complexity alone. But when you further considered that it was strictly observance—the "lessor's" guarantee and his irresistible selling point—that no renter, and surely not the lessor himself, would have, *could* have, access to another renter's premises, his wandering "parcel" in the giant machine—you understand why Drexel kept his notations to a single sheet of paper and why that sheet of paper resided in the U.S. Safety and Protection Corporation stronghold under a security defense-mechanism immeasurably better than lock and key.

To be sure, there was much Drexel had not uncovered from *Walnut*, but there was also much that he had, and how he had engineered his way into its labyrinthine systems of perpetually reshaping fault-lines and turned up so much information was known by no one else in C.I.A. The composition of the Central Intelligence Agency was intricate beyond belief. And it followed from this that no one there *could* know everything (wasn't this the motive behind the Agency's Chinese-puzzle architecture?), but Morgan Drexel knew more than anyone else did. For he had penetrated *Walnut* and therefore knew many truths no one man was comfortable knowing. He shared this burden with no one else in the Company. He dared not—for any one of them— even Deputy Director Warren Miller, a man Drexel himself had brought in and brought along to even higher office, and still Drexel's most trusted aide —any one of them might in fact be some other domestic or foreign agency's counterintelligence, a *mole* perhaps, a "sleeper" agent, or worse, just an ambitious man, a private adventurer.

Drexel sighed heavily, swept his hands apart as if in bewildered disgust with the items before him, then briefly buffed with his coat sleeve where the steam of his palm had fogged a patch on the sheen of the walnut. When he had done this he fingered the reception key on the intercom.

"I'll see Miller now," he said, and then brought himself forward in his overstuffed chair of cracked crimson leather and propped his arms on the desk top in a pose of thoughtful attention and, he hoped, fit enthusiasm—for the fact was that even so outlandish an occasion as this bored Morgan Drexel. For Morgan Drexel intrigue was fundamentally tedious, a child's game of hide-and-seek graduated to seek-and-kill, and just as pointless. But whatever the work, for Morgan Drexel work was nevertheless a grand aesthetic, the thing one did and did unimpeachably well because—well, because there was really nothing else to do.

Miller, a man in his midforties, was only moderately less colorful than Drexel himself. But Miller's fourth-carbon resemblance to the original article seemed, by comparison with the original article, a crime deserving punishment. He entered and quickly took the seat opposite in a chair purposely angled from the desk so that Drexel could enjoy the full view of his visitor's legs—for how a person composed his lower extremities Drexel thought intensely revealing.

Morgan sat and did not speak until the secretary had left. "What's up?" he said brightly once the door was closed.

"Come here," Drexel said, and when he had Miller standing attentively at his elbow, Drexel smoothly slid the paper·in a perfectly lateral direction as if the measured gesture were in itself a message that spoke multitudes. "Read," Drexel said, and kept himself leaning forward in his chair so that Miller had to bend at a clumsy incline.

Miller saw exactly this:

TRIPLE TEST CONFIDENTIAL

TO: General A. M. Underwood

FROM: Amann, Covert Unit (U.S.)—Israeli Strategic Services

RE: Decommission of C.I.A. personnel, Cartwright County, Illinois

1. Reference is made to your impending program concerning terminating of President of the United States. You are advised hereby that your two agents supervising training in respect to above were killed. Also killed was one rifleman. Presently at Cook County morgue, Chicago, Illinois are the corpses and corpses remain unclaimed. Our source indicates coroner of Cook County can be regarded cooperative and as likely to cooperate with regard to cover requested.

2. You are further advised also that your operation is penetrated, with regard to all phases, by Defense Intelligence Agency, agents of which responsible. The ambition of D.I.A. in this is counteroperation and other reasons you will know.

3. You are finally advised at last that accord-

ing to D.I.A. timetable crucial period of disintegration of the Central Intelligence is begun. Selective elimination of other key control and supervisory agents for the mission will be anticipated shortly. This to be followed by dissemination to media of data revealing it is C.I.A. who will assassinate Chief of State. At that time, credit for interruption and disintegration of the termination mission is given Secret Service.

4. Enclosed herewith both with original and with copy is bullet. Bullet obtained by our representatives. Preliminary examination indicates not only that the subject bullet is frangible water bullet, but also type of bullet used against the two supervisors inasmuch as there was fragmentation in skull of each leaving nothing but fragments to be collected at autopsy. Rifleman was killed by other means yet undetermined by this agency.

5. While Amann does not engage in action operations within the territorial limits of friendly nations, necessarily it engages in fact accumulation and monitoring of unusual activities. Your pertinent mission—assigned to you by Pentagon —is monitored by our organization. Our purpose notifying herewith of the internal operation against your organization hopefully is to prevent the discreditation of you, which agency is always cooperative with us and has been to our cause always friendly. Having informed you of facts above, our organization takes no further action, because of our policy requirements limiting activity within the borders of nations which are friendly nations.

6. It is unnecessary to add that under no circumstance is our service to you acknowledged by our home government. It is hoped aforedescribed information will be useful and will further prevent interference with and damage to your agency.

Sh'mor tsa-ad-cha may-o-hev shesar may-dar k'cha!

AMANN,
Covert Unit (U.S.)
I.S.S.

cc/
R. Morgan Drexel,
Director
The Central Intelligence Agency
Langley Field, Virginia

General Saul Grad
Controller of the Mossad
Tel Aviv

Saul Haas
International Research
The Foreign Ministry
Tel Aviv

"What is this crap?" Miller said.

"Is it crap?" Drexel said.

"How the hell do *I* know?" Miller said, and returned to his chair.

"What's your educated guess?" Drexel said, unable to stifle the ironic inflection the sentence seemed to want. "You might begin, for example, by telling me how the hell the Israelis come to be sticking their hairy noses around on U.S. soil."

"Who says they *are?*" Miller said.

"*This* says they are," Drexel said, tapping the paper with an elegantly bloodless finger.

"Then that means you believe it," Miller said.

"Don't be so precious clever, Warren. I am not interested in fencing with you. I want opinions from you, and I want them now, and I want them without decoration."

Drexel returned the sheet of paper to a position directly in front of him, picked up the bullet, and set it down in the precise spot from which he'd just raised it, and waited.

"All right, Morgan. You won't like it, but here are my opinions, if you insist on calling simple guesses 'opinions.' I don't know if it's legit or not. If it is not legit, then *who's* fucking around and *why?* But if it *is* legit, then it follows that we begin by first researching the shape and composition of the facts right on down the line from here to Cartwright County, and so on. If we get that far with it and it looks like we're going somewhere, well, then I'd say we blow a whistle somewhere fast and loud before we get it blown on us. As for whether or not the Israelis are into *us*, I don't see why *not*, because *we* know the yids are into everything else. As to the question you are probably most concerned to have my opinion on: Why Underwood? Why would this Amann outfit want to spill all this to *Underwood?* And I'm going to give you my best opinion on that one, Morgan, because that's the one that convinces me our heads are in the oven. That thing went to Underwood because the yids really *do* know something, which something they *do*

know that we *don't* know is undeniably made credit-
able by their *addressing* the goddamn thing to
Underwood and merely *carboning* us. My guesswork
working for you, Morgan?"

Drexel replied with royal simplicity. He said,
"Yes." This reply, Miller could readily see, pro-
nounced an end to talk, to allow for the really deep
thinking to begin.

Drexel swiveled in his chair, idly tracing a crack
in the leather with his finger, and then finally faced
forward with great pomp.

"Listen, my plan is this. We will proceed as
you've outlined, along those rough directions. We
will also stop Underwood. He was O.S.S., and that
outfit, I am beginning to suspect, is enjoying some
sort of insane renaissance.

"Next, we go to *Walnut* and make an entry into
D.I.A.'s leg of the box. I can get over their fault-line,
and I will do it. We do not report to the President.
His destiny has nothing to do with ours. We do not
report to the Pentagon. Their destiny has nothing to
do with ours. We do not report to the State Department. Their destiny has nothing to do with ours.
We do nothing but cover our flank and continue
advancing our information spearheads. We have one
aim; to know what is happening, to find out who is
making it happen, and to wrest control from whoever
it is and transfer the power into our own hands.
Are we agreed?"

Miller nodded weakly, stunned by the speed of
his superior's backpedaling.

"I take it we are agreed, then. I will want you
in this office at eight tomorrow morning. I want you
carrying every tidbit from the files that might bear

on this matter. You will confer with no one on anything even remotely related to this matter. All right,"
Drexel said, and indicated with a gesture of the hand
that Miller might go.

When he was gone and the receptionist had been
waved away with her offer to bring coffee, Drexel
entered upon the elaborate and complicated procedure necessary to open the stronghold and place the
document inside. It was dangerous to base a plan on
even educated guesswork, but he was increasingly
willing to concede that in the ambiguous world being
flung up around him, guessing was the best anyone
could do—and the madder it all got, the more one
guess, educated or not, was as good as another.
Sometimes, the crazier the guess, the better.

23

"Kick the goddamn thing on!" McFerrin said.

"It's busted," Greenfield said. "I already told you, you, the fucking switch is *busted*. Now hold still, goddamnit!"

Room 415 of the Marriott Inn was hot, hot enough to pass for the boiler room in summer at the Yuma Desert Arms. And the air conditioner gave no relief, because the air conditioner would not work. What *was* working was Greenfield, with hacksaw and pliers—the hacksaw to rid McFerrin of the manacles, the pliers to steady the bite as Greenfield cut.

"Jesus, hurry," said McFerrin. "Can't you move that thing faster?"

"Just calm down, buddy—calm down," Greenfield said. "If I slip with this blade you'll need more than a Band-Aid."

The sweat ran off them as the two men labored against the support of the bathroom sink. McFerrin had the come-along slung back over his right shoulder, and as he strained with Greenfield to hold the

175

steel against the shove and draw of the blade, a small flower of blood began to show in the center of the bandage on his forehead.

"You're bleeding a little," Greenfield said.

"Where?"

"Up there—where that bastard tapped you with the pistol butt."

"Well, he maybe tapped his last," McFerrin said.

"You didn't say you snuffed him," Greenfield said.

"I don't know *what* I did. I ran over the creep. I tried to cool him and maybe I did. Who knows? I'm past caring."

"No shit," Greenfield said, through one cuff now and motioning McFerrin to place the other in position. "I'd say, good buddy, we maybe both better be past caring."

"I need a shower," McFerrin said, abruptly changing the subject, "but not here. No telling where our drag strip racing friends picked up our trail, and I don't want to be around when that door comes crashing down."

While McFerrin shucked the case from one of the pillows on the bed and dumped in the come-along and cuffs and the hacksaw and pliers and shoved the sack of it under the bed, Greenfield paid the bill at the office and brought his Datsun station wagon around.

It was after midnight now. Their room at Howard Johnson's Motor Lodge was almost a duplicate of the Marriott. The two men sat as they had earlier that day, Greenfield using the chair, McFerrin, his legs stuck out in front of him, seated on the bed. He looked pretty fair now, though his bandage was water-soaked from his shower and bloody and needed changing. He fingered a Schim from the flat tin he carried, jabbed it between his teeth, and set it aflame.

"I'd like some coffee," he said.

"I'll get room service," Greenfield said.

"No, don't. What I want is my homemade Turkish brew, my sage special. Besides, let's leave off with any additional spectators right now. Frankly, man, I feel——"

"Watched," Greenfield said. "I know. Me, too."

"Yeah," McFerrin said. "To tell you the truth, Dan, that Montague dude really gets to me. He's some special treat, that boy. I can't get a real fix on him."

"I'll be happy if I *never* have to meet the man."

"Take it on faith," McFerrin said, "that is one very weird customer. And he's got a face by Special Effects to prove it."

"So all right—he's a bad-ass guy." Greenfield got up, turned off the television, and went back to his chair. "So? What now?"

"What now," McFerrin repeated and puffed a bit on his cigar. "One, I've got to get word to Val not to go to my apartment here. And the Philly apartment is hereafter off bounds, too. Two, we've got to keep you out of your place so long as your wife and kids will be okay without you, and get both of us to a more secure setup. Three, I've got to talk to Quiller, which means try some new tack because I don't figure it's such a hot notion to use the Arlington gambit anymore. Cousin Montague seemed

177

to know all about that number. He *seemed* to seem to—because that little buster is such an inscrutable *strange* bastard there is no goddamn telling *what* he *does* know. Christ, the guy is all suggestiveness, all ironic *implication*. Anyway, I need to talk to Quiller; I need his guidance now, because, Danno, I tell you, I am getting a little goddamned *confused*. Montague's after me, but who the hell *is* Montague and who's he working for? D.I.A.? Who's pushing his button? Underwood? Christ, we don't even know if there's any connection there. Poucher? Well, why the hell not? Just a lousy break that my stakeout notion got messed over by my flakeout notion to wait as long as I did. But I guess Montague would have had my ass either way. Where was I, five?"

"Four," Greenfield said, "but I think I can follow without the bouncing ball."

"I can't," McFerrin said. "I need to see this thing in as orderly terms as I can manage. So if you don't mind, pal——"

"Okay, four," Greenfield said.

"Four," McFerrin said, "we stay buttoned up but good from now on. From now on we figure whoever the hell he is, he is onto us and he wants to defuse us."

"I'm with you there, friend."

"So okay! We play it all the way *in* now," McFerrin said, relighting his cigar. "We play it as if it were Nam, Turkey, Greece, Guatemala. An *assignment*, for Christ's sake—one we assigned ourselves. We play it by strict field-operation *rules*; we keep it buttoned up and *secured*—only we also keep ourselves loose to spring for the action, to *anticipate* the action and lay in a shock hit, a hit they can't anticipate. All right!"

"All this *four?*" Greenfield said, trying to construct a smile.

"Come on, Dan, cut it *out*. I know you're scared, man. I'm scared a piss bucket and a half too—but we've got to come straight on this. We're *in* it, man. We're fucking around with something big, I know— a Government plan to waste the President of the United States of America—*do you hear me?* Do you get what this really *means?* You understand people who would go after a number as big as that you don't make jokes about?"

"Let's have five," Greenfield said.

"Okay—five," McFerrin counted up. "Five, we put it like that to the press; we put it just that way. We go public! They won't believe us, of course— they'll take us for crackpots, but it will maybe at least get the ball rolling *public*. We lay out the whole story about the action back at the mock-up site in the woods; we get the rehearsal action out there in black and white—the *Times* maybe and maybe C.B.S. and the *Washington Post*—whoever we can get the story to without uncovering ourselves, and we get some *noise* going, we keep warming it up, right?"

"Right," Greenfield said. "Turn the flame up under it, right." He was all seriousness now, a student of the excitement that was coming over McFerrin.

"Right is right! And *six*, we've got it cooking pretty good under Poucher and the J.C.S. and there's the memo to the Director and the copy to Underwood. So we let it simmer, and we watch it come on up. And meanwhile we get something on with the media. I don't care *who* or *how*, so long as it's done with zero exposure of us."

"I'll handle media," Greenfield said.

"I know," McFerrin said. "I know you will."

"Right," Greenfield said. "You keep to four walls for a time, okay? You could use a little R and R, old buddy, is what I'm thinking."

"I need Val," McFerrin said.

"You need quiet, Colin—we'll get Val to you after some nap time. Okay, good buddy?"

"How the hell can I crash when I'm this keyed up?"

"You'll be okay," Greenfield said, getting up, going to the television to switch it on. "Let's ease off with the late late movie; then tomorrow we can schlepp around for a place to lay low." He fiddled with the dial until he had something tuned in. He sat on the floor in front of the screen, and in a bit McFerrin slid from the bed, and propping his back against the sideboard, he too sat watching the old British spy drama as it unfolded in too-orangy color before them. It was not long after this that the screen gave way to the sign-off news, and among the head-lines the announcer read, there was included an item reporting the death of Arthur M. Underwood, distinguished associate of World War II O.S.S. Chief "Wild Bill" Donovan, distinguished Major General, U.S. Army, retired, distinguished former Deputy Director of the Central Intelligence Agency —dead, in his home, of natural causes.

"My God, they aced him," McFerrin said. "They aced him when they got our little love letters."

"Somebody moves fast. Poucher? The J.C.S.? The Agency?"

"Who the fuck knows?" McFerrin said. "It figures, but who can count on what figures anymore?"

24

It was a high white house of clapboard construction, its broad and evenly spaced windows shuttered in forest green. The front of the house looked out onto a sweeping lawn that in Edward Burlingame's absence was marked only by the geometry of croquet wickets and, under a tall elm, the weathered shed where the mallets and balls were kept. This was the President's summer cottage, a house that overlooked the Atlantic on every side, in a place called Mount Desert, an island a few miles off the coast of Maine.

But today the gracious lawn was combed of croquet wickets; the butler had removed them early that morning in preparation for the corps of press and Secret Service that would crowd the front of the house in anticipation of the Presidential party's arrival. For the President had decided to celebrate his son's fifth birthday with an old-fashioned country picnic, and his family, along with a dozen or so honored guests from the capital, had flown up from Washington to Portland the day before on Air Force One and then cruised over to Mount Desert on the Presidential yacht *Serena*.

The *Serena* now lay moored several hundred yards offshore, and the family and guests stood in the shade of the large yellow-and-white-striped tent that had been erected out back. In front, where the press milled around and were kept from overstepping their welcome by the two dozen Secret Service men that had been flown in for the occasion, tables had been set up for them with a spread of sandwiches and soft drinks. Out back, the fare for the guests had of course been more appealing, but now it was mostly litter that attendants were clearing away in expectation of the serving of the cake. When the cake was brought from the kitchen—a very large affair, also flown in from Washington—the five blue candles that topped it blew out in the late afternoon ocean breeze. The President himself relighted the candles at the big round table where the party sat, and then he led the group in singing Happy Birthday to Stephen.

The cake was cut and passed around, and now the children and their friends and most of the women retired to the spacious interior of the house, for the sea was giving off a good wind now and the hour was early evening. Cigars and brandies were produced, and as the servants gathered up the remaining dessert plates and utensils and restored the large table to order, the talk began in earnest.

General Poucher wanted to know what the President was going to do about Greece, and the President, accustomed to Poucher's bluntness, was beginning his genial reply when Secretary of State Danforth interposed himself to say that he thought a toast in order. He stood, raised his glass of Courvoisier, and

THE STAR SPANGLED CONTRACT

said. "To Stephen Burlingame, and to the good man that is his father."

Franklin Quiller rose quickly, saluted with his glass, and said, "Gentlemen, to the President and to his son."

Everyone was on his feet echoing Quiller's words, and it was Commandant Thorne who quickly thereafter said, "Hear, hear!" and was joined in this by Morgan Drexel, who went Thorne one better at pomp and rapped the table with his knuckles.

"Thank you," the President said, "thank you, gentlemen," and when he saw Admiral Jark preparing to rise from his chair, the President smiled warmly and said, "I'm very touched to have these sentiments, and I think we can now proceed to the concerns expressed by General Poucher. There's no reason why I can't respond to him here. I want my position abundantly clear."

"Thank you, Mr. President," General Poucher said, "and let me for everyone thank you and Mrs. Burlingame for your generous hospitality today. Now, about Greece——"

"Yes, of course," the President said. "I am happy to restate my position, and I am sorry it does not find favor with you and your colleagues, General—but I must again say that I choose to see a Greece that is strongly supported in the direction of democratic rule. It is my judgment our best interests lie in backing a popular government in Greece. Now, as to specific points of how I see us proceeding in the current unstable situation there——"

"Mr. President," General Poucher interrupted, "you will forgive me if I say that I cannot be persuaded by this line of thinking, that I——"

"Excuse me, General," the President said, "I believe you asked for my thoughts concerning Greece. Your ideas on this subject are well known to all of us. Now I——"

"As are yours, sir!" General Poucher said.

"Gentlemen," Franklin Quiller said, "I see no advantage to a discussion that so early arouses temper. I might add that it would do well if we were to bear in mind the occasion that brings us here, to the President's private home, as his guests, I remind you."

"I will not be patronized by you, Mr. Quiller," General Poucher said. "The President is well aware that I appreciate his hospitality. The President is also well aware that you are not the only man here in possession of respect for the proper courtesies. My remarks to the President are in the spirit of open debate, a right I enjoy as an American, sir. I needn't be shy of giving my opinion in any arena in these United States. As a patriot, a man who has fought honorably in this nation's great wars, I needn't be reminded how to act before the Chief Executive of this land. The President has my respect, and he knows it—and I will not be instructed in behavior by you, sir."

"I think you're making a fool of yourself," Quiller said.

"You will apologize for that remark," General Poucher said, standing now.

"I don't believe that's necessary," Quiller said, sitting back nonchalantly in his chair and reaching into his coat pocket for his pipe while Poucher stood across from him, glaring.

"I think we would like to hear the President's specific suggestions—as to Greece," Morgan Drexel said, his pale eyes hidden behind the virtually black sunglasses he wore whenever he was out of doors.

Poucher, still on his feet, shifted his angry expression to Drexel, and said, "Your business is collecting information. Period. Keep to your business."

The President stood. "I hesitate to say this, Mark, but I think you're out of order. I am sensitive to the fact that there is serious disagreement over the making of policy with respect to Greece—but I will not have disagreement escalating to discord so soon after my son's birthday party. Now I ask you to remember the occasion—and although I welcome our using the rest of the evening on the nation's business, I will not have my backyard turned into a battleground."

"I'm sorry, Mr. President," Poucher said. He gave Drexel and Quiller each a hard look in turn and then sat down and quickly drank off his brandy.

"Thank you, Mark," the President said. "More brandy, gentlemen?" The President looked around in signal to the attendants to replenish glasses. As the pouring began, he turned to Danforth, half nodded, and then said, "Perhaps the Secretary of State would choose to comment on this matter, now that it has landed in our laps here. Otis?"

Otis Danforth might have passed for Franklin Quiller's brother. Where Quiller had close-cropped steel gray hair, Danforth's was long, rather theatrically waved, and very white, but aside from this distinction, the two men were remarkably alike in their bearing—both tall, taller than the President by a very noticeable degree, both bony in the face, with the open countenance that frowned handsomely or smiled easily, both the slouchy, loose-limbed, aristocratic sort. These were men who looked like architectures that only New England restraint, hardiness, and tradition could make, men you liked instantly if you happened to admire the virtues of careless excellence which generations of patrician rearing fostered; men you disliked instantly if you knew yourself their natural inferior no matter how great your worldly achievements.

Not only did Danforth and Quiller look strikingly alike, but in style and substance they seemed to cast uncannily twin figures—with shared political and social views that appeared to have evolved as naturally in them, to be as much a part of the patrician stamp that marked each man, as did the soft and woody tweeds they always wore, the sylvan browns of their well-waxed British shoes, the inimitable flare and the slight touch of fraying of the button-down collars of the faded blue Oxford cloth shirts these men appeared to have in unending supply.

Despite the chill wind that now blew briskly off the water, Otis Danforth was coatless, the collar of his worn blue shirt open at the throat, his sleeves rolled carelessly to just over the elbows. He teetered back in his chair, managing to hold a brandy snifter and a Camel cigarette in one hand while he gestured with the other, and smiled broadly around the table.

"Gentlemen," he said, "I guess it needs saying that the President and the Joint Chiefs of Staff aren't all that far apart in their positions. After all, it is the good of this nation that both positions seek, and I think we are none of us any longer willing to believe that the nation's good can exist apart from the nation's security. Hold it," Danforth said and then swallowed some brandy, coughed amusingly, and began again. "The President sees our security in the Mediterranean enhanced by our adopting an open policy with respect to Greece; that is, by our not interfering in favor of either the military junta which apparently aims to seize control or in favor of stabilizing the popular government that currently holds the reins of power. In the President's judgment and, I must say, in my sincere judgment too, American *self*-interest is best served by our keeping hands off to the greatest extent we're able. Sorry," he said, and took another pull on his brandy. "And when I talk about self-interest, I'm talking about protecting the national economic interests, in oil traffic and so forth, *and* strengthening the nation's defense posture as well. I grant you, the President's *methods* may be at slight variance with those proposed by the Joint Chiefs. But I see no substantial difference in the ends really, and only a very subtle distinction in means." Danforth concluded with another generous smile spread evenly around the big table.

"That's utter eyewash," General Poucher said, the back of his neck flushed with color. "Eyewash and double-talk—and I for one, sir, am not fooled."

Danforth ignored the remark, the majesty of his smile never fading in the least degree. "The Vice

President's presence in Greece these last few days has helped immensely to secure our interests with the provisional government—and, moreover, the world sees in his presence there a U.S.A. that is concerned but benevolent. The resultant utility of good public relations in this, with both friendly and unfriendly nations, must not be overlooked and cannot be overstated."

"More double-talk," Poucher said, bristling. He stood up from the table. "With your permission, Mr. President, I believe Mrs. Poucher and I will spend the night on the *Serena* and forgo your kind offer to put us up here at the house. The sea air will do me a world of good at this point. With your permission, Mr. President——"

"By all means, Mark," the President said, relieved to see an end to the conflict and rising to clasp the General's hand.

Those remaining at the table seemed to take this for a signal that the festivities and its unscheduled aftermath of debate were over. All were standing now, shaking hands and again congratulating the President on his son's birthday, eager to be free now to wander casually around to the front of the house and meet there with reporters from the television networks and the nation's major newspapers.

The sun was well into the trees to the west, the sky flaming up there to a brilliant display of color. The President stood among the remnants of the celebration, still shaking hands and bidding his guests good night. Franklin Quiller had placed himself close by, and when the lawn was empty of all save the President and, several yards to his either side, two Secret Service men, Quiller came up to the President and slapped him gently on the back.

"Can't believe Stevie's really five, Ed. My God, how time does fly."

The President turned to face Quiller, and he was not smiling.

"They mean business, don't they, Frank?"

"The J.C.S.? I guess they do, Ed—but what the hell. Has there ever been a time when those boys weren't all spit and thunderation? They'll cool off. They'll come around in time for the election, and if they don't come around, then so what? We don't need their support and they know it, and that's what's eating them, too. Put it out of your mind."

"Sure," the President said.

"Want to step around front and have a little chat with our friends from the fourth estate? This is July—a little electioneering wouldn't hurt any this early in the game."

"I'm tired, Frank," the President said. "I believe I'll catch Stephen before Mary puts him away for the night, and then, I guess, I'll make it an early night myself. Make my apologies for me, all right?"

"You bet," Quiller said, "and tell Stevie old Uncle Frank says, 'Keep 'em flying,' okay?"

"Will do," the President said, and turned to enter the house—and as he did this and as the two Secret Service men moved with the President to the high wooden stairs that gave access to the large screened porch entryway at the back of the house, Quiller, as if prodded by the sudden spark of an afterthought, loped after the President and caught up with him just before he'd reached the stairs.

"One moment, sir," Quiller said, brushing the President's sleeve.

"Yes, Frank?"

"Have you changed your mind about the Kansas City appearance?"

"Why do you ask?"

"I've heard some more scuttlebutt. Not good."

"Where'd you hear it? Who? What?"

"Vague stuff," Quiller said, searching the President's face. "Not anything I could pin down, evaluate."

"I said, who? what?" the President said.

"More of the same—that there'll be an assassination attempt."

"Who's saying this?" the President said impatiently. "Is C.I.A. saying this? Is Secret Service? Who?"

"I told you before, Ed, I don't think the usual sources are going to be much good to us in this."

"Come on, Frank—spill it—what the hell is going on?"

"Mr. President," Quiller said, whispering now, "I'm doing my best to warn you."

The President cast a glance at the two men who stood some yards away, looking conspicuously in the other direction.

"On the basis of *what?*" the President said, not whispering.

"Ed, the damn thing is so foggy, so hard to put your finger on and prove, there's just no answering your questions in the straightforward way I'd like. The point is, I'm hearing things, things I can't dismiss, things that could involve one of our own agencies. When I get a better sense of the shape of the information, I'll let you know. In the meanwhile, I think you should cancel out the Kansas City appearance."

"I will not be intimidated," the President said.

"Put off the Kansas trip or scrub it entirely. I beg you to take these precautions, sir."

"I've heard you, Frank, but I don't see how I can stick my head under a pillow. These threats are always in the air; someone somewhere *always* wants to kill the President. I am well protected. I will not alter my plans because there are threats abroad or because you're hearing some sort of unspecifiable intelligence. I cannot conduct the responsibilities of my office in a state of fear or out of negative thinking. I will not be scared off, Frank. And I will not be persuaded that I must discount the reliability of my routine channels of intelligence and my routine protection force. Frank, you're my friend, and I want you to know I appreciate your concern. If you've got facts, route them to the Secret Service. But I don't want to hear any more about this. Think on it, Frank. I believe you'll see I'm right in taking this position."

"As you wish, Mr. President," Quiller said, unaccountably whispering still.

"Good night, Frank," the President said, and put his hand on the railing and raised his foot to the stair. Before the President had taken his second step, Quiller called out loudly:

"Tell Stevie Uncle Frank says 'Sleep tight—and keep 'em flying!'"

"I will," the President said, and made his way

wearily up the tall set of stairs, his hands on the railing all the way up, the two Secret Service men climbing behind him at a safe but respectful distance.

25

Morgan Drexel's descent began at an unmarked door—a simple lock, no one standing guard—then carried him down two flights of stairs to an elevator too small to accommodate more than one person at a time—even with the roof set so low the passengers must crouch. The elevator took him several levels farther down.

He came out into a room blazing with light, a gray-walled room empty of any fixture except the perfectly smooth door opposite. He stepped onto a floor whose surface was of a kind of foam sheeting, a substance that imprinted a sharp and lasting impression of the traffic that moved across it. It too was gray, this foamy material, and could be made blank again only by the action of an erase mechanism whose control was operated from Morgan Drexel's office. It was Drexel's practice to erase his own footprints as soon as he returned to his office. Otherwise, he would let whatever the floor had printed remain visible for twelve days, a practice made known to all the personnel having access to the *Walnut* Room.

Adjacent to the door and one inch up that wall from the floor, there was a slender slot—and it was into this that Drexel inserted the plastic card he had slipped from the slit pocket cut into his lapel. The door rolled sideways, withdrawing itself into the wall, its ponderous movement suggesting the remarkable density of its composition.

He stepped into a cubicle the size of a small bathroom. There, at table height, stood a platform that rose from the floor in one continuous sweeping mold, and on this platform, so closely fitted to it that one could see no point of joining, one there saw the *Walnut* console, Console #2.

Its panel revealed no more than six controls, and slanting forward from its base was a simple keyboard of the sixteen IDEK symbols, the language *Walnut* heard and spoke. Everything in this compact room, even the stool that came up from the floor in a creamy wave to provide seating for the technician, looked as if it had grown there, a kind of garden of unnatural plants. All of it was gray and seemed of a piece—all, of course, except the technician, who spun the stool to face you as the heavy door locked closed behind you.

"Say hey, chief!" the technician said cheerily.

"Starwell," Drexel said in greeting.

The technician, a dwarfish fellow with a withered arm, spun back to face the console.

"You chattering or auditing this morning?" Starwell said, his eyes never leaving a two-inch display screen that at first seemed a mere gray light when you entered the room. An IDEK "purge" was underway, a newly developed automatically cued program for purifying the machine's language of the steadily

195

evolving mutants of linguistic material the language itself had been discovered to generate.

"A little of both," Drexel said, returning the plastic card to the slit pocket in one lapel and extracting a second such card from the other lapel. He held it ready in his hand, and when Starwell turned and said, "Okay, let's hit it," Drexel gave him the plastic card.

"Are you a member of the Mock Turtle Club?" Starwell said, and smiled.

"You bet your sweet ass I am," Drexel rightly replied, not smiling.

"When did you join?" Starwell said, still enjoying himself, the litany of the elaborate password one of his few amusements in life, and when Drexel gave his mother's birth date, Starwell paused a moment, seemed to be fingering through file cards stored in his head, and then he grinned again and pressed Drexel's card into a slot concealed below the console's keyboard. A single symbol flashed onto the display screen, and Starwell now spoke mechanically into the tiny grid just above the two-inch square.

"*Walnut* friendly. I have seven, twenty-five stroke" (now his gaze shifted to the massive chronometer he wore on the wrist of his good arm), "four ten post-em, a *Walnut* friendly at Post Two, Langley Drexel Drexel Drexel." The symbol on the screen blipped off and blipped again. "Thank you, *Walnut*," Starwell said. "He's carded, *Walnut*—and I have Drexel Drexel Drexel and sixteen wives going to St. Ives."

A new symbol showed on the screen. Starwell kept his attention fastened there. "Okay, chief, we're in," he said, and waited for Drexel's instructions.

"Let's have *Israel* stroke *Intelligence* stroke *U.S.* stroke *Covert*," Drexel said.

Starwell punched a sequence of keys, and in the count of two a narrow band of paper started to feed out into a well-like affair that bloomed from the floor under the platform. About five inches of the tape skimmed out, there was a microsecond's hesitation, and then another inch or so was burped into the well.

"Next?" Starwell said.

"That'll do for now," Drexel said.

"Check," Starwell said, and directed his attention to a pad of notations that rested on the platform before him.

Drexel bent to retrieve the output from the well and rolled it into a tight cylinder. He began to slip the plastic card for the door from his lapel and returned to his other lapel the one the technician had just handed back to him. "Yes, that's it, I suppose," he said. "Oh, yes—meant to ask next time I was down—someone in the Counter Intelligence staff was asking at a C.I.A. council the other day did I think it at all possible for someone to get into our premises in the box, and so I naturally said how the hell would *I* know, ask Arnie Starwell if you want to know."

"Who?" the technician said, finally looking up at Drexel.

"Oh, anyone—D.I.A., N.S.A., or some other renter."

"No," said Starwell, "I meant, *who* asked?"

"Hell, I don't recall who," Drexel said. "One of the usual busybodies. Who the hell can remember?"

"Well," the technician said, "you send him to me

when you come up with that feller's name. Arnie Starwell will straighten his ass out."

"Sure will," the Director said, flustered, trying to hide it. "Point is, I guess, you could do it—you know, I mean, right?"

"I'm a company man, Mr. Drexel," the technician said. "I do the Company's work." He returned his attention to his log, and speaking into his log he said, "You send that feller to me, sir. I'll grind his sausage for him."

"I'll do that, Arnie," the Director said. He placed his sunglasses over his eyes, worked his plastic card to roll back the security door, quickly strode across the yielding floor, ascended by elevator and stairs to ground level, hurried to his office, and once there, a man of habit, activated the control that erased the printed surface below. It was only then that Morgan Drexel smoothed out the cylinder of paper tape that had never left his hand. The data on it were of course set forth in IDEK, not a difficult semaphore, really. What it said drained what little hint of color there was in Drexel's virtually colorless face.

He signaled the deputy director on the intercom that sat to the far side of the handsome French desk.

"Yo" came Warren Miller's reply.

"Warren?" Drexel said.

"Yo" came the repeated reply.

"I have an appraisal here on our Israeli friends."

"I'm listening," Warren Miller said.

"It seems," said Morgan Drexel, "that in the opinion of the large nut below, the Israelis are into us about as far as you can get. It also seems, according to the nut, that the proof count in their whiskey makes it pretty close to pure alcohol. The nut says nothing about the correspondence we received, its authenticity, but it does give I.S.S. an A-plus for its activity here. You'd better get over here so we can chat a bit."

Miller's voice came through the intercom. "I'm on my way."

Drexel snapped off the key and reflected. If the memo was legitimate—and it seemed safest to assume it was—intervention on his part could make him a target for the intelligence machinery sponsoring the operation. Elimination or discreditation. With his coat sleeve, Drexel rubbed at a smudge on the glowing wood. He organized the papers in front of him, lining everything up in stacks that were parallel to the edges of the desk. For the first time in his career in the clandestine professions, first espionage and now this, he spoke aloud to himself. It seemed to him, in that instant, something he must do, a reflex that insisted it go the full distance of its arc.

"I will save myself," he said. "It can all fall down, but I will stand."

If he felt foolish in this, the making of this little speech, you could not have detected it. Morgan Drexel sat comfortably back in his cracked crimson leather chair, clasped his hands behind his neck, and began to plan. His plan was simple, really, an uncomplicated objective: *survive*. That was all he planned for now—his own survival.

26

The July 26 morning edition of *The New York Times* carried the story. Copies on the street were sold out in less than an hour, and an additional printing was ordered. Under the front-page headline were photographs—six of them—spotted throughout the text and very sharp in their register. Who supplied these photographs? *The Times* wasn't telling. "Sources," the national desk editor said—and by then the story had been picked up by the wire services and the networks and the syndicates, and it was changing as any retold tale changes.

But *there* were the photographs—and they stayed the same: the most convincing of the lot, an aerial view of the practice site, the replicas keyed with arrows, numerals, and a legend that interpreted the translation into the topography of Kansas City's Foley Square and the approach roads. The other five photographs showed the M-16's and Mausers, the limousine, the Defense Intelligence Agency credentials, and a bucket of spent rounds collected in the area. The text reported that more than a thousand of these were gathered, and went relentlessly on into every reportable detail.

The Chairman of the Joint Chiefs was quoted. "I can't say exactly how," General Poucher stated, "but I am in possession of information supporting the theory that a liaison of radical and Communist groups are behind this vicious plot." In reply to the question "What information?" the General was quoted as having said he was not at liberty to say. He cited national security and secret classification as his regrettable reason for silence.

A statement was sought from Brigadier General Ralph Willets, chief of the Defense Intelligence Agency. But *The Times* was obliged to report that the Brigadier General was unavailable for comment and that he would not comment until more facts were known.

Statements were sought from the President, the Vice President, the Secretary of State, the Secretary of Defense, the Justice Department, the F.B.I., residents of Cartwright County, the sheriff of Cartwright County, and the Cook County coroner.

The President said his press secretary would have a statement later in the day.

The Vice President said that inasmuch as he was out of the country on sensitive international business, he would have to wait until he had returned home before commenting.

Secretary of State Danforth said that the nation was being overtaken by lunatic groups of every stripe, called for unity and reason to bring about a better America for all people of every rank, pointed out the overwhelming need for uplifting the poor and the disenfranchised, and argued that it now was overwhelmingly apparent that gun-control legislation was the first priority of national business.

The Secretary of Defense said he had no idea why he was being asked to comment and that he had no comment.

The spokesman for the Justice Department said most certainly Justice was prepared to prosecute wherever and whenever any crime involving violation of Federal law was involved, most especially —as appeared to be the case here—where the potential for violence existed.

The Director of the Federal Bureau of Investigation said the matter was under investigation and that any full comment would be held for such time as the inquiry had gone sufficiently forward. He did state, however, that enough information was available from confidential sources to indicate a design pattern pointing to possible radical terrorist activity.

Three residents of Cartwright County were quoted in *The Times* coverage. One said he was sick and tired of longhairs coming into the region and spoiling the woods with their mess; the second said he was moving to Louisiana; the third, an Iroquois living on the land nearby, complained of the U.S. Government's failure to live up to its treaty obligations to return Long Hill to the Indians and to protect the Conservation Area streams from being fished out by white trash who had no respect for the local ecology or anything else.

Sheriff Melvin "Slim" Anderson talked at length about a telephone call from a man named Scarlotto and another telephone call from an unidentified man. He remembered nothing specific in what the second man had said but was sure the man was crazy and was in some way connected to the whole shameful affair. He also said the man on the phone had a foreign accent and that it could have been a Russian accent but that there was no telling, seeing as how he had never heard a Russian talk before.

The Cook County coroner acknowledged that he also had received a suspicious phone call but said he would discuss the matter only with the F.B.I. and police authorities and not with the press and certainly not with the Eastern Liberal Establishment press.

The Times editorial page was given over to the amplification of a single thesis: a nation violent abroad must expect violence at home.

By the following afternoon, the media were carrying news of increasingly bizarre developments, items of progressively remarkable content. Yet the sources for information were not disclosed.

ABC-TV aired a long statement from the Pentagon public relations officer. The statement set forth the commissioning of a special board of inquiry to undertake a full and complete investigation of the effort to implicate the Pentagon in a Communist scheme to assassinate the President or some other person in the Presidential motorcade planned for Kansas City on August 1.

Then CBS-TV reported a story, cited as coming from an authoritative source within the Agency, that the C.I.A. had received an Israeli Intelligence memo warning of the affair but had failed to pass it on. C.I.A. Director Morgan Drexel was not immediately available. Two hours later a statement issued in his name was forwarded to the press by his news secretary. Drexel himself was unavailable for direct comment. The statement that he caused to be issued read in part: ". . . I did not convey the presumed Israeli memo and an evaluation of its contents to the White House Secret Service because the memo was clearly bogus from beginning to end. I therefore chose not to risk alarming the President with a patently false document. But now that other aspects of the matter have reached the media, I thought it wise to add the memo to the general store of information accruing in the case. , . ."

Admiral David Jark, a member of the Joint Chiefs of Staff, tendered his resignation on the grounds of extreme stress in his personal life. His letter to the Pentagon and the Department of Navy, the full text of which was reported in the *Los Angeles Times*, explained that Mrs. Jark was about to undergo radical surgery for uterine cancer. In an accompanying item, there was a bylined interview with Mrs. Jark which was conducted in her room at Cedars-of-Lebanon Hospital. In the interview, Mrs. Jark expressed faith in God and, in reply to a specific question, reported: "The cancer was discovered late last week."

By the following night, when the three major television network newscasters and commentators had consolidated the various stories and adorned them to heighten the drama, the nation was in uproar. And on the morning after that, business offices everywhere, classrooms, trains and busses, the whole waking United States was abuzz with the excited talk of what had been planned, what had nearly happened, what a hell the nation was coming to, what with the killing of public officials getting to be in the nature of things.

Teachers lectured on the violence in our national character, the brutalizing influence of crime shows, advertising, the movies, the comic books.

Businessmen chatted over lunch about the probable impact on the economy from a sudden shifting of the reins of power. Would the Vice President deal favorably with business interests? And how would the stock market perform?

Parents turned it all into a history lesson, reciting earlier instances of violence against Presidents, praising mournfully the virtues of Lincoln as if they had lived at the same time and their personal aspirations had been crushed under the heel of his murderer. And then they turned it into a conversation piece between themselves: should children be made aware of the harsh realities of contemporary life? What do you think Spock or Gesell or one of those fellows would say about a six-year-old's potential delinquency as a result of his confrontation with the traumatizing event of the destruction of one of his hero figures?

And the nation was kept busy and attentive and very interested for about twenty-four daylight hours. It didn't matter what your political camp was or what your age or where you lived. For this was high drama on the high seas of the national imagination; this was intrigue and killing and it all involved people of real importance. This was the best of theater: it was *news*.

But by the end of the week, although the story continued to unfold in somewhat sluggish fashion now, the national imagination had returned to its normal states of boredom, unfocused irritations, semi-paralysis. And the great breath that had been inhaled a day or so before came ballooning out, dying into the fading whisper of an apathetic sigh. Whatever it was, it was over—and all one could in truth now say about it was that it didn't last *long* enough, whatever it really was. But this was a truth no one dared utter. All you knew was that you were bored again and had used up a commodity again, had *consumed* what America gave you to consume—and it never lasted long enough anymore. Things lasted less and less.

But what you didn't know, what no one save a handful of people knew, was that *nothing* was over. On the contrary it was getting solidly underway, just beginning to move ahead on the unimaginably complicated and invisible wheels that had been invented to roll a spectacular train of objectives all the way down history's track.

What you didn't know—what not even Colin McFerrin knew—was that whatever the recent flurry of excitement was really all about, even more was happening than met the eye. Nor did you know that what was happening represented the completion of the second stage in an elaborately contrived orchestration of events, all planned, all controlled, all aimed at one ultimate objective.

There was something else Colin McFerrin did not know. It concerned a *Walnut* printout displaying his name at the top of a relatively short list of names. It concerned more than that now. A woman. A woman referred to familiarly by certain key persons in Intelligence as Adele. In her quiet way she was famous by this name—famous and feared. In fact, no more than two or three officials in the Defense Intelligence Agency could tell you what this plump, middle-aged woman actually looked like, so guarded was her identity over the many years of her career with D.I.A. Colin McFerrin could pass her anywhere and not know whom he passed. But now that *Walnut* had done its work and General Poucher had conveyed the assignment, it happened that the plump, middle-aged woman could scan an array of misleading photographs and pick out Colin McFerrin's ten times in ten tries, one hundred in a hundred. The fact was she stopped practicing after sixteen tries.

27

Commonwealth State College was a "streetcar" school—a place students commuted to and from on a work-day basis. And although that was what the expression suggested, Commonwealth State was in fact a four-shift college, handling loosely matriculating students of all ages, mainly from the inner city, in clusters of classes concentrated in the morning, in the afternoon, at the dinner hour, and then at night. It was an arrangement set up so that students could also hold down eight-hour jobs, a thing most of them needed to do.

It was the place McFerrin worked, the place where for the last few years he taught history: two sections of the introductory course in American History and one in Modern European History. It was the place where he was addressed as "Professor," and where, beyond that basic identification, he was, like most of the teachers at Commonwealth, little known. For Commonwealth was not the sort of school where the connections between students and teachers were very great. Everyone's real life existed off campus, and the life on campus was, for those who went to classes and those who taught them, strictly business. At Commonwealth State College, one kept to himself—and such an environment was ideal for a man of Colin McFerrin's far-reaching and complex background and "interests." It had been a good place for him to work, and now it was a good place for him to hide out—so long as he used its premises selectively. Of course the school was carried in the computer as his employment base, and thus his office cube might be subject to a routine check. Yet in his present circumstances the school grounds could provide a momentary haven.

Before Illinois, hiding out at Commonwealth was a figurative idea for Colin McFerrin. Now it was anything but. Now, since the chase on the parkway and the little exchange with Montague and the man named Ben, hiding out was a very literal matter, no longer a metaphor, no longer an idea—even though you knew that eventually they'd find you if you stayed there too long. Still, you needed a time out, away from the heat, clear of Washington and all the crap that was coming down.

Commonwealth had seemed the place for a breather, a place where McFerrin and Greenfield might set up shop for a day's rest and see what's what, what move was next in line. And if no move were next in line, if the whistle had been blown loud enough, the plot dynamited into small enough pieces, there nevertheless remained the fact that McFerrin considered himself a hunted man, a man running—and a man running, no matter what his direction, needs to stop to draw a breath.

They now occupied a large lecture room, a double classroom, on the fourth floor of the Liberal Arts Center, one of the few Commonwealth buildings not in use during the summer months. The news package Greenfield had insinuated into the press through the skeptical cooperation of a *New York Times* friend in the Washington office was still breaking, ramifying itself into now dozens of splinter stories and human-interest sidebars. Greenfield's resourcefulness did not end there. Nor did his pride in his work. For the lecture room was outfitted with a tiny Sony TV Greenfield had "borrowed" from the A-V department so that he and McFerrin might follow the geometric growth of the item that had been planted. The lecture room had just about anything a man might need and want in a situation of this kind—two dozen hard desk-chairs to sit in, a floor to sit on, three walls to look at because you dared not expose your face at the row of windows in the fourth, and a bathroom down the hall with no shower, a near-empty soap dispenser, and a diminishing supply of paper towels. The security wasn't exactly perfect, but it was a place he knew and liked, and what better place to hide for the time being. Besides, there *was* a blackboard *and* a good deal of chalk, and when you wanted to order your thoughts, a blackboard and chalk were good things to have.

The blackboard was covered with notations—jottings of this or that reminder, lists of persons and agencies, cross-checkings, arrows, times, dates, places, everything either man could think of to try to put the total picture in better perspective. And as further news items were declared on the little

Sony television, a score or oo of new notes and marks were added to the blackboard.

And the floor was covered with twelve hours' worth of used cigarettes and the butts of McFerrin's small cigars and Styrofoam cups of coffee that came from the corner market three blocks away and the crusts of tasteless sandwiches that came from there too. The two men sat amid this litter in the first row of desks, talking little now, each staring at the verbal litter strewn across the blackboard, each waiting for the clutter on the slate to surrender up its secret.

McFerrin glanced at his watch.

"She's late."

"She'll be here," Greenfield said.

"When she gets here, you beat it, okay?" McFerrin said.

"Yeah, yeah."

"For good, I mean," McFerrin said.

"Okay."

"I'll hang here awhile, and then I'm checking out too."

"Back to D.C.?"

"Yeah. I want a meet with Quiller, another look around, and then we'll see. I don't know."

"You want me to set up the Quiller meet?"

"Right," said McFerrin. "Just about to ask. How do you figure you'll do it?"

"Not sure, but I'll do it, don't worry. What's his number?"

"Don't know," McFerrin said. "He always discouraged that. But try to fix it for ten tonight. Behind the Kentucky Fried Chicken joint on Northwest Sixteenth."

"You got it," Greenfield said. "I'll have him there if he can be there."

"Ten sharp. I'll wait two minutes, fade for five minutes, then come back for another two, and so on."

"Way we did in Turkey?" Greenfield said.

"Yeah. Turkey."

"What if he can't make the gig?" Greenfield said. "How will I let you know? Want me to show up instead?"

"Hell, no!" McFerrin almost exploded. "We don't want everybody's ass in the wringer. You stay away."

"Okay, but if I can help——"

"We'll contact through *The Washington Post* personals. *Professor seeks researcher. Call et cetera.*"

"Or me to you, *Journalist seeks researcher.*"

"Check," McFerrin said. "Read the papers. Keep abreast of the news."

"I always do," Greenfield said, squashed out a cigarette on the writing board of the desk-chair he sat at, and poked a fresh one between his lips, lit it, took a deep drag, coughed, said, "Shit."

"You have a nice way with words," McFerrin said.

They were still sitting this way, the two of them smoking, talking in abrupt and weary chunks, still staring at the blackboard and getting nowhere with their staring, when they heard her footsteps on the marble stairs, and then the clicking of her high heels as she made her way toward them down the hall.

"I'm set," Greenfield said, stood up, reached his

hand out to McFerrin. "Take care, pal," he said.

"On your way," buddy," McFerrin said, rising too, taking Greenfield's hand in his. "You be good, now," he said. "You watch your ass, okay?"

"Yeah, dad. I'm looking behind me, don't you fear."

Valerie Craig stood in the doorway. Both men stood gazing at her, a beautiful woman, set off by the drab, clinical setting of the lecture room, like an apparition of loveliness standing there, or some specimen that had been collected to serve as a model for a lesson on the Aesthetic of Womanhood. She was wearing white sandals with heels and a simple white jersey, a slip of a dress, casually stylish, sleeveless, and open at the throat. To both men she looked somehow naked—all that white against the deep tan—and waiting there for *use*—an ideal example of something called Woman, a creature of parts and depths all of which accorded with some ideal, all of which were being made available for *use*—so that something could be learned—and *using* was the only way to do it.

"I'm set," Greenfield said again, abstracted now, still standing where he was.

Valerie glanced at the sandwich remains, the chalk-marked blackboard, the two men standing there, and the concern in her eyes snapped them out of their reverie.

"Okay," McFerrin said. "Luck, Dan. You be good."

Greenfield shook McFerrin's hand again, moved to the door, muttered a few words to Valerie which McFerrin could not hear, and then called back, "Clean off that blackboard before you clear out!"

McFerrin grinned. "Who's the teach, old buddy?"

Greenfield gave McFerrin the laugh he wanted, turned away, and was gone. And now the two of them, Valerie and McFerrin, stood where they were, listening to the diminuendo of Greenfield's footsteps along and down the marble surfaces of the school building. Even when the echo of the closing door four flights below had faded in the empty building, McFerrin and the woman still stood where they were. Neither moved for a long moment. And neither spoke for a long moment—until McFerrin looked at his watch again, and said, "We have one hour."

She came into the room, and he closed and latched the door.

She said, "Here?"

He grinned and moved toward her.

"Wait," she said, stepping back and setting down the handbag she carried and beginning to undo the buttons on the light summer dress. "I dream of doing things this way," she said. "Of undressing for you, of making myself naked for you in a room full of light."

"And me?" he said, "what am I doing?"

"Just standing there," she said. "No nearer than you are. Just looking, just watching, while I make myself naked, and the room is full of light."

"Does it matter that I have things to tell you? Very important things?"

"It matters," she said, "but later."

"We'll take the train back together," he said. "I'll tell you later."

"That's right," she said, gathering up into her hands the skirt of her dress so that she could work

214

the buttons that ran to the hem. "We'll make this a dream hour."

"An hour we will do everything in," he said.

"We are already doing it," she said. "You're watching me while I remove my clothes, and that is something I've always dreamed of—your watching me the way you are, with the room like this, very light, and you standing at a little distance, just looking."

"We haven't touched yet," he said. "It's strange."

"I know," she said. "That strangeness is something I want. It excites me."

"Tell me everything you feel," he said.

"I will," she said. "I promise. I want to."

"Tell me now," he said.

"I am excited. This, what I am doing, what you are not doing, what we are saying to each other, the dreamy way we are saying it—it all excites me."

"Say it makes you hot," he said.

"It makes me hot," she said. "It arouses me. It fills me with sexual desire," she said.

They talked as if transfixed, as if, though the room was brightly lit, it had become dusk, that unreal time after sundown but before true night when a jittery, sleepy magic covers the shapes of things. It was like that for them—*magical*—and now the hypnotic effect of their movement and nonmovement and their speech and nonspeech was firmly fixed in them. They had become children playing—playing at the large-bodied thing that was the anticipated spasm between them.

Valerie had dropped her dress to the floor—it seemed to float there—and had stepped away from it. She wore no panties—she wore no bra—and in the July heat she wore no stockings either. She stood next to her dress, her shoes on, her heels high enough to define her calves and to effect that gentle bunching of her lower thigh muscles that certain women with excellent legs display to just the subtle degree to drive men mad.

"Say everything," she said. "You too."

"I've never seen that before," he said, not moving his head to indicate what, not pointing.

"What, darling?" she said. "What haven't you seen before?"

"There, above your knees, where the muscles tighten there in the front."

"You've never seen me naked with high heels before—that's why."

"That's why," he said tonelessly, going deeper into the fixation the moment was conjuring in them.

"Say everything," she said. "What else do you want to say?"

"The way your breasts dip and flare, the way they look heavy, will feel heavy, weighted, in my hand, even though they are really light."

"You're saying what you want to say, aren't you?" she said.

"Yes," he said, completely adream.

"What do you want me to do?" she said. "What now?"

"Ease down," he said. "Ease down and spread your legs."

She did as he said.

"What now?" she said.

"Touch yourself," he said. "Do it. Do it with one finger so I can see you do it."

As she did as he described, he took off his shirt

and his trousers and kicked off his shoes. They were both jolted from their dreaming by the harsh sound of the Voroshilov belt pack slamming the floor, but then he came forward to her in his stocking feet with his undershorts snug over his hard buttocks, jerked wildly out of order in front where the material was thrust out and to the side.

Valerie was still squatted below him, her legs wide apart, her finger slipping high along the crease between her thighs. With her other hand she reached up, tore the shorts down to his knees with one strong yanking motion and then reached up again to clasp her hand around the startlingly thick length of his intensely erect flesh. She squeezed—not rhythmically but in one long, steadily measured pressure. And when McFerrin looked down at her, saw her long slender fingers curled white against him, saw her looking up at him, and saw the glazed look that was in her eyes now, he bent over. He took her by the waist and raised her up to him. He said, "Tell me what I'm going to do now," and she said, "You're going to come into me and I want you to look in my eyes when you do it, as you go in and as I go over to you I want our eyes looking at what happens in our eyes."

He was holding her there, aloft, and now she took him around the neck and arched back and swept her legs up and around him so that she could hold him like that and be open and ready for him so that he could move up easily into her. And as he came up into her, she came down onto him, until they were fitted together, jammed together and holding there in a tightness that was overwhelming.

"Don't move," he said.

"I want it to last," she said.

"Tell me what you feel," he said.

"A fullness, a pushing aside, into."

"Where?"

"Deep. In deep. And buzzing—as if it were a nipple rubbed, played with. And you?"

"A wetness. An enclosing wet warmness. Make yourself tight."

"Squeeze? Like this?"

"Oh, God," he said.

"Do you want to come? Let me make you come."

"No, I want it like this, this knowing we can do it to each other whenever we want but not doing it yet—just——"

"Floating."

"Yes," he said.

She tightened again, and then she made a waving motion with the muscles that lined her inside, and he said, "Oh, God, Val," and she said, "*Now*—I can't wait—Colin—look in my eyes and see me come."

They thrust at each other's nakedness until the parts they rubbed together flamed into an all-enveloping blaze. The eye of a spasm began and then went winking agape through all the cells of their bodies. They both screamed in the fullness of the feeling, the immensity of the fusion that drove through their bodies. And the screaming, later, when they both remembered it, would seem eerie in that empty classroom in that vacant building, but now, as they sagged together on the floor, holding each other's sweated body as each drifted into sleep, they still heard the duet of their screaming—and they were still hearing it as they fell all the way asleep on the schoolroom floor.

28

QUESTION: Going pretty well, wouldn't you say?

ANSWER: Going terribly well, I'd say.

Q. Yes. My real thought, too. Though I'm disinclined to overstate my successes.

A. You're by nature a superrealist. So don't pretend modesty when you know better. You know perfectly well things are working out precisely according to plan—so why be reticent to see it that way? Especially with me?

Q. You're right, of course. A piece of superstition, I suppose—the old business of propitiating the gods, saying you expect the worst will happen as a way of inviting them to bestow the best.

A. The best *will* happen. You've *planned* for it. A plan of surpassing ingenuity. It will *all* happen.

Q. I know. Don't think I don't. Nothing can really stop it now—we'll scuttle the whole row of tin soldiers—and it's the knowledge of this that makes me virtually tremble with anticipation. To see the biters get bitten, the braided masters of the power tableau checkmated by the silent possessors of the ultimate power. It's a kind of exaltation, a grand, almost religious, passion.

A. I feel it too. It's why I'm with you—why I've always wanted to be with you. Because being with you puts me close to that energy, close to the very center of things. I touch you and it's like touching the furnace at the center of the earth.

Q. You're not afraid of being burned?

A. I *want* to be burned. I want to be consumed in the fire that whirls out of you.

Q. A trifle poetic this morning, aren't you?

A. I'm agitated—that's all. A little manic, I imagine.

Q. Why so?

A. Vlednik called.

Q. Montague?

A. I'm sorry. Yes. Montague. It's crazy, but that name makes him even more frightening. It's so, you know so——

Q. So solid, so reassuring. Exactly. An interesting dynamism in that—our being more appalled by the menace of ordinary solid things than by the off beat and alien. There's a motion picture fellow who's made quite a name for himself with the trick.

A. Alfred Hitchcock?

Q. Yes, that one. He discovered the terror that exists in the banal—the man named "Smith" more threatening than the man named, say——

A. Vlednik.

Q. Exactly. Montague seems so—reliable, so clubby, so thoroughly respectable. Hence, all the more frightening when he turns out not what his name suggests.

A. He'd frighten me whatever his name was. That

221

face—the colors, that incessantly modulated voice, always so empty of inflection, of emotion of any kind. The man is really monstrous.

Q. The man is nothing of the kind. He is merely the *best* of his kind—the purest professional imaginable—no feeling, no thought, just all task and performance. He's a kind of idealized instrument. The fellow is even better than that; he's a sort of extrahuman instrumentation, more a process, an event, than a thing.

A. At any rate, he called in—and, as always, he unsettled me, I guess.

Q. He's making a pickup today, is he not? The historian?

A. Yes. Late this afternoon or early this evening. He wanted you to be assured everything was on schedule. He said you would probably want to confirm your contingent arrangements.

Q. Good man. Good instrumentation, I should say, right? Good Montague. We throw another scare into our history scholar, we bring the chap around, right? This time a capital scare. This time we turn him upside down and inside out. Another good dose of castor oil, and we will have reduced the youthful historian to a good boy, a supple learner. And then, my darling, we will teach the lad some proper history.

A. Aren't you a little manic this morning too, darling?

Q. Perhaps. But I think I've earned it. Years of painstaking planning and risks of the highest order, and now it's all coming to pass. I think I owe it to myself. Yes, I admit it—I'm excited. Yes. They're all in disarray, the whole stupid,

stupid lot of them, like mongrels in a frenzy to rid themselves of the poisonous creature they gluttonously took into their mouths. You've seen that, haven't you?

A. When I was a girl—once, yes. It was horrible.

Q. The maddened filthy beast trying to throw the thing off, running himself into a fit of tightening circles until he is seized with a convulsion? You've seen that?

A. Yes. A neighbor's dog. It frightened me terribly.

Q. Our friends are entering upon the pattern now. Poucher and his manic playmates stumbling in headlong, Drexel and his smug lot dragged in ass backwards. They're like crazed dogs still chewing on the thing that kills them. See Spot— see Spot run?

A. He said he'd take him, at the latest, by this evening. I didn't press for more than he wanted to give me.

Q. Of course. One doesn't press Mr. Montague overmuch. All right. Call Lawn Crest. Tell them to be ready anytime now.

A. Anything else?

Q. Yes, coffee—and I want you to set up a breakfast with the major metropolitan newspaper editors—line people, city editors, and the like. Tell them that though I intend to speak off the record, I'll have some significant policy formulation to introduce. Media Control is still inadequate. Make sure we have Angstrom of the *Sun*, Bernstein of the *Star*, Ryan of the *Inquirer*, and Schissel of the *Times*. And, oh, yes, contact Archer of the *Post* and have him send over a man.

A. Anything eles?
Q. Yes, do be a dear and make sure coffee's sent in before you make those calls.

29

"Get the blackboard, baby, while I make neat, okay?"

McFerrln moved quickly around the room, gathering litter into the small brown bags the corner grocery used for packing sandwiches and coffee. His actions were noticeably lithe now, more athletic, an earlier energy apparently rising in him again. Valerie came back from down the hall with wads of wet paper towels in her hands and went to work wiping the notations from the blackboard, her movements languid, sinuous in the stretching she now and then needed to reach the upmost patches of lists and diagrams. McFerrin caught a glimpse of this as he moved along in a scavenger's low-slung lope, snatching up this and that, stubbed-out cigarettes and cigar butts, squashed napkins. He saw the calves define themselves as she reached high, and it was like an invitation to his blood. He felt the heat come over him and he wanted in that moment to hasten his lope across the room, place hands on those calves, move hands up, up along all the slick surfaces of her legs and then bring hands, fingers

225

together where her body began, where it centered at the dark forest of her moistness, still fevered from their touching moments before.

"I want that," he said from where he was.

"You just had it," she said from where she was standing at the blackboard, hair flipping girlishly as she turned her head to answer.

"I want it again," he said.

"Truly, darling?" she said, and stepped away from the blackboard to face him fully.

"Yes," he said, coming up to his height.

"We'll miss the train," she said.

"I know. But it might be a long time between tastes." He moved to take her into his arms, and she let her head go back as he tongued her throat and took her hips hard against him with his hands to let her feel the bolt of blood that sought a place inside her.

"Jesus," she said softly. "The size of him."

"Big crazy bastard doesn't know when to quit," McFerrin whispered into her open mouth as he kissed her parted lips.

She whispered back, "Colin, I think I'll give him a good talking to in the cab—because we mustn't. You'll miss Quiller."

"In the cab?" he said softly into her mouth, their lips and tongues missing as they talked.

"It'll be fun," she said. "Discreetly."

"Promise?" he said.

"Promise," she said, "if you chain down that crazed animal for now."

They both laughed at that and used the laughter to break their embrace and return themselves to the task of putting the room back in order.

At last he had the bags bunched by the door and the portable Sony there too. He went back to the blackboard and checked to see if the notations had ghosted there now that the slate was dry. He saw fragments but nothing worrisome, turned to face the room again, scanned it for anything missed, and then reached behind and snapped the Voroshilov from the belt pack and reset each shell in its chamber, spun the magazine, and set the revolver back in the belt pack.

"Okay," he said to Valerie, who stood waiting at the door, gathering her hair behind and securing it there with something she had in her fingers. She picked up the little Sony and gripped her handbag under her arm. McFerrin took up the garbage into a bundle against his chest, said, "Let's hit it," and together they went out into the hall and headed for the stairs. He stopped her at the second landing down.

"Look," he said. "We can't talk in the cab, and it's better if we don't talk on the train—and there's something I've got to talk to you about. *Now*."

"All right," she said, leaning back against the wall. "Go ahead—only watch the time."

"I'll take care of the time," he said. "You listen."

"All right. Start."

"You know just about all there is about what I'm into."

"I know enough."

"You know enough to get yourself killed. I'd say that was more than enough."

"Are you worried about me, Colin? Because don't. You needn't. N.S.A. gives me all the pro-

227

tection I can use. I'm safe, darling, if that's what's on your mind."

"Val, no one's *that* safe. And Fort Meade can't protect you from what they don't even know about. Besides, who the hell knows where this thing is coming from? Who the hell knows if N.S.A. doesn't own a piece of the action, too?"

She set the television down and searched in her handbag for a cigarette. "That's ridiculous, Colin—and you know it."

"Okay," he said quietly, lighting her cigarette. "Let's not hassle the point now—but that wasn't my point anyway. And now my point isn't your safety, either. It's too late for that now. You bought in —just as Dan bought in. You're grown-ups, both of you—you chose and you got it, right?"

"Right," she said, exhaling a long stream of smoke. "I'm not complaining."

"Good enough," he said. "No regrets."

"None."

"All right," he said. "You're in to the extent you're in—and now I'm going to ask you in a whole lot deeper. I'm going to ask about something it's crazy to ask about, but it makes sense. To me."

"Colin," she said. "Ask it. The train."

"I want you to talk to K.G.B. I want you to talk to the Russians."

Even as he said it, he knew it sounded insane, a preposterous long shot. But if he was going to survive—if there was to be any future for the two of them—he needed a greater balance of power than the good intentions of Franklin Quiller. The Russians were businessmen, utilitarians. They would be in no hurry to swap Edward Burlingame, a man committed to detente, for a new succession of cold warriors.

"I don't talk to the Russians, darling—I *listen* to them. With a number two pencil and a sheet of graph paper."

"I want you to talk to them."

"For God's sake, Colin," she said, "do you have any idea what you're asking me to do?" She shifted her position against the wall and eyed him sternly. He had never seen her adopt such an expression before. "Let me talk to *you* a minute," she said. "To begin with, you don't know a damn thing about Fort Meade. Granted, you were C.I.A., but Fort Meade is a very different ball game, sweet love. Second, we long ago agreed—tacitly, I know—never to get into my work. You have a broad notion of what it is, but that's all you have. Anyhow, that's been the ground rule between us—just as we also agreed to other rules. No talk of my marriage, no phone calls to my office, no pressures, no expectations beyond what we have and what I cherish. What we had upstairs and what I want from you and what I know you want from me. I don't want *depending*, I don't want *asking*. I want you to have my body when you want it and when I can give it. And, yes, I want your love. But in the way we've established, in the way that works for us. But let's get to the more important point for now. Number three. If I altered my routine in my work, a routine that is observed to a degree of thoroughness you couldn't even guess at—I'd be stopped in an instant. And Lord knows what they'd do. For all I know, I might be offed on the spot. Believe me, Colin,

N.S.A. is not organized by method and temperament in ways that resemble anything you know about. These are very heavy people. And now you ask me to contact the K.G.B. Jesus Christ, Colin, you want me dead?"

"You want Burlingame dead?"

"If it were to come to such a choice, I think I'd favor my own skin over his, yes."

"All right," he said, "you're entitled to your way of looking at things, Val. You're entitled, okay? But I am entitled to say that in my book your job comes down to protecting the President because the President *stands* for what your goddamn supersecret outfit is supposed to be all about. Right?"

"Wrong," she said without pausing to suggest that the question required some difficult measurement of practice against ethic. "What my job comes down to, my darling, is protecting the United States of America, not the *President* of the United States of America. You see the distinction?"

"Frankly, I don't," he said. "Not when that office happens to be filled by a man like Edward Burlingame—no, I don't. Burlingame represents the best of this nation. He *is*, if only as a symbol, the fucking United States of America!"

"Symbols are fine, Colin," she said, "but not that many people really care what happens to Burlingame as long as it doesn't happen to them."

"I care!" he snapped. "What does that make me? Some kind of asshole?"

She looked up at his gray eyes, coolly measuring their intensity. "Not that," she said, "but you're a very demanding man—for yourself, and others."

Then she reached up and ran a finger across the stubble on his cheek. "Still pissed at me?"

"A little," he said, "yeah. I want you to do it because the Russians just might happen to see where it's in their interest to block it."

"Too dangerous. How could I keep it clear of N.S.A.? My work, Colin," she said smiling, "is a thing apart. It has always come first."

"Okay," he said. "You use a pay phone, call the Russian embassy, and tell them you have special unit information, anything that gets their tape going. Pass on the details I gave you."

"If they buy all that, then what?"

"The K.G.B. liaison at the embassy would get the tape at once. From there it's a policy decision— whether or not they'd attempt an interdiction through liaison with one of our agencies. A long shot but worth a try."

"Colin, you're whistling in the dark. Let's drop it, my love, please."

"All right. But I'm going to say this. And you listen, for Christ's sake. If you change your mind, if you get a chance, if you see *some* way to do it, I want you to tip the Russians to what I'm guessing is going on. I'm asking you to do it, because they just might think it will pay off for them to block it. That's what I wanted to say, and I've said it. So, okay, let's beat it. The train."

He tried to motion her onto the stairs. She fielded her cigarette, took up the television, and touched his arm. "I just want some assurance you'll try to see it my way."

"I know the score," he said. "But you want assurance, find it somewhere else. I can't see it any other way but the way I named it."

"Colin," she said. "You're a big stubborn mick—and I guess if I could get you to come around as easy as all that I wouldn't be so insane to get you inside me all the time."

"The man who won't come around is the only man who makes you come, right?"

She flared in obvious anger. She did not reply. She stepped around him, and then he followed her, and they descended the two remaining flights of stairs. When they reached the landing and started for the basement door, she was still several strides ahead of him—but when he saw the square of paper stuck up against the pane of glass nearest the knob, he moved quickly past her. He dumped the garbage where he stood at the door, snatched open the door, and left-handed out the Voroshilov in one motion. He stood like this, not moving. Then he relaxed his stance and turned back to where Valerie was waiting, her hand just going now to take the paper from the pane.

"I'll handle that," he said, and stepped back and peeled away the Scotch tape that held the square of paper secured to the glass.

30

The sharp crease bisecting it perfectly, the sheet of paper was folded just once, to produce a square. McFerrin took Valerie roughly by the arm and steered her back behind the door.

"You watch, I'll read."

She placed herself so that she could observe the alleyway without being seen. McFerrin sat on the first step of the inside stairway, laid the Voroshilov beside him, and then unfolded the paper.

"What does it say?"

"Shut up a minute!"

"I'm in this too, Colin."

"Yeah, sure," he said. "Look, you just stand there and keep your eyes on that alley, I'll read."

Both sides were covered with tiny script. The handwriting was immediately familiar, and when McFerrin saw the way it opened—"Dear C"—and closed "The old hassler, Doug"—he knew it was either legit, really John Douglas' handiwork, or the best phony since synthetic rubber.

Dear C,

This is going to shock the hell out of you, man—but it's John talking. Don't ask me how I found you and don't ask me what's going on—just do what I ask you to do. This is red alert, man—no time for questions, no time for explanations, no time to come the hell up there and fill you in. Besides, three's a crowd. Just dig it, please. Tell Mrs. Craig to get out of there and then you follow about a minute later. In front of the grocery where you've been buying your coffee, there's a convertible parked, waiting. Go there and get in it. You'll be driven to me and then you'll get all the explanation you need. Okay, my threads are Brooks Brothers standard sack now, but I'm still the dude that rode with you and Danno through the wild East. Trust me, buddy. You, me, and Danno didn't come through every kind of shit together for nothing. We handled it in Nam and we handled it in Greece—and now we've got to still handle it—*for* Greece, for the liberation front—and *for* America, for Ed Burlingame. All right, man—move it! Let's go! This counts! Sit in the back seat of the car—*now*.

The old hassler,
Doug

McFerrin looked up, his face mapped with confusion. He folded the paper in fourths and fitted it into his pocket. He picked up the Voroshilov, hefted it, and then put it back down on the stair beside him.

"What kind of insane horseshit *is* this? Jesus!" he said.

"What is it, Colin? Tell me. What's going on?"

234

"Just a second. Please, Val. Give me a minute to think."

McFerrin removed the folded paper from his pocket, opened it, and scanned the crabbed lines.

"Douglas," he muttered to himself. "That's John's voice and John's crazy goddamn foreign scribble and only John called me "C." But the damn thing's *odd* in a weird sort of way. And yet it's the oddness that makes it convincing."

"Colin!" Valerie snapped. "I am not going to stand here and listen to you talk to yourself. What is it about? If you don't think I can help you, then I will have to help myself! Do you hear me, Colin?"

"I hear you."

"Well?" she said, not turning her attention from the alley.

"Just wait a minute."

"I'm not waiting any longer, Colin. Now, I'm giving you one last chance. If this is very heavy, then I'll call my office and they'll send help. Do you want me to call my office, Colin?"

He did not answer. He held the sheet of paper in his hands and moved his lips in silent recitation of its phrases.

"That's it, Colin. I'm not waiting. You seem to have forgotten what I do for a living. You wanted my help for something I cannot and will not do. But you don't seem to want my help for what I *can* do. Are you going to tell me what's in that message?"

"It wouldn't make any sense to you, baby—believe me," he said without the slightest hesitation. "Go ahead. Get out of here. Take care of yourself. I'll be in touch."

This time it was she who did not reply. Her eyes

still on the alley, she snapped her handbag under her arm and pushed at the door.

"I'm sorry, Val," he said.

"No problem," she said, and holding herself very stiff, she pushed open the door and moved out into the alleyway, stepping along at an even pace and keeping close to the wall. McFerrin was standing now, watching her progress through the glass, doing something in his head that was very nearly prayer. He saw her summer dress, the deep tan of her glorious skin, the long, high-hipped stride that always assailed his senses. And then he saw the white fabric flash as she reached the end of the alley and came into the bright sun—and then she had turned and he could not see her anymore.

He sat down again. He checked his watch. He listened.

Nothing.

He lit a cigar. He took a few puffs and then he said aloud, "Doug, you crazy sonofabitch, you and me got games to play—is that it?"

McFerrin returned the Voroshilov to his belt pack, again folded the paper in fourths, put it in his pocket, and stood.

"All right, John boy," McFerrin said. "Let's see what you got for me."

The car was an old Pontiac with a torn convertible top. It was empty, all right. For that matter, it looked abandoned. It stood in front of the little market where McFerrin could see clusters of students bunched nearby, talking and laughing and wolfing snacks.

He reached for the door handle and thumbed the

button, but the door did not give. He pulled harder. It stayed stuck. He yanked. When the door came open, he flung the front seat forward and rolled in back. He placed himself in the center of the seat and lit up a Schim. He leaned forward as if to study the dashboard, and with his arm low he went behind and lifted out the Voroshilov and eased it to the floor between his feet. He held himself forward for a time longer, still making a show of inspecting the dashboard. Then he sat back and waited. Every so often he would glance casually to the left and then to the right. But he mainly kept his attention focused straight ahead, a practice he'd long ago trained into himself for a case when you didn't know which way to look for the play that was coming at you. Just as he'd long ago trained himself to jump to the side opposite the handedness of the man shooting at you.

He waited. He smoked. Let's play it, John boy, he said once to himself.

31

When Greenfield arrived at Union Station, he went directly to a pay phone and called Alison Monroe, a *Time* staffer who covered the White House. Did she know Franklin Quiller? he wanted to know.

"No," Alison Monroe said. "Only to look at—and he's something to look at."

"Yeah, well—listen," Greenfield said, perspiring heavily in the July heat and dense air of the terminal building. "I need to get to Quiller and I figure that'll be pretty tough. You know anyone in his office?" He wiped at his face with his free hand. He could smell the bad air rising off him, the humid muck of the city mixed in his own sour salt from days without shaving and showering.

"What's this all about?" she said. "You onto something good, Dan, it's only fair to share it with a lady."

"Look, Alison, I swear to you it's not a story," he said, ignoring her flirtatious tone. "There is nothing in it for you, you have my word. Just give me a name if you've got one. Please."

"Somehow, Mr. *Greenfield*, I can't remember you

ever buying me lunch or a drink, or tipping me to anything, the way so many of the boys do. Does that fit your recollection too, Mr. Greenfield?"

"All right, Alison," he said, shifting his weight. "I am not fucking around. Are you going to come across with a name or not? Who's your contact in Quiller's office? You got one, or are you just fucking around with me?"

"I'll make you a deal Mr. Hotshot Correspondent," she said, her voice all business now. "I'll lay a name on you. And I will also lay a private telephone number on you. And I will even let you use my name to make your pitch. *But*, Mr. Pulitzer Prize Winner, *but* I want in return a permanent wire into your congressional stuff."

"That's crazy. Can't do it."

"I'm not asking for the works, Dan. I'm being reasonable. I don't want all your stuff. But anything that bears strongly on the White House beat I *do* want. That's fair, Dan. Believe me, buddy boy, there is no way in the world you'll get to Quiller in the hurry you seem to be in without my laying that private number on you. Deal?"

Greenfield shifted again. Then he punched the wall of the booth. "Look, bitch, you've got a deal— but don't you ever grab me by the balls like this again, you hear?"

"Why, sir," Alison Monroe drawled in the old Georgia syrup Radcliffe had boiled out of her. "I'm just a working girl doing her job, don't you know."

"Give me the goddamn name and number, Monroe!" Greenfield barked into the telephone. "I mean it! Come on, goddamnit!"

"I have your word, Greenfield?"

"I already gave it! Now come across!"

"Alison Agajadian. 663-3464." she said.

"*Your* name's Alison," Greenfield said.

"There some law against more than one? You going to file a petition to deport one of us?"

While Alison Monroe talked, Greenfield got out a stub of a pencil and on the inside cover of a matchbook wrote *663-3464, Agajadian.* Then he cut Alison Monroe off: "That A-g-a-j-a-d-i-a-n?"

"Just the way it sounds, yeah. 663-3464?"

"So who's she to Quiller, your namesake?"

"Confidential secretary. A very classy babe, too— not your usual confidential secretary type at all. Started University of Chicago when she was fifteen, did graduate work at M.I.T. Even worked with Watson out at the Cold Spring Harbor lab and Harvard for a while. Plus she looks great—a knockout, in fact."

"So what the hell is she doing lackeying around for Quiller?"

"Digs the slavey role, I guess. Digs Quiller pure and simple. Admires the man, his politics, the whole bit. She adores the guy—believes he's the Second Coming."

"Yeah, I know somebody else who feels the same way."

"A lot of people do. Franklin Quiller's a remarkable man."

"Yeah, but he's a *man* is the point. Puts his pants on the same way I do, right?"

"I'd like to see that sometime. Like to see how you do it sometime, Mr. Greenfield sir."

"I got a wife, you know? Look, one last thing,

Monroe," Greenfield said. "What's your connection with Agajadian?"

"Friends. We go to the same gym. And then it turned out our dads were in medical school together. She's very keen on staying in shape—and of course I've got to improve myself to merit the likes of you. Anyhow, that's how we first got together—and it's worked out okay even though she knows I'm press. She gives me a little stuff every now and then. But she's not exactly what you'd call the cozy type. Very cool, very remote. Anything else I can do to assist you on your way to the Hall of Journalistic Fame?"

"Check with you later," Greenfield said. "Thanks."

"My pleasure, Mr. Greenfield, sir," Alison Monroe said and hung up before he had a chance to do it, first.

He had an answer on the first ring.

"Yes?" the icy voice said.

"Yes," Greenfield said. "Alison Monroe gave me this number. She said to mention her name. I'm trying to get a message to Mr. Quiller."

"Your name?"

"Greenfield. Dan Greenfield."

"State your business, Mr. Greenfield."

"It's a private matter."

"I handle Mr. Quiller's private matters," the woman said.

"Yes, well—let's say it's a *personal* matter," Greenfield said.

"I also handle Mr. Quiller's personal matters," the imperturbable voice said.

"I see," Greenfield said stalling. "All right, look —you're Miss Agajadian, Alison Agajadian—and

Alison said you'd put me through to Mr. Quiller. She said you'd take care of it for me."

"I *am* taking care of it for you, Mr. Greenfield. What is it you wish to tell Mr. Quiller?"

"You won't put me through?"

"My instructions don't permit it. But please be confident your message will be conveyed to him exactly as you state it."

"Is that your last word on it?"

"A pointless question, Mr. Greenfield. State your message."

"You have a pencil?"

"I'm holding one, Mr. Greenfield. I am waiting for your message." The blasé voice had not altered in the slightest.

"Tell him Colin called——"

"You mean *you* are calling for this Colin."

"Right," Greenfield said. "Colin will be at the rear of the Kentucky Fried Chicken outfit on Northwest Sixteenth at ten sharp tonight. He wants Mr. Quiller there. It's urgent. Mr. Quiller should be there at ten sharp and if necessary wait there for no more than ten minutes. If Colin doesn't for some reason show up, he'll contact Mr. Quiller tomorrow. This is very urgent, okay?"

"I have the message, Mr. Greenfield. Good-bye," she said, and broke the connection.

"So long. Nice talking to you," Greenfield said to the dead line, and then he said, "Some beauty that one—a real sweetheart," and then he replaced the receiver and turned to leave the telephone booth.

He didn't hear anything.

They say you never do. Of course even with a silencer there's always an audible report of some kind. But to hear a sound, it must register in the brain, and Dan Greenfield's brain had been utterly destroyed.

Greenfield apparently had picked an unpopular phone. It was almost an hour before the body was discovered where it had sagged to the floor of the booth.

32

They were young men, early twenties, their short hair curling close to their skulls. They approached from the rear of the car. If they were armed, it would be small-caliber weapons or perhaps knives. McFerrin couldn't see them come—but he sensed it—and with his feet he altered the angle of the Voroshilov where it lay on the floor so that he need only straighten his elbow to take hold of the grip.

The young man to McFerrin's right struggled with the door as the other young man slid into the driver's seat. While his companion still jerked at the door, the driver turned around and smiled broadly at McFerrin. McFerrin smiled back. Then the driver made a sort of salute to McFerrin, and McFerrin nodded. The driver again smiled expansively and then reached across the front seat to punch the door opposite with the heel of his hand. The door flew open and the other young man got in.

The young man at the wheel started the engine and pulled the car away from the curb.

"Where's Douglas?" McFerrin asked. "Where's the meet with my old pal?"

There was no reply. The car sped along through the outskirts of Philadelphia and then took the alternate highway toward Baltimore.

"We going to Baltimore?" McFerrin said, still leaning against the back of the front seat. "Douglas hanging out in Baltimore these days?"

Finally the young man at the wheel nodded, and then he flipped on the radio and busied himself tuning in the loudest rock music he could find. "Sureness," he yelled abstractedly, and then sat back in satisfaction with the hard, clashing beat that filled the car.

The noise made further talk clumsy, and McFerrin was willing to give up on it. Besides, he'd already decided to take his chances, to launch himself into the zone of high risk. The whole thing was screwy enough to be true. Wasn't the world of power-play laid over power-play mad to begin with? And wasn't it getting crazier every whipstitch?

McFerrin was willing to understand that one oughtn't expect the readily rational, the easily explained, when it was at bottom an effort to assassinate the President of the United States which set the whole damn carnival in motion. And was there anything more unhinged than that? To think you could off the most powerful political leader in the world and get away with it? Wasn't *that* already such a maniac proposition that anything it entailed would submit to no logic? Yes, McFerrin concluded, it would be crazy to expect anything but craziness, anything less than the most bizarre possibilities imaginable.

Despite his knowing that he would never figure things out until he knew *more* and that the only way to know more would be to stick his neck out even further—to do, in fact, exactly what he was right now doing—McFerrin couldn't quit wondering, couldn't quit trying to reduce the puzzle to something that made sense. Doug? How the hell would Johno factor into all this? McFerrin was still absorbed in the effort to dope things out when the convertible swung out of the Baltimore street traffic and stopped abruptly in front of a tavern with one of those fake Tudor facades so popular in the thirties.

The driver wrenched around in his seat and grinned back at McFerrin. "Getting out, please," he said.

"This it?" McFerrin said. "Okay, fellas. Why not?"

The driver was still grinning at him. "Take gun is okay," the driver said, and then crooked his finger over the seat and flickered it at the Voroshilov gleaming on the floorboards. "Fine gun to take is okay, yes?"

"You bet, Jackson," McFerrin said. He straightened his elbow, took the pistol in hand, and then slotted it back into the belt pack.

The driver hopped out, jerked the seat forward to let McFerrin follow, and as McFerrin came clear of the car the driver touched his arm to assist him. Instinctively, McFerrin went into a kind of defensive spin, and with lightning speed the driver snapped into a karate stance, feet planted, arms leveled in front of him. McFerrin grinned, and then he laughed and relaxed his body. Whoever these boys were, McFerrin felt like hammering them a little, felt like showing them some real work. He figured he could do it—and wouldn't mind doing it just for the sport of it. But in an instant all of them were laughing, the other young man laughing loudest as he came up behind McFerrin and emptied the belt pack of the Voroshilov.

33

Her name was Adele Dietz, and she had recently turned sixty. She made no effort to hide the gray hair. In fact, she rather fancied the gun-metal shade and wore it to great appeal, cut very trimly in a boyish bob. The effect was vaguely oriental for some reason having, perhaps, not a little to do with the almond cast of her eyes. She was a little heavy now, though still petite, tanned year-round, and possessed of magnificently white, even teeth. She was also immeasurably intelligent, was privately proud of this immense intelligence, and though she gave off the studied impression of great warmth and charm, she was as cold and ruthless and solitary as a scalpel.

In gangster parlance she was a hit man. In the argot favored by the Defense Intelligence Agency she was a *cooler*. But Adele Dietz was not any ordinary cooler, for hers was a career distinguished by an uncommon role—namely, that her work as a cooler was confined primarily to what was called "housecleaning." She was one of four such persons who rid the D.I.A. ranks of troublesome employees.

She had grown up in Alabama, and after an outstanding scholastic record at the University of the South and later at Vanderbilt, where she took a highly unusual doctoral degree in Chinese studies, she entered the foreign service and, in the normal course of events in those days, was later graduated to the Office of Strategic Service, and went on to work closely with "Wild Bill" Donovan in England. After the Second World War, it was thought she had been planted somewhere in Asia, that she might even have been deployed there as a short-term *mole*, but no one knew for sure. She surfaced again in the early sixties, now as a cooler for the D.I.A.—a part-timer, it seemed, who did this sort of piecework with great aplomb and possibly even relish.

She was the best at the sort of work she did, a specialist of unparalleled skill and the only one of the four specialists with enough power to have broad access within the D.I.A. As such, she had the admiration of many men, and General Mark Poucher accordingly had been eager to meet this extraordinary woman who for years had been indirectly in his employ.

"Mrs. Lambert will have the veal piccata, and I think I'd like the chicken Bolognese," Mark Poucher said, and then ordered his third Wild Turkey and Adele Dietz's fourth Metaxa.

"Will monsieur want wine?" the captain said.

"Wine, Amelia?" General Poucher asked.

"I don't think so," Adele Dietz said, holding her cigarette angled toward the captain and smiling in gentle benevolence when he quickly bent to light it as if this were the one act he had waited all his life to perform.

"Very good," the captain said, and turned away.

It was well after the waiter had brought their drinks that the silence that covered them was lifted again. Not that Mark Poucher was not a talker. On the contrary, he loved to exercise his vast command of the language. But he was more than a little awed in the presence of this strange and silent woman. But talk was *not* Adele Dietz's custom—talk being, in her estimate, an impediment to thought and action, the only significant modes of conduct.

"This place to your taste, Mrs. Lambert?" Mark Poucher said, downing his bourbon, the contours of his face now slackening just enough to reveal the havoc the alcohol was accomplishing on his brain.

"Satisfactory," Adele Dietz said.

"I'm glad," he said.

He was about to launch into instructions when the waiter and captain appeared with the serving table. The lavish display they made of warming and spooning and arranging food on the plates and the plates on the table insisted that all attention be focused on the serving ritual. And so it was not until they were alone again that General Poucher was able to say: "Look, Mrs. Lambert, I know you don't feel the need for further guidance——"

"You're right," she said, looking down into her veal piccata and, using her utensils continental style, cutting away a dainty bite.

"How's your veal?" Poucher said, flustered. No one talked to him like that.

"Passable."

"The chicken's excellent, I can tell you," Poucher said. "Another drink?"

"No," she said.

Poucher signaled the captain and pointed to his glass. The captain delivered himself of the mildest form of recognition imaginable and in turn signaled the waiter.

"Arrogant swine," Poucher said, and pushed his dish away from him. "Have a drink, Mrs. Lambert, please."

"No." She chewed her food with precise little bites. She seemed not quite present.

"The funeral's on the second," the General said.

"Underwood?" she said.

"Yes—did you know him?"

"By reputation," Adele Dietz said, and reached to the pepper mill.

"It's a shitstorm," Poucher said. "I suppose we just dig in and hold tight." He promptly took up the glass of whiskey that the waiter set down and drank off half of it.

"I'll increase the visibility for you," Adele Dietz said. "I'll thin out the precipitation. You just point me in whatever direction you want."

"One must adopt a philosophical attitude in matters of this kind. First things first, Mrs. Lambert. I have utter confidence in you. As for the large questions, well, Presidents come and go. Men come and go. Nations come and go. What matters in this is two things. Does the best survive for the best people? And do *you* survive to enjoy it? The general question and the particular question. Everything else is irrelevant, mere child's play, the day-to-day world that keeps the mechanics busy with their useless fretting and pointless tinkering."

"I am a mechanic, Mr. Poucher."

"*General*," he corrected.

251

"Yes," she said, and now reached to sip some water. "You see Burlingame as a mechanic?"

"He's something more, perhaps. But not an engineer, no. A foreman, perhaps," Poucher said. "At most, a foreman. But dangerous as such."

"If he makes it to a second term," she said.

"Precisely," Poucher said. "But I wouldn't worry about that if I were you, Mrs. Lambert. That's being handled, shall we say."

"Underwood, you mean. But Underwood's dead."

"Yes, of course," Poucher said. "But Underwood's plan lives on; the apparatus he erected continues to do its work. It's self-perpetuating, you might say." The General smiled.

"How interesting. As for myself, I've never been one to work and play well with others. I prefer the solo performance, the lone stalk." Something new must have been working in her, been suddenly triggered, for she seemed lost in a reverie of some kind —and she began to talk, more generously open talk than normally heard from her. "Dear General," she said, "I like especially to kill with a gun. But you must have heard that. When I was O.S.S., I killed with knives and wires and things that went into your beverage, but I still liked especially to kill with a gun. All sorts of guns, but I like most to do it with an MP-40 or an AK-4 or an Uzi or a Stoner or a Luger. You know, I once used a Browning Highpower with *wehrmacht* proofs? On a woman, too. And once an Artillery Luger with a snail-drum magazine and a mag-charger. One shot, in the chest. A vicious brute of a fellow, too—but that was long after O.S.S., a mole in Guatemala who simply refused to unmole himself. The ridiculous lout had the gall to think he'd just keep on with life as a hotel operator. Said he really got a kick out of hotel management and didn't see the reason to jeopardize his place in the community after all those years of sleeping. The poor fellow was really absurd, thinking the Pentagon would simply forget him, forget his obligation to the nation."

"You needn't prove yourself to me, Mrs. Lambert. You needn't prove yourself to anyone."

"Thank you, General," she said, "but I want you to feel assured your work will be done."

"I have every confidence," Mark Poucher said.

"McFerrin," she said, trying to catch the captain's eye. "What an implausible name. It is the name that adorns the butler or the chauffeur in some slapstick film with Peters Sellers or some such. *McFerrin*. My God, it is the name one assigns to a servant."

As the captain approached behind the billboard of his smile and just before she ordered coffee—*two, café filtre, please*—Mark Poucher said, "My thought precisely, dear woman. A clown's name, a clown's role. Finish it. Soonest. The man is—well——"

"Tiresome," Adele Dietz said, and at this the General and the small, chubby woman across from him both smiled in perfect agreement.

"But first," Poucher said, "I want this other fellow, the one with the shabby loyalty rating."

"Vlednik," she said.

"He calls himself Montague now," the General said.

"No matter," she said, and sipped her coffee. "He'll be nameless within twenty-four hours."

34

The sign said DEMOS—short, McFerrin figured, for Demosthenes—but pretty clearly Greek any way you looked at it. Inside, the long, zinc-covered bar was lined from end to end with workers, from the look of their clothes—machinists, pressmen, truckers, longshoremen, and the like. The air was pungent with a sour cloud of cheap beer and exotic tobaccos, and the instrumental screaming from the jukebox was distinctly Middle Eastern—balalaikas, finger cymbals, much whistling, that sort of thing.

The two youths seemed immensely pleased with the setting, though their trendy clothing looked to McFerrin comic in this somber, brooding atmosphere.

Dark booths of high-backed wooden benches ran along the opposite wall, and it was to the far end of this line of booths that the driver motioned with his head. The three of them made their way across the plank-board floor. It was not until they were almost there, just paces from the last booth, that McFerrin saw who was waiting for him. Even in the dim lighting, there was no mistaking the disastrous organization of parts and colors that was Montague's face.

Montague nodded in welcome, and although he did not rise to greet McFerrin, he made a great show of extending his hand. McFerrin almost recoiled—indeed, something inside him *did* shrink back—but he took the hand held out to him and then sat down. His escorts continued to stand alongside the table, the two of them now humming with the exuberant chorus that drilled from the jukebox, each gazing down at McFerrin and grinning.

"You going to call the roll, or do I just start right in asking questions? You suckered me—right, mister? I don't know how you brought it off, but you did it, right? Or is your messed-up kisser some party mask you wear and deep down you're just my old buddy Douglas."

"Possess yourself, Mr. McFerrin. Be calm, sir. I appear in John Douglas' place, John Douglas needing to be elsewhere at this particular time. But I appear in his place, sir—with his authority, I assure you."

"Sweetheart, force you got—I grant you. Authority you got *shit* of—take my word for it. At best I can get you the *Port* Authority, cleaning out the toilets with a short stick."

"Don't be flip, Mr. McFerrin," Montague said. "There's no call for joking."

"I agree. The Boy Scout took my gun—that's no joke."

"Precaution," Montague said.

"Against what?" McFerrin said.

"You're a hothead. When you have a hothead who's not sure which end is up, you have a dangerous situation. My young friend there was simply subtracting the danger from the situation."

THE STAR SPANGLED CONTRACT

"All right, where is Douglas? When do I see him? What am I looking in your slop-face for?"

"Presently, Mr. McFerrin, all will be unraveled presently, I assure you. But first I'd like to trust you better—and naturally it would please me to have you in turn trust me."

"Trust you?" McFerrin said evenly. "How about ask me to eat a centipede?"

"So be it. Meanwhile, you are here, young sir, and you will listen."

"Get me a beer while I tune up my ears," Mc-Ferrin said, withdrawing one of his sleek little cigars and lighting up.

Montague signaled, and the driver sauntered off to the bar.

"He understands you pretty good for a fella that doesn't handle English," McFerrin said.

"You came—now listen," Montague said, ignoring the remark.

"I got a problem," McFerrin said, puffing coolly on the Schimmelpenninck. "I came here to talk to somebody else, you know."

"Exactly," Montague said. "And so you *shall*— in due course. Poor Ben and poor Clyde, they had other plans too—and disappointments. The way these things are played out, Mr. McFerrin, there is ample surprise for all of us. Some people call it destiny, fate."

"I like that," McFerrin said. "Never took you for a philosopher, pal. Always took you for a simple thug. But now I can see you're the real brainy type, a regular deep fella. You got a first name, deep fella —or do I just call you Commander Montague?"

"Cyril," Montague said as the driver returned with four glasses of beer.

"That's cute," McFerrin said. "I like that too. Cyril. Come to think of it, Cyril, the better I know you, the more I'm just crazy for everything about you. So fill me in, okay? So I can really get a case on you. I'm waiting for your story, Cyril. My ears are ready to go to work."

"It's complicated," Montague said.

"Somehow I knew it would be," McFerrin said. "So try to simplify it for me. And do me a favor, old pal—make it snappy, because I'd like to take a leak sometime this month."

"I'll condense," Montague said. "If I go too fast for you, stop me—ask a question."

"You bet," McFerrin said. "I'll raise my hand and let you know. Okay, spill it."

"Burlingame is to be burned up on August first at K.C. Crossfire into the motorcade. You know the plan, because you put the boots to one of the shooting teams. But there is a second shooting team remaining. They practice even as we talk. Today is July twenty-sixth. The order originates with the Joint Chiefs. The contract went to Art Underwood. Underwood signed his supervisory people out of C.I.A. but mainly D.I.A., and they in turn picked up further supervisory people all over the place, pros and semipros from various agencies and para-agency organizations. The objective is to burn up Burlingame before he makes it to a second term."

"My hand is up, pal. Who wasted Underwood?"

"Don't know. D.I.A. operating on behalf of the Joint Chiefs is my best guess. Your trifling in Illinois must have exposed Underwood in some way. They saw him compromised, so they wiped him."

"So who replaced him?"

"I did," Montague said.

"You're shitting me," McFerrin said.

"I was Underwood's guy-behind. When he went out, I went in. I'm still running that program. To the extent anyone really runs it anymore. The thing is a fantastic cross-hatching of capsules and insulations, each operator knowing only what he needs to know, and so on. You've been around—you know how these things work, how they're set up."

"All right, good buddy, it's getting pretty complicated—but I'm still with you. Next question—why snuff Burlingame?"

"Foreign policy. He made it in on a mandate vote to get us out of Indochina, and now he's going to score a second term with a hands-off approach to Greece. The J.C.S. want bases there; they want the military junta back in power."

"And the J.C.S. are getting their marching orders from the good old oil and armaments and heavy-industry boys."

"That's the easy part," Montague said. He finished his beer, checked McFerrin's glass, and raised two fingers to the grinning driver.

"No, make mine strong black coffee—Turkish coffee if they have it—and tell them to stick some sage in it."

The driver went off.

"Look how fast he learns English," McFerrin said. "Your kids nowadays are something else. Regular internationalists. Smart as a whip."

"Your kids nowadays know the score," Montague

said. "They know it's all economics, all the distribution of resources. They see politics as crap, a smoke screen, something to keep people like you and me entertained but confused. It's all your multinational company—your conglomerate, your consortium, your syndicate and cartel. There are no real political interests anymore. It's all dollars and petro-dollars, the rate of exchange and the balance of trade—and nations are simply the deck of different-colored cards in a worldwide game of monopoly. The kids know it. The kids believe it."

"Do you?" McFerrin said, stubbing out the Schim.

"I believe it," Montague said. "But I don't believe *in* it."

"What do you believe *in*, Cyril? How about you tell me that? You believe in snuffing the President of the United States?"

"There is no explaining how I became Underwood's guy-behind—except to say that I always admired the man. When he and I were with Wild Bill Donovan in the war, there was no one better. Art was a great agent. A man of true heroism. As for his subsequent politics, well, he became, shall we say, unbalanced on the communism issue. He failed to realize that there really was no issue—that capitalism and communism are the same thing—material solutions to material problems—and therefore highly compatible systems that are destined to overcome their superficial differences. A family. That's what Russia is to the U.S.—family."

"You got a cute name, Cyril—and you got a cute way of looking at things."

"That's not how *I* look at things," Montague said.

"That's how the kids do—and others who are un-afraid of reality."

"You were talking about Underwood, good buddy. You can skip the philosophy lecture and let me hear some facts."

"As you wish," Montague said. "Your coffee is here."

The driver put a mug of coffee in front of Mc-Ferrin and a glass of beer in front of Montague and then stepped respectfully back to his position next to the other young man.

"That's all there is," Montague said. "I admired him immensely—when we were both O.S.S. He needed a number two man in this thing—the pay was extraordinary—and I knew it was the only way to stop him."

"*Stop* Underwood?"

"Exactly. Only from the inside could I interfere with the program to terminate the President. At least that's what I thought. But no one man can stop it—the plan is much too elaborate, too many self-propelling elements—and it's already gone too far to defuse it now. Edward Burlingame will be shot at Kansas City on August first, and a man named Billy Joe Dooley will be discovered with the weapon of assassination, and no one can do anything about it."

"Except the President. The President need not go to Kansas City, or has that simple thought not crossed your mind, Cyril, old pal?"

"Exactly," Montague said, raising his glass to his lips, and for the first time, he smiled. McFerrin wished he hadn't. Montague's face was even more repulsive when his lips were stretched back from his teeth.

"Now, you tell me how it is one persuades the President not to go to Kansas City? The man is thoroughly headstrong. The man has been thoroughly warned. The man is unafraid. So tell me, Mr. history professor, how? And then, when you've told me how, tell me by what means you even get a message to the President? A message that is safe with the messenger? Speak, Mr. history professor. I am willing to listen."

"I know a man," McFerrin said simply.

"And who is this man?" Montague said.

"Franklin Quiller. He could do it," McFerrin said. "If he had all the facts and he believed them, Quiller could do it."

"My thought exactly, young sir. Quiller. And this is Douglas' thought, too. But Quiller must be persuaded—and John Douglas can do it. Because Douglas knows things none of us knows."

"That's crazy!" McFerrin said. "I've heard some crazy shit from you this afternoon, pal, but that's the craziest yet!"

"I warned you, yes? Did I not say complicated? Do you not know that in today's marketplace of intrigue, nothing is as it seems?"

"Including you, handsome."

"My face is my badge, Mr. McFerrin. I earned it at war. When you were dreaming of growing up to play a child's game of football in Iowa City, I was playing a man's game with the gentlemen of the Gestapo. It is the only medal I have, my young friend."

"I'm sorry," McFerrin said. "But I don't get how John figures in this, how John knows stuff."

"Precisely," Montague said. "*What* do you know!

You know *nothing!* You are an infant full of illusions and bad temper. You are a babe in such matters."

"Prove it!" McFerrin snapped. "I'm tired of this horseshit. Put up or shut up!"

"I am prepared to put up. I am prepared to put up John Douglas, and he, young sir, will in turn put up Franklin Quiller. All will be provided because Douglas and I are colleagues. Is that not ironic? Your partner all through Vietnam and Greece and Turkey —the third of the McFerrin, Greenfield, Douglas trio?"

"John's still Agency. He never quit. And he's so deep in the goddamn Mediterranean—how the hell would he be in any of this?"

"I told you, Colin—you know *nothing.* Douglas and I have been working together for almost three years."

"You telling me John is hooked up with you in this Presidential gig?"

"I am telling you," Montague said, "that John Douglas and I are as tightly tied as you and Greenfield and he once were. I am also telling you that when you and Greenfield checked out of the Middle East and went into private practice, D.I.A. assigned me and the Agency assigned Douglas to keep an eye on the Greek liberation boys. Our assignment called for simple observation. But John and I wanted to fight. We helped. In fact, we went into the hills and soldiered—and it was the best of my life since the big show in Europe. Things mattered to me again. I was—alive. Do you understand what I'm saying?"

"Yeah, sure—" McFerrin muttered, his mind staggering under the bulk of so many contradictions, so many revelations, so much to try to figure out. He drank down his coffee, and Montague raised his eyebrows in inquiry.

"You wish another?"

"No thanks," McFerrin said. "I've got to take a leak. Okay if I go?"

"Go," Montague said.

McFerrin stood up. He started toward the rear of the tavern, and when he glanced back, just before pushing open the door to the men's room, he was surprised to see that he was not being followed. The two youths still stood approximately where they had been standing. As for Montague, the high-backed bench concealed him from view.

McFerrin stood at the urinal, his brain reeling. Run? From what? And if running were really necessary, what would it accomplish? It would simply leave an even greater mystery behind him. In six days someone—Poucher?—was going to try to off the President—and no one but this fantastic bastard —liar? lone good soldier?—this bastard Montague was talking. But Douglas with Montague? Incredible! Yet the note was unmistakably Johno's—his style, and who the hell else would know about "C" except Dan? And as for John, there was no one— not even Dan or McFerrin's dead brother Bill—that he held in as high regard. No one was more solid than Doug! And if Montague could *produce* John—?

McFerrin zipped up and stepped to the basin. He splashed cold water over his face, combed his wet fingers back through his graying hair, and washed his hands very carefully to give himself more time to think, to make a last giant effort at deciding. But how to decide anything when everything was getting more preposterous by the minute? He checked himself in the mirror. The strain was showing. His forehead had nearly healed, but his eyes looked as if they'd been painted on with poster colors. The fatigue was surfacing again, the leaden feeling that gave him to wonder was it all a long lousy dream you were in and when you woke up at last you were dead.

Montague was sitting in the same spot, his hands folded tranquilly on the table in front of him, his arms looped around a fresh glass of beer. And the two young men had not moved from their stations, although they too held full glasses of beer. The juke-box was still doing its ear-splitting business, and though customers were leaving, new ones, dark and grim-faced men of the same stripe, were taking their places at the bar and tables.

"Produce John Douglas," McFerrin said when he was sitting across from Montague again.

"Exactly," Montague said.

"The real world may be getting away from me, but John is solid. You show me John."

"Exactly," Montague said. "It is all coming together now. The point of his note to you. What John and I are working on. Why we want you in with us. And Greenfield too—if you think he's solid. Together we are going to save the President and save Greece and, in doing so, save ourselves. We are working for the Greek people, and that means we are working for their defender in the White House —and it is only by fighting with friends that we know our flanks are safe."

"And while all this is going on, you're still running the program to *terminate* the President? That's what you're telling me, isn't it?"

"Exactly," Montague said. "Shall we go?"

"Go?" McFerrin said. "Go where?"

"To see John Douglas," Montague said. "What else?"

"It's six forty-five now," McFerrin said. "At ten o'clock I'm scheduled to see Quiller in D.C. And I believe I'm in Baltimore now, right?"

"Mr. McFerrin," Montague said, "you will see John Douglas *and* Franklin Quiller by no later than seven-thirty if we leave right now."

"Cyril, you are a man of infinite surprise. And you probably are the biggest bullshitter drawing breath."

"Exactly," Montague said, rising.

"And these Boy Scouts are just going to scoot us to wherever it is in their jalopy out there, right?"

"Exactly," Montague said. "I had a very pleasant current model Ford sedan, but it was taken away from me a few days ago. An unfortunate incident."

"Yeah," McFerrin said, "that brings up another item, just one of your minor details, you know. How come you've been hassling me—those little numbers on my living room rug and on the free highways of America? That something else I'll understand when I get to be a grown-up like you?"

"Your irony is a bore, Mr. McFerrin—I suggest you work on it, get it up to par. My colleagues and I were obliged to beat you about the head and shoulders because your head is thick and your shoulders burdened with matters too weighty for you. You were messing up, getting in the way. We are all going in the same direction, have the same finish line, but you are running on the track and stepping out of your lane. Such discourtesy keeps snagging other runners in the ankles, tripping them up, so to speak. In plain language, young friend, it was my job to put a little fear into you—keep you cleared off so stronger runners might have a chance to finish ahead of the opposition. Smacking has taught you nothing. Now we will instruct you by example, punishment having proved useless in your particular case. And, of course, to stop all this foolery, we need you. John says we need you, and that means we need you. Let us argue no more, please. John awaits us. Please," Montague said, gesturing toward the exit.

"But no hard feelings—right, Cyril, old pal?" McFerrin said, rising too.

"I am past all feeling," Montague said. He raised his glass of beer and downed it in one draft. "Hard or otherwise. Let's go."

They pulled out of the booth, and as the four of them stood sorting themselves for the walk to the door, McFerrin said, "How about my gun?"

"By all means," Montague said. "Give him his pistol."

One of the young men came up close to McFerrin and then looked down toward his feet. When McFerrin also looked down, he saw the silvered Voroshilov glittering in the man's hand held low at arm's length. McFerrin took the thing into his own hand and then quickly folded his arms and started toward the door through the dense curtain of smoke and noise.

As the four of them came out into the sultry heat of the early summer evening, Montague touched McFerrin on the elbow.

"Feel better?" he said.

"Not really," McFerrin said.

"It will all come clear in due course," Montague said.

"That's good," McFerrin said, knowing that he was well past worrying whether it came clear or not or how it came out in the end—knowing that he was all the way in it now and that he was taking one deadly step after the other.

The blue convertible waited. McFerrin chose the side with the troublesome door. He nearly tore it from its hinges yanking it open—and as he shouldered in to the back seat where Montague was already in place, he said, "For the record, pal—these boys really Greek or are they just more of your general showmanship?"

"What does it matter?" Montague said, looking straight ahead. "Consider, Colin—what does it *really* matter?"

35

On the morning of July 28, Washington newspapers
and broadcast media carried the story of the death by
shooting of Daniel Jay Greenfield, age thirty-four,
nationally know war correspondent and free-lance
journalist lately covering the congressional scene
with a series of profiles for *The New York Times
Magazine* and other Sunday supplements. The news
revealed that at approximately 4:30 P.M. on July 27
Greenfield was killed instantly by a single shot fired
at close range into his head. It was surmised that
Greenfield had been using a public telephone in
Union Station when the shooting occurred. It was
also revealed that Greenfield had been attached to
the Central Intelligence Agency for an undetermined
period of time, in the late sixties and early seventies.
Finally, it was admitted that the police had no leads
as to the assailant or the motive for the shooting.

*Colin McFerrin did not read this story, nor did
he hear it over the radio or television.*

Valerie Craig, however, did. And therefore at
11:45 A.M. on July 28 she left her office at Fort
Meade and drove home, complaining that she felt

unwell. When she arrived at her apartment in Georgetown, she pulled out the phone directory and riffled through the pages for the number of the Russian embassy. She stared at the page for a long while, then slammed the book shut and tossed it on the sofa. She wandered across the living room, adjusted a lampshade askew on its base, then gazed idly out the window, the filigree curtain draped on her shoulders like a shawl.

Then she went back to the phone book, copied out the number, and walked briskly out the door and two blocks down the street to a corner phone booth. She dialed the number and was startled by the bright clear voice at the other end.

"Good afternoon, Russian embassy," the woman's voice answered in flawless English. Valerie did not reply, the phone unfamiliar and remote in her hand, as if it and not the voice at the other end were an alien. The embassy's switchboard operator repeated the greeting, and then Valerie carefully replaced the receiver in its cradle.

She walked slowly back to her apartment, the veins in her temples suddenly throbbing, the pressure behind her eyes building in earnest now. She closed the curtains to dim the sunlight streaming in the window. She would take two Valiums and nap. The day was long, but right now Valerie Craig had to bring July 28 to a close. She swallowed the tranquilizers with some diet cola, washed off her makeup, and with bra and panties still on, she crawled into bed and slept.

Colin McFerrin did not read or hear any news of anything on the morning of July 28. Nor was he anymore in touch with the world by the afternoon of July 28.

By the afternoon of July 28, General Mark Poucher was at his retreat on Hiltonhead Island, South Carolina. The General's aides and attachés had strict instructions that his five-day fishing and nature-walking respite from the stress of the Pentagon was not to be disturbed for any reason short of business concerning national emergency.

Commandant Thorne was in Carmel, California, resting up from a bout with the flu.

General Grissle was in the Ozarks on a bird-watching tour.

General Keller was vacationing with his grandchildren at the Del Coronado Hotel at Coronado, California.

On the afternoon of July 28 only Admiral Doggett Anson—Admiral David Jark's replacement as Navy Chief of Staff—was on hand at the Pentagon as a representative of the Joint Chiefs of Staff.

There was a bed where Colin McFerrin was on July 28. The bed had no legs. It was a fixture that came out from the wall, held there by steel braces. The mattress was a solid slab of tough rubber one inch thick, and it was fastened to the bed frame so that it could not be removed.

Billy Joe Dooley spent most of the morning and some of the afternoon of July 28 in jail. He had been picked up on a possession of a dangerous and unauthorized weapon charge and booked by the Kansas City police. Bail was set at one thousand dollars. It was paid by a local bondsman in the early afternoon. Forty minutes later Dooley was released. The weapon—a .357 Magnum—was of course confiscated and held as evidence.

Dooley returned to his room in a boarding house on Trannick Street. He left his room at the dinner hour, went to Barney's Best Beef downtown, ordered a K.C. Special, squabbled noisily with the waitress about having to pay extra for fried onions and then left the restaurant in the company of two men who had joined him for coffee and pie.

Colin McFerrin saw a doctor on July 28. He saw three doctors. They said they were psychiatrists. They examined him, chatted briefly with him, and then the third one returned to the room where the steel bed was and explained that it would be necessary to restrain him for a time, inasmuch as he was undergoing a severe reality dislocation occasioned by an intense manic-depressive episode. The bed was the only furniture in the room. It was a white room. There was a four-by-four-inch window in the door, with chicken wire running through the laminated glass. There was no doorknob on the inside.

In the early evening of July 28, Edward Burlingame read a chapter of *Robin Hood* to his two children. His five-year-old Stephen cried when Will Stutely was about to be hanged and Robin had not yet shown up to save him. Burlingame comforted his son, skipped quickly in his reading to the happy outcome, and then kissed his children and sent them off in the care of the First Lady.

The President then had a brief conference with his special advisor, Franklin Quiller, and thereafter went into the White House garden on the west lawn to study the speech that had been prepared for his Kansas City appearance on the first of August.

He retired at 11:15 P.M. but did not fall off into actual sleep until well after 2 A.M. July 29.

In the dawn hour of July 29, Adele Dietz drove to the hill country of Maryland. Before the sun had cleared the treetops she had arrived at Lawn Crest Sanatorium and parked the car not far from the front of the sweeping pastoral entrance. She remained in the car. Alongside her, on the front seat, there was a shopping bag filled with packages of candies and a half-dozen paperback novels. They covered what was at the bottom of the bag.

Colin McFerrin read nothing all day July 29. As for what he heard, it was chiefly the remarks made by the three men who briefly interviewed him and a word or two from the attendant who brought him his meals and three times gave him an injection of phenobarbital and once obliged him to drink down a little cup of paraldehyde. As for what Colin McFerrin saw that day, outside of the four persons noted, it was through the chicken-wired glass in the door, and it was the dim corridor outside that door, the white wall that was opposite, and no one passing by.

Secretary of State Danforth was in San Francisco all day July 29. In the morning he addressed the California Bar Association at the Mark Hopkins Hotel. The title of his speech was "Crime in Government: Seed of Crime in the Streets?" That afternoon Danforth and his official party toured the sights—the Presidio, Sausalito, the Palace of the Legion of Honor. Danforth had dinner that night with his wife, the Governor, and the Governor's wife. They ate at the Blue Fox and then all returned to their rooms at the Mark.

Franklin Quiller worked all day on July 29. He

had lunch and dinner sent in. The door to his office in the Executive Office Building was kept closed and locked through most of that day. Only his confidential secretary, Alison Agajadian, had direct access to him.

The Vice President was continuing his goodwill tour on the twenty-ninth, planning to depart Cairo at noon for a short stay in Tel Aviv. Afterward he would return to Athens for more talks with both factions in the belligerence now dividing Greece and threatening her strength among the N.A.T.O. nations. The Vice President had been abroad for almost forty days.

Colin McFerrin woke up the morning of July 29 in the same white room whose monotony had helped to keep him asleep most of July 28. The steel bed was the same, the walls hung with white canvas mats, the sort found in gymnasiums to protect players from bruising themselves—the chicken-wired laminated glass in the door, the same—it was all the same—and moments after waking, he felt the little nip in his arm again, saw a man's face smile comfortingly and then move away, and again McFerrin fell thunderously into a deep and perfect sleep.

36

It was not like any room you ever saw. And yet
there are in the world many rooms like it—rooms
that are blunt squares and tall in the ceiling, their
surfaces on all sides, around and above and below,
tile—little white hexagonal tiles. But you can't see
the tiles going around until a point six feet up the
walls, because canvas mats cover the tiles, fitted
there by rivets whose rims are covered too. There
will always be a bed that juts from one of these
walls—a "bunk" it would be called. There will be a
sink that runs cold water because you could hurt
yourself with hot. On the floor where your feet would
be you'll find a chrome button; step on it and the
cold water runs. There will be a toilet—more a bowl,
really—bolted to the floor, and just in front, another
chrome button. Step on it and the white porcelain
flushes out. And there will be a door—with no knob
on the inside—and up at eye level there will be a
little four-by-four window with chicken wire running through the sheets of laminated glass. Or maybe
it will be plastic. A light will go off and on in a thick
globe well recessed into the tiles above your head,

but you will not be able to control either of its two simple phases—for control will come from somewhere in the world beyond the chicken-wired glass, a switch that is perhaps down the hall where you can't see or perhaps very nearby, perhaps on the wall just outside your door, but you cannot see that either. Nor could McFerrin.

Colin McFerrin could control nothing on July 28, not even the periods of his sleep. He slept the durations someone wanted him to sleep, and when he waked and stared for a little while at the crook of his arm where it hurt, little waves of anxiety would wash over him. Then the man would come again and stick it quickly with a needle again, and there would be a pin dot of pain, and then Colin McFerrin would sleep again, a sleep that rolled through some huge, empty echoing place.

On July 29, McFerrin did not sleep so much. And once when he waked, the light overhead off and one end of the room suffused with a dusky glow from the little window, he tried to stay awake, although he did not have the strength to sit up. He lay there staring at the crook of his arm where it hurt. If he could keep on staring at the pain, jam the feeling of that pain into his brain, make the hurting hurt *enough*, then maybe he could keep himself awake. He was working at it, had maybe held himself conscious for eight or nine minutes, when the man came, and it was the man with the needle and he said, "Easy, big fella—take it easy now," and took McFerrin's arm and held it steady in a steely grip and was saying, "Easy now, big guy," and, "How's old Marty's sleeping beauty today? You okay, friend?" and, "Pleasant dreams now, little darling," and was just touching the point of the needle to the vein that stood out from the grip pressing above it and was saying, "Bon voyage, little soldier, old Marty's going to launch you to the stars," when there was another voice, a very hollow and resonant and very assured voice from somewhere farther back in the fog, and it said:

"All right, Ames! I'll see to it now, thank you!"

And the man in white with the needle faded back into the misty light and vanished, and then the fog parted and revealed another man coming forward, this one older, wiser, nicer, *father, father, father*— and McFerrin started drifting off again into that huge, empty, echoing place.

"All right, Mr. McFerrin," the voice said. "I want you to wake up now, please. You don't mind my calling you Colin, do you? That's right. Wake up."

And the face focused, and it was not such a nice face, after all—and of course it wasn't——

"My God," McFerrin said, "for a minute there I thought you were my father."

The man chuckled. He patted McFerrin on the shoulder and then moved his hand down to McFerrin's wrist, the fingers taking it in the way that somehow comforts us, and McFerrin could see that the man was clocking his pulse.

"Have I been hurt?" McFerrin said. "I was riding in a car—with—with a man—with one, two—with one, two—with *three* men. Did we hit something?"

The man held the forefinger of his free hand to his lips and made a hushing expression with his face and then checked his watch.

"That's good," he said. "Very good," and he released McFerrin's wrist. "So many questions. Suppose I ask one. Tell me, Colin, what is the tallest building in New York City? Can you answer that for me, please?"

"You're kidding," McFerrin said, trying to sit up but falling back to the hard rubber mattress.

"Would you like me to repeat the question, Colin? I'll repeat the question if that's what you'd like."

"Hell, I don't know," McFerrin said. "I guess the World Trade Center buildings are taller than the Empire State. Yeah, sure they are. What kind of question is that? Why does my arm hurt?"

"Your arm hurts because I've been obliged to order sedation for you. You've had a few injections."

"How long has this been going on? Where am I? I was in a car—I remember that—three other guys. What happened?"

"Never mind about that. That will come later. You're hungry and you're thirsty and you're growing irritable. Shall I go now? Would you like me to go now, Colin—so you can go back to sleep?"

"I thought you said I was hungry and thirsty. Why should I sleep?"

"You're confused, Colin," the man said, and stood to leave, and McFerrin could see the fog behind the man and the muted glow that shone in the fog, and he reached out a hand to show the man he wanted him to stay.

"Hey, come on—stick around," McFerrin said. "Are you a doctor? How sick *am* I? What's wrong?"

"Ames!" the man called, and stepped back into the fog, and the tuck his body made as it folded into the haze bellied out as the man in white came out of the fog. He came at you, and his fingers took you hard around the arm. The needle went in again, made its long journey in, and the pain wasn't a pin dot anymore because now you were wide awake to feel it, and what you felt was true pain now and then the wide world opening to drop you miles and miles asleep, and the last words you heard were: "Now you just sail on off to dreamland, big fella. Old Marty's here wishing his big friend nightie-night."

37

It was the morning of July 29, not yet eleven o'clock, when Dr. Agajadian came striding down the long white corridor, turned right under a bank of fluorescent lights, and then turned right again. He pushed through the swinging door, his white smock flapping, and entered a pleasant room that could have been the kitchen of a country inn. But it wasn't. It was a kitchen, yes—but it did not serve a country inn.

The doctor, his skin swarthy and with a perceptible sheen to it, sat heavily at the scrubbed pine worktable that stood in the middle of the floor, and when he was seated, the old woman at the stove picked up a large steaming pot, the kind whose finish looks paint-spattered. She turned, selected a gleaming mug from the drainboard, and scuffed across the highly polished random planking. The old woman set the mug before the man and filled it to the brim. Then she leaned across the table and scooted the sugar bowl and cream pitcher closer to him.

"Will you be eating something, then, sir?" she said.

"Thank you, no, Winnie," the doctor said. He

pinched the bridge of his large nose, rubbed his eyes, and then spooned a little sugar into his coffee.

"More coffee for you, then?" she said flatly to the other man who sat at the table, his chair directly opposite the doctor's.

"An excellent breakfast," the man said, and when he raised his face into the morning light to look at her, you could see how severely it was disfigured, the scars and slight repositioning of its parts marked by an inhuman coloration of the skin. "Some more coffee would be fine."

She poured his cup full of hot coffee from the pot and waddled back to the stove.

The doctor blew gently on his coffee, and then he searched his pockets for a cigarette.

"Here," Montague said, producing a long, slim silver case from his breast pocket.

"No, thanks," Dr. Agajadian said. "I prefer these," he said, producing a crumpled pack of Gauloises.

Montague struck a match and reached the flame across the table, and Dr. Agajadian had to stand up a bit to put his cigarette within range.

"Thanks," he said, and sat back down. "Ames make you quite comfortable last night?"

"Just fine," Montague said. "But I would have preferred had my men stayed here."

"Of course," Dr. Agajadian said, testing his coffee. "But quite enough security here with Ames and his people—and, as I explained, we're at capacity. Isn't that right, Mrs. Fitzgibbon? Not a free bed in the house?"

"It's the truth, sir," the old woman said, not turning from her tasks at the stove.

"I'm sure your people were very comfortable at the motel in town. It's rather new, I believe."

"I told them to go ahead," Montague said. "They're restless boys."

"They're not waiting for you? What about transportation?"

"I can always grab a cab," Montague said.

"Okay by me," the doctor said. "Now that you've delivered your package and the bill of lading."

"Incidentally, how's the goods?"

"Progressing nicely," the doctor said. "I meant to ask yesterday, by the way—how you got him here without a struggle. He shows no signs of recent injury except a wound a few weeks old on his forehead and some abrasions on his wrists."

"Sodium Amytal—a shot in the arm just before we got here, and it was done."

"Sodium Amytal? Then it's good we've had him sedated. He'd still be having a headache the size of the Goodyear blimp."

"So be it," Montague said, bored with the chitchat. And with that he scraped back his chair, dropped his cigarette into his empty mug, and stood. "Time to press our fortunes elsewhere, good doctor," he said.

"Shall I call for a cab?" Dr. Agajadian said, also rising.

"No need," Montague said. "I believe I'll stroll for a bit."

"Stroll back to *Washington?*" Agajadian said.

"I can get a cab down by the station," Montague said, impatient to end the encounter.

Dr. Agajadian stood. "Enjoy your hike, Mr. Montague," he said, smiling and extending his hand.

Montague touched the doctor's hand lightly, then pushed through the swinging kitchen door and headed down the carpeted hallway and out the front door.

As Montague strolled through the tall, arched iron entrance gate and turned down the road toward town, a car pulled out of an adjacent driveway and moved up alongside him.

Montague waved, the motion not a greeting but a signal to stop.

He needn't have signaled. The car stopped, and Montague came up to the open window.

"Where you headed?" he said.

"Into town," the woman said. "I was just turning around. I forgot my son's chocolate."

"You've got a kid in that place?" Montague said.

"My son," the woman said, her face grim. "He's almost forty. But yes, I imagine one would call him a kid, yes. Candy—that's all he wants when I visit, and I completely forgot his favorite—those Hershey things—kisses they're called. I'll have to go all the way back and get them."

"Bad luck," Montague said, smiling. "Want a passenger? I need a lift into town."

"I'd love company," the woman said, and patted the seat beside her.

Of course she had waited for company for some time. She would not have missed this man's company for all the world. She knew this man by reputation, and she had even met him a few times in the forties, twice in Glasgow and once in London; and once there had almost been a meeting in a farmhouse in the Ruhr Valley when they shared the same section chief in the O.S.S. Of course his name hadn't been

Montague then. No, it was something Eastern European—*Vlednik*—although he had affected British dress and accent and even decorated himself with a Royal Guards moustache. He'd been quite handsome then, this man, rather dashing really, and very brave. As for his face now, she would never have believed it possible. It was so clearly what it was, even from this distance, one did not need a photograph to be certain one had the right man. One needn't worry that one might be pulling the plug on the wrong man.

As for Montague, he of course did not recognize the middle-aged woman who greeted him so cheerily as he took a seat alongside her in the car. The woman who hospitably slid the shopping bag closer to herself to make plenty of room for him on the seat was no one he had paid much attention to almost forty years ago when their paths crossed a few times during the war. It would have amazed Montague to know that this genially smiling, petite woman, this ostensibly giddy chatterbox who now sat beside him, this warmly appealing stoutish middle-aged woman who was his driving companion through the graceful summer hills of the sovereign state of Maryland was, at least insofar as he was concerned, the angel of death.

And like the angel she was, she proved herself merciful. The bullet entered the left side of his head at the point of the mastoid gland, pursued its vigorous journey upward at an angle that took it traveling grossly through the midbrain before it exited the skull and continued through the roof of the car.

It is doubtful Montague knew what had hit him.

Certainly that was how the gaily talkative woman had wanted it, and how she reported it to Mark Poucher.

38

A. Cigarette?

Q. What? Are you serious? I have my pipe.

A. I know you have your pipe. You *always* have your pipe. I thought you might want a change, a tiny break in custom.

Q. I'll stay with my pipe, thank you. I don't favor sudden changes, as you know.

A. Of course. I was teasing, I suppose.

Q. Don't. My nerves don't seem very elastic these days.

A. It will be over soon. You can rest then. Perhaps we could get away for a week or so.

Q. It will have reached a minor climax in a few days, but it will not be over. Not for years yet. And you know that. But, yes, I *am* tired. Let's look forward to a brief holiday around the fourth. Canada perhaps. What would you say to the Algonquin?

A. In Saint Andrews? Wonderful, darling! That would be wonderful.

Q. How different everything will seem then, a few

285

days hence. Even now everything is so much clearer, the lines so much more clearly drawn.

A. It's in sharper focus, yes. You can *see* the thing now. Poucher and a few diehards isolated, and the key management of their spearhead decapitated. The central core of the Company in disarray, Drexel paralyzed, Miller numb. The President still determined but indecisive now, really. And D.I.A. completely in chaos, like a brute stunned by the slaughterhouse rod.

Q. Exactly. You select whatever idealist is handy, take him firmly by the ankles, and laying about you with his snarling romantic Irish convictions as your ax head, you swing him in a circle and chop randomly away. The man's been a veritable battle-ax for us, in one way or another enabling us to cut down the field on all sides.

A. And now to turn the battle-ax into a bomb.

Q. We're seeing to that. But first, since the President will follow through on his itinerary despite all arguments to the contrary, and since the Poucher-Zero program will likely trigger automatically, regardless of the loss of leadership and the crippling of the primary shooting team, we must turn the event to our advantage. At this stage that's really very simple to accomplish.

A. But Burlingame may still be killed in Kansas City.

Q. *No*, darling. He will *not* be killed. He will *go*. He will publicly show his resolve to be unafraid, "to meet the people," as he boyishly puts his advertising—but he will *not* be killed. He will be pulled back from the edge of the precipice, and the net effect will be in our favor.

A. You'd have to crack the Pentagon's *Walnut* annex to interdict the Poucher program, and I don't see how we can do that. We've tried. Everybody, I think we can safely assume, has tried. Those fault-lines can't be crossed.

Q. I'm not thinking in *that* direction at all, darling. It's much simpler than that. In fact, it is such an elementary notion, it astonishes me no one's used it before. Or if they have, no scholars in the subject have ever seriously speculated in this regard. For it occurs to me, my sweet, that the only political weapon of ultimate force more conducive to public relations than assassination is—ah, but shouldn't you deduce it yourself?

A. I don't like this side of you, and you know it. Don't tease me.

Q. You teased me earlier, did you not?

A. Over a *pipe!* And only to relax you, to get you to let loose a little. I'm not inclined to love you when you're like this. *Tell* me or I'm going to bed.

Q. Very well then. Let's arrange it this way. I'll tell you, and you nevertheless *will* go to bed and I will too. If you want to relax me, darling, there is nothing very difficult about it.

A. I thought you were expected downstairs.

Q. In the morning. I won't be needed until the morning.

A. Then the schedule has been delayed?

Q. Not grievously. These things take time, but immensely less time than one would think. A few hours longer won't matter very much.

A. Shall I have Mrs. Fitzgibbon send up a little light supper, then?

Q. She's incapable of that—but, yes, I won't be going down, so let's eat up here.

A. I'm waiting.

Q. Call down your order first.

A. If I have to do that first, then you, my love, will have to eat supper first. Do I make myself clear, Franklin?

Q. Perfectly. I have the power to shape history, but, alas, I am in the thrall of the shapeliness between your legs. Your answer, beautiful woman, is this. The only political weapon of ultimate force that is more conducive to public relations than assassination is—?

A. Stop it now. Please, dearest. This is silly, Franklin.

Q. Of course, Alison, darling. *Attempted* assassination. Don't you see, Alison?

39

Franklin Quiller was seated on the couch, a sort of
Victorian affair covered in a rich mauve brocade.
Next to him sat a slender woman, a woman so stately
and so still in her bearing that she seemed to have
been carved from stone. Her fine, gleaming black
hair fell evenly down from the part combed precisely
from front to back and framed the translucent white
of her skin. The rose glow that marked her full and
perfect lips was natural—yet there seemed nothing
natural in this woman. She was a vision from dreams
or from nightmares, something a man might imagine
yet never really see.

She was Alison Agajadian.

A third person stood to the side and rear, leaning
against the carved mantelpiece that hooded the large
fireplace. As tall as Quiller, he was dressed expen-
sively in a white linen suit, oddly vested considering
the season of the year. Despite impeccable tailoring,
one could sense the pack of muscle in the shoulders
and the lunge of powerful neck at the collar. His face
was heavily freckled, and in one hand he held a glass,
and he now and then sipped the Scotch it contained,

purposely tinkling the ice cubes between each leisurely sip.

He was John Douglas.

It was very hot this first day of August, as hot here in the hills of Maryland as it was on the streets of Kansas City. The windows in this room were shut, and the room was very cool, as were all the air-conditioned rooms on the second floor of Lawn Crest Sanatorium.

None of these people spoke. Nor did they once look at one another. Their attention stayed fixed on the screen of the large television set that stood against the wall the couch faced. The three had remained silent through all the precoverage color, through the on-the-scene reports from this or that C.B.S. newsman with a breathless slant on the coming event. The three had stayed silent through the coverage at the airport, through the brief remarks to the crowd when the huge plane had touched down and when Air Force One had emptied out its august personage and his entourage. They had stayed silent through all of it, right up to the time the motorcade assembled itself and the long line of limousines and motorcycles went screaming in from the countryside toward downtown Kansas City.

It was only when all hell had broken loose, when the bomb had exploded on the highway a safe thirty yards before the first vehicle reached the spot, when the motorcade had come to a shrieking halt and Secret Service men were vaulting over car hoods and running in every direction with guns drawn and faces haggard with anxiety, when the C.B.S. announcer reported that official word had been passed that the President would return to the airport for immediate departure back to the nation's capital, it was only then that one of the three spoke.

It was Quiller.

He said, "Exactly."

And Alison Agajadian extended her elegant arm in his direction and handed him his pipe.

And John Douglas took a long pull from his Scotch.

It was only moments after this that the C.B.S. anchorman at Campaign Central in Washington broke in to say that Calvin Goodman, in downtown Kansas City, had a fast-breaking development that might throw light on the shocking incident the nation had just witnessed, and then the anchorman said, "Go ahead, Calvin," and the picture changed and the reporter was saying, "This is Calvin Goodman in Foley Square. It was minutes ago that the metropolitan police revealed they have arrested a man discovered on a rooftop in Foley Square. He was armed with an M-16 rifle and is identified as one Billy Joe Dooley, a former Marine, twenty-nine years old, white, of slight build. Dooley, it has been learned, was arrested days previous on a charge of illegal possession of firearms and was released shortly after when bail was posted by a local bondsman. Dooley has been returned to City Jail, where he was held just a few days ago, and is being kept under maximum security. C.B.S. has been told that Dooley has a record of radical left-wing and pro-Communist activities in this city and in Houston, Oklahoma City, and Miami, and that he received a dishonorable discharge from the Marines, where he was trained as special high-performance sharpshooter and small weapons expert. That's it from downtown Kansas City—and now back to you, Roger."

"Thank you, Calvin," the anchorman in Washington said, and Franklin Quiller said, "That goes double for us, Calvin," and all three persons in the cool room in Lawn Crest Sanatorium not far from the small spare room where Colin McFerrin still drifted in sleep, all three of them laughed.

40

"Rise and shine, cupcake!"

Was this *sound?* Was it the sound a *voice* made? Was it a *language*, something that could be figured out—or fitted into the long-ranging silence of the stark-white dream you knew you were in?

"Come on, cupcake—rise and shine! It's a great day for sheet-metal workers and seekers of the ultimate wisdom. Come on, big fella—on your feet."

It—was—language! And McFerrin could just make out the relatedness between the words and what was happening—could just begin to see that his being lifted to his feet had something to do with the words he was hearing. And then he was standing, groggy still, having still to be held upright by the man who'd lifted him and was steadily talking to him, saying, "Okay, look alive, big fella—time to get out there and earn your chicken and peas. Wake up, my sleepy friend; old Marty wants his buddy bright-eyed and bushy-tailed because company's coming."

And as these words slowly arranged themselves into a pattern of meaning, there came the stab of pain in his arm again—only this time it was not followed by a headlong descent into stupor. This time it was a sharp quick prodding, whose result was a blue flame that brought all of McFerrin's cells brilliantly awake to an electric alarm ringing frenziedly along the trunk lines and branches of his nervous system and ending with a sustained clangorous tympany in his brain.

"Jesus!" McFerrin said.

"Some jolt, cupcake. You got to be a buster to take a jolt like that—but we know you're a buster, all right. That's what you are—you're a buster, aren't you? Speak up. Are you old Marty's buster?"

"What was that?" McFerrin snapped. He was fully awake now. For that matter, he was superawake.

"Shut up!" the attendant said, and took McFerrin firmly by the arm and led him out of the blunt white room of mats and tiles.

They went down a short hall into a sitting room furnished with an abundance of dark, overstuffed chairs, a heavy odor of what seemed to be garlic steaming in the air. In the center of a circle of chairs stood a low table with three empty ashtrays and a large bowl of pistachio nuts.

The door opposite opened and a plump, round-faced man glided into the room. He gazed at McFerrin, moist eyes blinking, and then he waved a fleshy hand toward one of the chairs.

"Please sit down, Mr. McFerrin. Ames, you may leave, thank you." When the attendant had left, the fat man lowered himself into one of the chairs. "I hope my associates did not inconvenience you. I trust you will excuse the widespread rudeness and our unorthodox means of bringing you here." He sat well back in the oversized, overstuffed chair, his short, fat legs crossed clumsily in front of him.

"I am Dr. Agajadian."

"Doc, I think we've met before," McFerrin said.

"Yes, of course," Agajadian said, placing the bowl of pistachio nuts in his lap, his little, soft hand burrowing among its depths. "We met weeks ago when you first had your breakdown."

"Is that a fact?" McFerrin said. "*Weeks* ago? *Break*down? You're the clown who wants to know what's the tallest building in New York, but I'm the whacko, right?"

"Then you remember me, Mr. McFerrin," the fat man said, prying apart the pink-shelled nut and with a long fingernail scooping out the meat and raising it to his liverish lips.

"Oh, yeah," McFerrin said. "Crazy as I am, I've got amazing powers of memory. I also remember I was promised my friends would be here. You know what a promise is, Dr. Freud? Can you explain that?"

"I believe I can, Colin," a voice to the rear of him said.

McFerrin froze.

He did not turn to see the face that went with the voice. He did not need to. McFerrin knew the voice the instant he heard its distinctive coloring of his name, the familiar New England swallowing of the second syllable.

That voice, in this place, paralyzed McFerrin— and when he felt the hand on his shoulder, the presence of the man behind him, McFerrin felt the blood grow cold in his veins.

295

Quiller!

"Good morning, Colin. You look very rested, old son. Mind if I sit in on this?"

Quiller patted McFerrin's shoulder and then stepped around into view. After a moment's pause, when he seemed to be making a difficult decision, Quiller took the chair nearest the man who called himself Agajadian. Quiller pulled out his pipe and filled it from a tobacco pouch. He lit it with slow, easy puffs, his eyes fixed on the flame.

"I'm waiting, Frank," McFerrin said.

"Soon, old son. I'm here," Quiller said, "to explain everything. I'm not sure you'll appreciate it at first."

"I'm not sure I'll appreciate it at all."

"Just hear me out. It was necessary for us to talk about some things. But there was no way for us to talk about anything sensitive until some form of insurance was established."

"Insurance? I've heard that crap talk before. Talk *straight*, Frank. Now's the time."

"Protection, if you prefer."

"Whose protection? *Your* protection, Frank?"

"Our protection. Yours, too, really." Quiller puffed on his pipe. "You see, I have a proposition I've been wanting to make to you. A proposition that can elevate your entire life, give meaning and size to your destiny. However, the matter could not even be broached—just in case you happened not to see its merits—until insurance, excuse me, protection, was created."

"What you're saying is, you wanted something on the record to make me look unbalanced if you have to."

"That's roughly the picture, old boy. But of course you really *are* unbalanced, you know."

"Look, Frank," McFerrin said, "let's cut this horseshit fencing, hear? What's on your mind? Let's get it all out on the table. It's about time, don't you think?" McFerrin looked hard at Quiller, hating the pompous face, wanting to smash it, to smash away at him for years of deception. "A mole," he said, "Frank, I never dreamed you'd turn out to be a goddamn mole."

Quiller's face was placid, pleasant. "It takes all sorts, Colin. The Intelligence community thrives on a great variety of participants—workers and managers of every stripe."

"And to think I used to run to you with the inside dope on how the agencies operated," McFerrin said. "Jesus Christ!"

Quiller smiled. "Naïve, perhaps, but not unforgivably so. You were always a perceptive and earnest student, my friend."

"I'm still waiting, Frank," McFerrin said, struggling to control his rage. "*Talk!* Enough bullshit!"

"Certainly. You and I can discuss *any*thing now —can't we?" Quiller smiled agreeably—then turned to Agajadian. "Would you bring down my briefcase from upstairs? I'd appreciate it." Agajadian rose quickly and left the room. "I recall," Quiller continued, "your once expressing your displeasure with the Company. If I recollect accurately, you said you'd come to feel insignificant in your work—the meaning had gone out of it for you—you failed to see the impact of your labors, its relation to the great American enterprise, and so forth, and so on. Am I paraphrasing you fairly enough, Colin?"

"Something like that," McFerrin said. "And so?"

"The point is this, lad. I propose to insert you into history. Nothing less. You will *make* history, not merely teach it. You will achieve something significant, shape large events."

Quiller was talking like a madman, it suddenly occurred to McFerrin, and he very nearly told him so. He could not understand how Quiller had managed to misread him so wide of the mark—and he so wrongly misread Quiller. My God, McFerrin thought, my God. Yet he was a dead man if he played this one too much one way or the other. This would require the trickiest handling. McFerrin stared at the man across from him. The match was on.

"I'm still waiting," he said.

"Good," Quiller said. "Let me particularize. While you have the capability for action, which is a valuable asset, you are, above all, my boy, an intellectual—and I think I can demonstrate that with the proper exercise of your considerable talents, the future I've designed for you will prove satisfying in the extreme."

Dr. Agajadian returned to the room and handed Quiller his briefcase. Quiller removed a thick manila envelope and studied its contents. Entering the room with him was a tall, dapper-looking man who carried an air of authority in his stride.

"John Douglas!" McFerrin said. "This is some show you boys are putting on. I'm impressed. How're you doing, man?"

"Cooking on all burners, Mac. How's yourself?" he said, holding out a pair of cigars to McFerrin.

McFerrin sensed immediately the change in his old friend, the slight strain in his chummy speech.

"Can't complain," he said, then added, "Pretty fancy threads, man. I remember denim and beads."

"I'm afraid that went out with my hair," Douglas said, running his hand over a balding forehead backed by carefully trimmed gray hair.

What had changed most, McFerrin thought, was his face. It was fuller, perhaps, but it was more than that. It was the face of a man who had come to savor the fullness of success in his field, of a man who possessed power and knew it.

"What have you got there, Frank?" Douglas said as Quiller examined the papers in front of him.

"My dossier," McFerrin said.

"Yes," Quiller said, smiling, "and it's filled with good reports about you, extending back to your time in Vietnam and Greece."

"Mac was a good friend of Demosthenes Pelias," Douglas said, taking a chair at the table as Dr. Agajadian simultaneously rose, his bowl of pistachio nuts at last empty, and strolled out of the room.

Quiller silently watched the fat man's passage to the door and then again looked down at McFerrin's dossier. " 'Demosthenes Pelias, professor emeritus at the University of Athens, former premier of Greece. Resigned Premiership to return to teaching,' " he read aloud.

"Pelias was just a history professor when I met him," McFerrin said. "I took a course he was teaching, and we got to be pretty close. He helped me with Greek history, and I helped him with American history. I guess you could say we were buddies of sorts."

"Your good buddy merely became the Premier of Greece," Quiller said, tapping the page with his pipe.

"He's just a history professor again," McFerrin said. "Things change, you know."

"As they have with your friend Greenfield," said Quiller, lowering the folder and gazing at McFerrin.

"Is Dan all right?"

Quiller shook his head. "He's dead, old son. I'm sorry."

"You killed Dan?"

"I kill no one," Quiller said. "That was the work of the D.I.A."

"They're your friends, aren't they?"

Again Quiller shook his head. "Not in that sense, Colin. They're too quick on the trigger, perhaps because it's a new game for them. It's an old game for the Company—maybe that's why we find it a bit boring. But I feel bad about Greenfield. I know he was your friend."

Quiller paused, looked down a moment, then tapped his pipe against his teeth. "In any case, old son, there's a great deal of unrest in Greece right now. If a change in the government were to occur, the voice of Demosthenes Pelias could bear significantly on the question of a new government's survival. He is still the most popular democratic leader in Greece, retired or not. Now, I hope you are with me in my thinking to this point. Please follow closely. As a general proposition, Pelias dislikes Americans. As far as our information indicates, you are the only American he's shown any regard for. You could be a—how shall I say—a moderating influence on him, help him to see that it's only fair that he give a new government a chance to get started, that he withhold his judgment for an appropriate interval." Quiller paused and jerked up his eyebrows in contemplation of McFerrin. "Are you with me, lad?"

"Oh, I'm with you, all right, Frank. But you only mean, of course, if something *happened* in Greece."

"Of course, of course," Quiller said, gazing at McFerrin with a wide-eyed expression. "But, as I say, there *are* signs of unrest in that troubled cradle of democracy."

"No shit," McFerrin said, his anger rising against the other man's complacency, cutting down his own control. "I'd say there are signs of *unrest* here too. You know, little stuff like somebody trying to bump off the President and the President's closest advisor turning out to be some kind of megalomaniac. Shit, Frank, I'd say that when you have one of your best buddies croaked somewhere and another showing up some kind of fink—I'd say there's enough *unrest* around to keep a tidy fellow pretty busy. You agree, Frank?"

McFerrin studied his man, the thought suddenly in him that he had gone too far, said too much. But the rage was in McFerrin too, and he was glad now that he'd said it, said that fancy word that in simple language meant your garden-variety screwball, your basic madman—a Napoleon, a Hitler, demented, sinister, treacherous.

Quiller chuckled—a deep, genuinely amused roll of soft laughter. He glanced over at Douglas. "Do you hear that, John?" He scratched his short-cropped hair, his eyes twinkling in what seemed real amusement. "I believe you caught the drift of that. Our friend here thinks we—ah, well—the word is inescapable—our friend thinks me *mad*." Again Quiller chuckled—and then his expression abruptly changed.

He faced McFerrin, and McFerrin could see true contempt in Quiller's eyes.

"Colin, you are such a boy. Your vision is so dreadfully narrow. Madness is your only means of explaining what you do not understand. You parse the world into such earnest, simplistic terms—this over here, that over there—this black, that white, no grays. No *grays,* Colin. Shame on you, boy—you pretend to intellect, but in you there is the fundamental American flaw, a failure to entertain ironies, contradictions, complications. You want it all apple-pie easy—the good guys and the bad guys, one either this or the other and everything, *everything,* must be labeled, identified, pigeonholed one way or the other. That's your madness for you, dear boy—that *will* to categorize, to place everything in a slot that seems to define it, even if the critical, the operative, edges must be knocked off it in the doing. Don't you see, old thing, that *that* is where the national insanity begins?

"Listen, the effort to restore the military to power in Greece is the Pentagon's doing. It is what they want. And a plan I happen to applaud but am not involved in. Still, I wish to see it go forward. As for the President, his termination, this too is Poucher's plan—because the Joint Chiefs will not tolerate Burlingame's re-election—and his re-election is a certainty unless he is humiliated in some fashion beforehand. Poucher considers me a distant ally of sorts, thinks I'll play his game, but I don't want Ed killed. I don't want Ed shot down like a dog. If only because I don't want an abrupt fracture of any kind. But I do want Ed out. I am fond of the man, but he is wrong for the nation, wrong for our long-term best interests. And I know how to get him out, by *using* the Pentagon, by letting Poucher do what he wants with Greece and thereby shaming Burlingame into stepping down before November. Look, boy, it's complicated, all this. Shakespeare himself would have been impressed with the subtleties and ironies."

McFerrin was convinced now. "You know, Quill, you're something new under the sun, in your tweed jackets and your leather patches and your American-as-all-hell prep-school white-buck swell-gay style. You're a goddamn madman creep, Frank. You follow me? I mean, I hope you'll pardon the harsh language, Frank, but you take the fucking *cake*, old buddy. You want me in with you, mister—then cut the high-flown patronizing horseshit and give it to me *straight*—from the top! You tell me what the hell has been going on from the start. You tell me why my world is made up of either finks or dead folks, and then maybe I'll be prepared to play ball in the game according to Quiller. Are *you* with *me*, Frank? You want to teach your old student something, then you've got to first gain his confidence—and right now I guess I'd have to say my confidence is just a wee bit shaken, you know?"

McFerrin knew he was trying for a large one, making a downfield play for total disclosure, but he also knew he had nothing to lose by trying. Things couldn't be worse—and he for sure wasn't getting out of here alive without some extravagant stunt. If he came around easily, Quiller would never buy it. On the other hand, if he tried the man's patience a degree too much, that would be the end of it. You're dealing with a nut, McFerrin counseled himself, an extraordinarily intelligent, wildly dangerous *nut*.

Every word must be the right word; every maneuver must seem logical, consistent, innocent, earnest, sincere.

Quiller turned to Douglas. "Tell him," he said—and McFerrin could see that for the moment it was still okay, that whatever he was improvising, it was working.

"It's not that complicated, Mac. I'll make it fast." Douglas spoke softly, his gaze throughout his speech always somewhere just to the side of McFerrin's eyes. "Frank was double deep-cover Agency since his college days. He's always been Company, one way or another. I mean, he's had *two* roles with the Company, what you see and what you don't see. There are a number of us—highly placed enough to influence not merely the course of the Agency but the direction of the Government. We don't advertise—we're rather modest that way. But we do press our objectives, and we do what has to be done."

"Like terminating a President?"

"That's not our style, Mac. That's a desperation act, an admission of failure, really. As Frank said, that's where we part company with people like Poucher."

Douglas leaned back in his chair, smiling pleasantly. Quiller seemed equally unruffled by McFerrin's outburst. "Do you feel up to it, then, lad?"

"Up to what?" McFerrin said.

"Pelias, old boy!" Quiller said, screwing up his eyebrows in mock amazement at McFerrin's apparent obtuseness.

"Oh, *Pelias*," McFerrin said.

"We'd like to have you with us, Colin—and Pelias would be your way of proving your mettle, don't you see. But be realistic, think about it. I think you'll find we have a common objective."

McFerrin blinked. "Which is?"

"Why, of course, the preservation of the good life for those best able to enjoy it—though that is of course stating it in less than the noblest terms. We want America strong. We want America to move forward into the twenty-first century still the dominant force among nations. But one doesn't achieve this end through the means that worked in centuries past—oh, no. Matters are more subtle now, lad, enormously more complex. The upper hand will be held by those most skilled at the subtle manipulation of power, those most gifted at perceiving world problems in their abundant complexity. American interests, the husbanding of our self-interests, cannot be left in the hands of bullies like Poucher or innocents like Burlingame. That Greece be returned to the control of capitalist rule—a military junta, say —is essential to our interests—but Burlingame refuses to see the point, whereas poor Poucher would put bombers over Greece to prove it. Power must be altered in *gradual* steps— increased and decreased by prudent degrees. One can't have revolutionaries running amok, on the one hand. Nor, on the other hand, can one have international gangsters and adventurers and policemen crushing helter-skelter every legitimate outburst of governmental reform. *Pelias*, Colin. Work on Pelias for us, and you will be doing immense good for the American enterprise—true patriotic work. Don't you see that now?"

"And then what, Frank? After Pelias, then what? Kill the President? Or is he already dead?"

"Great God, Colin—*we* don't want Burlingame

dead. But we don't want him re-elected either. He should, however, be persuaded to step down, in which case, Otis Danforth would step forward. Danforth will obtain the nomination at the next convention—and he will win. Accept my word on that."

"Danforth's *your* man?"

"Yes," Quiller said. "Otis is with us. Which is to say, Otis will take his instructions from us."

McFerrin leaned forward. He placed his hands on the low table—and then he turned them over to expose his palms. He raised his eyes to John Douglas and tried to capture his old friend's gaze. When he could not, he moved his head to face Quiller full on. He said it very quietly, very evenly.

"You are telling me these things—you're telling me everything—because you can kill me. Your convictions are not strong enough to stand alone. Otherwise you would leave your case to my free judgment based on the merits. But I am a prisoner here—and I am a prisoner only because you don't really trust what you say and believe in, because you're afraid your beliefs can't compete in the free marketplace of ideas. That's it. I've said my piece. What do *you* say, Frank?"

Quiller looked at McFerrin as if he were just discovering his presence in the room. He studied McFerrin's face for a long, hard moment. The room was very still, charged with a silence that was thunderous. At last Quiller spoke, never once unfastening his lock on McFerrin's eyes.

"I say *go*, Colin. That's it, old son. Just go. Ames will drive you back to Philadelphia or to Washington—to wherever you want."

"And?" McFerrin said.

"That's all," Quiller said, smiling. "Call me in a day or two at my office—and give me your reply."

McFerrin stood up. "That's fair enough, Frank," he said.

"I think so too," Quiller said. He gathered together the materials into the briefcase, stood, gave McFerrin another stern look, then turned on his heel and left the room.

41

Was this happening?

Was he free?

Of course he was not free. He would never again be free. He would be hunted or he would be dead—and if you thought death a kind of freedom, that was the only way he was ever going to get it.

McFerrin sat in the back seat. Ames sat in the front—and drove. And that was the way it was going to be: you sat back while they drove you where they told you *you* wanted to go. They sat there in front driving—so unconcerned with your power to do anything about it, they just turned their backs to you and went about their missions: driving you back to your apartment in Washington or driving the whole American nation into the future ruled by the invisible machinery of power-crazed men and computer-deduced international planning.

Ames eased the car to the curb that fronted McFerrin's building and let the motor idle.

"On your way, tiger," he said, and winked at McFerrin in the rear-view mirror.

"See you around, jumbo," McFerrin said, and

popped open the door and stepped onto the sidewalk.

As McFerrin made for the entrance, Ames called out to him. McFerrin turned and saw that the big man was out of the car now, leaning massively on the roof.

"One thing!" Ames called, and beckoned with his finger.

"I can read you from here!" McFerrin called back.

"Whether or not this thing works out, cupcake, old Marty wants you to know he figures he's one day going to get a crack at opening you up. Can you read that, boy scout?"

"Ram it up your vein, jumbo," McFerrin shouted.

He checked the apartment for bugs. But what was the use? If they wanted to listen to him take a leak, all they needed was a shotgun Sennheiser with a pre-amp and they could pick up his sizzle from blocks away. He went to the kitchen and worked up his special Turkish brew. He downed it with two aspirins. He dialed Val's number. No answer. He showered and shaved. He called Dan Greenfield's wife. She cried when she heard his voice, and then he started to cry, so he hung up. He tried Valerie again. Still no answer. He turned on the television. It was screaming from every major channel: the explosion on the highway, the arrest of Dooley, the growing establishment of Dooley's complicity, congressmen and senators of both parties pleading for a return to sanity. N.B.C. had an in-depth interview with Special Advisor to the President, Professor Franklin Quiller. McFerrin stood there transfixed. "A scandal," "an outrage," "a nation bent on destroying itself," were the only words McFerrin registered. And then on A.B.C. he heard that the Congress had empaneled a special investigative commission to bring serious pressure to bear on executive assassination attempts. The head of the World Bank had been named chairman. Sitting with him would be a former director of the National Security Agency, a former director of the Defense Department, two retired admirals, and a deaf but conscientious congressman. McFerrin switched off. He dialed Valerie's number once more —and on the second ring the receiver was raised. He waited.

"Who is this?" she said.

"Thank God you're there."

"Colin! My God, Colin! Are you all right? Where are you?"

"I'm okay. I'm home. Here, in Washington, I mean. Can you come over?"

"I just this minute got in the door," she said. "Give me a half-hour."

"I need you *now*," he said. "Come right away."

"All right, darling," she said. "I'll come."

He made himself another cup of Turkish and sage —and then he thought better of it and let it stand on the kitchen counter and went to the living room. He got out the Jack Daniels and poured a long shooter and swallowed it off in two scalding drafts. The whiskey partly restored him. And then there would be Val—her long, cool legs, her warm wave of belly— and *she* would thoroughly restore him.

McFerrin checked his watch. It was 8:46 P.M. and it was August 1. She should arrive around 9:00.

Together, their bodies naked and together, McFerrin and Valerie would see the dawn of August 2. And *then* he would think. Tomorrow.

42

It was just after nineteen hundred hours at the Pentagon. But in the inner Command Operational War Room it was brighter than an Arizona summer at high noon. The Joint Chiefs stood before a papier-mâché replica of Greece, its mountains, valleys, beaches, and harbors shown in ample detail. Nearby, an auxiliary extension of *Walnut* received questions and returned answers. In the adjacent G-2 tank—separated by windows and connected by intercom—strategists from D.I.A. Tactical Operations gamed the projected counter-revolution in Greece. They worked out problems with roads, communication nets, unit-protection facilities, supply routes, and whatever else they could think of.

D.I.A. was programming a day or two ahead of the Joint Chiefs, calling probability answers into the main room over speakers. It was hard for the Joint Chiefs to think in the midst of all the buzz and clatter—and the wreckage of the K.C. plan didn't help matters any. The tension in the Command Operational War Room was at Mach 2 and gaining.

General Grissle made rapid notes. General Keller

312

gazed at the ceiling in an effort to steady himself. Admiral Anson kept glancing at his watch. He felt they were wasting time now. They had gone over the rehearsal of the beachhead assault and it was solid. Admiral Anson hated to waste time. Commandant Thorne looked again at the large operations clock on the wall, its numerals and hands set off in red. What it indicated was not the time in any U.S. zone but the time in Athens, a scarlet hand sweeping away the seconds there.

The chairman, General Poucher, made a final, exhausting review of the artillery available to back up the beachhead assault.

Then Poucher spoke. "We were fucked over in Kansas City. But, gentlemen, you have my oath—we will not be fucked over in Athens."

"I don't want to hear about Kansas City," General Keller said. "I don't want to hear about it. I am a soldier. My profession is warfare."

"Well, the problem is still there, and it will come up again," General Grissle said. "Kansas City was a fiasco because we were too busy keeping our fingernails clean—jobbing the work out to Underwood instead of sticking with our own people, with D.I.A."

"I want to focus on immediate objectives, gentlemen," General Keller said, pointing to the gaming model of Greece. "In warfare, one performs the work of a soldier, not the conniving of a cutthroat. That was our error in Kansas City. It will not be our error again."

"Agreed," said Commandant Thorne.

"Agreed," said General Poucher. "Hereafter, we conduct our affairs like the soldiers we are—here and abroad."

"Agreed," the other men said in something close to unison.

As they filed out of the room, Poucher turned to General Grissle. "There's still this piece of impudence, McFerrin. The cutthroat gets the cutthroat's death. It remains in the capable hands · of Dietz." Again the other man said, "Agreed."

The porticoed gingerbread house on M Street stood in darkness. But in the large basement room the shades were down and the curtains drawn and light flooded into every corner. Here the Washington contingent of British M.I.5 was meeting in emergency session. On the large worktable lay a map of the Mediterranean. The gaming out of a war between Israel and Egypt and of a new crisis in Cyprus had been completed, and now concentration was turning toward speculation on a counter-revolution in Greece. Someone said, "The bloody Yanks," and someone else said, "Do shut up."

In Sound Chamber 234, at the National Security Agency, Cryptological Command at Fort Meade, *Do shut up* was duly recorded onto tape.

At the Russian embassy only night lights shone here and there. The staff had retired early. There was nothing to keep anyone awake. Second-strike nuclear capability on the part of both superpowers meant diplomats and tacticians could sleep when they wanted to. Moreover, the U.S. and the U.S.S.R. had long ago acknowledged large joint interests. The respective militaries had established fundamental sweetheart agreements. Of course, a steady display of seeming antagonisms had to be maintained for reasons of arms-industry profits, general good showmanship, and simple diversion. The Russian military and the K.G.B. had been fully briefed by the Pentagon well in advance of the scheduled American enterprise in Greece. In exchange for a promise of foot-dragging in the matter of further American arms support of Turkey, the Russians had approved the Greek venture and would not make an issue of it in the United Nations. So far as the Russians were concerned, the seizure of the liberal Greek government was as good as accomplished, and they had moved their attention on to other, more critical, matters.

It was nearing ten-thirty when C.I.A. Deputy Director Warren Miller retired for the night. He knew he would not sleep. He had taken two phenobarbital tablets, but he knew he would not sleep this night—just as he had not slept these many nights.

Adele Dietz slept perfectly well the night of August 1. She had gone to bed shortly after a light supper of hardboiled eggs and Ry-Krisps washed down with what was left of a bottle of white wine. She had sat for a few moments on the silk comforter, looking at the stylized metal that lay at the foot of her bed. Then she got up, adjusted the air conditioner to High, and returned to her bed. She lifted off the Ingram-3 subsonic, held it in her hands for a few moments, and then placed it on the floor next to the MAW-3 silencer and the brown and white spectator pumps she planned to wear in the morning. She fell asleep atop the comforter and pursued a sleep vacant of memory and dreams.

Morgan Drexel was working late at Langley Field this night. It was shortly before midnight—but the handsome antique lamp threw a circle of orange onto his nineteenth-century French Boulle desk. The C.I.A. director knew he was not accomplishing very much. He knew he was accomplishing nothing at all. Yet sitting here relaxed him somehow. His door was locked against the sounds of office labor the night staff sent up. It was wonderfully quiet in here —and whatever was going on out there, Morgan Drexel now understood he could neither control it nor escape it.

Edward Burlingame spent the night of August 1 in Bethesda Naval Hospital. He had been put to bed at seven o'clock, sedated, and visited drowsily with Mary Burlingame and the children until 7:30 P.M. He was unharmed, of course, and not very shaken really—but his personal physician thought the night's stay in order, and the First Lady was asked to urge the decision. She did. The President of the United States kissed his son and kissed his daughter and held his wife's hand until the sleep of chemistry came.

Franklin Quiller made the rounds of the television networks the night of August 1. So did Secretary of State Otis Danforth. They told a nation that lay awake, bright with the excitement of a near-kill, that order must be returned to the national landscape, that goodness and justice and reason must prevail.

"Extremism," Professor Franklin Quiller stated, "cannot be suffered in a free and open society when it places in jeopardy our nation's leaders." Otis Danforth, speaking in reply to a question calling for his personal reaction to the assassination attempt, declared: "I am deeply shocked and aggrieved to think that the President of the United States of America cannot travel the byways of this land in perfect safety and tranquility."

Alison Agajadian lay in a scented bath the night of August 1. It was after midnight now—but the miniature Panavision on the tubside stool still showed her she needn't hurry from the perfumed waters. He was still addressing the question of the prospect before us. She would have at least another hour to wait, another hour before she could take his handsome head in her hands and kiss the fatigue from his princely features, from his aged yet vigorous body.

It was well past 2 A.M. when Colin McFerrin and Valerie Craig fell asleep, their legs twined together into a lacing of bone and muscle which only the twist of passion spent and exhaustion achieved could produce. They slept like this for hours, neither moving, neither feeling—and when each came briefly awake by turns, each remained in absolute stillness, not daring to move, not daring to break an embrace that was impossible and perfect.

43

He would never get used to seeing her back like that
—those taut planes and the cleft of her spine and
those winking Venus dimples just above the buttocks
—seeing her back going away from him as she toed
across the bedroom carpet to the bathroom, the little
trot she did as she leapt from the tangled morning
sheets to hasten to the bathroom—and he went up
on his elbow watching, watching her skip-dance
across the carpet, the long, incredible velvet-bronze
length of her flashing in the misted bedroom morning light. Two, three seconds—and then she disappeared from the line of his vision. Then a pause,
the golden light of her back still printed on his eyes.
And then the hiss of her morning water giving him
something else to cherish, something else that meant
Valerie and that he would never want to give up.
She made him want life. She made him want life on
any terms he could get it. And the thought of this invited the thought of Quiller and all that Quiller
meant.

It was morning, the next day, the tomorrow he'd
set as his deadline to *think*. But McFerrin did not

want to think—not just yet. He wanted never to think again. He wanted mornings always like this, his first vision the drape of her chestnut hair against pillow white, then the cascade of her skin as she unfolded herself from his body and touched toes to the carpet and the brilliant undulation of hips and back as she slow-sprinted from the room. Then the pause —and the long sweet hiss of water that announced his woman was here.

"Awake?" she said when she came back into the hazy light.

"I don't sleep on an elbow," McFerrin said.

"Awake enough to talk?"

"I just gave you a demonstration. You want further proof, come here."

"You just want me for my body," she said, taking the comb from his dresser and starting on the dark gloss that was her magnificent hair.

"You bet your sweet ass," he said, patting the bed. "Do it over here."

"Haven't you read Germaine Greer? You think white-slaving is still in fashion?"

"Pussy is always in fashion. And, lover, you got the high-stylest cooze in history."

"Is that the opinion of a scholarly historian or just your average lug with a hard-on?"

"You got a dirty mouth—you know that, baby? Is that what you get from reading Greer and the rest of that swill? Is that your idea of a better world, a lot of dirty-mouthed chicks teasing horny historians?" McFerrin gave a grim laugh and flipped over on his back. "Christ," he said, and laid an arm over his eyes.

"Hey!" she said. "That's not like you."

"I'm okay," he said. "Just been trying to postpone my brain for a while more and then had to go and remind myself. *A better world!*"

She came to him. She sat and ran her hand under the sheet and grabbed the hair on his belly.

"It could be a better world, Colin. If I were free now. If we were together, maybe somewhere else, maybe things wouldn't matter so much, maybe the Quillers could just do whatever the hell they wanted to and we'd just close the door on it all and love and love and love. If I were free. I could make that count for a life. *Give* the Quillers the goddamn world. It stinks, anyway. We take our acre of it and build an electric fence and a wall and lock the gate and lock the door and love each other until we drop. Is that so bad? It's more than most have, Colin—and it could be enough."

"Baby," McFerrin said, and circled her waist with his arm and drew her down to his chest. He held her that way for a time and then he said:

"It would be a life if it existed—but it doesn't. There is no acre anymore. There is no wall tall enough, no fence hot enough, no lock strong enough. There is nothing to get behind and bolt, because they are already on the other side. There is no getting away from it, because they are already wherever you're going. The world may stink, but the smell is from the sweat of trying, not the rot of dead hope. That's the mistake the Quillers make, the insistent flaw in their grand designs. They sniff the air with their aristocratic noses, and the stench they smell they take for the smell of death. They just don't know honest sweat when they smell it, the heat the race of men give off when they're laboring at the hard task of making a life and a place and future the best they know how.

"The Quillers smell something, they smell mankind burning with life; and they think it's rot setting in, the body going to corpse, time for the vultures to come on down off their lofty perches and get *theirs*. But it's just mankind burning, the wild heat of his efforts, of all the trying he's always done since all the world's blaze of human endeavor began. Oh, shit, baby—I know how goddamn corny all this sounds— but the plain fact of life is that when you say what matters, there's no way out but to say it corny. Maybe that's the heart of it: we're *ashamed!* Embarrassed. What we feel and trust in comes out cornysounding because we've talked ourselves into being embarrassed by feelings and faith. Trust! Honor! Faith! Privacy! Family! The home! A moral center! Grace! Nobility! Dignity! Jesus, just listen to that! Well, screw it. I *am* listening. I've always listened— and I'm not stopping *now!* Not for nothing! There's no playing ball with the Quillers, because you'd trip over your goddamn heart every single play. And there's no *not* playing ball with the Quillers, because they've turned the whole world into their field."

She moved against his chest and took his hand from her hair and brought it to her mouth.

She said, "All right. But what will you do? What can you do? If you can't join and you can't run, what in the name of God can you *do*, Colin?"

He pushed her away from him and got to the floor. He walked slowly across the room and grabbed the doorjamb as he made it to the threshold. He squeezed it hard and then let go, and then she could not see him anymore. She wanted to hear him in the bathroom, but suddenly he was back in the doorway.

He looked at her. "Hit," he said.

"They'll kill you."

"I know," he said, "or defuse me in some other way. Get me certified or something. It all comes to the same thing. You neutralize the hostiles. Well, I've neutralized a few in my time. I've got no gripe coming."

"*I* do," Valerie said, "I love you."

"Then love me now," he said, and stayed there in the doorway unitl she came to him.

She was in the shower when he called Quiller, and when he gave his name, the woman on the White House wire punched him through instantly. "McFerrin," she said in her frosty voice, and then McFerrin heard Quiller say, "Yes?"

"I'm ready," McFerrin said, and that was all he said.

"I'll send a car," Quiller said, and that was all he said.

The line went dead. McFerrin was still holding the receiver when Valerie came into the living room, a small towel turbaned around her hair, a large one swept around her body.

"So? Making another date? A little something on the side?"

"Quiller," he said. "You stay here. I'm splitting."

"I have a job, Colin. Have you forgotten? I'm already late."

"Hey," he said, "all that talk about us running off. A job. *The* job. Let's not kid ourselves, baby. That work you do matters to you like nothing else going. All right. Forget I said that. You just be a hero when you can. There's a ring with both keys on the hook over the can opener. You know how to work a Medico lock?"

"Colin, I happen to be a decoder, you know—I guess I can come up with something. All right, I'll be here—sometime this evening, at any rate. They can find me at home as well as here. And is my office any safer?"

"What's *your* guess?" he said, and at last he replaced the receiver.

"After what you've told me, I guess not. Here's as good as anywhere else. And if you're here, then it's the only place. *Will* you be here, Colin?"

"I don't know, Val," he said. "Val, I don't know."

"All right," she said, "I'll be here."

"They won't harm you," McFerrin said, coming to her, gathering the warm, moist bundle of her into his arms.

"They iced Dan. For nothing more than working with you."

"You're not working with me," McFerrin said. "You're not in it—you're just with me, is all." He took the towel from her head and playfully, then wistfully, rubbed the hair as if to dry it when all he wanted was to touch it and touch it. "They know the difference."

"Do they?" she said.

"Sure," he said, taking her shoulders now and holding her away from him, trying to cheer her. "We ain't nothing alike. Who the hell could mix us up but a Chinese waiter?" He took away the bath towel. "Look at that," he said. "My chest is a whole lot hairier than that. Just show them your chest, and they'll know you're no kin of mine." At last she smiled a little, and when she did he knew that it had to be now. "Okay, I'm off," he said. "Car's coming —I'll wait out front."

"Off *where?*" she said, trying to hold him with explanations.

"Quiller," he said. "To the White House, I guess. I want the whole story, the whole picture—all I can get from him, clear in my mind."

"And then what?"

He was moving to the door.

"And *then* what, Colin?" she repeated.

"I don't know," he said. "I'm thinking about it. There's only one thing to do with a story, and that's to tell it, right? So, I'm getting the story—and then I'll find a way to tell it. That's not so bad for a beginner's plan."

He was backing to the door, grinning at her, trying to keep it light, trying to fix the last look of her into a faraway place in his heart.

"See you," he said, his eyes printing, printing all they saw.

"Tonight," she said, standing there in the towels that he had let fall to her feet.

"You bet,' he said. "We'll eat some franks and beans and potato chips and drink Coke and sit around watching dumb-ball and stupid-throw on the good old TV. Okay, babe?" he said.

"Okay," she said, and when McFerrin heard her say it, he left her no space to say more. He opened the door and shut it behind him and took the stairs— because if he chanced the elevator, he chanced her following him with more questions, more touching, more gestures at covering over what they both guessed were good-byes.

It was on the first landing that his hands reflexively went behind to check for the belt pack and the Voroshilov. There was nothing there, of course. But of course what had been taken from him would be no weapon in the combat he was going into—and who the hell was getting into the White House with a pistol, anyway? Besides, you didn't kill a cancer with a gun. You exposed it to the amazing light of a laser maybe, a beam of very great intensity.

Or maybe you did not kill it at all.

44

The woman who told him to wait and then told him Mr. Quiller would see him now was beautiful. Beautiful in a way that no man could really touch or take to himself, McFerrin thought. One stood off from a woman like this, but one never forgot what he saw. Or perhaps there were men who could reach women like this. But then, McFerrin speculated, it would take a man like such a woman—a man that was complete, whole, interior, turned inward, so absorbed with himself that he was not really *with* anyone and could therefore be with *anyone*.

The beautiful woman held the door for McFerrin, and as she ushered him through he had a fleeting visual echo thrum in his memory—something reminiscent in her face and something not at all beautiful. But the echo was muted, seemed overlaid with the heavy blanketing of a long and suffocating sleep.

"Close it," Quiller called from behind his desk.

The woman shut the door. She shut it to make three in the room, not two.

"I don't talk with her here," McFerrin said.

Quiller laughed. "She's all right, Colin. She's

326

better than all right. Alison Agajadian, meet Colin McFerrin, one-time Iowa farmboy and U. of Iowa fullback, one-time Agency field-agent and Indochina counter-revolutionary expert, one-time Middle East deep-cover operative, part-time historian, full-time pain in the ass, and one of the lousiest law students ever to set foot on the Yale campus."

"That was constitutional law, Frank. What the hell would a cow-flop kicker like me know about constitutional theory?"

"Now, now,. Colin," Quiller said, laughing. "Enough of that." He put his arm around McFerrin's shoulder and wheeled him toward the woman. "Say hello to Dr. Agajadian's daughter. You owe her more than you can imagine. You might even say you owe her the breath you just took. She's been plotting you, Colin. You've been her project more than mine, really. But don't let it bother you, lad. She's come to have a real affection for you. You might even call her a fan. Be nice. Say hello to Alison."

"Hello," McFerrin said. "Your dad hear any good dreams lately?"

"Only the rantings of angry Iowa boys who can't believe the city won't work like a farm."

"Be nice, children," Quiller said, holding up his hands in a comic gesture of concerned parenthood. "Don't fight."

"That's okay," McFerrin said. He took a chair and then removed the flat tin of Schims from his breast pocket. "I had it coming. Well, the farmboy is ready to move into the city, Miss Agajadian—it *is* Miss, isn't it?—he's ready to move in, get adjusted to the noise, then maybe occupy a place with a balcony, way up in one of those steel-and-glass jobs you city types seem to favor nowadays."

"*That's* the spirit, that's the fullback. Win, lad. It's winning through for those that can *do* it. That's all that counts."

"Oh, there *are* rewards," McFerrin said, eyeing Alison Agajadian broadly, making the degree he pitched it just edged enough but not too much. He was playing it, playing it for all it was worth—because it was worth *everything*. He checked Quiller again, a casual glance to measure his progress.

Yes! Quiller was taking it, nibbling, testing, playing with it. Oh, he was a big fish and an old fish and a wise fish, and he had been in this pond a long time and he was not biting anything that he hadn't nosed and turned in every direction first. But McFerrin was in no hurry. He'd just let the line out easy, slipping it out an inch at a time. No hurry. Big and old and wise—but going blind—blind with the arrogance of unchecked power—and proud.

"Good lad," Quiller said. "See it in its totality, lad. Rewards up here men dream about, long for all their studied lives, and then try to die with the quieting thought that *no* men get such things. But they *do*, Colin. Some. A very few. A mere handful. Conquerors, tyrants, princes—and now, in our time, your latter-day visionary, the applied and theoretic *manager*—the futurologist, Colin. It's all *systems*, old son. Systems and teamwork and technology of an ever-widening, ever-heightening capability, and the futurologist to manage the theory and the application."

"Show me the dotted line," McFerrin said, casting it with just the inflection of sarcasm that would loop the line out further. *Take it!* McFerrin roared to himself. *Believe*, you crazy sonofabitch.

"Good, good," Quiller said. "Now let's put these pleasantries aside for the moment. Alison—please, sit down. On second thought, get me that new Algerian briar from over there and *then* sit down."

The woman strolled over to a rosewood hutch, spun the piperack that sat on its apron, and then ambled back to Quiller's desk with the pipe he wanted.

"Now sit down, please. Everything is all *right*, Alison. Isn't it, Colin?"

"Just great, old buddy. I could watch her walk all day." Risky—but he'd done it now.

"Farmboys are famous for male chauvinist piggery, Mr. McFerrin, but it's been my experience few have bigger than the cock of a duck. Are you one of the rare exceptions, Mr. McFerrin, or is your phallus all in your mouth?" She settled herself on a couch that was upholstered in sleek brown leather, crossed her long, shapely legs in a movement of impeccable grace, and stared at McFerrin.

"Children! Children!" Quiller said. "*Please*. To *business* now. Colin, Alison—*business!*"

Perfect, McFerrin thought. He gave himself a grade of perfect on that one. Nothing on his mind but nooky and horsing around. Just a good old frat boy funning with a pompom girl while the concerned housemother looked scolding but indulgently on. He was taking it, Quiller was running with it—and if you just didn't blow it, he'd *bite*.

Quiller gestured with his pipe. "As I said, enough pleasantries."

But before he could begin, the beautiful woman

said, "Still no call from Vlednik. I'm worried, Frank."

"About Montague? Don't be absurd, darling. That old workhorse, there's nothing to worry about. He's iron, *steel*—a survivor. He'll be in touch."

"Nevertheless, I'm worried," Alison Agajadian persisted. "I work him and it's my job to worry about him."

"Of course, of course, my dear," Quiller said, and turned to McFerrin. "Now then, here's the situation, Colin. Because I must be candid with you. If you tried something foolish, you would promptly be discredited as mental. Records at Walter Reed have been manufactured to show that you were once admitted there as a psychotic—that, in fact, you received extensive shock therapy regimens last year. There are three psychiatrists who will swear to a diagnosis of manic-depressive psychosis with severe paranoid delusion. So much for your thinking you might go from here and spill our growing stack of beans to the *press*."

McFerrin drew on his small cigar and grinned. "To tell you the truth, Frank, I get to feeling a little spacey and squirrelly every once in a while. For my money, the phony rap sheet is probably right. My hat's off to—it is *Doctor* Agajadian, isn't it?—my hat's off to him and his excellent guess."

Quiller made a wry face. "But why are we talking this way? You're coming aboard. I just want to point out that there's no going back. You'll have money—more than you can imagine—and you'll have power. More than you can imagine."

"It almost seems too good, Frank." A show of caution.

Quiller laid down his pipe and put his fingertips together meditatively. "No more than you deserve, if you produce for us. After all, you've been passing your tests very well."

"How so?"

"Your following the Underwood lead to the Illinois practice site. Your robust handling of the situation there. And the screwing you gave the Joint Chiefs and the Agency—and especially Underwood. A-1 very fine, very fine. You're first rate, lad—always were." Quiller leaned forward. "But did it never occur to you that you couldn't have made it as far as you did without a little help? Did it never occur to you to wonder why you were put on to Underwood and Poucher in the first place? Did you never wonder why I didn't go to the Secret Service with what I knew? We *knew* Underwood would send Reiner out for a firsthand account of the new frangible bullet, and we wanted you to follow. We've been using you to create a rumpus, old son. We could have stopped Underwood and Poucher's assassination plan right at the start—but we wanted turmoil —and you helped the turmoil along. Moreover, we *wanted* Poucher to move ahead on his Greek enterprise. So we were in a tricky area—send you out to set back the assassination thrust but preserve Poucher to go ahead on Greece. What we did *not* take into account was the supreme excellence of Underwood's work, the enormously clever termination program he would evolve, and then *its* evolution into something self-operating. But, hell, boy, we've been managing you all along! Don't you remember the helicopter that passed over you while you lay there in the woods? Oh, Colin—did you *really* never once consider that you were being worked? Every move plotted? Old son, you passed the test of a top-flight field-agent, yes—but you have a way to go before you're trained to the vastly less simple labors we require."

McFerrin knocked the ash from his cigar onto the floor. "And there I was—fat, dumb, and happy all the time," he said. "Hell, maybe I'm just too trusting to go back into Intelligence at my age."

Quiller laughed. "We'll drain that out of you, have no fear. Bury trust, Colin. It has no place in the world that's coming, that's almost here." Quiller stood up, hands in his pockets, shoulders hunched. "You find it hard to digest all this, and I don't blame you. You can't kid me, Colin. I'm not fooled."

McFerrin's mouth went dry at this. But then Quiller continued, and McFerrin could see that the bait had not been dropped. On the contrary, the blind fish was taking the line farther and farther than the hand could play it out.

"You're amazed, lad. You're astonished at our management of you and too damn boyish proud to show it. I understand, old son. It is wondrous, isn't it?" Quiller moved around the desk and came to McFerrin and tapped his knee with his pipe. "I understand," he said. And then he strolled to where the woman was sitting stiffly in the deep brown leather and touched the top of her head as if bestowing a priestly blessing. "He's all right," Quiller said. "Our boy is all right."

The woman gave no sign. She just sat in cold containment and let her head be touched.

At last Quiller said warmly, "A man to manage Pelias." Quiller seemed overcome by emotion, and then he *was* overcome by emotion—and McFerrin could see tears begin to well up in the man's large, handsome eyes.

He's insane, McFerrin stated matter-of-factly to himself—the man is utterly insane. Does she not see it? Don't the others? Douglas? The doctor? Whoever these other people are? Don't they know this man is insane? How could they not? And then McFerrin realized: of course they know—and that's what excites them, inspires them. Were not Hitler and the rest exciting *because* you *knew* they and their schemes were insane? Was that *not* why these men inspired their closest lieutenants to the maddest actions?

Quiller put his hand on McFerrin's shoulder. McFerrin wanted to leap from the touch. "Let me show you around a little before we eat."

"I've been here before," McFerrin said.

"But never had the grand tour before, lad. I just want to show you a couple of things. Let you get an idea of the big step forward you're about to take."

This indestructible good humor began to alarm McFerrin. For the idea came to him then that it might all be an act. Quiller suddenly seemed *too* congenial, *too* uncomplicated, too much the coach signing up the high school star and clownishly rejoicing, showing off the stately campus, the knockout cheerleaders, the fat steak dinners.

"Let's go downstairs to the War Room and see what's happening in the twentieth century and a forecast of how the twenty-first is shaping up."

McFerrin stood. The woman stayed seated. Quiller took McFerrin's arm and guided him toward the door. But just before Quiller opened the door, he paused. The tall man winked at McFerrin, increased the pressure on his arm rather considerably, and said, "You're not recording, lad, are you? Because I hope not. It is one thing to call you crazy if *you* speak out. But all this in my *own* voice! Well, I'd have to terminate you, wouldn't I? I'd have no choice, would I?"

McFerrin grinned. "Hell, Frank," he said, "there's no tape long enough that could keep up with all the greenery that runs out of your mouth. You're still the professor, man. And like every good student, I'm taking notes—but so far they're all in my head."

"Good, good," Quiller fairly crooned. "That's good, lad. Keep them there. So long as you keep them there, you'll keep the thing that contains them, right? Right, lad?" Quiller chuckled at what he thought a wonderful amusement. And then he opened the door. "Keep your head, old boy—that's the thing!" And he laughed loudly. And then he leaned to McFerrin and whispered, "Notice how freely I talk in here, boy? Here in the *White* House—in the President's playpen, as it were? That's because I keep my head, Colin. And because I make very sure nothing that comes out of it gets onto anybody's tape. You *are* clean, aren't you, lad?"

"You got a safer bet on me than on your office," McFerrin whispered back.

"That's *good*," Quiller said, still whispering, "because my office is as clean as a whistle—which means you're clean as a—as a——"

"How about a cunt hair on that broad you're so bananas about?"

It was going all the way. It was a run for home-free or a fall to your grave.

"A cunt hair on that broad," Quiller repeated, his voice coming out of the whisper now. "When it comes to cheek, boy, you could give cards and spades."

"I just speak what's in my heart and on my mind, Frank," McFerrin said aloud—and then laughed heartily but not too long—and made Quiller laugh by working him with his eyes—and then, when it looked good, when it felt to him that just the right mood had been achieved, McFerrin let himself be led along the stately hallway.

45

They had turned a corner and were heading down a flight of stairs when McFerrin heard a high-pitched intermittent tone sounding from somewhere on Quiller.

"Hold it," Quiller said, and reached into his coat pocket to punch the response button, the signal that he was calling in. "All right—come with me," he said to McFerrin.

They continued down the stairs, and when they reached the landing, Quiller stepped into a shallow alcove and raised the receiver of the telephone that rested on a shelf there.

"Four," he said into the receiver and waited. And then he said, "What is it, Alison?" And then he hung up. "The President," he said to McFerrin.

"What?"

"He wants me. It's all right. Come along. Time you saw how these things work, lad."

"I'm all ears," McFerrin said, smiling grandly and striving for the look of the earnest learner.

Together they returned to Quiller's office. "Okay, get him," Quiller said to Agajadian as they passed her desk. "Close it," Quiller said to McFerrin once they were inside the office. "Close it and sit there."

McFerrin kicked shut the door and took a seat where Quiller indicated. Then there was an intercom signal and the beautiful woman's voice saying, "He's on."

Quiller snatched up the receiver from one of the three telephones arranged on his desk—the blue phone, McFerrin noted.

"Yes, Mr. President," Quiller said.—"I can talk, sir, yes." —"I hadn't heard that, sir, no." —"May I ask where that information comes from, sir?" —"I see." —"How long ago?" —"Has Fort Meade verified it, sir?" —"Do we dare ascertain through D.I.A.?" —"My suggestion, sir, is do nothing." —"Obviously, it's a matter of gravest concern if the Pentagon is acting independently and, moreover, in defiance of national policy—your Administration's objectives.

"On the other hand, until we can actually prove Pentagon management of the operation, to all intents and purposes it's still a civil matter confined to Greek soil and Greek combatants. In other words, so far as the world will know, these are Greeks revising their own government by force, and we've got to stay out of it unless we can prove otherwise. Unless we have the provable facts of U.S. military connivance with Greek military forces, we'd sound like hysterics if we went after the Joint Chiefs publicly.

"You agree, Mr. President?" —"Assuming the Greek military *succeeds* in gaining the government, we'll put our people on Pelias and protect them so that he can speak in open opposition to the military junta. Assuming the Greek military *fails*—well, then we have no problem, none save getting ourselves in gear and slapping back Poucher where he belongs." —"I don't see what else we can do at this stage, sir.

"Yes, sir, that's my thought too, we'll simply have to hold our water and see how things turn out." —"Has C.I.A. been informed or done any informing?" —"Well I don't understand that, either, sir. We cannot run an effective show if we must depend on British Intelligence and Israeli Intelligence for stuff we should be getting from our own people." —"Oh I assure you, Mr. President, they *are* our own people still. Things haven't gotten *that* far out of hand, except D.I.A. perhaps and Poucher's crew.

"Tonight? At what time? All right, eight-thirty. All networks?" —"That doesn't give me very long, Mr. President, but I will do my best, of course." —"Yes, I naturally agree."—"I'm not hedging, Mr. President—I agree that it is probably important that the nation see you are uninjured and in good spirits and that they have a statement of your continuing will to go into the streets and meet the people and discuss the issues face to face.

"All right, sir. If you wish. Yes, I can come by now, sir, and we can make a few notes. And then I'll do a first draft of the speech for you to go over." —"Shall I come directly, then?" —"All right. While I'm at it, I'd like to bring by one of my old boys from Yale. You met him briefly once before, and I think you passed one or two sentences between you on your mutual interest in Lincoln scholarship." —"That's right—you remember him, the historian. He's doing his doctoral dissertation on some aspect

of Lincoln, yes. Your memory is amazing, sir."
—"Yes, I'd be delighted to bring him by for a
minute if you're feeling up to it, sir." —"He's in my
outer office now, yes." —"It's good to hear you
laugh again, Ed. No, really, I guess I'm still the
proud teacher who likes to show off for his students."
—"Thank you, Mr. President—he'll be thrilled, I
know." —"Thank you, Mr. President, we'll be right
over, Ed."

"What the hell was *that* all about?" McFerrin
said when Quiller put down the phone.

"Simple," Quiller said, standing now and fumbling around on his desk top for his pipe and his
tobacco. "Poucher's proceeded exactly as I projected. When he failed to bring off the termination
in Kansas City yesterday, he moved on his plan to
set the Greek generals in motion against the G.L.O.
With Pentagon backing, the popular government
will fall in a matter of hours. Our objective precisely—and now that the J.C.S. have tipped their
hand there, we get their asses, too. Lovely. Meanwhile the Agency's obviously sitting back as long as
they dare to because they want to get back that
foothold in Greece for countless reasons. Only
problem for the Company is that management has
waited a few hours too long. So now Drexel and
Miller get their nuts nipped off because all the info
is coming from the limeys and the yids. C.I.A. has
kept silent. N.S.A. is talking, but all they're doing
is confirming what the British and the Israelis have
already told Danforth's office. Lad, lad, it's a great
day for us—it shows how our team can put a package together and sell it right into reality."

"Sounds great, Frank." McFerrin stood up from

THE STAR SPANGLED CONTRACT

his seat on the couch and took a pack of matches from Quiller's desk and fired up one of his little cigars and then struck a second match to hold to Quiller's newly packed pipe.

"So when do I meet the rest of your cadre and who the hell *are* they? A grouper likes to know who the other groupers are. I don't like working with shadows."

"All in good time, old thing—all in good time," Quiller said, again putting his arm around McFerrin's shoulder. "It seems to me you've met quite enough of our people for now."

"Well, Frank," McFerrin said, "to tell you the honest to God truth, that broad out there with the legs and the rest of it could be your whole group and I'd enlist for a lifetime hitch. Am I right, old buddy?" And McFerrin slapped Quiller on the back and said, "Okay, leader, take me to your President," and laughed heartily.

"I *thought* you'd get a kick out of it," Quiller said. "Good. And none too soon, too. I mean, charming Eddie's not for the Presidency much longer."

"How so? I thought your motion was not to off him."

"True, lad. But *now* there's no need to, even if one might have now and then thought there *had* been. With the Poucher move, we've accomplished three objectives with one blow, just as we planned it. The Pentagon's ass, the Greek coup we wanted, and Burlingame's humiliation and therefore his defeat at the polls in November. I mean, if I can't persuade Ed to step down before it comes to that. I told you all this at Lawn Crest, and now it's coming *true*, boy. You see? The machinery's already lined up to assure the nomination of his successor—but you have a few chores to perform before I can go into that with you."

Quiller glanced at his watch. "Meanwhile, however, Edward Burlingame is our President, and we don't want to keep a President waiting, do we?"

"I hear," McFerrin said. "Let's hit it, then."

"Just a minute or so, Colin—and then I'm afraid you'll have to pop off. Call me late this afternoon, and I'll have instructions on your entry into Greece and some detailed guidance on handling the Pelias assignment. And if I'm still working with Burlingame on his speech, then Miss Agajadian will convey my instructions."

As they left the office, McFerrin made certain Quiller saw him eye the beautiful woman sitting elegantly and coolly at her desk.

"That's choppin' in tall cotton, Professor Quiller," McFerrin said, punching the older man on the arm, lightly, with seeming envy, advertising himself as a man with nothing on his mind but irrepressible lust.

46

"My pleasure to see you again, young man," Edward Burlingame said to Colin McFerrin, coming from behind his desk and holding out his hand in greeting.

"I'm honored, sir," McFerrin said, and shook the President's hand firmly, his legs weak with the possibility of the moment. Was this happening? Had Quiller, in his manic enthusiasm, actually put him in touch with the one man who could stop it all and with whom a hearing would be otherwise out of the question?

"Sit down, gentlemen," Burlingame said, and waved McFerrin and Quiller to chairs.

"Mr. McFerrin will occupy no more than a moment, Mr. President," Quiller said as he seated himself and began searching his pockets for pipe and tobacco and matches, his manner, McFerrin observed, purposely slouchy, offhand, theatrically professional, just your crumpled, regular-guy egghead, harmless and cute. Well, McFerrin thought, I'm playing my game too—the bushy-tailed womanizer and now the wide-eyed citizen agape at meeting the President of the United States, stunned by the reality of being here in the famed Oval Office. I'm stunned, all right, McFerrin considered, but it's expectation that has me overwhelmed, *how* to do what I must do? *When? How?* McFerrin could feel the current rising in him, a streaming electric excitement coursing up from his groin.

This was it! It has all been pointing to *this!* But *when? How?*

The President was chattering on amiably, charmingly, asking McFerrin how his work on Lincoln was coming along, had he turned up anything new, something that would shock the very foundations of Lincoln scholarship or, more happily, shore them up—and McFerrin was responding with the usual forms, making the sort of polite small talk that he knew was expected, that would flash no alarm in Quiller's direction. But the time was elapsing, and McFerrin knew it was limited time that was elapsing, that only moments remained before Quiller would make McFerrin's excuses, say that he had to rush off to something, then see that McFerrin was ushered from the room.

And then he did it. Quiller did it!

"Colin's already late for a meeting with the Lincoln librarian at the Smithsonian, Ed. I hate to break this up, to tear you Honest Abe maniacs apart, but the young professor is late, and you and I have hurried business, Mr. President."

Now! Start now!

"Mr. President," McFerrin said, rising from his chair to elude Quiller as he came toward him to escort him out. "Mr. President, I never got a chance to ask you how you're feeling since the Kansas City incident. I mean, I hope you're feeling in proper spirits, sir."

"Young man, that's the subject, in part, of an address to the nation I plan to make this evening," the President said. "I want to assure the people that I'm in the pink and raring to get on with the business of government—our government and the government of Greece—that is, my anxiety over the possibility of trouble for the popular government now holding sway there. In any event, I'm fine, young man—and I thank you for your kind concern. I'm glad to have had a little visit—and I do hope you'll stay in touch with old Franklin here so that I might see you from time to time. Good luck with your Lincoln work and with your teaching. That's what the kids need now—level-headed fellows like you in the classroom."

The President was coming forward to grasp McFerrin's hand. His face was fixed with a generous smile, and it was clear to McFerrin that there was no extending this conversation in any graceful way. The three men were standing now, the President holding out his hand to McFerrin, Quiller taking McFerrin by the arm to steer him away once McFerrin had shaken the President's hand.

The President's hand was out, had already been held out there too long.

"Mr. President," McFerrin said, "I wonder if it would be at all possible for me to arrange to see your Lincoln memorabilia sometime? I mean, if it's accessible in a way that would not inconvenience you, sir, I'd be grateful to have a look one day."

"Yes, yes, of course, Colin," Quiller was saying, taking McFerrin's arm by the elbow.

But then the President said, "Why, yes—that would be no problem, none at all. As a matter of fact, Mr. McFerrin, I keep a few items right here in the office, three or four of my favorite artifacts—if you'd like to———"

"Yes," Quiller said. "We could see to that some other time. I'm sure, Colin———"

But the President raised his hand from where it was poised to grasp McFerrin's, raised his hand to McFerrin's shoulder to guide him away to the cabinet that stood against the wall behind his desk. "I see no reason for you not to have a look at these right now, so long as you're here. Have you ever seen the map of Booth's flight to the Garrett farm?" And as the President was turning McFerrin away with him in the direction of the cabinet, he called back to Quiller: "Frank, this won't take long. We'll get to that damned speech straightaway, my word. In the meanwhile, see how we stand on the Underwood funeral procession this afternoon. My secretary has the routine facts, but maybe you could find out how the hell long I'll really have to hang around, what's the latest I can show up without looking disrespectful, that sort of thing."

"Ed—" Quiller said, his voice edged now but not following the name with anything more. He stood in the middle of the floor for a moment, then gave a barely perceptible shrug and left the Oval Office.

McFerrin gave himself all the time he could. The instant he heard the door close behind Quiller, he wheeled in a half-circle to face the President square on. He locked on the President's eyes, held them in

345

his, invested in his own eyes a signal of dire urgency and utter sincerity, and then he said:

"Quiller. He's a traitor. He's insane. He's manipulating you and international events. He's an Agency man—deep, *inside* Agency. His group has penetrated to the heart of the government. They'll ruin you. The Pentagon wants to kill you, and Quiller wants to ruin you. I beg you, sir, believe what I say. Now smile, Mr. President, and look amused, because he could come back at any moment.

"Do you realize what you are saying, young man?" the President said. But he was smiling, beaming broadly, as a matter of fact—no less the stage actor than the other two men in the drama that would bind them all together in history. "Give me proof. Perhaps *you* are insane. Perhaps you're not. Let me see proof."

The President was still smiling, still looking as if what was unfolding before him were an immensely amusing entertainment. As for McFerrin, he was stunned that he had gone this far, stunned too that he'd *gotten* this far.

Proof? What proof did he have? Certainly he had no proof connecting *Quiller* to anything. His mind ranged frantically over the weeks of his pursuit and flight.

What proof? What one thing could he offer as incontestable proof?

And then he had it. Good Christ, how obvious! Good Christ, how obvious and inescapable and Jesus God Almighty true!

"My death," McFerrin said just as Quiller re-entered the room.

"All set, lad?" Quiller said jovially. "Feel better

now that you fellas have compared toy soldiers. Forgive me, Ed," Quiller said, taking McFerrin's arm again, "but I guess I've never been much of a Lincoln buff—except where he surfaces in constitutional law."

"Thank you, Mr. President," McFerrin mumbled as he made for the door under Quiller's escort. McFerrin was conscious of his breathing and wondered if his voice had held to its natural pitch.

"All right, old son, on your way now," Quiller said, shaking McFerrin's hand. "Don't forget—call in later this afternoon, and I'll let you know if I can squeeze you into my Georgetown class."

"You bet," McFerrin said. "Good-bye, Mr. President," he called out over Quiller's shoulder.

"Good-bye now, young man—and good luck!" the President called out, back behind his desk now.

Once into the hallway, McFerrin quickly sought an exit. But he needn't have worried. The security man who promptly moved in to take him under tow guided McFerrin swiftly along the route out. Lingering was not welcome in the White House these days, and in no time at all McFerrin was on Pennsylvania Avenue waiting for a cab.

"An unusual young man," Edward Burlingame said when McFerrin was safely away. "What do you know about him, his background?"

"Oh, yes," Quiller said. "First rate—a truly earnest scholar and an outstanding performer all around. A fine record of intelligence and espionage work in Greece and Vietnam until he resigned to go into teaching. Much respected by Pelias, by the way. Fact is, Ed, it occurs to me to suggest Colin as the perfect emissary to carry word of our support and protection to Professor Pelias. We might consider it—see what Otis thinks, since that's his bailiwick."

"Not in the cards, I'd say, Franklin." The President pushed back on his reclining desk chair and folded his arms. "The fellow's unstable, I'd say— clearly strained himself to the limit.- Too much study, I'd guess—those airless library research cubicles. If I were you, as his friend, I'd check his medical background."

"Oh?" Quiller said, touching his fingertips together meditatively, his pipe jutting from his patrician jaw. "What gave you such an extreme opinion?"

The President unfolded his arms and clasped his hands behind his neck.

"Come on, Franklin—time to get cracking on a draft of that speech. Make some notes, please, while I just run through the points I want to cover."

"No, really, Ed—I'm worried," Quiller said. "I'm very fond of McFerrin, and inasmuch as I've been thinking of a way to bring him back into government work, your remarks concern me. What gave you the feeling the young man is unwell?"

"Hell, Franklin," the President said. "I'm no psychiatrist."

"But I haven't the vaguest idea what tipped you to trouble, Mr. President."

The President brought his arms down and started toying with a pencil on his desk. He tapped it neatly against a clean pad, beating a cadence, his eyes cast down to the pad. He looked up.

"We're wasting time with trivia, Franklin," the President said, abruptly coming forward in his chair and discarding the pencil with a sharp toss. "Now let's *go*, my friend, and get to *work* here. We've already consumed precious minutes on something I really don't have time for. Take this pad and pencil, man, and let's get *busy. Please.*"

"My apologies, sir," Quiller said, reaching out to take up the note-taking materials. "I had no idea the fellow was off his bean." He dismissed the subject with a self-deprecating shake of his head. "Now, then, Mr. President," Quiller said, the pencil poised to begin, "let's sketch out the highlights of what you'll be saying tonight."

"Begin," the President of the United States of America said, "with a statement of my good health and the general tranquility of the union, *et cetera, et cetera*——" And then Edward Burlingame laughed.

"Come now, Mr. President," Franklin Quiller said, "let's be serious."

But the laughter did not drive out the tension now between them. For both men now knew that they would do well to know more—and both men now suspected there was more to be known.

But the President of the United States would not elevate suspicion into something conclusive until he was given cause; he could wonder, yes—yet he would let what was very likely a foundless charge rest where it was until there was reason to do otherwise. But now he would look for that reason.

Franklin Quiller, however, converted suspicion into conclusion as readily as milk soured into curd. Franklin Quiller did not need to prove his guess. He *knew* it!

He knew the starry-eyed flag-waving doublecrosser had *talked!*

Quiller contained himself. He took notes for three or four minutes, and then he excused himself from the Oval Office, begging the President for a few moments to return to his office to secure the secret file on Greece. He apologized for having come not entirely prepared and quickly left the room.

As he went along the corridor, he knew that now he had no choice. The fool had talked—Quiller was sure of it! There was no other option now—because now there was no telling what the President knew— or how much he would presently believe—or try to prove if he were given the *time*. Now it was finished! There was *himself* to save—because at the least Burlingame would *suspect*, and at the most Burlingame would in time be able to prove.

As Quiller passed Alison Agajadian's desk, he said, "Any word from Vlednik?"

"None," the woman said.

"All right. Get me Poucher on the phone. Use the Red Alert line. *Fast!* And get me the Greece file."

Quiller was behind the desk when she buzzed. The nylo-strap was off the receiver. He raised it. He said, "Poucher?"

"Speaking."

"Quiller here."

"I know."

"Get him now. He's having you arrested within forty-eight hours. As soon as he's cleared it with the Justice Department. Do you understand me?"

"Yes. But why should I believe you?"

"Take your chances, then. I have no time to argue. Get him. Soonest."

"I heard you. Is that all?"

350

"Yes."

"I'm hanging up."

"One minute. McFerrin. You want him, you can have him. He left here minutes ago. He's a walking bomb—he could blow us all up."

"You're talking from the White House?"

"Of course."

"Good-bye," General Poucher said, and cut the connection.

Quiller replaced the heavy red receiver and smiled. Then he rose from his desk and moved rapidly along the route back to the Oval Office. "I'm sorry, Mr. President," he said when he got there and opened the folder Alison Agajadian had handed him on his way back.

47

"So where to, fella?"

"Just drive for a while until I make up my mind," McFerrin said.

"Come on, buddy—this ain't the movies. Now, where do you want to go? I need a destination for the log."

McFerrin gave Greenfield's address, the cabbie threw the clock, and as the taxi shot away from the curb, McFerrin could hear news coming over the radio.

"Hey, kick that up louder, okay?" he called to the driver.

It was a bulletin coming through—the fall of Athens to General Akonimedes, eighteen months exiled in Spain, now in power again and triumphantly welcomed back to the helm of government by the free people of Greece. Also returning with Akonimedes were eight other exiled generals, eleven colonels, and fifteen hundred combat soldiers (trained in Fort Benning, McFerrin guessed), forty infantry-landing craft (built in Alabama?), forty gunboats (built in Delaware?), and several dozen Tiger Cat aircraft (built in California?). A Pentagon spokesman announced it had had no previous indication of the coup. The Joint Chiefs of Staff, it was further announced, had examined the situation and concluded that this appeared to be a genuine and spontaneous uprising of the Greek people against a Kremlin-dominated government. It was acknowleged that some elements of the American Sixth Fleet, which had just completed maneuvers near Cyprus, were located off the coast of Greece but that their presence there was without significance.

The announcer went on to report that Wall Street reacted promptly to the news coming out of Greece, that stocks were rising across the board, with important gains being made by Grumman, Northrop, Sperry Rand, Dow Chemical, General Dynamics, General Motors, I.T.&T., Boeing, and Lockheed.

Secretary of State Danforth issued a statement expressing grave concern. "Peace in the Mediterranean," he said, "like peace everywhere, is the primary desire of the American people. We deplore the present outbreak of violence in Greece and hope that the civil war just concluded there will secure the best interests of the people of Greece and of all mankind." The Secretary of State ended his remarks by calling upon all Americans to join him in his prayers for a just and lasting peace. There was an interruption for a brief commercial message followed by an updated Washington forecast, and then, strangely, the voice of the Secretary of State was heard again, urging the Security Council of the United Nations to restrain itself from taking any precipitous action, to postpone action for at least ten days in order to allow the situation in

Greece time to seek a calmer level and to give
the people of Greece an opportunity to express their
preference for leadership between the competing
factions. "Self-determination," said the Secretary of
State, "is the keystone of freedom," and then the
news item ended, five commercials followed, and
rock music started screaming from the speaker.

"Turn that shit down, okay?" McFerrin called to
the cabbie.

"Make up your mind, mister," the cabbie snapped
back—but lowered the volume.

The car was wheeling through increasingly heavy
traffic. McFerrin stared out at the clogging streets
and the lowering sky. Rain seemed to be building up,
a downpour. He slapped his pockets for his tin of
cigars and then realized he'd smoked his last Schim
in Quiller's office.

All right, McFerrin listed his schedule, three
things: get cigars, get a gun, get Valerie. Get the hell
out, too. But where? He'd figure that later. First
cigars—he was crazy for a smoke. Then a gun, and
there was every chance that Dan had kept one at his
place and that his wife would know where it was.
Money! He'd need money. Valerie? She'd be at her
office, and there was no calling her there. And his
checkbook was back at his apartment. Go there?
No, better not. Valerie was the best bet for money
if he could get through to her at Fort Meade and
if she could get away to cash a check before the
banks closed.

"Stop here," he shouted to the driver when the
traffic had come to a standstill on a busy commercial street. "Here," McFerrin said. He handed the
driver the exact fare and tip, stepped quickly from

the taxi onto the sidewalk, trotted down the block several doors, and then cut in under a canopy and hustled through the lobby of the Buckley Hotel. It was then he remembered the room at the Marriott Inn, but just as suddenly he realized that that was no good either. No, nowhere in the metropolitan area would make any sense. He had to get the hell out and be long *gone.*

The lobby was eerily quiet, ornate walls papered black and gold, the rug that spread out from him in all directions blood red and thick and very deep. McFerrin turned into the darkened bar, walked to the far side, and sat in one of the booths, picking the side that faced the entrance. It was even quieter in here—"hushed" was the way to describe it. The only other customers were a man and a woman seated at opposite ends of the bar.

The waitress came up—dressed like a miniskirted French maid, a bit of flouncy black and a white doily for an apron, black net stockings adorning her very evident thighs and legs.

"Coffee," McFerrin said.

"We don't serve coffee here," she said. "You have to go to the dining room for that."

"You have Irish Coffee?" he said.

"Yes."

"Okay. Tell the bartender to make me an Irish Coffee—and leave out the whiskey."

The waitress hesitated, then made a note on her pad and left.

A small, stocky, middle-aged woman in brown and white shoes entered and took a booth to McFerrin's right. She began fumbling through her purse, found the pack of cigarettes she was looking for, and lit one. McFerrin remembered. Cigars. He stood up and quick-walked to the newsstand in the lobby. "I'll take these," he said to the woman behind the counter. He threw down a bill and moved swiftly back to the bar.

A short, skinny man entered, looked around, and went over and joined the woman in the booth. They started laughing almost immediately. McFerrin studied them a moment. The man patted the woman's hand and she giggled. The waitress came back and set his glass in front of him. McFerrin sampled it. It was Irish Coffee, whiskey and all. Shit! He wanted his head very clear. But what the hell. He stoked up a Schim and downed the Irish Coffee before it had time to cool. He felt better, more alive than he'd felt in months, in years.

Okay. *Think*, man. *Call* Valerie? No—no good. Too risky. Gun, cash, Val—and then figure out things from there. Did the President believe him? *Would* he? Probably not. But there had been no choice, nothing else McFerrin could have done. It was a long shot but the best shot. And if the President did believe him, what would he do? And if he *didn't*, what then? Who the hell knew!

McFerrin's mind teemed with questions. He smoked his cigar, considered another glass of Irish coffee, and then thought better of it. Just sit quiet for a while, *that* was the thing—collect your thoughts, man.

Two men entered, one considerably older than the other. McFerrin examined them as they sat down, heard them talking, the younger man about his child, the other looking pleased. Probably father and son, McFerrin guessed. Then two more men, in

Ivy League suits, entered the bar, made their way to a booth nearby, sat, and began chatting about the improved stock market. Broker types, McFerrin decided, or lawyers.

Then McFerrin suddenly noticed that the little hefty woman and her friend had stopped talking. He glanced their way in time to find her looking at him, her almond eyes clearly studying him. She looked away quickly, as if caught at something. McFerrin froze to attention.

Then three men entered the bar, laughing loudly, and their laughter flashed an alarm through McFerrin's stomach. For he suddenly realized that, in the less than ten minutes he had been there, nine people had been added to the lounge. And no one had departed. The population of the lounge had increased at the rate of one patron per minute. Where there had been two customers besides himself, now there were eleven. For a quiet bar off a nearly deserted hotel lobby, and in the early afternoon, such a rate of increase could not be accidental.

McFerrin glided out of his booth, his manner indifferent, nothing changed in his movements. He strolled over to the bartender, loudly ordered another Irish coffee, and loudly said that he would be right back.

Once in the lobby, he quickened his pace. No, not the street! He headed for the mezzanine floor. He took the stairs—and when he reached the second landing, he looked back and saw the two Ivy League types were at the foot of the stairs and starting up. Were the others coming too—or had they fanned out and covered the exits? McFerrin ducked into the men's room, saw the glazed window at the far end, raced across the tiled floor, and jerked the window open. Even as he saw the alley below, he was sliding out. He hung by his fingertips for an instant— long enough to hear hurried footsteps on the tiles and to register his stupidity: Quiller was no fool. From the start he must have given instructions to tail McFerrin when he left the White House! Then McFerrin let go. He landed hard, buckled onto one arm for an instant, and then was off and running. He headed toward the laundry truck parked squarely in the middle of the alley, saw the two men loading up laundry bags from a side door of the hotel, had almost reached the truck when he heard the soft pop of a silencer.

McFerrin saw the red dust spray as the bullet slammed the brick wall opposite. He raced past the truck, his mind snatching up the image of the two laundry workers jammed into statues by their fear, eyes wide, mouths yanked open.

He ran even harder now, head low, heard the cushioned pop of the second shot but didn't see where it hit. He veered sharply, to fake out the shooter, and bounded hard off the building to one side. He made it to the end of the alley, blasted into a right-angle turn, and then felt the pain stabbing in his shoulder. Had he been hit? No, the pain was too large. It must have been from the jolt he took when he ricocheted off the wall.

He sprinted onto the sidewalk, slowed to a fast trot, had not yet caught his breath when he saw a cab coming, flagged it down and rolled in, still trying to catch his breath.

He wanted to look back to see if anyone had seen him get in the cab, but the taxi had already pulled into traffic and McFerrin's view was blocked.

"Lincoln Memorial," he snapped—just to name a place. He let his head back onto the seat, shut his eyes, felt the pain putting out fingers into his right arm now. He rested this way for a while, and then he opened his eyes and saw that rain was falling lightly, the windshield sprinkling with rain that the wipers now scuffed away but that covered the glass again, the cycle repeating and repeating.

"Jesus," McFerrin muttered. "Is there anything stopping the shitfall? Is there any making it now?"

He wrenched around in his seat to check through the rear window. It was hard to see. He made a memory print of the cars he saw so that when he checked again he'd know if any of them were especially constant, part of a pattern.

The cab turned onto Constitution Avenue. After two blocks McFerrin looked out the back window again. The taxi had moved into a new flow of traffic, and McFerrin saw no cars behind that looked familiar. He faced forward, reached for his Schims, and then reminded himself that he'd left them in the booth to underscore his announcement that he'd be back. Goddamn! He was right where he'd started —in a goddamn cab going nowhere at all and without a smoke!

All right, for*get* the goddamn *smoke!* Think, man! McFerrin screamed at himself. What move would be the right move when they got to the Memorial? Stay with the cab and give him a new destination? If there were enough visitors at the Memorial, it might be a good place to switch from this cab to another.

Now—beyond the spire of the Washington

Monument just ahead—McFerrin could see the marble temple at the far end of the long, grassy mall. It was glistening in the growing rain, and now he could make out the colossal figure seated there. The car closed on the marble structure, and McFerrin could see tourists beginning to move away from the statue toward shelter. Some were going up the steps inside the monument itself; others jogged toward the sight-seeing busses parked nearby.

Underneath the large oak tree just ahead, a man was waving furiously. McFerrin hunched forward. "Pick that man up! I'll get out here!"

The cab pulled off the road under the tree. The other man got in. "Thanks," he said. "Pretty darn wet out there."

McFerrin stuck a five-dollar bill in the driver's hand and got out. As he shut the door, he heard the man name the Holiday Inn in East Arlington, a fare that would take the cab across the Potomac.

McFerrin loped toward the Monument, and then he ran on past it and bolted for the tourist busses, made it to the nearest bus, and pressed in among the other passengers. He slipped into a seat in the rear, and the bus lumbered off behind two other busses. Somewhere in front someone blew a party horn. Now half a dozen men produced red and white cardboard horns and joined in. The others in the bus yelled, "Yeah, Bama!" A moon-faced man next to McFerrin began unscrewing the cap of a pint bottle. McFerrin slumped into his seat and stared at the rain washing over the windows. His shoulder ached, his right arm throbbed. The boozer next to him tipped the mouth of the bottle in invitation. McFerrin took it, raised it in a gesture of gratitude, and then drank off a long pull. And then another.

The bus was finally headed home now. The Birmingham Boosters were singing "Stars Fell on Alabama" and then "Oh! Susanna," and then they fell into drunken silence. The moon-faced man next to McFerrin kept staring at him. At last, his speech boozy, he asked how come McFerrin was sitting next to him since he wasn't any Birmingham Booster the moon-faced man had ever before seen. No, McFerrin said, he wasn't a Booster but worked for the tour service and was making a spot check of the operation. The man tried to focus his eyes on McFerrin, finally gave up, and fell back against his seat in a drunken stupor.

The first bus trundled across the bridge. Now McFerrin's bus crawled forward, following the second bus. Suddenly the Boosters broke into a howling chorus of "Go Alabama, Go Crimson Tide," and the moon-faced man opened his eyes and joined in the general uproar.

At last the bus came alongside the two already parked in the lot of the Howard Johnson Motel on Virginia Avenue. Huddling in with the others, McFerrin ran through the pouring rain into the lobby, then separated from the group, took a stairway down to the basement, found the right door, and came out into the hotel garage. Against the far wall he saw two attendants in coveralls. They were lounging against a limousine, their backs to McFerrin. McFerrin shouted, "Hey! Hey, chief! The key's not in my goddamn car. I left it on the dash, and now it's not there.

Both attendants turned, startled.

"Which one?" the younger man shouted.

"Right here, dammit!" McFerrin shouted, touching a purple Plymouth, the automobile that happened to be nearest him.

"Hold it, buddy. I'll check the board. You ain't supposed to leave your keys in the car. Somebody must've caught it and took them to the office. Just hold your horses, I'm coming!" the attendant called as he approached. "What stall is it?" he said as he got nearer.

"Fifteen," McFerrin quickly answered—and then to sell it all the way, he added—"Come on, fella, make it snappy. I got me some class stuff waiting, the best you can get in this goddamn town. Let's *go*, man."

The attendant disappeared into the office while McFerrin smacked the hood in rhythm in a show of vast impatience, keeping it up until the attendant reappeared.

"Here you go, man," the attendant said, tossing the keys to McFerrin. "Gonna nail yourself a little nooky now, are you? Sheet!" The attendant laughed and turned his back on McFerrin, going into a jive-ass skipping routine across the garage floor, sing-songing in a voice loud enough for McFerrin to hear, "Ain't he the bad-ass now! Ain't he just the *baddest!* These motherfuckers gonna be the *death* of us, they all so groovy and *bad!* Sheet!"

McFerrin cut toward southeast Washington, holding his speed as high as the traffic would let him. He glanced in the rear-view mirror, saw no sign of pursuit, turned right, and drove two blocks until he came to 24th Street. Now he was far enough away to return to Virginia Avenue. But his return to the Avenue was slower than his departure. The traffic had begun to thicken. Back on Virginia, he headed southeast.

He knew where he was going now. He drove slowly through the immense downpour. Yes, he knew where he was going.

48

But it was going wrong at the start.

The A.P. receptionist said the bureau chief was out; come back later.

Some assistant manager at U.P.I. listened to a couple of sentences, asked to be excused, and never returned.

At the Washington office of *Time*, McFerrin waited fifteen minutes until a secretary reappeared with the word that no one was free at the moment; call first before coming next time.

He went down the line, now racing against the clock—because Valerie would be getting out of her office any minute, making the drive back from Fort Meade, and he wanted to catch her, across the street from the building if necessary, before she returned to his place. That was out of bounds for them now. He had an hour, an hour and a half at most.

The traffic was impossibly dense in this rain, slowed to a crawl on every thoroughfare.

He tried *Newsweek*. No go.

At the Washington bureau of *The New York Times*, he got as far as the man who handled the national news desk—but as soon as McFerrin got into it, the man began grinning tolerantly. He nodded, muttering, "Yes, of course—yes, of course —just *imagine*——" and McFerrin could see he'd wasted his time again.

He rose to go. Standing now, he said, "Fuck you, Jack!" and then almost had to laugh at himself for confirming the bastard's impression.

He tried the *Star*. Useless.

What did he have left now? Forty minutes at best.

The *Post!* Why hadn't he thought of *The Washington Post* in the first place? Had not it proved its courage with its hardheaded investigative work on Watergate?

The *Post* was the place!

He parked a block away, as near as he could get, and ran through the torrential cloudburst to the entrance of the building. He was soaked. Who the hell would pay him any attention looking like this?

But they did!

After two brief preliminary interviews—with the assistant to the national news editor and then with the editor himself—McFerrin was quickly ushered into the office of the managing editor.

The man came smiling forward from behind his desk, his cozy-lined office so assuring that McFerrin wanted to weep with relief.

"I'm Archer—Harry Archer," the pleasant man said. "Everybody here calls me Harry. You're Mc-Ferrin, right? Mind if I call you Colin? The boys say you've got one hell of a story to tell—and I'd like to hear it."

He shook McFerrin's hand as if McFerrin were the one person in all the world he right now most wanted to see.

"Have a seat, McFerrin. You look all out, young man, really done in. And you're drenched. Can we get you a drink? Coffee? Which is it?"

"Some bourbon," McFerrin said. "No ice."

"You got it," Archer said. "And I'll join you—though at my age," the older man said as he walked over to the wet bar built into the wall, "you don't take it neat anymore. But I'm still a bourbon man, I don't mind admitting."

"Can I use your phone?" McFerrin said.

"Feel free," Archer said, his back to McFerrin as he poured the whiskey.

McFerrin dialed his apartment. He let it ring and ring. No answer. He checked his watch. Five past five. Okay, he could still maybe catch her downstairs.

"I'm in a hurry, Mr. Archer," he called to the gray-haired man at the bar, and without turning, Archer called back: "It's Harry—Harry to all my boys here and Harry to you—Colin?"

"Sure, Harry—call me Colin. But come on—let's get into it."

"All right, son," Archer said as he turned around with two glasses. "Here's yours. Let's hit it, Colin. You talk. I'll listen. What exactly is this story of yours?"

Archer returned to his large, comfortable brown leather office rocker, put his feet up on the desk, and rolled the glass of whiskey between his palms, casting an encouraging look in McFerrin's direction.

"Okay, Colin. You tell your story. Tell it any way you like. I've got all the time in the world."

Archer smiled and took a sip of his drink and then cradled the glass on his paunch, his feet up, his head leaned comfortably back.

McFerrin talked. He told it all. He told it in all its incredible breadth and fantastic detail. And when he had finished, he checked his watch. Thirteen minutes. It had taken thirteen mniutes to get it all out, a blueprint for power that could force the direction of human history for who knew how many years, decades, generations. And only thirteen minutes to tell it.

He looked up at Archer—and raised his eyebrows in question, in supplication.

Archer brought his feet to the floor and came forward in his chair. "All right, Colin—if the story checks out, I'll print it. I'm with you, boy—and I'll print it! What do you say to that?"

"Thank God," McFerrin said—and noticed a buzzing in his legs. From excitement? From relief? From disbelief at being believed? He checked his watch again. Val. He had to head off Val before she stepped into the elevator and went upstairs. Get Val. How much time left? He looked at his watch. He studied the little numerals, the little markings that scaled the minutes. What—time— was—it? He couldn't tell, the numbers had gone running, were blurring, and now as he tried all the harder to read them, they began moving on the face of his watch, were now swimming in front of his eyes. The buzzing spread in widening waves up his legs and into his back. He groped upward, shoved himself up from the deep leather chair, his mind roaring with the knowledge of it.

"Drugged! You laid one into me!"

"Just a little tranquilizer to calm you down, boy."

McFerrin lunged across the desk, caught the man Archer by the neck. Then he drew back his arm, stiffened its length, and with fingertips straightened into the same iron plane, he drove forward into the man's throat.

Archer sagged in his chair.

McFerrin pulled back across the desk, pushed himself erect from the force that had dropped him to the desk top. He grappled for the telephone and slowly, slowly dialed.

It rang. It seemed to ring forever. And then he heard her voice.

"Hello?"

"Val! Colin. *Washington Post.* I've been whiffled. Archer, managing editor. Must be deep-cover media control. Don't know how long I can stay awake. Had to off him. All right, I killed the sonofabitch. Now get away from there! Get to lobby of the Sheraton Park. Wait there. I'm coming. You be there. Have cash. Gun. Gun too. If I make it, I make it."

"The Sheraton? A gun, Colin?"

"Go!" he yelled, and slammed down the receiver. He pushed away from the desk and staggered around it to drag Archer from his chair. He yanked the slumped form to the floor and hauled it across the carpet. The buzzing was into his chest now and moving out in a tide of vibrating bands into his arms and legs. But his head was still clear, still working. He got Archer to his private bathroom, jerked the dead weight in a short burst across the tiles, and slammed it against the shower stall. Then he stepped into the shower and turned on the cold full blast. His clothes were already soaked, and the explosion of water wet quickly through to his skin, the frigid shock-waves running against the rising tide of stupor that was moving in numbing advances toward his brain. He could feel his face going lax, his lips thickening, his eyelids slowly, slowly closing. But he could also feel the freeing water raising a shaft of life in his spine, little shrieks of stunned nerve-ends blitzed, holding him aloft in consciousness. He could feel the cold smack against the heavy torpor rolling through him, cracking small crevices in it, opening it up here and there, sending it back. But then he caved in, folded onto the floor of the stall, the blazing cold water crashing over him as he collapsed slowly and then, headlong skidding, passed out.

But it only took feeling himself slam into the porcelain to rouse him, to carry him flashing back to consciousness. And then, the exertion of mind and spirit and muscle like nothing he'd ever willed in him before, McFerrin was on his feet, his brain squeezed into a single jamming frequency, the one thought: *On your feet, you're on your feet!*

Now move!

He killed the streaming water, stepped soaking from the stall, stepped high over the crumpled body piled there, the movement of his flooded clothing now like knives of ice cutting slits of wakefulness into his legs and back.

Whatever it was the bastard had slipped him, it was receding, a temporary knock out rather than the real thing. A media man wouldn't handle a termination. Then the thought was shoved back by the enormous cold and the gross effort to move.

Move! Keep moving!

And he did. He dragged himself to the door of the bathroom, kicked it closed behind him, and then he was slogging across the carpet, water drenching from his shoes, pumped out into a trail behind him until his hand was on the knob and he was ready to go, no notion how he'd handle it, but he'd handle it.

He turned the knob and came out—into a crowd of newsroom workers arrayed before him like spectators, and he heard someone cry out, a woman, "What the hell is going on in there? Is Mr. Archer all right?" And then someone else, a kid's voice, a copyboy, shouted, "Hey, the guy's clothes are all wet! Look at the guy!" And then the woman again: "What the hell is going on in there?"

McFerrin couldn't focus their faces, but he could see them all coming forward, moving crazily at him, and he moved too, bellowing at the top of his lungs, howling and hurling himself through them: "Move it! Move it!" Bellowing the command, he ran through them, howling, "Move it! Move it!" and keeping it up until he was into the hallway and down the hall and then down another hallway, not knowing where this was leading him but sensing that if he kept it up, kept moving, something would lead him out—and then banging his way through a heavy plated door, he rolled through and was *out*.

Men in workmen's caps bustled around, and delivery trucks were lined up at a kind of dock—and McFerrin was coming awake enough now to see what this was, to see that this was the loading platform for delivery trucks, to see everything around him in growing detail, the rain splashing against the concrete ramp, the dollies piled with wired bundles of newspapers, and now even to see the banner headline, heavy black there at the top of each stack: JUNTA SEIZES ATHENS GOV'T.

He jumped from the platform, hit the concrete below, and quick-walked until he'd made it into the alley the trucks fed through, and then he was running.

And now he *ran.*

49

The rain had stopped.

He had been running—four, five blocks, he didn't know how many—when the rain shut off as if a faucet had been abruptly spun to.

And just as abruptly the late afternoon sun lit up the world around him, the fire of the angled sun turning everything orange and red and brilliant.

McFerrin felt exposed now, felt that the rain's ending and the light flooding back had exposed him, had lifted a cloak of invisibility from his back. He felt himself the lone player on an empty field, the stands all around filled to overflowing with the thousands that had come to see him traverse the yardage from one end zone to the other—with nothing to bring him crunching to the turf but the blazing light that shone all around.

And then he noticed that the streets were filling— not with men and women on their way home or men and women on their way to evening shifts but with people who just milled about as if waiting for something.

For *what?*

And then he heard the street noise growing, everything coming very alive, an activity preparing itself, a hum gaining volume, something situating itself into a state of readiness.

But what?

He was overcome by a strange feeling of being amidst preparations, as if something theatrical were about to be inaugurated by all the people that now stood expectantly around him, crowding the sidewalks and the street in increasing numbers—their voices colored by a kind of holiday expectancy, people getting ready for something—but what?

"What's happening?" He caught at the arm of a teen-age boy who stood beside him waiting for a crossing signal.

The boy turned on McFerrin, took in the condition of the man, the clothing, bunched into wet lumps, the wild expression of the face.

"Hands off, wino!" The boy sneered and jerked his arm away. "You never see a parade before, dad?"

"What parade? For what?"

"Some brass hat croaked. How the hell should I know? A funeral thing—a, you know—like for a funeral when you're a big deal. Fuck off, Jack—okay?" And the boy cut quickly into the crowd crossing at the intersection, turning to give McFerrin the finger when he'd gotten far enough away.

All right. Then it would be all the harder getting to the Sheraton Park with the speed he knew he'd have to make. There was no going back for the car. No chance moving it in this kind of crush and crazy to go back to anything he'd touched. Not now! Not anything ever again except Val. And that's all he wanted now—to touch her again—because now there was nothing else to want, nothing more to do —but get the hell away, get to a hole somewhere and put it all the hell behind you even if you never really could.

The Sheraton Park! Which way? Which direction? Where was he? He crossed just before the signal changed again and stood on the opposite corner, trying to get a fix on his position, collect himself, get his bearings. And then he slowly turned to get a feeling for what was all around him. They were after him, yes—but how close were they? Were they watching him now; did they see him standing like this, slowly revolving to see if he was seen? He couldn't tell, of course. All around, the street was dense with people milling. Who could tell anything in this? Who could conceivably have noticed anything out of the ordinary among the citizens lining the sidewalks all around for a look at what was coming by? The stocky, middle-aged woman that stood in brown and white shoes no more than eight paces from him was just a stocky middle-aged woman to even the most practiced eye. You would have to know her, have seen that face, see it when it contorted in pleasure as the body it went with was doing its special work, have seen it *that* way to recognize that this was no ordinary sidewalk pedestrian out to witness a funeral procession. Even if you'd seen her before, this very day, sitting comfortably at a hotel bar, you'd never isolate someone so ordinary from a crowd like this.

McFerrin saw this stocky, middle-aged woman just as he saw everyone else thronged about him, a creature of no significance, a human being on routine human business.

He had to push his way to the middle of the block. And then the press of onlookers was so great that his forward movement was stopped. Again he was seized by a feeling of strange suspension, the installing of something stagelike, a designed event about to begin. And then he heard the muffled dirge, slow drums. And very quickly the sound grew louder, the rhythm beating up to a fullness on down the block beyond. And then he suddenly remembered! Remembered the President's command to Quiller. Get the details on formalities and courtesies for— Underwood This was what it was! Underwood! A funeral cortege! The irony curled along McFerrin's spine and made him almost laugh.

Those who jammed the sidewalk to see now stood eight to ten deep, and McFerrin went up on tiptoes behind them to see too, to see the caisson-borne coffin draped in a rain-soaked flag and drawn by pairs of dun horses in tandem, an honor guard moving forward with it in solemn, stately march. But now a heightened energy suddenly charged through the people all around him. The word raced through the spectators, streaked along the walls of bodies flung up against the curb.

The President! A block to the rear! Walking there right in the middle of the street. Edward Burlingame was approaching, and everyone was going up on tiptoes and children were catching at their parents' clothes—what? What? What's coming? Who? And fathers reached down and carried the children onto their shoulders.

The President.

"You'll see, you'll see. Any minute now. Look that way, down there—he's coming, just be patient."

And in fact the man in front of McFerrin had just raised his young son aloft, was locating him comfortably on the saddle of his neck and shoulders, and McFerrin was seeing this little display and just beginning to register a feeling of *good* things, *old* things, *American* things, when a voice to his rear said:

"Colin McFerrin."

Reflex turned him.

"You make a move, I tear a hole in you that would make a wind tunnel."

It was a voice like none he'd ever heard—flat rolled steel running out from a spool. And seeing the face it issued from, a rather ordinary face, not unpleasant, almost agreeable and gentle really, the immense distance between the look of the face and the sound of the voice gave the words a quality not unlike something borne shrieking from hell.

"That's right," the stocky, middle-aged woman said. "Just freeze and keep it frozen."

He cast his eyes down—saw in the fold of her raincoat the weirdly freakish snout of the MAW-3 muzzle silencer poking brutishly three inches from his side at waist level.

He said, "The bar. At the Buckley," and the woman actually winked.

"Check," Adele Dietz said. "I like a little rye as much as the next one. Stand easy now, Colin— hands a little way out and back. You know how. You've been around. Do it."

The crowd was leaping all about him now, the

flame of anticipation sweeping higher as someone called out, "I can see him! It's him!"

McFerrin could hear a wave of applause rising far to his right and moving toward him. "Let me look. It's the President," he said.

"In a minute," Adele Dietz said.

"Yes," she said, first glancing away at an angle to her left. "More like thirty seconds now. Thirty here and twenty-five there." McFerrin followed her glance. He saw the orange umbrella, furled, raised high.

"It's what you call 'serendipity,' Colin—things just fall into perfect place for no apparent reason at all." Again, incredibly, the woman winked. "I call it 'serendipity,' " the woman said. "Now stand calm, boy. You blink an eye and I blow you away. Test me and you flunk," the stout little woman said.

McFerrin heard the drum roll fade, the caisson moving down the street, its creaking wheels and the treading pace of the honor guard overwhelmed now by the edge of applause that flashed closer, advancing from his right. Somewhere, on rooftop or in parked van, there would be rifles. And then he turned to the umbrella again, that brilliant orange, a beacon in sunlight.

"It's the generals" someone nearby shouted. "Will you look at the fruit salad on those babies!"

"Go Navy!" someone yelled.

McFerrin counted. His thought in that moment was that there was something useful in counting, in calling off the silent numbers into the listening microphone of his brain. He counted and watched the umbrella.

"You see it?" the woman said, glancing to that leftward angle.

But McFerrin did not answer.

Then the father standing in front said, "Billie, can you see him now? Can you see the President?"

The child had seen the generals and the admirals marching in solemn ceremony, had seen Poucher, Thorne, and Anson and Grissle and Keller, but then the child had seen something else, and in a seizure of delight he yanked at his father's hair to turn his attention to the thing he saw on television and bigger than the one at home, a little funny-looking, so long in front it was and probably not as easy to stick in your belt because it was very big and would jab you, but he wanted his father to see and get him one just like it anyway, and so he yanked on his father's hair and tried to turn his head around and down.

"Okay, okay!" the father howled in proud delight. "Take it easy, son. That's the President of the United States, all right, but for God's sake don't tear your old dad's hair out!" And he pulled his son's hands away and glanced briefly at McFerrin and the woman, wanting to acknowledge his pride and the embarrassment that rightly attended it. He would have said, "My son, some kid, huh?" or something on that order if he'd been able to catch the attention of these people—but they seemed utterly absorbed in the spectacle, and so the father faced forward again, shoving upward now to see the man his son was seeing for the first time in his life, a President, the President of the United States, right out there just over the heads of all these Americans who were also thrusting up and forward to catch a fleeting look at the man walking there, an ordinary man but their living idea of government, for better or for worse, the human embodiment of this nation's sense of itself, for better or for worse.

"Look now," the woman said.

McFerrin stretched himself up to see the President. And saw too the umbrella spring open, an orange dome aglow in strong sun. He was still counting, had counted to twenty-three and was holding himself stretched to his height and was on his toes for a count of two when the first crack split the air.

The first shot took the President to his knees, and the second two whirled him around and sent him skidding, skipping forward along the dark macadam still wet from summer rain. It was as if, though dead, the body would nevertheless keep pace with the procession that had now flung itself out in all directions in a panicked flight for cover to escape the cross fire that had shouted down on them and slammed them into silence—the huge quiet that gunshots leave behind.

But McFerrin did not see the President walking or falling, his line of sight blocked by the boy Billie riding on his father's shoulders in a pitch of near-frenzy to make him see the wonderful thing the woman held.

And then no one saw anything but people running.

And in the eye of that chaos there was now the tableau of two unmoving figures, only those two, and then the woman said:

"Hold it frozen, Colin. That's good."

And then the words hurried, as if she must insert

this speech in keeping with a precisely fixed schedule; she leaned close to McFerrin and hissed; "Don't you see *you* made this happen? Don't you see that when you warned him you forced our hand? Who's the fool? Who's the real assassin?"

But McFerrin was counting seconds, not caring anymore, not hearing anymore, just emptying himself out into the numbers whispered through him, each a warm wind blowing on his back—ten, nine, eight, seven, six, five, four—when the world opened a vast fold of space and time before he got to three and the count of two never happened because just then an ocean of ebony void rushed up and took him in when the amazing toy the woman held made a little rushing sound.

When the MAW-3 did its work, it was like someone puffing on a straw.

It was pandemonium there in that Washington street. That was how the press described it. Pandemonium helped explain the failure to uncover the assailant promptly. Or assailants—if there really *were* others. The firing had rained down from an odd elevation, and it would all take time before more was known. But the Secret Service pledged that more would be known. And damn quick. Meanwhile, the best that could be done had been done. For at least one potential assassin had been removed from the vicious ranks of those that would dare shoot down a President in the public thoroughfares and in the midst of so auspicious an occasion. This second or third gunman reportedly had not fired his weapon, thank God, and thanks too to the alert action of a government agent concealed among the throng to protect the Chief of State. That this additional gunman happened to be a former Intelligence agent only confirmed the Secret Service's publicly expressed opinion that these were insane times we were living in, when actual Communists could in fact penetrate our nation's most guarded agencies. What had become of the potential gunman's weapon, the evil instrument of this bold assassin who had placed himself among patriotic Americans paying their last respects to a great military figure, God only knew. Speculation had it —and it was only reasonable to agree—that some souvenir hunter had snatched it. In any case, the next President would rest easier knowing that a madman named Colin McFerrin also lay dead this tragic night.

Valerie Craig speculated for a while too. Had she been wrong in not going to the Sheraton? She had barely heard him on the phone. A gun? Where? For what? Surely common sense was on her side. And the way things had turned out, she obviously had been right. It was plain he had never gotten anywhere near the Sheraton.

In any case, her conscience was clear—she had reassured herself for two days now—she had tried to tell him he was attempting the impossible. Some things are better left alone. If only he had listened. She lowered herself into the warm waters of her bath and tried not to think about Colin.

Again and again in the days that followed, commentators across the nation sounded the alarm on radio and television. It would have to be clearly

THE STAR SPANGLED CONTRACT

understood that no core of bodyguards, no matter how vigilant, could ever protect a President who insisted on going among the people, so many of whom in these lunatic times were maniacs inflamed by vicious drugs and unruly passions and the insane will to achieve instant celebrity.

Regrettable as this was, Secretary of State Danforth said that he was obliged to agree—and then he solemnly announced the names of the members of a judicial panel called to undertake the assassination inquiry, the body of eight eminent men and women to be guided by the just and prudent chairmanship of the distinguished advisor and close friend of the late President, Professor Franklin Quiller.

The Congress gave its advice and consent, and the people accordingly approved.

382